safe within

Also by Jean Reynolds Page

A Blessed Event
Accidental Happiness
The Space Between Before and After
The Last Summer of Her Other Life
Leaving Before It's Over

safe within

JEAN REYNOLDS PAGE

wm

WILLIAM MORROW
An Imprint of HarperCollinsPublishers

P.S.™ is a trademark of HarperCollins Publishers.

SAFE WITHIN. Copyright © 2012 by Jean Reynolds Page. All rights reserved. Printed in the United States of America. No part of this book may be used or reproduced in any manner whatsoever without written permission except in the case of brief quotations embodied in critical articles and reviews. For information address Harper-Collins Publishers, 10 East 53rd Street, New York, NY 10022.

HarperCollins books may be purchased for educational, business, or sales promotional use. For information please write: Special Markets Department, HarperCollins Publishers, 10 East 53rd Street, New York, NY 10022.

FIRST EDITION

Designed by Diahann Sturge

Library of Congress Cataloging-in-Publication Data has been applied for.

ISBN 978-0-06-187694-3

12 13 14 15 16   OV/RRD   10 9 8 7 6 5 4 3 2 1

To Joyce Ross and Ralph Reynolds

And as always . . .
With love, for Rick

Acknowledgments

Years ago, when I had three very small children and one very busy husband, it was difficult to justify (to myself) the time spent in the writing of fiction. In those days, publishing seemed as likely as winning the lottery and, even with encouragement from Rick (the very busy husband), I had trouble validating my own identity as a writer. The Durham Arts Council in Durham, North Carolina, changed that. Based on several chapters of a novel in progress, they awarded me an Emerging Artist Grant. The money went toward a few hours of childcare three days a week. The grant not only gave me time to write, it gave me the courage to see myself as a writer. The chapters the committee read (and the book those pages became) went into a drawer as a first effort, but faint echoes of that story—both characters and setting—can be found in *Safe Within*. That book gave me the beginnings of this narrative. And all those years ago, the Durham Arts Council gave me another kind of beginning. I am still filled with gratitude.

Years later, my extraordinary agent Susan Ginsburg offered me the ultimate validation as a writer when she called to say she would represent me. Ten years down the line, Susan remains a professional wonder to me—and an equally remarkable friend. I couldn't be more grateful. In addition, many thanks to Stacy

Testa and everyone at Writers House for always looking out for me.

This book has been a longer journey than I expected. A move that took us more than halfway across the country—from Seattle to Madison, Wisconsin—put the writing on hold for a while. I would like to thank my patient editor, Lyssa Keusch. She made this book better (as she has the previous three). In addition, she provided a workable timeline and cheerful encouragement all along the way. With Lyssa are all the wonderful folks at HarperCollins who have mounted the effort to get this book out into the world. I would like to thank Seale Ballenger, Jennifer Hart, Jean Marie Kelly, Mary Sasso, and Joanne Minutillo, not only for their efforts to promote this book, but for taking the time to talk and brainstorm. Amid my disorganized process, Wendy Lee kept me on track early on, and later, Amanda Bergeron stepped in seamlessly, offering ideas and assistance at every turn. Many thanks.

In terms of a writing community, I was fortunate to land in Madison, Wisconsin. Susanna Daniel, Michelle Wildgen, Judy Mitchell, and Jesse Lee Kercheval read (and reread) drafts. For their time, suggestions, and insights, I am tremendously grateful.

To my tireless Texas readers, I also offer a big thank you. Ian Pierce and Jeanne Skartsiaris have remained constant for many years and continue to offer valuable thoughts and treasured friendship. Thanks for making me and my books better. Mary Turner, Kathy Yank, Chris Smith, and Lou Tasciotti were all with me in spirit.

When it came to an accurate portrayal of Greta's eye problems, Dr. Paul L. Kaufman, chair of the University of Wisconsin Department of Ophthalmology and Visual Sciences, offered valuable information. I would like to thank him and Dr. Barbara Blodi for being generous with time and knowledge.

Any mistakes are my own, but their input gave me a much better sense of Greta's struggles.

I would also like to thank the wonderful folks at Desert Mirage Alpaca Ranch in Marana, Arizona, for sharing their wonderful animals with me and my adventurous pal Jan Bremner. (And thanks, Joe, for always being game!)

A few people appear in my acknowledgments book after book. That is because I am fortunate to have the consistent love and support of family and friends.

I will never cease to be grateful to Colleen Murphy and Victoria Skurnick. No matter how many books I publish, they will always be the ones who offered to help and came through for me when I was looking to find my way into print. Hilda Lee was an early champion who encouraged me to venture out into a bigger world. Never underestimate the importance of an amazing teacher. And to Andy Ziskind, continued thanks for making me smile for the camera.

My life is rich in family. My sister, Joyce Ross, and my brother, Ralph Reynolds, and their families, along with Lynn Saunders, Bob Reynolds, and all my other Reynolds family and Blue family loved ones, remind me that I am not alone in the world.

And, as always, love and gratitude to my kids—Franklin, Gillian, and Edward—and to my still very busy husband (I wouldn't have it any other way, dear). You all make writing possible and life a journey worth taking.

safe within

One

Elaine pulled into the lot beside the Roseville Municipal Building. One wing of the concrete structure made up the police department. She sat in the car, angry with Greta for putting her in this position, angry with Carson for asking her to go.

Just get it over with.

The evening's humid mist covered her as she got out of the car and it calmed her a bit, but a moment later when the damp warmth on her skin met the shock of cold air inside the building, she got pissed all over again. She wished she had a sweater. She wished she had a normal mother-in-law. And more than anything, she wished that Carson wasn't dying.

A plump woman with a frosted bob sat perched behind a high counter in the lobby.

"I'm looking for Greta Forsyth," Elaine said. "A woman brought in earlier?"

"Oh, Lord," the woman said. "She's a piece of work, huh?"

The tone sounded admiring of Greta's obvious misbehavior. Her full, teased head of hair, which, best Elaine could tell, had been shellacked, moved as a single unit when she shook her head.

"What do I need to do to get her out of here?" Elaine said, leaning on the counter.

"It won't take much," she said. "They can't wait to pass her off to somebody." The woman's nametag identified her as Donna.

"What happened, exactly?" Elaine asked.

"Depends on which officer you talk to," Donna told her. "She said to one of them, 'I am a good Christian woman you understand, but after meeting you, the notion of evolution doesn't seem all that far-fetched.' That was my favorite." A slow smile spread across the woman's face. "She told another one that bathing was not as painful as he must imagine. When she said that, he told her—"

"No," Elaine interrupted the narrative that seemed to be gaining steam. "I mean, why is she here in the first place?"

"Oh, sorry." The woman deflated a bit as the story left her. "You can talk to Officer Harlow. He talked to the state trooper who brought her in. I heard that the trooper found her standing in the middle of the highway just outside of Lowfield. She didn't seem sick or crazy, he said. She told him she was from Roseville, but wouldn't tell him anything else, so he brought her here."

"Why was she in the middle of the road?" Elaine didn't know if she should be alarmed, angry, or amused. Greta wasn't even from Roseville. It all seemed too confusing.

"She wouldn't say." Donna looked away as her phone began to ring. She stopped long enough to answer and put the caller on hold. "Might have been some kind of big animal there, too," she said to Elaine. "The trooper saw something running into the woods. Said it might've been a deer, but it looked too big and furry."

Alpacas. That's what Mattie—the woman who lived in and

helped at Greta's—had told Elaine over the phone. Elaine didn't even try to explain that one to the police receptionist. The woman had returned to her phone call, anyway.

Elaine watched as two men in uniform walked through the lobby and exited to the parking lot. They couldn't have been much older than Mick. A year or two at most. Twenty-six. Twenty-seven. How would she feel if Mick rode around with a gun seeking out trouble all night? Those boys had mothers somewhere, too. And fathers.

She thought of Carson back at the cabin. She hadn't wanted to leave him, but he'd been insistent that she go help his mother.

"The policeman told me someone from the precinct could drive her home," she'd explained to him. "Why don't we let them do that?"

"Because she's my mother," he said. "And the thought of the police telling her they'd found her family, but no one wanted to take the trouble to get her . . ." He took a deep breath and brought his eyes up to meet hers. "Thinking of her being driven back in some squad car . . ." He shook his head. "I'd go myself if I could, Elaine."

Elaine should have been worried about him—in his condition, alone so late, so far out from town—but for some odd reason, she felt okay. In the tree house, he would stay protected. Placed high in the branches of two oaks, the tree house had been her father's vision of a home. She'd had her beginnings from that unusual vantage, a childhood spent looking out on the lake from a shingled nest.

A couple of weeks before, Carson had decided that he wanted his last days to be there. So the two of them had driven away from Chapel Hill. His friends and colleagues from the university had said their good-byes already. He taught all but the last two months of the semester, something his department and his doctors found remarkable. When he got too sick to continue, he'd endured a receiving line of visitors, day after day. Everyone from the department chair to the janitor had come to the house.

"You ought to sell Tupperware or something," he told Elaine. "Make use of all this traffic. The sympathy factor alone would move a ton of merchandise."

"You're horrible," she said.

"Tupperware's a fine product."

She smiled, wondered if his gallows humor would seem as funny as the actual gallows drew near.

Even as he lost weight and his appetite, he *had* kept his sense of humor. An hour earlier, he'd even found the news of Greta's little stunt amusing. She'd apparently released a neighbor's herd of alpacas before getting herself picked up by a state trooper and taken to the police department in the next town over. The Roseville police didn't know about the animals. The trooper brought her in because she seemed to be in the middle of the road for no reason and she wouldn't tell him where she lived.

"Except for the problems with her eyes," the officer told Elaine over the phone, "she seems as sharp—probably sharper—than the fellow who dragged her in here. And she speaks her mind, that's for sure. But she won't give us a clue about where to take her home. Just says she's from Roseville. I'm lucky I found this number in her sweater when she went to the bathroom."

He'd called Carson's cell phone, the jangling tone startling her as Carson slept in the other room.

"She's going to be mad as a badger when she finds out I went through her pockets."

He still didn't know that Greta wasn't from Roseville. She lived less than a quarter mile from where the trooper found her, just outside of Lowfield. Why she'd allowed herself to be carted to the next town over was anybody's guess, but Elaine imagined it had something to do with the fact that she'd set loose a half-dozen alpacas that didn't belong to her. Elaine was surprised that with her failing eyes—sight dim with macular degeneration—Greta had been able to pull off the liberation of the odd livestock. Then again, her stubbornness made up for any amount of physical compromise.

Elaine might have even found it funny if she hadn't been dragged away from Carson in the middle of the night. Still, she was where he wanted her to be, helping his mother—a woman he loved, a woman who had not exchanged so much as a hello with Elaine in two decades. But Elaine had gone to retrieve her—not for her mother-in-law, but for Carson. And she'd left him inside the tree house, inside the walls that had seen her become the person she was. She trusted the cabin in the ways she'd trusted her dad when he'd told her that—improbable as it seemed—their home was as rock sturdy as any house built on the ground. The place would hold Carson safely until she got back.

The receptionist switched from one call to another, then put the receiver down. "He's bringing her out now," she said. "Bet they're all relieved that you showed up." Then she added, "She liked me, though."

Elaine tried to decide if the woman was joking. In what world would Greta and Donna become friends?

"She leaned in real close to me and told me that my hair looks like cotton candy." Donna smiled, touched her head.

A door at the far end of the reception area opened and an officer came out.

"You off for the night?" Donna asked.

"I wish," he said. "I'm just leaving to get a bite."

Elaine pegged him immediately as the butt of Greta's "evolution" remarks. All pasty jowls and longish brown hair, the tall man moved his ropelike arms in a manner that did bring to mind rather simian imagery.

"I'm here to pick up my mother-in-law," Elaine told him. "I'm Elaine Forsyth."

"Well, God bless your heart," the man said. "I was thinking that if she was a relative of mine, I'd have to think long and hard about coming to get her. You know, she had the nerve to tell me to get her a pack of Nabs while I was out."

"So, where is she, exactly?"

"She's in one of our holding rooms," he said. "Donna, you get out the paperwork for this good lady to sign, and I'll go get the other one and bring her out."

He seemed all too eager to skip his snack run in order to get Greta out of his precinct. Moments later, he emerged through the door with Greta. The woman's eyes did a vacant scan of the room—the lifetime of seeing that preceded her vision's demise led her to maintain the effort, it seemed. But other than this particular decline, Greta looked nearly the same as she had two decades before.

Her hair was different. The shoulder-length brown had become a soft, silver gray, shortened into a stylish, sporty cut. She'd stayed slim. Elegant. Entirely entitled. She wore tan slacks and a pale blue knit top. Even in police custody, Greta appeared to be the one in control.

As her mother-in-law drew closer, Elaine could see that her skin had the etching of seventy-plus years. Still, she could have been one of the mature, silver-haired models so prized by J. Crew or Talbots. Women who demonstrated that stylish possibilities needn't diminish with the years. Greta's dignity and preservation came as something of a surprise. Given what Elaine remembered of Greta's temperament, she had expected the woman to grow harsh with age.

Elaine stepped forward and Greta, keeping a hand on the rail along the wall, seemed to look in her direction. The jowly officer, walking a few steps behind, winked at Donna and made a show of pretending to feel with his hands in front of him—eyes squinted. He stopped when it obviously occurred to him that

Elaine was watching, too. Greta inclined her damaged gaze in his direction, as if she sensed what she couldn't have seen going on behind her.

Elaine went toward them. "I would appreciate a show of respect for my husband's mother," she said. She felt the rapid pulsing of blood in her neck, in her temples.

The ample cheeks of the officer went from putty to pink. He didn't respond, but the grim line of his mouth suggested the effort it took to hold back his words. Over at the desk, Donna looked down and busied herself with paperwork.

"Greta," Elaine said, "it's me. Elaine. Carson asked me to drive you home."

Greta offered a small nod. If she was surprised at Elaine's presence, she didn't show it. They signed the necessary papers and then Elaine took Greta's arm and walked with her mother-in-law out the front door.

Carson heard someone humming in the next room. Just waking, he had to think for a moment. He was in the tree house. He'd sent Elaine to get his mother, and Linnie must have gotten home.

Linnie Phelps, the only sibling of Elaine's mom, had been a huge help since they'd come to the cabin. She'd lived in the tree house for four years—ever since Elaine's dad had died.

Linnie, a former dancer, had spent most of her life traveling from one performance to another with a modern company based in Chicago. She danced into her forties and stayed on with the company to direct rehearsals after that. The cabin had been a familiar place for her to land when she gave all that up.

After Carson and Elaine arrived, the woman's constant influx of exercise-induced endorphins provided an infectious cheer. It was difficult to keep things upbeat when you had Hospice on speed dial, but somehow they were making it all work.

He hoped Elaine would stay on at the cabin for a while after he was gone and allow Linnie to help her ease back into life. Elaine's mom had been gone for seven years. A malignant breast had taken her with just four months between diagnosis and her last breath. For Elaine's father, it had been his heart and an even more sudden exit. Carson wished to God he could spare his wife another loss, but pancreatic cancer had not left him in a position to negotiate.

A year and a half before, he'd carried 172 pounds on his six-foot, one-inch frame. When he'd dipped under 150, he stopped getting on the scales. The diagnosis had left them with no illusions. Still, he'd lived twice as long as they predicted. When it became clear that they were no longer looking at months, but weeks, he said he wanted to travel to Lowfield. To the tree house cabin—the house her parents built high in the oaks on the shores of Lake Riley.

He listened for any sound of an approaching car. He couldn't remember how long Elaine had been gone. Pain meds rendered time a fluid thing. He felt no worse than he had earlier. That was good. He'd promised Elaine he wouldn't die while she was off rescuing his mother.

And he wasn't going to die. Well, he was, but not acutely. Not while she was gone. The pharmaceutically induced half sleep that kept his pain to a whisper also brought memories that arrived as visitations. He didn't recall them so much as reanimated them. In the previous twenty-four hours, he'd been seven again, fishing on a pond in a boat Greta's father had built. His granddad made him bait the hook himself, and he mourned for the worm as if it were a pet.

Later, he found himself watching a movie in the basement of his dorm at Duke. Three buddies sat with him, each with a beer in hand. Even in his weakened state, he felt the real-time beginnings of an erection as his younger incarnation took in the naked woman on the screen. The moments varied in significance. There seemed to be no rhyme or reason to the selection, no linear sequencing to these rehabitations of his earlier life.

And, contrary to popular assumption, they did not flash by in a rush of projector-like reels. Rather, the scenes became available to him, the past momentarily becoming his present once again. He remained aware that he'd lived beyond them, but there seemed to be no separation of decades, no relevance of his current age—only the perception of "now" as Carson, once again, embodied his own story.

He sat in the bleachers. He ought to be on the damn field, but Coach said all freshmen had to play a year of JV. The first football game, second week of September, but it still felt like August. He watched the receiver fumble. If that idiot Gaines kept playing like that, Coach would reconsider. The only thing the old guy hated more than changing his mind was losing.

"Hey." Alex sat down beside him, passed him a can of soda spiked with rum. He nodded toward the field. "What's going on?"

"Asshole Gaines just dropped it again."

"Shit."

They sat and watched. It was nearly halftime already and they were a touchdown behind. A girl climbed midway up the stands and sat with some kids a couple of rows down.

"Who's that girl?" Carson asked. He got a glimpse of her face before she turned away again. She looked familiar, but he couldn't place her. Even from the back, she looked beautiful.

"Elaine Tyson." Alex grinned, tipped up a brown bag of concession popcorn and shook a few pieces into his mouth, then took a long swallow of his drink.

"Are you kidding me?" Carson knew who Elaine Tyson was, but this girl looked like a much older, prettier version of the kid he knew.

"That's her," Alex insisted. "Looks like she went to the boob farm over the summer and picked a couple of ripe ones."

"Jesus, Alex," Carson said, still looking at the girl. Alex loved to say the word *boob*. He worked it into the conversation at least fifty times a day.

Elaine stood up again and moved over to sit beside a girl in the middle. As she made her way, she looked up and saw Carson staring at her. She smiled.

"Careful, buddy," Alex said—a little too loudly, "she's still in eighth grade. You got to give it a year or two, man. If she doesn't get fat or something, she'll look incredible by then."

"Shut up, Alex," Carson said under his breath.

"You'll have to wait longer than a couple of years for me." Elaine Tyson looked up the stands and addressed the two of them. She spoke without any sign of embarrassment. "Try, um . . . never."

"Why?" Carson volleyed back. "You have a boyfriend?"

"No," she said, sitting down beside her friend. "Just standards."

"What a bitch," Alex mumbled.

Carson grinned, shook his head. "Damn."

"I know," Alex said, passing the soda over again. "Like I said. A major trip to the boob farm."

Dave, another JV player, came running up the bleachers toward them, the sound of his feet loud and hollow on the metal steps. Something was wrong.

"Carson," he said. "They sent me to get you—Mr. Gray and some people. Come on."

"What the hell'd I do?" Carson said. Mr. Gray was the high school principal. He always lurked at football games, hoping to catch kids getting up to something. But Carson knew he hadn't done a damn thing to get on the man's radar.

"Seriously, man," Dave said. "Come on."

Carson stood, aware that he probably smelled like booze from Alex's drink.

"Okay." He followed Dave. As he went down the bleachers, he glanced over at Elaine Tyson again. She was watching him, but when he looked her way, she looked down. She had a smile on her face.

Just wait until you're a freshman and I'm on varsity. The thought cheered him all the way down the bleachers.

But the look on Mr. Gray's face made him forget about Elaine Tyson and football—and everything else. Blaine Richards, one of the town cops, stood beside Principal Gray.

"It's your dad, son," Mr. Gray said. He glanced over at the policeman. "Officer Richards came here to find you."

"What's wrong?"

"I need to drive you to the hospital," the principal told him. "He was working, getting a dead tree down on your property just before dark when a branch came down on him. Your mama is with him there. I don't know any more than that."

They were already moving toward the parking lot. They were already moving toward something so big and horrible he had to push hard to keep going, like walking waist deep in water, fighting a strong current.

When they got to the hospital, one of the nurses took his arm and led him to a room where his mother sat beside a man with a tube coming out of his mouth. His face was so bruised and torn that Carson wouldn't have recognized him as Taylor Forsyth. Greta turned and looked at Carson as he came in. She was crying, a sight that frightened him more than his father's injuries. He'd never seen tears on her face before.

"He can't breathe on his own, son," she said. "He's not gone yet, but he will be." Her voice was hoarse. "You need to tell him good-bye."

The current he'd walked through before had found its way inside of him. He felt it rising and pushing up through his chest. *No. No. No.*

"Come here, Carson," she said.

He still couldn't move, frozen at his place just inside the door. Mattie stood up from a chair in the corner. He hadn't seen her there before. She walked over to him and, with one arm around his back and a hand on his arm, she guided him toward the bed.

His father's eyes were open, but they didn't seem to see anything. "Can he hear?" Carson asked.

The corners of his mother's bottom lip pulled down. She was trying to hold back her sadness, but the effort seemed useless. He'd always thought his mother could hold back the tide and here she was as helpless as anyone else.

"Your daddy is between this world and the next," Mattie said. "It's generally understood that he's still with us. You tell him you love him and he'll hear it. He'll feel it."

Carson did as he was told. He said it, but even though the words were true, he didn't feel much of anything. God had mercifully sucked out all feeling from him and stuffed something full and numbing in its place.

Later, when it was all over, Greta told him to go outside. She said she'd meet him out there presently. He walked out the lobby door and around to the bay where ambulances brought people in. The small hospital sat on a hill and, from the landing outside the emergency room doors, he could see the high school ball field. The game would be over, but the lights were still on. He wondered about Elaine Tyson. Who had driven her home? She lived outside of town on the lake, up in a weird tree house her folks had built.

Did her dad come pick her up, wait in the car for her to come out of the gates after the game? His dad wouldn't pick him up anymore. Carson had the selfish, absurd thought that if the accident had happened a year later, he would already have his license.

"Hey, buddy." One of the EMTs approached him. "Are you okay?"

Carson knew most people in town, but the guy didn't look familiar.

"My dad just died," Carson said. There. He'd said it out loud. He could do it. He could say the words.

"The tree accident," the man said. "I was with him coming here. He said he had a son."

"He talked to you?"

"A little bit," he told Carson. "He was going in and out. But he was thinking about you, talking about you, when he said anything at all."

Carson's hands held on to a rail, and he couldn't get them to stop trembling. He bent over to look at them and felt wet drops land on his fingers. Jesus. Now he was crying.

"I'm sure sorry we couldn't do more for him," the EMT said. He was standing close to Carson. Carson could smell cigarettes and something else—an antiseptic smell. He seemed like a decent guy.

"Yeah," Carson said. "I know you tried."

"Hey, Bobby." Another EMT came out of the doors. "We got a call. Let's go."

The EMT, Bobby, gave Carson a pat on the shoulder and left him there alone by the railing. Carson couldn't stand to think about his dad, so he kept pushing his mind back to the moments before. Before he knew. Before he was a kid without a dad. In that moment, the girl, Elaine Tyson, seemed to represent everything happy from that before.

He knew he should be thinking about his mom. And he would. He'd be everything he needed to be as Taylor Forsyth's only child. But in those moments, he only wanted to feel how wrong things were for *him*. An hour before, he'd been a high school kid watching a football game. He'd been sneaking booze with his best friend and flirting with a girl who seemed to like him back. He'd been what he was supposed to be when you're goddamn fifteen years old.

And Elaine Tyson with the attitude and the dark hair. Elaine Tyson with the unanticipated smile. She was the last one to see that person that he would never quite be again.

Greta had not spoken. After they got on the road, Elaine asked her if she was okay. Greta nodded. Elaine asked if the air conditioner was at the right temperature. She nodded again. Beyond that, the woman stared—seeing God only knew what—out the window. Even with 20/20 vision, a person would see only acres of dark woods in the twenty miles between Roseville and Lowfield.

For a while, Elaine listened only to the hum of the car. She turned on the radio and smiled at the song that was playing. "Witchy Woman." Glancing over in Greta's direction, she thought she saw some amusement on the woman's face, but in the shadowed light, it was hard to tell.

Their mutual animosity almost brought them full circle—to a certain brand of camaraderie.

"How is he?" Greta's voice broke into her thoughts.

"Weak," Elaine said. "Not a lot worse than he was when you saw him the other day."

Greta had been to the tree house every few days. Mattie would drive her out and, according to Linnie, who stuck around while they were there with Carson, the two women were quite a sight on the gravel drive below.

"With Mattie's knees and Greta's eyes," Linnie had said, "it was the lame leading the blind or vice versa."

Elaine hated to be away from Carson, but everyone agreed that it was best if she left before Carson's mother arrived.

"He's still able to keep down soup and grits," Elaine continued, reminding herself that Greta loved Carson, too. "He tries to take in those awful cans of high-calorie protein drinks, but that's harder for him. He doesn't like the taste."

"Has he seen the blue lights yet?" Greta posed the question as if it made all the sense in the world.

"What blue lights?" Elaine was in no mood to decipher Greta's cryptic comments.

"The weather blues. They'll likely come. That's always the way with our family."

Her explanation stopped there. Elaine didn't know what to say. In spite of her apparent sanity, maybe Greta *was* finally losing it. Opening the gate to set loose a neighbor's livestock, running on about blue lights. Still, nothing about her seemed crazy. She seemed to know exactly what she was saying and doing.

"Is the boy there yet?" Greta changed the subject.

"Our son has a name, Greta, and you know it," Elaine said. She could feel the anger rising in her arms, pressing toward her lungs.

"Is Mick there yet?" That much concession was unusual for Greta—maybe a small show of gratitude for Elaine's efforts.

"Mick flew down and back from Rhode Island last week. He'd planned to drive down this time and bring enough of his stuff to stay awhile, but something's wrong with his car, so he's catching a ride with a friend of his who's going on through to Florida. I don't know how far along he is. He'll get here sometime tomorrow and he plans to stay . . ." The words ended there. Mick planned to stay until there was no reason to stay any longer. He'd told them at the boatyard where he worked that he didn't know how long he'd be gone. So Mick would be with her through to the end—and beyond. Elaine couldn't even think about that, much less say it. "It'll be good for Carson when he gets here."

"Carson's a saint to have accepted that boy at all." Greta still faced the window, but her words came hard and clear. "A saint." And so, the cease-fire ended.

"Don't start, Greta," Elaine said. "I swear to God I'll put you out right here and you can spend the rest of the night walking back."

"Go ahead." Greta called her bluff.

Elaine's impulse was real, but her threat, empty—and they both knew it.

Elaine kept her anger in check. She wouldn't argue her son's paternity with Carson's mother. If Carson had never been able to sway the woman's opinion, Elaine had no prayer of changing her mind. Mick was twenty-four, and nothing short of the entire story would convince Greta that she was wrong. Elaine and Carson had agreed long ago that revealing the entire truth of it was not an option. Wallace Jamison had been a painful chapter in her relationship with Carson, but that part of it was her business—and Carson's.

"Why'd you let them loose?" Elaine decided to shift the topic to more neutral territory.

"Let what loose?"

"You know what I'm talking about," Elaine said. "Those animals that belong to your neighbor. Why'd you open the gate?"

Greta looked down and made a low noise, almost a growl. "Hellish beasts if you ask me. All you have to do is look at their faces to see there's evil in them."

"With your eyes, Greta, you can't even make out their faces."

"If I'm anywhere near that fence, they come over right next to me. I can see them well enough." Greta pursed her lips. "That land used to belong to my uncle. Good farmland. Then it was sold to a fellow who grew Christmas trees on it. That soil would grow anything you planted, and he filled it with Christmas trees. Then he passed, and it got handed off to this oddball from Atlanta. An actor who comes up on weekends and thinks he's some kind of Dr. Dolittle. He wants to buy me out, too, and let those things loose all over my land."

Elaine wasn't even sure Greta was talking to her anymore. The woman could have been in a room by herself, letting off the same steam.

"Turning respectable acres into a circus," she said. "No. Not a circus—a zoo. Wild-eyed things stand right at the fence, and people traipse all over my property to get a look at them. Park on the side of the road and walk my land like it's a national park. I'd had enough of it. That's all. How'd you know about the animals, anyway? They didn't arrest me, so I'm guessing the law didn't tell you."

"Mattie told me," Elaine said. "The Roseville police found Carson's number in your pocket and called his cell. I called Mattie after that. She was out of her mind with worry, you know. You'd gone missing and, on top of that, the guy from next door was screaming at her through the front porch screen. She was beside herself."

"Did you tell her I'm okay?" Greta's hard tone softened to one of genuine concern. The sudden shift surprised Elaine.

"I told her I was going to get you," Elaine said. "She couldn't even leave and look for you because she's babysitting her grandkids."

"Great-grandchildren," Greta corrected her.

"Whatever. You gave her a real scare." Elaine thought of Mattie—at first frantic with worry and then—when she knew Greta was okay—simply pissed that Greta had been up to such foolishness with the alpacas.

"Something about those creatures sets her off," Mattie told Elaine over the phone. "Says she can't stand their eyes. You believe that? The woman can't see my brown face from across the room, but she don't like their eyes?!"

"I do regret upsetting Mattie," Greta said, raising her fingers to brush a few stray strands from her forehead. "That man, Morales is his name, was screaming and chasing those things. I figured he'd have me arrested on the spot, so I let that trooper drive me away. I didn't think much beyond that." She actually smiled, but seemed to catch herself. It faded back into a neutral scowl.

They'd gone through Lowfield, and Elaine turned on the highway that would take Greta home. They didn't try to make more conversation. The ride had gone about as well as either of them could hope for.

After a stretch of silent miles, Elaine turned into the dirt drive that ended at the house where Carson grew up.

Greta took in a sharp breath and let it out, as if bracing for what came next. "I'd like to see him again," she said.

"Let Carson know when you're coming," Elaine said. "I'll make myself scarce."

Carson loved his mother, in spite of everything. He didn't excuse her behavior. They had all allowed it to become a stalemate. Over the years, he'd gone alone to visit her every couple of months. He'd share a meal with her and Mattie, and they'd talk about everything under the sun except his family. He would want to see her again.

"Take the boy with you when you go," Greta added.

Elaine gave herself a second, let the surge of anger pass before she answered. "Don't worry. Mick has never requested an audience with you. I don't intend to inflict one on him now."

Greta nodded. She opened the car door. The screen door slammed shut on the porch, and Elaine saw Mattie coming down the stairs. "Tell Carson I appreciate him sending you out," Greta said. That was as close as Elaine would get to a show of gratitude from her mother-in-law. Fine. She wanted nothing from the woman anyway. Greta didn't wait on Mattie before she got out of the car. She stepped away, striding boldly across property that she knew by feel.

Mattie reached her and put out a hand. "Stop it." Greta brushed her off. "I know my own front yard, and my legs are in better shape than yours."

As Carson's mother made her way toward the house, Mattie came over to Elaine's side of the car, her brown skin blending with the surrounding night. Elaine rolled down her window.

"God bless you for going over there and bringing her back," Mattie said. "She won't say it, but I will. I would have been there myself, but I had charge of those kids. Thank you."

"I'd say it was my pleasure, but my nose might start growing."

Mattie smiled. "Give my love to Carson," she said.

"Greta asked to see him again."

"I'll bring her over whenever it's convenient," Mattie told her. With that, she stepped away and began walking toward the house.

Elaine backed out of the bumpy drive. Carson would most likely be awake, waiting for news of his mother. She thought of calling him, but on the off chance he *was* resting, she decided to wait. Linnie would be home, too. If Mick's friend decided to drive straight through, their son might even have arrived.

The gathering had begun, and so had the leaving. And even as she drove toward home, Elaine could not escape the notion that no amount of acceleration would keep her from being left behind.

Moments of Carson's life continued to come back to him—to take him to other places, other times.

He stood beside his car outside the cabin, looking up and waiting. He had two months left before he graduated from

Duke. Two months before he had to have a plan. Elaine, a junior
at Chapel Hill, took so much for granted. Things would work
out for Carson. They always did, she said. He'd applied to three
grad schools—Georgetown, UVA, and Vanderbilt. A letter came.
No from UVA. He didn't tell Elaine.

The next day, two more letters. Yes and Yes. Vanderbilt was
an offer of acceptance. Georgetown, an offer of acceptance with
a teaching assistant position to offset the costs. Georgetown
it was. He still didn't tell Elaine, this time saving it as a surprise. One of two surprises he had planned. The day before,
he'd swung by Chapel Hill to pick her up, and they'd driven to
Lowfield for the weekend.

He'd been tempted to blurt everything out on the drive
down. But he'd waited. Home, in Lowfield. That's where he'd
tell her. That's where he'd *ask* her, too.

As he stared up at the tree house, the nerves set in. High
above, Elaine waved from the kitchen window.

"I'll be down in a second," she called to him. "You want to
come up?"

"I'll wait here," he said. His big news, his even bigger
question—both of them threatening to tumble out of him the
second he had her in front of him. He needed to settle down.
He wanted the afternoon to be perfect, and that meant pacing
himself. He pushed his thoughts away from momentous issues
and looked up—way up into the trees—at Elaine's house.

No matter how many times he saw her place, it always amazed
him. A weathered wood cottage settled among the branches of
two huge oak trees. It was the most improbable, impractical habi-
tat he'd ever seen, and yet Elaine had grown up there in all the
normal ways. It looked as if some kind of Oz-like storm picked
the place up from the shores of Nantucket and dropped the whole
thing intact in branches overlooking a lake in North Carolina.

"Daddy was stationed on Cape Cod during the war," Elaine

had explained the first time he saw the place up close. That had been when they were both in high school. "So Daddy fell in love with the houses up there"—she'd gone on to explain—"dormer windows, shingles, white shutters—all that stuff."

"Why the hell'd he build it up in the trees like that?" Carson asked.

"I think he and Mom planned to build it as a regular house in town. They decided to practice with a weird little tree house on the lake. Kind of like a fort. They loved it so much, they gave up on town and built the whole thing here. Once Mom had her kiln built in the yard, there was no going back."

Carson had wondered at first if it could possibly be stable. But he'd studied it at times over the years and realized the supports that crisscrossed underneath were a marvel of engineering. Doug Tyson, Elaine's dad, had hired an architect from Raleigh, an old friend from school, to draw up the plans. The gables that ever so slightly curved out like a girl's skirt gave the impression of whimsy, but Carson saw that the bones of the place had been designed with serious intent.

Elaine's parents were both like that. Responsibly weird. Bohemians who paid their taxes on time. The house suited them perfectly. Doug taught English lit at the high school and Ginnie turned dirt into pots and vases. Elaine was both of them and neither of them—more complicated in every way than her parents.

"Hey." Elaine came down the stairs at the side of the house. Tan legs and blue-jean shorts, her dark, wavy hair forced into a ponytail. Her family reflected a mix of English, Irish, and Italian blood with a dose of Cherokee thrown in. The amalgam gave her high cheekbones, a full mouth, and those dark, dark eyes. His own family tended toward light brown hair and blue eyes. If they ever had kids, he hoped they'd get her particular cocktail of features. Skipping across the distance between them, she could easily have been sixteen, which made his plans for the day even more disconcerting.

"Where are we off to?" she asked, leaning on him to shake a pebble out of her ratty Top-Siders.

Carson grinned at her. He tried to look confident—anything but nervous and scared. Nervous and scared was no way to convince a girl to marry you. He'd planned the whole thing out, never considering that she might think it was crazy, but as he looked at her standing in front of him, that was all he could think about. They'd dated since his sophomore year of high school, then through all of college (with the exception of one breakup during his sophomore year—four months he'd rather forget). But in all that time, they'd never talked about getting married. What if she didn't want to be anybody's wife? Hell, her parents only made it legal to please their own folks. They'd told him as much.

"Carson." She raised an eyebrow of warning. "Where are we going?"

"Down the hill," he said, gesturing toward the pier.

He'd asked her dad if he could borrow the boat for the afternoon. *Bring it back with gas* had been Doug Tyson's only comment. Unlike his daughter, Elaine's dad wasn't big on questions.

She didn't move—just stood there, angled her head to the side. "What's going on with you?" she asked.

"Would you let me surprise you, for God's sake," Carson said, sounding more desperate than he intended. "You're as bad as my mother." That ought to do it. Any comparison to Greta should send her flying in the opposite direction.

She stood her ground for a second longer and then relented. "Okay," she said.

She shrugged, turned to head down the hill.

Carson felt more at ease once they were under way. The noise from the motor, churning a wake behind them, kept conversation short. He steered toward Merle's Marina. Merle, who ran the marina and grill with his wife, had agreed to put a picnic together for Carson—to have it ready for pickup by noon.

From the water, he looked back at the tree house. Mostly hidden by leaves, it seemed to float, the weathered shingles taking on a pale blue cast against the deep green of early spring growth.

How could you not fall for a girl who lived in a tree house? Elaine *seemed* like a fairy tale to him sometimes. By turns headstrong and humble, stubborn and vulnerable. The weather changed less often than Elaine Tyson. He loved it. He loved her.

"So at least tell me there's food involved," she said. "I'm starving."

By then they'd turned into the cove that led to Merle's. Carson slowed the engine. A fish jumped near shore and he absently calculated the possible length and weight of it before turning his thoughts back to the task at hand.

"Burgers?" She smiled. "This is your surprise? I mean, I'm not complaining—I love Merle's fries, but . . ."

"Stop guessing," he said, pulling alongside the dock and stepping out to tie up. "Stay here. I'll be right back."

Before he got off the dock, he saw Merle heading down the path from the restaurant with a cooler in his arms. He waited.

"How much do I owe you?" he mumbled to Merle as the man reached him.

"Oh, I don't know. The ticket's upstairs," Merle said. His expression gave the impression of chronic indigestion. "You can pay me when you bring back the cooler. Better get it back here, too. I'll tell your mama."

"Won't be any need to get Greta involved," Carson said with a grin.

"Yeah, I don't blame you. I fought in two wars and that woman scares the piss outta me," Merle grumbled. His apron had stains a decade or more in the making, but Carson could smell the Clorox coming off the white cotton.

"I appreciate this." Carson took the cooler from him.

Merle responded with a nod and a grunt. He turned and went back up the hill.

Carson put the cooler in the back of the boat. He had a bottle of wine in his backpack along with a joint—just in case his nerves completely took over. He untied the lines and pushed off from the dock. Elaine sat in the passenger seat beside him.

"Mind if I get something out to munch on?" she asked. She raised her eyebrows, a half smile on her lips—daring him to say no.

"I've got some news to tell you," he said, speaking loud over the motor, "and you won't hear it today if you so much as crack the top of that cooler."

She settled back in her seat, and he figured the only thing greater than her hunger must be her curiosity. He wore khaki shorts. The ring he'd bought her was too bulky in the box, so he'd taken it out and put it inside a silk pouch he found in his mother's jewelry box. He casually put a hand on his leg, suddenly afraid that it might have fallen out when he landed the boat. But his finger found the small, hard stone and he pressed it lightly, smiling.

"What?" She was looking at him. "Why are you smiling?"

"I'm just happy to be with you," he said. An honest answer.

He passed Point Zion and as he cleared the rocky bank at the tip of that spit, he could see Landers' Island up ahead. Elaine leaned her head back on the seat, her eyes closed. The rush of wind pushed at the hem of her shirt, and he could see her smooth, tanned belly made golden by the strong sun that covered her. He throttled down as they neared the island, the shift in momentum rousing her from dozing.

"I haven't been to this place for ages," she said. "My dad and I used to come here to fish when I was little."

"Yeah," Carson said. "I'd come out here all the time in high school with a few buddies and a couple of six-packs."

"I always wondered where you guys snuck off to."

The dock looked like a ramshackle assortment of posts and boards, the far end sloping into the water. Carson pulled in to a sturdier section near the shore.

Elaine stepped out and tested the dock. Shaky but holding. She tied up to a post and he handed her the cooler, then climbed out of the boat.

They stood there for a moment, and he began to feel nervous all over again. He'd been so sure she'd want to be engaged, but as the reality of asking the question settled on him, he began to entertain doubts.

What if she didn't want a ring on her finger during her last year of college? What if she wasn't as sure about the two of them as he was? Where did that leave them? Where did that leave *him*? Would they break up or try to maintain what they'd been for nearly seven years? Could they even go back after he'd asked the question and been rejected? *Jesus, Carson, stop it. You haven't even asked her yet and you're already working through getting turned down.*

"What's wrong with you?" she asked.

"I'm fine."

"You look pale." She put a hand on his neck. "You feel sick?"

"No." He laughed, pulling away. He reflexively felt for the ring in his pocket again, then took a deep breath to clear his doubts.

"Come on," he said, with a little too much enthusiasm. "Let's find a spot to set up."

The path was well worn, meaning new generations of high school kids had discovered it. As they walked around the periphery of the small island, they crossed over a stream on a footbridge with fancy woodwork along the handrail. Below, the slow-moving stream turned a waterwheel that activated a carved figure of a farmer that raised and lowered a hoe.

The wooden figures could be found throughout the island, animated by the movement of water or windmills. Some previous owner of the island had obviously had a mission—and a little too much time on his hands.

Nearly halfway around the island, Carson saw the spot he remembered, a raised clearing that overlooked the lake from a slight rocky bluff.

"How about here?"

"Great."

He wondered if she suspected. As she laid out the blanket and he opened the cooler, he tried to decide what he should do first. Tell her about Georgetown or propose? Georgetown. He had to go with that first. He could gauge her reaction and then bring out the ring.

Merle had outdone himself. Carson asked for sandwiches. Maybe potato salad. Merle had packed containers of roast beef and shredded pork, along with fruit salad, potato salad, and pickled cucumber. There was a slice of pie—it looked like chocolate chess—and some kind of berry cobbler.

"Wow." Elaine looked down at the picnic as if the sight of it made her full. "If you've got anything romantic in mind, you better get me before I get too stuffed to move."

"Pace yourself," he said, smiling. He opened the wine and poured it into clear plastic cups. He was out of his mind. This whole thing was crazy. He could just tell her about Georgetown and they could celebrate. He didn't have to settle their entire future all at once. But he wanted to. He wanted her. She made him feel as if he'd found his place in the world—no matter what else happened around him.

"Cheers," he said and handed her a cup.

"I can't believe all the waterwheels and carvings still work," she said. "When I was little, I could watch those things for hours."

"I guess people used to whittle things like that for fun. No telling what we'd do if we didn't have television."

They made sandwiches and ate on paper plates Merle had packed, along with plastic utensils.

"This is perfect," Elaine said, lying back and letting the full sun cover her.

Perfect. It was, he thought. "I got into Georgetown," he said without preamble. He'd never been good at leading up to things.

"Oh my God!" She sat up, a huge smile on her face. "That's great! I mean, it's what you wanted, right?" The smile looked convincing.

She *was* happy. So was he. But the distance would be hard.

"Yeah," he said. "I got into Vanderbilt, too, but not UVa. Georgetown has a TA job to cut my tuition, so . . ."

"I'm so proud of you," she said. The words trailed toward melancholy notes at the end, but maybe it was just the wine and the sun.

"Elaine," he said. Then he stopped. He could feel his heartbeat in his cheeks, and he wondered if his brain might simply explode. "I thought . . ."

"What is that?" She turned to look behind her. "There was a weird noise."

"I didn't hear anything." He didn't know whether to be relieved or irritated at the distraction. "What did it sound like?"

A mewling moan came from the woods behind them. Carson turned. Slowly, he picked up a stick nearby and stood up. He positioned himself between the noise and Elaine.

"Sounds like a sick animal," she said.

"Could be a bird," he told her. "They make some crazy-ass noises during mating season."

"Don't we all," Elaine mumbled, her eyes still locked on the woods beyond them.

Then it sounded again. Louder, and clearly coming from inside a thick patch of trees. Carson walked toward the edge of the woods. As a smaller gurgle of sound arched and fell, he looked deep into the shade and made out the movement of something large as it rolled over crunching twigs and dry leaves. It shifted again and groaned, then sat up. Jesus, it was a person. He didn't know whether to call out or grab Elaine and run like hell.

"Hello?" he ventured, motioning for Elaine to stay back. "You okay?" He took a step forward.

"Hey." The man's voice that answered him was hoarse and strained. "I'm alive," the man said. "I guess that's good." Then, he added, "And you can put down the stick. I promise I come in peace. Actually, it feels like I'm in several pieces at the moment."

Carson realized he was still holding his makeshift weapon in a ready position. He put it down and walked toward the edge of the trees. The man had pale skin and brown hair. He stood up with some effort and walked in Carson's direction. As he emerged from the shade, Carson made out the familiar face of Wallace Jamison.

"Jesus, Wallace," Carson said. He felt the throbbing thud of his pulse in his neck. "You scared the shit out of me. What are you doing?"

Wallace's tall body moved in a shuffle-and-lurch sort of gait.

"Trying to die, I think," Wallace said, squinting at the light. "Managed to screw that up, too."

Wallace was a friend of Elaine's from high school. They were in the same year and had always been buddies. Nothing more, she insisted. Just good friends. But Carson figured that wouldn't be from lack of trying on his part.

"Wallace!" Elaine ran to him and put her hand on his shoulder. "Are you okay?"

"Yeah," he said. "I just tied one on last night. Really outdid myself."

"Were you here all night?" she asked.

"Half of it," he said. "It was two in the morning when I got in the canoe to row across. I remember starting out, but I don't remember getting here—or where I left the damn boat." The last part seemed to be a new observation. "Shit. Where did I put it?"

They all looked toward the shore as if the boat, or at least some reasonable clue as to its whereabouts, would appear.

"Were you by yourself?" Elaine asked. She was standing too close to Wallace for Carson's tastes.

"Yup," he said. "Just me. Alone."

He seemed to mean something by this, but Carson didn't know what the hell it was. "Are you just home for the weekend?"

"Yeah. I skipped my Friday classes and drove down yesterday."

Wallace was at Washington and Lee, so the drive meant a long trip from Virginia for a short weekend.

"Christ, Wallace. You reek." Elaine made a face.

"Sorry," he said, running a hand through his tangle of hair. "Not sure what I ate yesterday, but I'm pretty sure I lost most of it."

"Okay," Elaine said, taking his wrist and pulling him toward the blanket. "We've got some food over here. You need to get something in your stomach, then we'll help you look for your canoe."

Carson watched the two of them. He tried to muster sympathy for Wallace, but he couldn't quite manage it. All he could think about was that this asshole was now sitting on *his* blanket, with *his* girlfriend, getting ready to eat *his* goddamn picnic. He walked over and sat down between the two of them. He scooted closer to Elaine with some intention of making a point, but Wallace didn't seem to care—or even notice, really—that Carson had become territorial.

Stop acting like a fifth grader. Carson sat back, tried to relax.

"So what happened last night?" Elaine asked Wallace. "I know you. You're not exactly a party animal and last time I checked, you weren't suicidal. What the hell were you thinking, getting into a canoe by yourself with a blood alcohol level that would stun a buffalo?" She handed him a bun filled with shredded pork.

Wallace looked down at the sandwich in his hand, but made no move to eat it. "I got dumped," he said. "I didn't see it coming. It felt like somebody dropped a fucking cinder block on my head. I just had to get out of there."

"Had you been seeing her for a long time?" Carson asked, his sympathies warming.

"A little over a year," Wallace said. "I was thinking we'd even get a place together for the fall semester. Then *boom,* just like that, it's over. Blew me away."

Elaine leaned over and put her hand on his arm. "I'm sorry, Wallace," she said. "I remember when I talked to you at Christmas, things were going so well."

"She say why?" Carson asked, trying to tell himself that he was just concerned for Wallace, but feeling a deeper vein of fear pulsing inside the question. If it could happen to this guy out of the blue, it could happen to anybody. Carson looked at the line of Elaine's profile. She wouldn't do that to him. There were things about her he didn't understand, but she had no cruelty in her.

"Apparently," Wallace said, "there's somebody else. A guy I thought was a friend of mine. I'm such a fucking idiot."

"Wallace," Elaine said, her voice kind, "you're not the idiot in this scenario."

"Thanks," he said.

"Eat your sandwich," Elaine said, the directive gentle and encouraging. "We'll hike around with you and look for the boat."

Carson felt bad for the guy, but he also felt helpless. The ring in his pocket had gone from a prize to a trinket—at least for the purposes of that particular afternoon.

"Listen," Wallace said, "you've got this whole spread laid out and I'm screwing everything up. I'm sorry. I'll go find my own fucking boat; you two do . . ."—he suddenly looked embarrassed—"whatever it is you were doing."

"We're celebrating," Elaine said. "Carson got into graduate school at Georgetown." She smiled as if the reality of the news had just dawned on her. "Can you believe it? How great is that?"

"Congratulations!" Wallace sounded genuinely happy for him.

"Have something to eat with us," Carson said. "Then we'll help you. If the canoe floated off, we can give you a lift back across to your folks' place. You're right across, aren't you?" Carson had been to the Jamison lake house with Elaine, but that had been several years before.

Wallace nodded. They were stuck, staring at each other, suspended in the arrangement for a moment longer, then Elaine took control and began to make a sandwich for herself, and Carson followed her lead.

Afterward, they set off walking the perimeter of the island, keeping an eye on the shore. The canoe, Wallace said, was red, and should be easy to spot. They crossed over an ornately carved footbridge, the handrails fashioned to look like a series of rolling waves.

"My granddad did all this," Wallace said.

"You're kidding?" Carson looked at the woodwork, then back at Wallace. "All the stuff on the island?"

"Yeah. This place belongs to my dad and his brothers now. But Granddaddy used to come out here with my grandmother when they were first married. Must have had a lot of time on his hands because . . ." He gestured toward the detail on the bridge. "Damn, look at it."

"Why is it called Landers' Island then?" Carson asked.

"My granddad was Landers Jamison."

"I never knew that," Elaine said. "Why didn't you say anything in high school?"

"I don't know," he said. "I only thought of it as a place to get wasted back then. I practically lived out here with Raiff Pascal and that jerk Thomassan who followed him around all the time. I wasn't paying much attention to the decorative carpentry." He veered off the path without warning, stepping into the dense growth. "Hold on a sec," he said. He reached a stump, knelt down, and stuck his hand inside a rotted opening in the side. When he stood up, he was holding a bottle of Wild Turkey.

"This used to be Raiff's hiding spot for his booze," he said. "Looks like the secret has been passed down to a new generation of Pascals." He brought the bottle with him, opened it, and the three of them, taking a ceremonial sip, passed it from person to person. Carson wondered if they were celebrating his grad school acceptance or toasting their former teenage selves. Wallace secured the top and put the bottle back in its hiding spot.

Carson felt his annoyance with Wallace subside a little. Poor guy. Dumped by a girl he loved.

"Hey, look," Elaine said.

Carson turned and saw the red canoe, brought up neatly onto a patch of leaves at the water's edge, the oar resting across the seat.

"I'll be damned," Wallace said, grinning. "That's a better job than I usually do sober." He walked over to the boat. "Okay, you two. I'll get my ass home now before Mama calls the law," he said, pushing the boat gently into the water. "Thanks for the sandwich—and for listening to my sob story."

"It's good to see you, Wallace," Elaine said. "Been too long since we've talked."

"Yeah, it has," he said. "I'll be around this summer."

"Me, too."

As he got the boat afloat and stepped in, he said, almost as an afterthought, "Good to catch up with you, too, Carson."

Carson nodded, his goodwill ebbing. He offered a small wave and tried to smile, but it felt, and probably looked, more like a grimace.

Elaine took his hand and began walking back toward their picnic spot.

"Elaine." He stopped, and she turned back to him. He had his other hand inside the pocket with the ring. He could just do it. Ask her to marry him.

Off to the side, the head of a grinning wooden gnome looked away from them and turned back. Away and back. Carson had the notion that he would not—*could not*—propose while Pinocchio's creepy cousin was glaring right the fuck at them.

"What's wrong, Carson?" She looked genuinely concerned.

"Nothing." He looked away from the figure but could hear the wooden pop of movement with every rotation of the wheel. "I just love you," he said. "That's all."

"I love you, too," she said. "I'm proud of you. Come on, we're by ourselves now. Let's go use that blanket for something other than a picnic." She smiled, raised an eyebrow.

"I want to marry you, you know." It felt like a breath he'd been holding too long. It just came out.

"I want to marry you, too," she said. She seemed confused, but not surprised by his pronouncement.

She thought it was a general notion, a theoretical assessment of their relationship. That was the bad news. The good news was that she didn't appear at all opposed to the idea. He'd give her the ring. Not at that moment. He'd make it special another time. But the worries he'd had were eased by her response.

"We'll have an amazing marriage someday, Carson." She put her arms around his neck. Her eyes were warm, and a little teary.

"So," he said, "back to your idea." He gestured his head toward the direction of their picnic spot.

She nodded and he pulled her up to him, lifting her off the ground. Then he put her down. They took off running, racing, like kids in a game, making their way back toward the place where the blanket waited. Still running, Carson glanced toward the water and saw Wallace Jamison in his red canoe, rowing away and leaving the two of them at peace—at least for the afternoon.

Elaine slipped back into the house. Linnie's truck was in the drive, so her aunt had gotten home. No sign of Mick, but at least he was on the way.

The small lamp was on in the bedroom and Carson had fallen asleep. She didn't want to wake him, so she slipped off her shoes and walked back into the den. A low, three-quarter moon had come up, laying a wide beam over the water. From her vantage, it looked possible to step onto the light and follow it like a road—Dorothy, with nothing to go on but advice from strangers, moving deeper and deeper into the bizarre.

If Elaine stayed on that light, it appeared she could make her way straight on up to the moon. And the moon would rise and take her away. Maybe she could leave Carson before he left her. Maybe she could get there first and greet him when he arrived.

Instead, she tiptoed in her bare feet back into the room where he slept, turning off the lamp as she went. Softly, she climbed in bed beside him, nodding off to the lullaby of his breath going in and out. In and out. Safe for now.

Two

Most people think of blue as cold. Lips and hands, blue in the frozen air. A fresh blue ocean stretching broad against August. But Greta knew there were other blues—the bottom of a fire blue, running low and hot under the yellow-orange flame. And the blue lights. She'd heard of those before she saw them. Her granddaddy called them the "weather blues." She'd seen them two different times in her life, burning in the sky. They were the kind of blue that takes every notion of pretty and puts it to shame. Hanging in the night, bright, close, and without a sound, the pattern they made looked like a puzzle it would take God to solve. How else could they even be there?

The lights had come. Three nights before. That was the talk. She hadn't seen them herself this time. But they came, and then Carson was gone. She'd expected as much, which was some distance from actually accepting it, she found.

But the lights. She wanted to touch them herself someday, had planned to do that long before Carson was gone. She longed to know how that blue felt. Would it give her shivers, or scalding pain? Could be both. Maybe cold and hot were all the same out there. Maybe everything, finally, is all of one piece. She liked to think that. Stubborn as she knew she was, she liked to think that the devilish quarrels that dogged her thoughts might one day be reconciled inside the different seasons of blue.

But, in spite of her desires, she had more living to do before she was released to the lights. Must be a reason for that, she decided, although she couldn't fathom what it might be. Not anymore. Her only child would be buried that very day, leaving her to wonder why she still lived and breathed.

"So help me God," she said out loud to the early morning air. "It is not my choice to stay."

Mattie watched from a distance, up beside the church. She'd left Greta in a seat by the grave—away from Carson's wife and boy. Even though Elaine Forsyth had taken the trouble to drive all the way to Roseville for Greta, that stubborn fool of a woman would not mix with them at the funeral. In the church, she sat on an otherwise empty pew until a woman from her church slipped in to make it less awkward. Mattie would have stayed with her, but it was an unfamiliar white church and Mattie didn't want to sit up front, drawing all kinds of attention.

Then again, at the graveside, Greta had Mattie position her off to the side. "For heaven's sake, sit with your kin, Greta. You ought to at least act Christian toward the two of them on this one day," Mattie whispered.

"I'm burying my son, Mattie," Greta said. "I won't make the ordeal harder on myself than I have to. Why don't you sit with me?"

"I told you I was uncomfortable with that. I'm going to stand up at the church like we talked about."

So Mattie had walked her from the chapel to the grave, following the procession of folks from the service. Then she walked back up to wait and to watch.

Behind the seated family, all the other white people gathered to pay their respects. Only the funeral home men, the ones who stood at the edges of the crowd, looked up in her direction. They must have found it peculiar that she stood there. Didn't matter what they thought. She'd made a promise, and she aimed to keep it.

She would be Greta's eyes from that vantage. She would stay sharp and try to memorize the faces, even if she couldn't remember the names. Later on, she would describe the whole thing as best she could. The young minister giving the eulogy had a voice so high and weak he might have been wind chimes, lost in the breathing of the gathered. Elaine's aunt and a man—a neighbor from the lake—sat in the family row beside Elaine and the boy. Way off to the side, Greta looked like she'd been put in the naughty chair. Ridiculous pride that woman had.

Mattie paid special attention when it was over, after all the talking was done and folks moved in twos and threes on toward the gravel area where cars were parked. She saw that a couple of the older people spoke to Greta. After that, one of the funeral home men leaned over to say something to her. He helped her up and walked with her in the direction of the car. Elaine's aunt and the neighbor fellow slipped out also. Mattie reasoned that they were heading off to be at the lake in case anyone cared to stop by after the funeral. Others lingered. Carson hadn't lived in town in a long time, but a sizable crowd came anyway. He was well thought of, even after so many years away.

Back in the old Buick across the street, Greta would be able to see the movement of people leaving, but she wouldn't make out more than general size and maybe the color of somebody's hair. Mattie didn't mind being a sharp set of eyes for her friend, but she wouldn't take up any part of the woman's feud with Carson's wife and son. Greta would have to fight that battle on her own.

Mattie nodded as if agreeing with herself on this particular course of action.

Greta knew even before the wife's phone call that Carson had passed. She knew as soon as Carl came up on the porch with the day's mail and started talking about funny blue lights people had seen just before the sun came up. When he said that, Greta, who was sitting with her coffee by the window, put the cup down and said, "He's gone."

Mattie didn't question that it was true. The world held more mystery than known fact. Less than ten minutes later, Elaine Forsyth called with the news.

Mattie found she'd lapsed, letting her mind wander. "Now, who would that be?" she mumbled, looking at the crowd. There were two black boys—one grown and one still little—walking back up the hill toward the church. Light-skinned boys, both of them. Mattie studied their features and decided she didn't know them. Other people were still making their way up, some passing close enough for her to hear the conversations. She straightened herself and took up her post again, drawing in everything she could.

A tall, middle-aged woman who Mattie recognized as one of the Hamilton girls was chattering to some older man. "At least seven people getting off the morning shift from the textile mill saw those things in the sky," the Hamilton woman was saying. "One of the fellows who saw them was retired military, and he said he knew for a fact that nothing out of Fort Bragg would look like that."

That had been one of the theories, that the lights were maneuvers out of the army base. Others just flat out called it a UFO.

But Greta had been expecting them all along. "Weather blues," she'd explained to Mattie years before. "That's what Granddaddy called them. They show up at important times for our family."

"How about other families?" Mattie asked.

"I don't know," Greta told her. "I imagine something happens for a lot of folks—lights, sounds, maybe a change in the climate or something with animals—they might not even make note of it."

Who knew for sure what all was out there in the big world and the sky? Every new thing seems strange until somebody comes along to explain it.

Mattie saw a crowd of the Jamison kin she hadn't noticed before. The sisters, it looked like, and some of the younger ones. That would set Greta off for sure if she got wind they were there. The Jamison boy—not a boy anymore—was the one in the thick of Greta's trouble with Carson and Elaine.

Even before all that happened, there'd been a falling-out between Greta and Tilda Jamison, Wallace's mother. Greta would never say exactly what happened, but Mattie knew the two of them had been good friends and then they were anything but. The business with Wallace and Elaine only made it worse. To Mattie's mind, Greta was better off keeping her distance. Mattie had never taken to Tilda in the first place, a woman with small shoulders and a small face—and a small-mindedness that fit with the rest of her.

Mattie made note of the Jamisons she knew and, to her relief, didn't see Tilda or Wallace. Maybe he *was* there but had gotten too fat or bald for Mattie to recognize.

Didn't matter, she was doing the best she could. She just hoped it would be enough to satisfy Greta.

Greta had been her employer since before modern times arrived in Lowfield, North Carolina. Mattie, five years older, had worked for Greta when they were both young women. Somewhere along that crooked road—Mattie couldn't even say just when—the woman had become more than her employer. Greta Forsyth had become her closest friend.

Elaine Forsyth turned Carson's wallet over in her hand, sliding her fingers on the soft leather. Everyone was leaving. She could hear the car engines turn as people made their way home. But she couldn't make herself walk away from the grave. As soon as the funeral was behind her, she would have to begin life without Carson. The billfold in her hand felt almost warm, as if he'd pulled it out of his pocket moments before so that he could pay for dinner or a bag of groceries. The dark brown hide had molded itself to the curve of his hip and it seemed abandoned now—an imprint of someone who had vanished. How can all the *things* that don't matter outlast the people who do?

Missing from the wallet was the picture of her he'd carried since before Mick was born. She'd slipped it under his hand the way he'd asked her to. The request had come just days before, when they knew time was closing in on them.

Elaine stood looking over the casket. He couldn't possibly be in there. They were two halves of a whole. How could she still be alive if he was gone? *We offer you today the body of your humble servant, Carson Forsyth.* That's what the ridiculous minister had said. Carson was a humble man, but he was nobody's servant. And she hadn't *offered* a damn thing. He was taken, plain and simple. One cell at a time, best she could tell. If it hadn't been for Mick, she might have wanted to follow him, to take herself apart, piece by piece, the way his body seemed to leave and travel with him into whatever unknown there might be.

Instead, she'd have to stay behind. She would have to—what

was it Carson told her?—reinvent herself. She was forty-seven. Young for a widow, but still she felt well past the freshness date for reinvention. She would manage. She looked up at Mick, standing beside the long, black car and fidgeting away his nervous energy. So much of him a boy, still, in a grown man's body. She had so much more to do for her son. Focusing on that would get her through.

Mattie's knees told her it was way past time for her to leave. Everybody had left the grave except Elaine. Her boy waited up at the funeral-home car looking twitchy as a squirrel. Last time she got a good look at that boy—Mick was his name—he'd been a little thing. Lord, that was an awful day. Now he was full-sized. Where had the time gone?

The funeral home men looked to be losing patience. They stood with the son by the black limousine, all wearing different sizes of the very same suit. They'd just as soon get on with the business of finishing up, Mattie knew that much. But Elaine Forsyth didn't make any move to leave. Mattie wanted to leave too, but no one was going to rush a woman who'd just buried her husband.

Mattie knew what would happen after the family left. Her son had worked funerals for a while—back before he left his kids to be raised by Mattie. He'd been one of the fellows who came in old clothes with their shovels. After that, others would collect the tent and the chairs. None of that could happen in front of the kin.

Carson was too young to be put in the ground when the likes of Greta and Mattie were still left standing topside. But things don't always happen in order. She and Greta had visited him one last time a few days before—two days before he died. Just the three of them in that strange house up in the trees. He seemed more at peace with leaving than Greta was with letting him go. It was a shame that Greta and that poor woman by the grave couldn't be of some use to each other. They both loved the man. That ought to make for common ground. Instead, Mattie would have to be the one to ease Greta through her grief.

"Lord, give me the strength for it," she mumbled.

Then her heart sank as she realized how long it might be before she got to go home. That poor widow looked for all the world like she planned to take a seat on the ground by that casket.

"Lord a'mighty." Mattie shook her head and watched, help-less, as Carson's wife sank down right where she'd been stand-ing. She sat on the cloth skirt they'd put around the grave like she planned to have a picnic.

"Lord a'mighty," Mattie mumbled to herself again, then leaned on the side of the building to take some weight off her poor, tired feet.

It seemed reasonable just to sit down for a minute, Elaine thought. Her legs wouldn't let her move away from him, anyway. No matter how much she wanted to leave, to be done with saying good-bye, her body simply would not cooperate. She looked up again toward the church where Mick waited at the car with the funeral-home men.

Up the sloping lawn, the white clapboard church sat in the shade, under the protection of three massive trees. Elaine thought of the first time she saw Stone's Throw Baptist Church. She tried to recall if the trees had looked smaller back then, or if the towering oaks had been old so long that the two-hundred-year-old church was young by comparison even then.

She and Carson had gone looking for a place to marry and, while the church was less than five miles from town, she'd never seen it before. They'd wanted to find a place of their own to have the ceremony. Elaine's parents meditated daily and put stock in a benevolent architect of the universe, but had no building to house their belief.

Greta's place of worship was out. She had made it clear she didn't intend to come to see them marry. Wallace Jamison's parents went to Greta's church, also. A ceremony there would have been contentious, at best, with congregants forced to choose sides.

So Carson had driven the back roads of the county with her, looking for a place that suited them. They rounded a curve and Stone's Throw appeared before them.

"Perfect," she said. Carson was already smiling.

"You think it's open?" she asked as he pulled up and parked alongside the chapel.

"Let's see."

She entered the unlocked door and stepped inside the small sanctuary. It looked bright, even though the stained glass on both sides left no view to the outside. The light seemed to come from the varnished wood and clean walls. The place had an energy of its own, and Elaine thought it might be strong enough to flush out Carson's sadness at his mother's objections. And the other sadness, the one that she had caused.

She felt an immediate ally in the church. A place that could help them heal—give them a beginning without the stains of the recent summer. No one could be anything but inspired standing in such sacred coziness.

She put her hands on her belly, felt a Eucharistic blessing settle on the baby inside her, and then felt Carson's hands cover hers as he wrapped his arms around her from behind.

"You'll marry me here?" he asked.

"I'd better," she said, leaning back, small against him. "Otherwise, we're going to have a little bastard on our hands in a few months."

"None of that." He bent and gave the lobe of her ear a little bite. "You'll be giving birth to a legitimate Forsyth. I promise."

"Tell that to your mother," Elaine couldn't stop herself from saying. She felt the muscles in his arms go slightly stiff. "I'm sorry," she said.

"She deserves it," he said. "Just don't take it out on me. I'm on your team, remember?"

Two months later they'd stood before the minister. Elaine's parents and Linnie were the only family in attendance. A few more pews were filled with friends—Wallace not among them—and four months later Mick had been born a Forsyth. She just hoped her son had a longer run in life than the other Forsyth men before him.

Elaine looked around the cemetery, wondered how long she'd been lost in thought. They could wait. She needed to keep her time with Carson sharp and present. Carolina clay caked the heels of her shoes, stained her skirt and legs.

Even the dirt conjured memory. Carson, coming up the hill from the lake with his tackle box in one hand and a bucket full of squirming bass in the other. The rust-colored clay, dredged up from the muddy banks in front of the tree house, caked his shoes and the bottom of his jeans.

"You're a mess," she'd say every time.

"War paint," he replied.

"Who're you fighting?" she asked.

"Biggest goddamn bass in the lake." He shook his head. "Still out there. Got some of his kin though." He'd grin. On those days, he looked more like Huck Finn than a college professor.

The postfishing routine played out over and over—a corny vaudeville bit that made them both smile. She knew their lives together by heart.

The breeze shifted. It had been at her side, but now came at her, more insistent and straight on. The rush of air seemed to signal a call for exodus. Hers? Carson's? For the first time, she felt nothing but alone—alone and sitting on the ground beside a grave like the crazy woman she guessed she was.

Mattie backed up a step or two and planted herself on a riding lawn mower that sat flush against the wall of the church. If Elaine Forsyth planned to sit and stay awhile, Mattie decided to give her own knees a rest.

Red dirt covered that poor woman's clothes.

At least the air was warm. Leave it to Carson to pass after it turned comfortable enough for folks to pay respects without freezing half to death. He was always a thoughtful boy. Mattie appreciated that about him—had always enjoyed his visits out to the home place. He'd come alone, every couple of months, and usually stay for supper.

He'd join Greta, Mattie, and Mattie's kin at the table and look grateful for any effort put into the meal. Sometimes, he'd talk about his work, teaching at that big college in Chapel Hill. Sometimes he'd steer Greta back into stories of the past. But they never talked about the wife. He never said a word about the boy. No use. Greta would have turned hard, and that didn't serve any purpose at all. Too bad Carson had gone and picked a woman Greta couldn't abide. Too bad Greta's stubborn side cost her so much.

After an age of waiting, the wife finally stood up.

"Praise Jesus," Mattie said, staying put until she was sure. "Get on back, Elaine, and tend to the living." Mattie's advice to Carson's widow was mumbled, but the woman turned her head as if she'd heard. For a second, she seemed to glance in Mattie's direction, but then she looked away again, leaving Mattie to feel invisible. Not an entirely bad feeling and certainly a familiar one. She'd gotten used to white people looking through her. Most of them, anyway. Not Greta.

She stood up and readied herself. Greta would want to hear

all of it, even though details of those mourning her son would be hard to take. Years before, Greta had been made a widow. A young one, too, just like Carson's wife. Forsyth men weren't long for this world, it seemed. When Taylor Forsyth had been put to rest, it nearly killed the woman, although Mattie was one of the few to see it. Now it was Carson. Shouldn't happen that way, mamas burying children. But that's what God had given Greta, and the good Lord didn't make mistakes.

Elaine got up and walked toward the limo where Mick stood waiting. Her son looked like a man. At twenty-four, with his dark hair and olive skin, he looked more and more like Elaine's father every day. But he wasn't nearly finished.

She glanced down at her ruined skirt. She planned to throw away every stitch she had on as soon as she got home anyway. She would keep no reminders of the day she said good-bye to Carson. She'd remember living with him, and that was it.

"You okay, Mom?" Mick asked when she reached him.

"Not even close," she said, touching his arm. "You?"

"Too soon to know."

One of the men from the funeral home opened the car door for them. He glanced at the mess Elaine had made of herself by the grave, but she guessed he'd seen just about everything in his line of work. What was his name? She'd been practically living with these people for nearly three days and she couldn't put a name on more than one or two.

Mick motioned for her to get in first. "Home, James," he muttered as he slipped in beside her. She smiled. Mick was like Carson. He always had a joke. He brushed his knee against the seat in front of him, back and forth in a nervous rhythm. He was barely keeping it together.

"Are people coming over to the cabin?" he asked.

"Linnie and Morty left just after the service and went back

in case people decide to show up," she told him. "But the lake is out of the way for people in town. I can't imagine that many folks would drive that far. I'm surprised there were so many at the funeral. Carson and I have been living away for a long time."

Elaine thought of growing up in Lowfield with Carson. Falling in love as teenagers. Staying in love for over thirty years. A long time. Not long enough.

"Mommy Dearest over there wouldn't even look in our direction." Mick stared out his window as he spoke.

Mick was Greta's only blood relative still alive. If that was God's idea of a joke, He needed to work on His material.

"Her eyes have gotten bad, so she wouldn't have seen us if she had looked our way," Elaine said. "And believe me, your grandmother ignoring us is better than the alternative. You don't want her to be paying attention to you."

The church receded from view, left behind on the rural road in a haze of pollen and gravel dust.

"Dad still went to see her."

"They loved each other," she said. "Carson told me he had a good visit with her when she came over this last time."

"Yeah," Mick said, "I know; he told me that, too. It's just weird. All my friends grew up getting birthday money and sticks of gum."

"Oh, honey, I'm sorry. It's never seemed to bother you much before." She looked closely, tried to figure out what he wasn't saying. But he only shrugged. She leaned over and touched her head to his. "All you've got is me. I'll try to be enough."

Mick attempted a smile, but she saw the wetness around his eyes and looked away. The boy hated to cry in front of anyone. She thought of how life had changed over the last year. The diagnosis, coming after a test that Carson almost skipped because of a tight schedule for final exams. Surgery and a round of treatment that would fly in the face of the Geneva Conventions if used as a military tactic. The hope. The disappointment. And after that, the time they had left. Oddly enough, the time after learning the worst of it was some of their best.

"You've never told me the whole story," Mick said, breaking into her thoughts.

"What story?"

"About her," he said. "The real reasons she won't have anything to do with you—and me."

For years, Mick took the situation with Greta to be inevitable. He didn't really ask. Elaine wasn't in the mood for full disclosure on the day she'd buried Carson. "She never liked me, my parents, the way we lived. My parents didn't belong to a church. She called them 'Voodoo Hippies.' You've heard this before."

"I never spent much time thinking about it before. What you've told me, that doesn't make somebody reject their only grandchild," Mick said. "Dad told me there was an old disagreement. Something that put bad blood between you. I still don't know what that has to do with me. Want to fill me in?"

"Not now, Mick," she said. "Can you give me a pass on it today?"

"Yeah, sure. I guess it's just that I really saw her today," he said. He rubbed his fingers together in rapid time, creating a whisper of a snap. He didn't even seem to notice he was doing it. "Looking at her up close . . . she looks like Dad."

The last seemed to trouble him, as if Greta didn't have the right to carry his father's features. It occurred to Elaine that for both Mick and Greta, family had become a scarce commodity.

"Try to get your mind off of her for now."

She'd always wondered when he'd want to know more. There was so much more for him to know, of course. But Elaine hoped Mick would let the subject of Greta drop. If Carson had any regrets, Greta was one of them. But the stubborn Forsyth matriarch would not let go of her crazy notions, and Carson refused to subject his family to her after Mick was born. Well, except for that one time when Mick was three. No, he'd just turned four. That was a disaster.

"Do you remember going out to Greta's once when you were little? You were really young."

Mick shook his head. "No," he said. "I remember seeing her a few times around town. Once, when I was at the grocery store with Grandma Ginnie. I guess I might have been eleven or so. Other times, from a distance. I mean, I knew who she was and all from the pictures Dad had. I got a good look at her today, though. There's such a resemblance."

It was good that Mick had no recollection of going to Greta's house. Carson had been sure that if he brought Mick to her, if he let the kid charm her, Greta would come around. She didn't. Elaine suspected that even after that awful day, Carson never quite gave up on the notion of reconciliation. That one day his mother would embrace his family.

After they moved to Chapel Hill, it was easy, at least for Elaine, not to think about Greta. Growing up, Mick spent most of his summers at the lake with her parents. But he never questioned his other grandmother's absence. She was mythical. Part of family lore. Nothing more.

"So I've been to her house?" he asked.

Elaine felt the mistake of bringing up the incident.

"I kind of remember Greta's house inside," he went on, scrunching his eyes as if to squeeze the memory into focus.

"Just one time," she said, forcing a light, dismissive tone. "You went out there with your dad when you were about four." She stopped at that. "I wonder if anyone brought food to the cabin?" She wanted to get his mind off Greta. If he had no recollection of her awful tirade when he was small, there was certainly no reason to jog his memory about it.

"I'm not hungry," he said.

She looked at the landscape outside the limo. Acres of woods gave way to the houses on the outskirts of town. Mick knew Lowfield as well as anyone. They'd moved away before he turned two, but entire summers spent with his grandparents made the town his second home. When Mick was little, he'd spend his days fishing and swimming off the dock with Elaine's dad. When he got older, he got a job as a lifeguard at the town pool and played baseball in the summer league. Most weekends, Elaine and Carson would come to the cabin, but for those hot months, Mick belonged to the place.

He'd stopped coming after the summer when he was seventeen. That was when his relationship with a local girl, Kayla Grimes, had ended. The relationship lasted through two summers with visits during the year in between.

Elaine never knew exactly what happened. Kayla had been a beautiful, thoughtful girl, and Mick seemed to be crazy about her. Elaine wondered at the time if the pressures of mixed-race dating in a rural Southern town had gotten to them. In her life with Carson, a life conducted among artists and academics, things like that never occurred to her. But mind-sets changed gradually in places that were small enough for all interactions to be more personal, more relevant.

Kayla had planned to come to Chapel Hill and go to Mick's homecoming dance that fall. Then, suddenly, she wasn't coming. Mick wouldn't say why, but after that, he seemed to have little interest in going back to the small town. About a year later, they heard that she had died. An accident, riding with her brother Kooper in the family's truck. Elaine knew the girl's death had shaken Mick, but he never talked about it.

"Was that Kooper Grimes at the funeral?" she said. "The fellow about your age with the younger boy?" Elaine had noticed the two of them standing at the graveside service.

"Yeah," he said. "The little one is Kayla's brother, too. I said hello at the graveside. Thanked them for coming."

"I didn't know she had a brother that young."

"He was born after we broke up," Mick said. "I remember hearing about him, but he wasn't around when I was with her."

"I guess that's right," Elaine said. "I forget how much time has gone by."

"Yeah," Mick said. "It's been a long time." He sounded desperate to leave the topic behind.

"It's nice that they made the effort," she said as an endcap.

Mick's leg went into double time again. He had something on his mind, but he didn't speak up. She shouldn't have brought up Kayla, especially given what they'd just been through. The loss of someone close to you, someone your own age, shouldn't come when you're a teenager. But then, life doesn't follow the rules. If it did, Carson would be grading exams from his spring semester classes, and Elaine wouldn't be a widow at the age of forty-seven.

"I think we should call her or something," Mick said, abruptly changing the subject. It took Elaine a second to realize he'd gone back to talking about Greta. "I know you don't like her, but she is his mother."

"I called after he died," Elaine said, "and Greta wouldn't even come to the phone. I spoke with Mattie, the woman who looks after her. She doesn't want to talk with us, Mick."

"We could ride out there," he offered. He sounded small, almost as if he thought the suggestion might cause an outburst of some sort. "I mean, what happened that was so bad she wouldn't even talk to us at his funeral?"

"Mick," she said. "I asked you not to push this right now. This has gone on for years. You just never had a reason to pay attention to it. She's never been part of your life. She's not going to be part of our lives now. I refuse to put myself through any sort of confrontation with her. Things are hard enough without adding that particular misery to my life. Let's talk about something else."

"Okay," he said. "I'm sorry."

They lapsed into silence. The rumble of the rough road beneath the limo's wheels filled the void. In counterpoint, Mick's twitchy leg played double time against the seat in front of him, trying to outplay his grief in an agitated, percussive frenzy.

They passed the mill before hitting the downtown drag. The flashing sign over Benny's Burgers looked too cheerful. Elaine had the notion that everything should be muted to show respect for Carson, but the world outside didn't seem to agree.

Once they got to the cabin, she would finally take the doctor's advice—his advice *and* one of the little pills he'd given her the week before. With any luck, she'd settle down to her first real sleep in days. The absence of Carson's hard-fought breathing was some comfort. It had taken so much effort for him to stay with her as long as he did. After she got some sleep, she'd pick herself up and figure out what should come next.

She'd also have to go back to work at some point, although she wasn't sure how to get herself excited about marketing the fall season at the arts council. Writing cheerful brochure copy, looking through stacks of press kits—none of that seemed relevant to her life anymore. She'd gotten a real charge out of her job before Carson got sick. Now she couldn't remember why she'd ever liked it.

And Mick. How soon would he head back to Rhode Island? With more than a little edge to the humor, Carson had teased him about the job he'd taken in Newport—working at a boatyard—after he graduated with a math degree from Middlebury.

"Imagine what I'd be doing if I hadn't graduated *cum laude*," Mick shot back.

"I don't know what direction he's going, Ellie," Carson would say when Mick wasn't around. "I thought for sure he'd take a year and then go back to school. But now I don't know. I wish I could see that he's going to be okay."

"He'll be fine," she'd say, without much conviction.

As the car made its way down Main Street, she saw people on the sidewalk staring at the limo, squinting to get a glimpse of her and Mick through the smoky glass. Some she recognized, most she didn't. It was a regular Thursday for people.

Just on the other side of town, they pulled in at the funeral home. From there, she and Mick would drive themselves out to the lake. Linnie would be waiting, trying to be of use to them. That's what family did after a death. They made themselves useful in the most useless of times.

One of the men opened the door for her, and she and Mick got out.

"Thank you," she said to the funeral director (still, the name escaped her). "You've made this day as easy as it could be."

"Thank you, ma'am," he said. "That's all we can do, really."

Her car sat in the same spot they'd parked it three hours earlier. Only three hours, but a lifetime in so many ways. When she'd arrived, there were still things to do. Put her picture in his hand, attend the funeral, lay a flower on the casket . . . Now there was nothing to do. The empty stretch of hours ahead frightened her. She'd pledged till death, but it didn't end there. Love didn't end anywhere. It simply endured the absence of the beloved.

"Me or you?" Mick held up the keys.

"You," she said, grateful to be a passenger.

They drove out toward the cabin where as a girl she'd dreamed she'd fall in love with someone like Carson. She wondered with an odd sense of detachment what she would be dreaming of from now on. There would be something. She wasn't old, and she wasn't given to pessimism. But her entire adult life had included Carson.

Mick's twitchy leg was now steady on the gas, his hand firm on the wheel. Given a physical task, he seemed almost to relax. Maybe the boatyard wasn't a bad option for him.

When they turned into the dead-end street that ran the length of the point to the tree house, she noted with relief the absence of cars. No visitors. She didn't feel up to facing acquaintances. She couldn't recall much of the drive. Time seemed to be switching back and forth.

"Thanks for driving," she said to her son as they pulled up into the gravel drive at the base of the tree.

"Anytime." He turned off the car and handed her the keys.

They got out and headed for the stairs that wound around the trunk. Above, Linnie waited on the landing up by the door wearing an oven mitt on one hand and a forced smile on her face.

Elaine took off her destroyed pumps and left them at the bottom of the stairs.

Three

Greta sat by the window, looking out as if she had something to see. Mattie intended to tell her the truth, whether she listened or not.

"Greta, you may have your quarrels with the wife, but that boy, at least, he never in his life raised a harsh tone against you. He's never done a thing. I heard you making promises to Carson before he passed. Sounds to me like all he wanted was for you to give his boy a chance, at least a kind word."

"Hmph."

Mattie tried again.

"Promise is a promise. And a promise to a dying man—that's a sacred thing." Mattie gave her a look that said she didn't intend to let a few grunts pass as a reply.

"I promised to keep my counsel, Mattie." Greta gave in. "I promised not to cause more pain than is there already. That's all I promised. Don't go putting words in my mouth."

"He asked you to *try*. He asked you to consider looking at the two of them as family. And you didn't say you wouldn't. I was there."

Mattie could remember the awful scene when that boy couldn't have been five yet. Little, bitty fellow, crying to wake the dead. It was the only time she ever saw Carson downright furious. *Had good reason to be that way, too.* Greta ended up on her backside with Mattie helping her up while Carson took the boy away. An awful day.

"Wherever Carson has gone, he has the truth with him now, Mattie. I had a cousin whose heart gave out and then they brought him back. He went to the blue lights and then came back to tell us there was nothing but love and truth waiting. Carson knows. There's never been a place for that woman or her son in my life. That hasn't changed."

"What you staying in this world for then? Carson's gone, and as far as you're concerned, the rest of your family's dead to you, too. So just get on home to Jesus then if you don't have plans to mix with the living."

"Hmph."

They were back to the grunting—only this time, Mattie could tell that Greta had gotten mad. Mattie had to smile. It was time for her to leave the room, let Greta think on everything she'd heard. Besides, that peculiar smell of Greta's tea was giving her a headache. Earl something. Mattie didn't know how she could drink it. She went into the kitchen to check on her casserole. *Ready.* She turned it off to let it cool, and then went back through the front room and onto the porch outside without another word to Greta.

Let her think all her own bad thoughts all by herself. Stew in her own mess for a while. Mattie watched the children running around. The sun high and warm. That's what led to happy thoughts. Watching children roll around and play, getting themselves covered in fresh, spring grass.

She used to watch Leonard, her son, play like that. But that was before. Before Hank decided he didn't care much about being Leonard's daddy anymore and took off to play his music anywhere away from home. His trips away got longer and longer until they became letters and postcards. Then nothing at all.

Seven years later, her boy Leonard did the same thing, leaving her with two granddaughters to raise. The only smart thing that ex-wife of Leonard's ever did was to turn those girls over to Leonard when she started with the needles. Smoking something was one thing, but even she knew that needles got to be a whole other matter. It was a blessing the girls had both been too young to remember that—or their mother, for that matter.

Then Leonard got to gambling bad. He would leave them with Mattie while he was off throwing away money he didn't have, then again while he was taking odd jobs to pay his debts. Pretty soon, he'd only show up for the holidays. Then not even that. He still called from time to time and showed up every so often for a day or so, but nothing more than that. Mattie knew it was just as well.

Two girls with no mama or daddy to tell them how to get along in the world. Mattie had failed Leonard somehow, but she hadn't failed those girls. Greta, alone by then—Carson already married with a child of his own—asked all of them, Mattie, Ayla, and Rae, to move in. They had a home. A place to be.

Greta waited a few minutes and then followed Mattie to the porch. "The boy," she said and then stopped like it was some kind of question.

"What about him?"

"What does the boy look like up close?"

"Carson's boy?" Mattie said it just to irk her. "He's fine looking. Just fine. You were close enough to see that he's a grown man himself now."

"Who does he favor?"

Mattie knew what she was asking. She knew that nothing she told the woman would bring her one moment of peace. Greta wanted to hear that the boy looked like nobody, or maybe that he had Jamison features. That way her quarrel could feed itself.

"He looks like his mama," Mattie said. "He favors his mama's family."

"Hmph."

Mattie felt sorry for her friend. Angry thoughts kept Greta's grief an arm's distance away. Feelings that burned and churned could keep a heart beating, but grief was likely to shut it down. If Greta wanted the truth, she didn't need blue lights to get it. *Family. That's the only truth she needs.*

"The only chance you've got, Greta, is with the ones who are left. Carson, he kept up the effort with you all by himself. Came to see you in spite of your ways. Now he's gone to the Lord. You've got to soften that heart of yours and make an effort."

"Mattie," she said, serious and tired. "You seem to be what I have left."

The words surprised Mattie, left her looking for something in reply. Instead, she made herself busy on the porch—wiping chairs and watering plants. *My hands are busy and my conscience is quiet.* That's what Mattie's mother used to tell her. She took up the broom and concentrated on getting the porch clear of dirt.

Greta hated being at odds with Mattie. She walked over and stood close enough to watch the black woman ignoring her. Mattie raised the blunt end of the broom to reach a spider's web in the corner by the window. That completed, she turned, stared hard at the windows of the house.

"Too hot now, so late in the day," she said. "But tomorrow morning I'm going to get out the vinegar and some water and give this glass a good clean."

Greta walked over and sat on the glider. In the yard, she could just make out the figures of three children, some of Mattie's great-grandchildren who lived in the smaller houses on the property. They were playing a game. She could hear the pop of a stick against a ball of some sort. Their mothers, Ayla and Rae, had lived in the main house until they married. Later, they moved with their husbands to the smaller houses on the property.

"He came by again day before yesterday," Greta said. Mattie would know that she referred to that man who'd bought the land next door.

"Even after all that mess you made letting those things loose? I watched him and that fellow who works for him out there for two days trying to round 'em up." Mattie acted like she was just making conversation. Greta knew her too well to believe it.

"What'd he say?" Mattie asked, finally.

It irritated Greta that the man still pestered her about the land. She didn't plan to sell him a sack of potatoes, much less her home. Mattie wanted the girls and their husbands to buy it all eventually. That seemed as good an idea as any.

But Greta was curious about Mr. Morales. He wasn't a real famous actor, Mattie told her. Mattie knew her television, and she said this man hadn't been any kind of regular on a show. He'd do little stuff on a program here and there. And she'd seen him in commercials. Darker-skinned fellow, but not black. From somewhere in South America originally, she seemed to recall.

Mattie fiddled with the broom in the corner, acted like she was only half listening.

"He said in spite of the trouble I'd caused him, he would increase his offer. He seemed to think I knew what that offer was, but it doesn't matter anyway." She rocked forward and back in the glider trying to stir the still air around her. "Told me he'd add ten percent to it."

Let her chew on that for a bit. Served her right, Greta thought, trying to talk her into making some kind of nice with Elaine

Forsyth. Wouldn't hurt her to worry for a minute, make her think that this place she calls home and that her family calls home might get sold out from under her. *Make an effort with those two that are left*. Hmph.

Mattie felt her heartbeat thumping all the way into her neck. She didn't turn around. She wouldn't show it. She wouldn't show how Greta's talk of Mr. Morales and his offers got to her. Greta had been generous, opening her home to all of them. Mattie's gambling son and that poor drug-craving woman he'd married had troubles that would have crushed those children. Instead, Mattie had been given a place to raise them strong.

Then Greta offered to let the girls live in the houses out back after they got married.

Those pretty green houses behind Greta's place, just perfect for two little families. Ayla and Rae had been able to stay with their own children while their husbands, Robeson and Dane, kept good jobs. Robeson worked at the mill, and Dane, with a local builder. All of them helped Mattie and Greta keep the property up. Couldn't be better than that. But the situation wouldn't hold forever.

She took the end of her broom and knocked down a wasp nest from the corner of the porch. The inhabitants flew out in a wild frenzy of confusion. "These things take over the minute you look away."

Mattie had hoped that her grandchildren would save up and buy the whole farm from Greta in time. But that man had a fortune to part with right away. A letter had arrived from him in the mail days before. Mattie knew it was wrong to open it, wrong to see that he made an offer of more money than Mattie could imagine anybody having. And then she'd done something else.

Mattie felt hot shame when she thought of that envelope sitting in a drawer in the kitchen. She'd slipped it in there, telling herself she'd pull it out when Greta felt up to thinking about it. It was a sin to want something that much. *I don't want it for myself, Lord. I want it for my family.* Deceit is the same color from either side. Mattie's mama used to say that all the time, and it was true.

Langdon, the littlest of her brood, had come out to join the three already playing in the yard. He stirred things up the way he always did, and an argument broke out about a minute later. Mattie shook her head at all the fussing and complaining.

She glanced over in Greta's direction. A small bit of breeze blew strands of fine, gray hair into Greta's face and she brushed it away. The woman had done plenty of work with her hands, but they looked delicate and soft—nothing like Mattie's calloused palms.

In spite of herself, Mattie had to ask the question. Better to know what was coming. "You thinking about selling?"

Greta stopped her rocking. She pointed her eyes in Mattie's direction, though the Lord only knew what she actually saw.

"Man like that," Greta said, finally, "with the zoo he's already built on his own land . . ." She shook her head. "Why in the world would I let him have my property?"

"Alpacas," Mattie said. "That's what they are." Greta had heard his story, but she refused to call the creatures by name. "He says the fur makes fancy coats and sweaters. Things sold for good money."

"The Forsyth homestead will not become a circus yard for glorified camels. This land has been in the family for over two hundred years. I've outlived all of them, Mattie. Can you believe that?"

"Not all," Mattie said.

"Not all what?" Greta asked.

"You've not outlived all your people." Words that would provoke. Mattie said them anyway.

"So help me God, Mattie . . . I might just up and sell this whole place out of spite if you don't let it go about that woman."

"I'm not talking about the woman," Mattie interrupted. "I said it before. The boy never did a thing against you."

"The boy is a Jamison." Greta sounded less riled than Mattie expected. "You really want to argue with me? You want that woman's son to inherit my land and then have him sell it off to somebody like that fool next door?"

Mattie had never for one minute put up with Greta's bullying. She didn't intend to start.

"Right is right," Mattie said. "If that means the boy getting your land, then so be it." She thought again of the note in the drawer. She wondered if saying one thing and wanting another would send her to hell. "You need family, Greta. We all do. You might find some comfort in that child if you tried." That's what she wanted to say. That was the truth.

"He looks like his mother," Greta said. "You just told me as much. That's reason enough to keep my distance." She turned and went back into the house.

Mattie leaned the broom against the window frame and sat in the glider. The children ran back to the shallow stream that passed between the green houses. They squealed and splashed as the cool water ran over their bare feet. Beyond, in the neighbor's pasture, she saw the hired man who helped with those alpacas—Timmer was his name. He worked on one of the fences while several of the creatures grazed behind him.

Mattie thought about her deceit. Greta didn't know exactly what the Atlanta man was offering, but Mattie did. And she knew for a fact it was more than her family could ever scrape together. On the one hand, she believed that Carson's boy deserved his birthright if he decided to claim it. On the other, she understood what the land could mean to her own family. A place to thrive and then to pass on. She'd never had that, but it was in reach for the ones just after her. She should speak up, tell Greta that she forgot about that note in the drawer.

My great-grandchildren follow me around like little ducks. I have a safe place to sleep at night and a good friend in the bargain. I'm blessed. Whatever happens, I'm blessed.

She got up and worked on getting the last bit of nest down from the porch ceiling, and she said not a word about the Morales man or any letter he'd sent. In the long run, it wouldn't matter what she did. The man had come more than once, and he would come again. Men like that kept coming until they got what they wanted.

Greta would most likely laugh if Mattie broke down and confessed. Still, she kept busy and said nothing, and the shame of that silence burned inside her.

Mattie went down the porch steps. She turned on the spigot and began watering the plants in front of the house. From that vantage she could see what her broom missed on the porch. Red dust that returned each day and settled, uninvited, between floorboards. She'd swept those boards more times than she could remember.

Greta could recall the first time the girl named Elaine had stepped onto her front porch. Carson had been seeing her for a month or so, and Greta thought it would pass.

Girls liked Carson. The girls his age at Calvary Baptist waited outside the service, trying to look casual. They made their parents park beside Greta's car. Elaine, the daughter of Zeb Tyson's loony son and the equally unstable woman from Burlington he'd married, lived in a tree house, for heaven's sake. Carson would get tired of that nonsense and move on to the next girl.

Elaine had gone on to show her stripes with Wallace Jamison in any number of ways. Greta's instincts had been right. And still, Carson had never moved on. And from that first day the girl stepped on the porch, Greta had never felt like Carson was her child in the same way.

Greta, thirty-nine years old, and already one year a widow, felt no closer to figuring out what her life would be without Taylor. After the heady rush of being courted by the most sought-after boy at church, Greta had settled into a strong, working marriage with Taylor Forsyth. She learned to ask for what she needed and to read the long silences that rested among his occasional bits of conversation. He'd been a good father—sometimes showing a camaraderie with Carson that she'd envied.

After Taylor died, she felt his loss throughout each day. Chores were harder, and her place in town and at church was undefined. All the men her age were settled and married. All the other widows belonged to her mother's generation. Even Tilda Jamison, Greta's best friend since fifth grade, feigned concern for the young widow, then acted like she'd won the lottery with a husband still alive beside her. Greta had no place. Except, she was still Carson's mother. That hadn't changed.

"I'm going to bring Elaine over after school," Carson said.

"Elaine?" She knew who he'd been seeing, but didn't want to let on. He told her more about his life if she pleaded ignorance.

"My girlfriend." He called her bluff. "Don't act like I haven't talked about her every day for the last month. Be nice. She's amazing."

Mattie had gone home for the day by the time school let out. Mattie was alone, too, most of the time—her husband, Hank, taking longer and longer stints away, performing in one town and then the next. If he finally left for good, Greta would just have Mattie move in. It'd be easier for both of them that way.

That wild son of Mattie and Hank's was mostly off on his own.

Greta heard Carson's car come to a stop. She stepped outside the front door to greet them. Elaine Tyson had gypsy looks. Curly dark hair that went every which way and a gauzy top that looked like the colors had run in the wash. The two of them walked up the drive together and, before they even got to the front steps, Elaine Tyson stopped, threw her arms around his neck, and kissed his mouth. Greta stood waiting, feeling dismissed before they reached her.

"Elaine," Carson said, his feet shuffling slightly side to side on the porch floor. "This is my mom. Mom . . . Elaine."

"Nice to meet you, Elaine."

They stood in the October afternoon. Greta noticed the leaves that had blown onto the porch just since morning. She wondered if the girl liked living up in the trees like a bird or a squirrel. Did she take after her hippie-dippy parents or was she a serious sort like her grandparents. Zeb and his wife—what was her name? Amy? The grandparents went to a newer church on the other side of the county, but Doug Tyson hadn't set foot inside a regular church since he'd gone off to college. For all Greta knew, he and his Burlington wife worshipped with a sundial.

"Come in the house," Greta told them. "I've got iced tea and some fresh corn muffins."

Every time Greta looked at Carson, he was looking at Elaine. The girlfriend was nice enough, she supposed, but a certain deferential quality seemed to be missing. Elaine Tyson spoke her mind without hesitation. She didn't take the temperature of Greta's opinions before she expressed her own. And the girl's physical ease with Carson made Greta downright uncomfortable. Together, the two of them took all the air in the room.

Greta had never missed Taylor so much as she did that day. She didn't know why exactly, but the weather was up and she didn't have the proper ballast to hold her own. Taylor would have given her some weight. She was caught up in thoughts of her lost husband when she heard Carson mention driving to Greensboro for a weekend concert.

"Don't forget the Harvest Sale is at the church Saturday night," Greta reminded him. The annual potluck evening auctioned everything from quilts to cakes to raise money for the Sunday school.

"Sorry, Mom," Carson said. "The Eagles are at the coliseum. I bought tickets a month ago. I told you. Remember?"

Greta saw herself at the church. She'd either sit with the couples and stick out like a bicycle missing a wheel, or she'd be with the gray-haired ladies, boxy purses perched on their laps.

"I guess I do remember that." She forced a smile.

They sat around the kitchen table. The girl ate half a muffin and drank her tea. Carson talked about football, about being on varsity as a sophomore starter. Greta felt as if she held on to a slippery shore with her fingers while the floodwaters raged beneath her.

After Carson left to drive Elaine back to the lake, Greta made herself keep busy—drying dishes that would have air-dried on their own, shaking out rugs that had no traffic to speak of. Maybe she'd plead illness on Saturday night. Maybe she'd simply take to bed and just never get out.

At the tree house, Elaine had gone inside and changed into shorts. As she buttoned them, she felt a jingle in one of the pockets. Reaching in, she pulled out a piece of paper and a handful of euros.

Go to Europe again. Don't forget to have fun. Carson's handwriting, his directive from beyond, caused a hot flush of nausea to rise inside her.

It should have made her cry, but it didn't. It made her angry.

Who was he to exit her life and then tell her how to live it? That wasn't fair.

Then she retreated. Guilt settled in. He'd fought leaving until they both knew it was time to relent. And even when he knew it was a losing battle, he'd kept on living. Making jokes, watching movies. He even made a pitcher of margaritas one afternoon after they'd come to the cabin. She came into the den to the sound of a blender and Jimmy Buffet. Carson wore an awful shirt with palm trees on it.

"Do-it-yourself Caribbean," he said, grinning. He was only telling her to continue what he tried to do.

A week after the margarita party she'd had to go off and retrieve Greta from the Roseville police station. Less than a week after that, even breathing had become a chore, and both of them knew that the end had to come.

On his last night, he'd felt too restless to stay in bed, so she'd let him lean on her, carrying his thin, remaining weight as they made their way to the den.

His existence had seemed synonymous with hers for three decades. Panic set in when she thought not of his absence but of her own existence beyond it.

"The water's calm," he said.

She'd pulled two chairs over to the large windows that looked out onto the lake. She insisted that he have the upholstered chair. He had almost no fat left to cushion his bones. They sat side by side, shoulders touching, her hand in his. Somewhere behind the house, a half moon threw shadows sideways onto the water. Down the hill, etchings of trees lay perfectly on the still surface.

"The wind's supposed to kick up tomorrow," she said, then regretted the reference to time he didn't have.

If he noticed, he didn't let on.

Through the night, they talked some. Recalled cities they'd

enjoyed, students he'd found particularly interesting. Nothing urgent. The big talks had occurred weeks before. Their conversation that evening reminded her of picking up shells on a beach.

He talked out of his head a few times. Not crazy talk, but talk that seemed to include people who were not there. She didn't know who exactly, just not her.

"I'll be damned," he softly exclaimed once to someone unseen. Then he smiled. "You're right about that. It's not far. The distance . . ."

Elaine glanced at him. He was happy to see whoever it was— or whoever they were. She could make out his features in the dark room, and his face seemed to have lost the strain and pull of the disease. He was leaving her. She knew it. She wanted to stop it from happening, then found it to be like trying to hold water. But in those moments, he was also shedding the pain, the physical hardship of the previous months—and that brought her close to acceptance. Even summoning all the love they'd shared in their lives, she couldn't offer his body an ounce of relief.

"Strangest thing," he said. He looked through the picture windows in front of him. "Really peculiar."

"What?" She only half asked, keeping her eyes on his face, his amazing profile, in the shadowed light. She wasn't entirely sure he was speaking to her again.

"Looks like a constellation," he said, his voice dreamy, "except the stars are blue—and too close. It's like the lights I always heard about as a kid. The pattern. There's a name for it in geometry—that peculiar shape. Three-dimensional. God, I can't remember what it is."

Elaine smiled. Always the professor. He stared out the window, but she couldn't take her eyes off of him. In profile, his features had stayed strong. She touched his face, pushed a stray section of hair off his forehead. His body was as familiar to her as her own.

"Beautiful," he said. "My God." His voice carried the innocent, amazed quality she still heard sometimes in Mick's exclamations. He turned to her. "It's all there."

"What?" She wanted to understand, but he already seemed beyond her somehow.

"Everything," he said. "It's all there."

"Except I'm here." Her words, almost a plea.

He shook his head. "There, too. That's the amazing part. You're everywhere." He leaned back, closed his eyes.

She didn't sleep, but she did let herself follow his breathing to a slower place. He had to work at taking air in and letting it out. She wanted to breathe for him, to give him a break.

They held hands, the lightest of entanglements. Time passed. She didn't think of it as lasting long, though.

"Never caught that damn fish." His voice had a low, raspy sort of wonder. Outside hints of pink touched the slick skin of the lake.

"You got most of his kin, though," she said. Call-and-response.

They sat in silence, still holding hands. Waiting. When she was the only one doing the holding, she knew. Still, she had stayed with him a while longer before she woke Linnie and Mick. When she finally slipped away to tell them, she looked back. With his head against the curved side of the wing-backed sofa chair, he could have been dozing.

She put Carson's note and the coins back in her pocket and walked outside to the landing again. Linnie came out to join her.

"Lost?" Linnie asked.

"I don't know what to do with myself," Elaine said.

Linnie, in her jeans and an oversized man's button-down, seemed to be an angel of sorts. A beautiful, tanned, bohemian angel—circa 1965. Shoulder-length hair, more salt than pepper, framed the remarkably unlined features of her face. Even at sixty-two, she retained her dancer's body, posture that reflected a lifetime of physical discipline.

"You can do any damn thing you feel like," Linnie said. "Scream like a howler monkey if you want to." Her arm rested lightly on the railing as if it might be a practice barre.

"Well, I don't know about howling, but I'm breathing. That's a start, I guess."

"Your mother would know what to say to you," Linnie said. "I'm sorry I'm all you've got, but I'll do my best."

Born fourteen years apart, Linnie and Ginnie, Elaine's mother, had been cut from the same cloth. Even their nicknames took on the twinlike cadence of a child's rhyme. The older Gelynda had been dubbed Ginnie before she could talk. When her baby sibling was named Belinda, Ginnie said that Linnie would do just fine. Over sixty years later, Elaine couldn't imagine her aunt with any other name. Even professionally, in all the dance playbills, she was known as "Linnie Phelps."

It had seemed natural when Elaine's parents were both gone that Linnie should move into the tree house. She'd lived the itinerant life of a professional dancer, then continued to work and travel with the company when she stopped performing. She wanted to stay in one place for more than a month, she said. What better home for her than her sister's grown-up playhouse? So she'd moved in, set up a studio in town to teach local kids modern technique, expose them to something more than tutus and satin shoes. She made a life for herself back in Lowfield.

At the time, Elaine had only been thinking of Linnie—giving her a place of her own. But Elaine now realized—having lost the person who defined her life entirely—that Linnie offered her a soft place to fall. It wasn't just the cabin. Linnie was her home.

"Hey, Auntie Lin." Mick stuck his head out the door. "Did

anybody bring that light green Jell-O stuff with the pears? I love that shit."

"Seafoam salad," Linnie told him. "Bottom row of the fridge. In the back, behind the seven-layer dip."

He offered a salute and closed the door again.

"You think anybody else is going to show up?" Elaine said. She'd missed a small contingent from the church that arrived just after the funeral. "I'm not sure I could even pretend to smile right now."

"I don't think so," she said. "People seemed to think that you and Mick would just as soon have some time to yourselves, so they didn't stay. Some people still don't know quite what to think of you." She smiled as if sharing a wicked secret.

"Greta," Elaine said.

"A lot of people in town have spent more time hearing her talk *about* you than they've actually spent *with* you. Not your friends from high school or folks on the lake here, but I think some people see you kind of like a character in a soap opera."

"Oh yeah, I feel glamorous as hell. Glad to be so entertaining, though." She looked down at herself, her cutoffs, a stray streak of graveside clay still cutting a diagonal up her thigh.

They leaned together, elbows resting on the rail. The sound of a buzz saw from nearby house construction sliced through the weekday calm.

"How did Dad rig up plumbing in this place?" she asked, suddenly curious about things she'd taken for granted her entire life. "Heating, electricity. How did he make this a normal house?"

"Every time I get repairmen out here for one reason or another," Linnie said, "they tell me over and over that your dad found a genius to design this place. All the utilities are managed in that storage shed over there somehow." She pointed to the wooden enclosure that sat just off to the side at the base of one of the trees.

"I know," Elaine said. "But how?"

Linnie shrugged. "Beats me." She was a performer. Impossible realities didn't trouble her. She simply accepted, with grace, the things that allowed her life to proceed.

When Doug and Ginnie bought the lake property, land was cheap because no one had figured out how to market the waterfront to out-of-towners. After the cabin was finished, her parents stayed every weekend in the summer, then every weekend in the fall. Weekends grew to four, five days at a time, and her dad would travel the twenty-five minutes into town from the cabin to teach at the high school. By the time Ginnie was pregnant, they gave up their rental in town and decided to build onto their playhouse by the lake.

For the expansion, Doug imagined a screened porch connected to the opposite tree, with another section of house built on the other oak. The Raleigh architect went to work again on a porch that spanned the two massive trees with a second, larger structure connected to that—two levels that held four bedrooms with a bathroom between rooms on the bottom floor—all in the same style as the original half. A minifoyer led to loft-type stairs connecting the levels. The only inconvenience was the washer/dryer unit that had to go in the storage shed on the ground.

Doug had always intended to build another set of stairs off the new section, but he never got around to it, so the only way up or down was off the original structure. As a kid, Elaine imagined herself Rapunzel, looking out the top-floor window with no obvious egress to the ground.

"So it's just us then. You, me, and Mick?" Elaine turned toward the door, ready as she would ever be to enter her new life as a widow.

"Morty's on his way back over," Linnie said, nodding toward the ground where Morty Connell was making his way between the two yards. "I told him you'd want him here."

Morty, who owned the neighboring cabin, could hardly be called a guest. "He's like family," Elaine said, then thought about the observation.

What did that even mean? Family. Linnie and Mick certainly qualified, but with dying came imbalance, shifting definitions. Her parents gone, Carson gone . . . The foundations of her world had become air under her feet. She could count on Linnie, but even her aunt would be gone at some point. Elaine herself would follow. Who would Mick have then? Family was an illusion. The irony was that she believed Greta might survive them all. Live to break records for longevity.

Stop it, Elaine Forsyth. This isn't you. Grief had turned her into a new creature, frightened and sad in every sense. She'd make sure Mick was okay, and then she would get back to her life in Chapel Hill. He'd want to go back to Rhode Island, too. The sooner they established a new normal for their lives, the further from grief they would travel.

She smiled as Morty made his way up the steep landings. His thick salt-and-pepper hair needed a trim.

"Lucky at my age to have hair," he'd say. "Shame to go cutting it." He never stopped moving, his lanky frame always clearing branches from his yard or power washing his decks. Constant activity kept him thin and fit but, he noted with dismay, nothing would rid him of the small belly that pushed at the waist of his pants.

The older man had owned the cabin next door since Elaine was a kid, and for most of that time, he had gone back and forth between North Carolina and his home in New Orleans. A few years back, he'd retired and moved to the lake full-time. He had to be seventy—or close to it—but he had the energy of a teenager.

There were stories that flew around about his marriage. Everyone seemed to know that he'd had a wife at some point, but he'd been alone for as long as Elaine could remember. Whether he was divorced, widowed, still married and living apart—it depended on who you were talking to. Knowing Morty, he probably started most of the rumors himself just for fun.

If you asked him, he'd shrug and say that women had more sense than to take up with the likes of him. She'd seen a woman or two at the cabin with him from time to time. They were always about his age and perfectly nice, but she'd never seen anyone more than once.

"Hey, Morty," Elaine said.

"Hey there, darlin'," he said, his years in New Orleans still bending his speech into a slightly foreign sound. "You done gone through the hardest day a your life, but we gonna do what we can. You hear that, don't you?"

"I hear you, Morty," she said, feeling herself relax. "Thank you."

"I do miss that Carson, though," he added, shaking his head. "Man was worth ten regular folk. I swear that to be the truth."

"You're right," Elaine said, because what else was there to say? "We were just heading inside. Come on in."

In the den, Mick sat slumped, elbows on his knees. "Hey, Morty," he said.

"Hey." Morty went over and put a hand on the boy's shoulder. "You did good," he said to Mick, "getting through the day and helping your mama. Saw your friends there, too. Nice of that girl's family to come and show their respects."

Mick nodded, but didn't look up.

"Go sit by your boy there." Morty gestured to her, as if she might be the visitor. Elaine obeyed, and Morty went toward the kitchen where Linnie had gone to pull out some food. Reaching up, Elaine brushed curly, dark hair away from her son's eyes.

"You look like hell," he said.

"Right back at you."

Dark circles gave his eyes a sunken quality. Still, he managed a smile. She pulled him into a two-arm bear hug, the same way she had when he was ten and it had irked the hell out of him. He didn't mind anymore.

Linnie had set places and put food out on the table. Elaine wondered what meal it would be. She hadn't been able to keep anything down at breakfast and with the funeral at eleven that morning, lunch had never happened. It was the middle of the afternoon, so she guessed they'd call it a late midday meal. Did it matter? Did anything matter?

"Thought Liza did a nice job with the music this morning," Morty said, dipping a serving spoon into a seafood casserole that sat steaming on a trivet.

"Beautiful voice," Linnie echoed. "Sounds like she had formal training, but her sister told me she's self-taught."

Mick nodded. All his nervous energy after the service seemed to have collapsed, and Elaine wondered if it would be okay to give him one of her sleeping pills.

"I'm going to see if I can manage a little nap when we're done eating," she said. "You should try to close your eyes, too, Mick. We were both up and down all night."

"Yeah," he said. "Maybe I'll try."

They ate in silence and when it seemed that everyone had stopped, Linnie got up to clear the plates. Elaine stood up.

"You go sit on the couch," Linnie said. "Both of you. Morty and I will take care of the kitchen."

Elaine obeyed. It wasn't a day to argue. It wasn't a day to do anything but try and survive. Five minutes, then five more . . . Mick sat beside her on the couch, his eyes red. When had he cried? She tried to remember.

Both of them turned toward the door at the sound of a car outside. Slow footsteps of someone making labored progress thumped up the stairs to the cabin.

Mick raised his eyebrows, eyes on the door. "I feel like we're in a horror movie all of a sudden."

There was a pause after each step that lasted ages. Elaine wanted to investigate, but didn't want to embarrass their visitor. Then progress seemed to stop. Mick inclined his head forward as if urging the new arrival upward toward the door. After a moment the thumping resumed, and finally a figure passed by the window just to the side of the entrance.

Elaine recognized Mattie. Through the smoky glass panel of the door, Elaine saw her look around for a moment. Finally, she knocked. By this time, Elaine had made it across the room to let her in.

The black woman was solid, but not overweight. Substantial, Carson once called her. She carried herself with the bearing of royalty.

Face-to-face with Elaine, Mattie didn't offer any news from Greta. Elaine doubted that Carson's mother would have sent her. In her hands, she held an oblong Pyrex dish with tinfoil on top.

"Thought y'all might could use some scalloped potatoes," she said.

"Thank you." Elaine took the dish, still warm to the touch.

"I made it this morning," Mattie said. "Had my granddaughter put it in while I was . . ." She stopped, both her sentence and her progress toward the middle of the room. She stood, looking uncomfortable. "Before I came over." She finished her sentence, then eased herself onto the edge of a sofa chair, sitting perched as if a sudden retreat might become necessary.

Mick hadn't said a word. He stood when she came in and sat on the couch again when she sat, but he appeared to be struck dumb at the sight of the woman.

"How's Greta?" Linnie said, coming into the room with Morty behind her.

Elaine was glad she asked. She couldn't bring herself to do it, but it was natural to inquire.

"She's grieving," Mattie said. "Losing her only child . . ." She shook her head. "That's not how it's supposed to go. Children ought to bury the ones that raised them."

"Amen," Elaine said. She looked over at Mick, tried to imagine losing her only child and then had to stop because it seemed unthinkable. "Would you like something to drink?" she asked.

"I expect a little water would be nice," Mattie said.

Linnie went back to the kitchen, while Elaine, Mick, and Morty assembled on the couch. It looked to Elaine as if Mattie held court and they, her awkward subjects, waited to hear her intentions. Maybe there were no intentions. Maybe she'd just brought food like decent people tended to do when someone died. While Elaine ran through and rejected several conversation openers, Mattie shifted forward, even closer to the edge of her chair. Elaine feared for a moment that she might keep going and topple onto the floor below.

"I was there today," Mattie said. She nodded once to further punctuate the statement. "At the service."

"I know Greta was there, but I didn't see you," Elaine said. But she had, she realized. Mattie was the figure Elaine had seen standing by the church after the graveside ceremony, only she hadn't registered the woman's identity until Mattie's confession.

"I wanted to pay my respects but I, like I told Greta, would have felt uncomfortable sitting with the family."

"No one else would have seen it as odd," Elaine said, "for you to be with Greta."

"I know that's true," she said, "and I appreciate your saying it, but all the same, I don't like to draw attention to myself in public. Just rather stay back."

"I understand." Elaine wished Linnie would come back. Mick looked as if he'd gone catatonic, and even Morty was uncharacteristically quiet. "And regardless of my issues with Greta, I'm glad you both had some time with Carson before the end."

Mattie nodded. "She made noise about not going to the funeral at all, but I knew she didn't mean it."

"There's no love lost between us, but I know that she had as much right to be there as anyone," Elaine said.

"She said it was because she thought he ought to be laid to rest at the church where he grew up. But I think she just didn't want to tackle the day at all. I told her it didn't matter if he was buried on the moon, his mama ought to be there. She had to do that for him."

"You're certainly right about that one," Morty chimed in.

Mick watched Mattie like a toddler watching television—absorbed but removed at the same time.

Linnie came into the room. She handed Mattie a glass of ice water and they watched her take a sip. When Morty asked her how she planned to handle the early spring with her garden, Elaine felt a flood of gratitude toward her neighbor. The conversation took a normal turn, and after a respectable amount of discussion on the matter, Mattie rose to leave.

When the older woman stood up, Mick stood, too. Mattie walked over to him, leaned in close, and inclined her head to look at him from the side. His discomfort became palpable.

"You do have some of Carson in you," she said. "From the side you can see it. And around the mouth some." She took a step back. "I'll tell her that, but she won't cotton to it. Most likely won't listen at all." This last part was mumbled, as if she might be talking to herself. Then she looked up again at Mick.

"You got emptiness in you," she said, without explanation.

"Well, he said good-bye to his daddy today," Morty said. "That'll empty anybody."

"I don't mean something new," she said. "I mean old. The kind of empty you get used to. You're too young to have that look, son."

Elaine looked at Mick. He offered something that might have been a nod of acknowledgment before looking down at the floor.

It was true, Elaine realized. What Mattie said was something she'd seen, too. He'd been rudderless for a couple of years. Mick looked back up at Mattie, but his expression faded into the pleasant mask he used to get through awkward encounters.

And Mattie was right about something else. Mick's face was shifting from boy to man and, in the transition, the resemblance to his father grew. That would fall on deaf ears with Greta. But it was good to hear Mattie say it nonetheless.

"I'll get your dish back to you," Elaine said, hoping to deflect attention away from Mick. At this, they all, Mick included, moved toward the door.

"Dish belongs to Greta," Mattie said when they'd all reached the landing. "No rush."

"Thank you for coming."

Again the nod from Mattie. She checked her purse for her car keys and put her hand on the railing to steady her descent.

"Mattie?" Elaine spoke up. "Does Greta know you're here?"

Mattie looked down toward the old-model sedan she'd driven out from town. She glanced over at the lake. Low-slanting sun gave the water a tangerine glow.

"No, ma'am, she does not," Mattie said, finally, without any suggestion of guilt over her actions. She didn't ask that Elaine keep it to herself. She asked nothing from any of them.

Mattie took one step down, still gripping the rail for dear life and, even so, looked too unsteady to negotiate the steep incline of the stairway. Greta must have helped *her* when they visited Carson. Going up had been an obvious struggle, but down was downright precarious. Elaine wanted to help, but she didn't want to embarrass the woman.

"I best be going home myself," Morty said, making his way

over to stand beside Mattie. "I'll head down with you." Without ceremony, he took her elbow and together, they descended the staircase.

"That was an unexpected visit," Linnie said when the departing pair had gotten out of earshot.

"Unexpected," Elaine echoed.

Behind them, the impending sunset simmered across the surface of the lake.

It wasn't lost on Elaine that, since the moment Mattie arrived, Mick had yet to utter a single word.

Four

ick sat in his boxers on the edge of the bed. He didn't *want* to get up. He didn't want to pretend that things were getting better. If anything, it had gotten harder in the week and a half since the funeral. At dinner the night before, his mom told him she thought she ought to go back to Chapel Hill.

"Maybe I just need to get back to work," she said. "Sitting here, I've got nothing to do but think about everything."

She had a point. The two of them couldn't live in limbo indefinitely.

Linnie said it was too soon, that they both should stay at least one more week, but after nine days of sleeping late, eating microwaved casseroles, and swimming in the too-cold lake, Mick felt the need to shake off the stale indulgence of bereavement and take a stab at something—anything—else.

Of course there was—how was it that Linnie put it?—

unresolved grief. Hell, *unresolved* described his whole fucking life. Another week hiding out in the trees wasn't going to make a dent. But a world without his dad in it . . . nothing made sense to him in that scenario.

He'd talked to his dad about it, about moving on when Carson was gone. They'd still been in Chapel Hill. A full week of unseasonably warm weather had brought out the bugs, and so they sat inside the screened porch behind the house. Mick let Carson talk, but in his own mind, something ridiculous, miraculous, would intervene and keep his father around. That made so much more sense than anything Carson was saying.

"I don't want to be an excuse," Carson said. "That'll fly for a little while, but everyone has to deal with loss sometime. I lost my dad when I was younger than you and it was a sucker punch. I won't lie to you. I wish I could make it come out another way, but I can't, son. I've got to count on you to make yourself move forward, think about your real future."

Carson meant his future beyond the boatyard. The things Mick really planned to do with his life. But if experience had taught Mick anything, it was that no matter what you planned, the world did what it wanted to. Hearing that Kayla had died in a wreck—that was his first clue. Carson's illness only confirmed it.

He couldn't change the way life worked. He had no big picture, no impressive list of goals. The boatyard kept him busy. Sometimes, his work there even made him happy. So Mick would go back to Rhode Island. That was the extent of his planning.

But he had come to at least one decision. Fuck the notion of family grudges; he had something he really wanted to do before he left town.

When he went into the kitchen, he saw that someone had cleaned the dish that held Mattie's casserole. The clear Pyrex sat on a dish towel where it had been left to dry. That seemed like a sign of some sort. No time like the present.

He didn't tell his mom he was riding out. He took the dish from the counter and found the car keys before Elaine got up. She was sleeping late every day, too. A bad sign. Linnie came in, already dressed in leggings and a tunic.

"You have a class today?" he asked.

"Saturday morning," she answered. "I've got three of them." She set to work, putting fresh grounds in the coffeemaker.

"If you're taking the pickup, do you think Mom will mind if I take her car?" he asked.

"Probably not," Linnie said. "Why?"

He told her he needed to ride around, see some different scenery. Linnie wasn't stupid. He could tell she didn't buy it for a second, but she didn't ask any more questions, not even when he left with the dish in his hand.

He drove fifteen minutes into town and then another five in the other direction. Lowfield roads were familiar, even after so many years. The road to Greta's took him along the route that led to the house where Kayla had lived. Maybe her family still lived there. He didn't know. He'd talked to Kooper briefly at the funeral, but he hadn't asked if they moved. Probably not. People in Lowfield tended to stay planted.

"Kooper with a K," he'd announced the first time Mick met him. The younger brother's name was Kyle, he found out. The little guy had eyes like Kayla. Only blue. Lollipop eyes. Hers had been green. Mick found the unexpected combination—brown skin and light, colorful eyes—mesmerizing. All three siblings had the same smooth skin—roasted almonds.

Kyle had been born after Mick stopped seeing Kayla. He was what? Six or seven. Had to be. Kyle, Kayla, Kooper. The folks had a naming system and stuck with it.

The GPS was telling him to make turns that seemed sketchy.

He'd gone off the grid for sure. He'd looked up the closest thing he could find to an address for Greta, then plugged it in. But even with the help, he didn't know where the hell he was. Modern mapping systems didn't seem to have a firm handle on the rural routes and country roads that formed the outskirts of Lowfield.

The surroundings had a familiar feel, though. He'd just gotten his license the summer when he was sixteen. He and Kayla logged the miles on every square foot of paved road in the county.

She'd planned to be an artist, so he'd drive with her to places she wanted to sketch—a covered bridge or an old barn. Early on, he expected to see a likeness of these things, but instead, she would draw the latch to the barn door that hung by one nail, or the rail that led to the bridge opening with only the barest hint of what lay beyond.

Spending time with her, he learned to see things in different ways. He learned to see himself in different ways.

They spent a lot of time hiking in the woods or driving his grandparents' boat on the lake. If they wanted to go on a real date, they avoided the local restaurants—because of the stares and whispers from the older folks. They'd drive to restaurants in Burlington or Greensboro, where they still got a few looks and mumbled comments, just not from people they knew.

He'd been happy that summer—and the next. Had he been happy since? Seven years. College, sailing, northern prep school girls who knew every bartender in Boston by name . . . a life in New England devoid of any of the familiarity of home. He'd had some good times. Still, on the occasions when he could no longer avoid himself, the frayed edges of his life nagged him. The biggest one? *How could he have treated Kayla that way?*

He passed a church with redbrick construction that dated it only to the 1960s or 1970s. Most of the churches outside of town were older, wooden structures. Some were even made from stone, which meant they were built about the time God got around to creating mammals. Just to the side of the "modern" church, he saw a roughly constructed cross—remnants of an Easter pageant most likely.

A board that read KING OF THE JEWS had been tacked to the top of the cross.

"Now there's something you don't see driving through New Jersey," he mumbled to himself.

Beyond the church, woods stretched on either side of the road, then on one side opened into pasture. There they were, grazing in the middle of the field. Alpacas. Those were the things Greta set loose. Must have been a half dozen or so. At least he was getting close.

"Damn," he said, craning to get a better look. In the distracted moment, his right tire slid off the shoulder, calling him to attention.

The GPS alerted him to an upcoming turn, but he saw no road in sight.

"Turn right now," the digital dominatrix commanded.

He slowed. There it was, a parting of the trees with poorly maintained asphalt running into the woods. A street sign read WHITESILL RD.

"I'll be damned. That's it."

Calling Whitesill Road a paved street was a stretch. The attempt had been made, but it had been a while since anyone had tried to keep it up. Mick bumped his way along until he saw a dirt driveway. The GPS had announced his arrival over a mile back, so he continued on faith that a house sat somewhere on the property.

Just off the dirt drive, he saw it. A sprawling farmhouse. Two smaller homes sat back on the property in the distance. Both had been painted the same shade of green. Unlike the road into the property, everything *on* Greta's land seemed to have been kept up with great care. Storybook patches of garden sat on either side of the two smaller houses. A neat pen with what appeared to be chickens inside had been set up behind them. It looked idyllic in a lot of ways, but the sight of the property sent a thread of uneasiness through him.

In front of the main house, two children played in the yard. The boy and the girl were both black, which made him wonder if he had the right place. But he recognized the sedan that the woman named Mattie had driven to the cabin after the funeral. Back beside one of the smaller houses, another boy—he couldn't tell how old—observed his arrival as well.

The closer boy, who looked to be about six, stared at him as he drove past, then followed the car as Mick maneuvered closer to the house. The girl, older and more aloof, stood back, but watched him with the same intense scrutiny as the boys.

"Not many visitors out here, I guess," Mick said to himself, positioning the car in the shade of a couple of trees.

He picked up the casserole dish from the passenger seat and got out of the car, looking around for any adults. Best he could tell, kids seemed to have the run of the place. He got a kind of *Lord of the Flies* vibe, feeling the eyes of the children bearing down on him. A circle of bricks in the ground formed a makeshift flowerbed. Yellow flowers grew inside. Not delicate, fancy flowers, but tough, stocky plants—just the kind to survive any threat of drought, bugs, or weeds. The right plants to keep company with Greta.

Just beyond the flowers, an old well with stone sides and a metal top sat baking in the sun. Recognition of the well startled Mick as he remembered a trip to Greta's with his father when he was little. Carson had raised the lid, lifted him to look down the well. He recalled the tight squeak of the hinge, the metallic smell from the water below.

He tried to remember more, but the images stayed just out of reach. He tried to imagine his dad as a kid, running around the yard, stomping up the porch steps with a jar of insects or whatever rural kids collected for fun back in the '60s. The property would have seemed old even when his dad was growing up.

Mick felt as if he'd gone through a portal and stepped back out into another century—no, another decade. Not time travel so much as that vague sense of memory. Holding his dad's hand—Carson's grip, a little too tight. Too protective. Mick remembered feeling queasy, asking if he could go inside. Rain. Stinging rain had begun to come at him and he wanted to go inside. *Not in my house!*

Carson was arguing with her. Mick rested his head against his father's thigh to shield himself from the rain. Carson's hand had been trembling, and Mick remembered thinking he must be cold, too.

"You looking for somebody?" It was the girl. She'd come up beside the smaller boy.

"Greta," he said.

The girl got an expression that seemed to say, *That's what I thought.* But she didn't make a move toward helping him out.

"Is she here?" he asked.

"Uh-huh," the girl said. "She inside." She kept her gaze solid and seemed to be daring him to ask for more.

"Could you let her know that Mick Forsyth is here?"

The girl held her position for a moment longer, then gave a slight nod to the boy. With nothing but that gesture from the older child, the boy ran off toward the house. In the distance, the other boy seemed to be a sentry, keeping his post.

Mick stood awkwardly with the girl looking him over.

"School out for the summer already?" he asked, trying to fill the moments as he waited.

"Saturday. No school." Her economy of words impressed him. "One more week to go before summer."

Seconds later, the boy came out of the house. The screen door slapped shut and Mick waited for the child to speak, but he hung over the rail of the porch, smiling, clearly playing a game.

"What did she say?" He took the bait.

"She say nothing," the boy told him, "but Granny Mat say to tell you to wait on the porch."

Before he reached the house, Mattie came out to greet him—if greeting meant standing at the porch rail with her arms crossed. When he got to the steps, the pungent smell of a flowering bush by the rail sent another, stronger shock of uneasiness through him. What was it with this place?

He walked up the steps with Mattie standing above him. She wasn't a particularly large woman, but Mick realized he'd hate to try and push his way past her. He stood, Pyrex in hand—a ticket to gain admittance, if he was lucky.

"The scalloped potatoes were terrific," he said. "I thought you might need the dish back."

"You come by yourself?" she asked as he made his way up the porch steps.

"Yes, ma'am."

"She might not have anything to say. You understand that, don't you?" Mattie took the casserole dish from him. Her face had an expression that might even be interpreted as benevolent.

"Yes, ma'am," he said again, then reached around to open the screen door for her.

"Well, you got your manners," she said, going into the house. "Wasn't sure you even had a tongue th'other day."

Through a window at the far end of the porch, he saw movement. Nervous fingers clutched a tissue, fidgeting. As Mick held his gaze on the sight, the arm retreated and was swallowed by the shadows, but not before he registered that it belonged to someone of his own race. Greta was really in there.

Why should going to see his grandmother be such a big deal? She was his dad's mother. How could he have spent *no* time with her in his whole life? He'd taken it for normal all along, but now it seemed strange. Really fucked up. With the exception of his mother, the woman was his closest blood relative. Southern families used to be such huge, sprawling things. How was it that his came down to a reclusive, hostile grandmother and his mom—with Linnie thrown in for good measure?

"Son?" Mattie stood just inside the door and waited for him to come in.

"I'm sorry," he said. "I got distracted."

Though it was ten thirty in the morning, the main room inside the door was all shadows. Pastel green curtains framed tall windows at one end of the room. Smaller windows looked out onto the porch. A sweater lay draped over the back of the couch and a teacup, half full, sat on a side table. The lack of sunlight in the room wasn't gloomy. Rather, with the windows open to the breeze, it seemed cool and airy—in contrast with the warming day outside.

"Have a seat," Mattie instructed. It wasn't a suggestion.

Mick looked around at his choices. Old furniture, but solid and in great shape. After two years spent working on boats in Rhode Island, Mick recognized integrity in construction. He sat on the couch covered in heavy, blue fabric. A subtle pattern of roses ran through the solid color of the material.

"You want something to drink?" Mattie asked.

"Water would be fine, thank you," he said. He wasn't thirsty, but he needed something in his hand to calm him. He realized the only noise in the room was the tapping of his heel on the wooden floor.

"Just made iced tea," Mattie said.

He didn't know if this was considered an upgrade, or if water wasn't on the menu.

"Tea would be great."

"Be right back," she said, retreating toward the back of the house.

A television in the corner of the room ran images of a game show. The sound was turned off, but Mick recognized it as reruns of an old program. *Let's Make a Deal.* The host—dated in his slick '70s suit—had to be older than God by now if he wasn't already dead.

"Here you go." Mattie came back in, handed him a glass of iced tea, and put a coaster on the small table beside the couch. She glanced over at the television and shook her head at the manic action on the screen. Crowds of people in the audience, most of them white, dressed as loaves of bread, Popsicles, and life-size dollar bills—all wearing obscene grins and hoping to get noticed.

"She loves this channel. They run all the old game shows," Mattie said. "I don't see it myself. I like my stories. She'll take a game show anytime, though."

Mick saw the hint of a smile on the black woman's face, a hard-won softening of her features. "Will she see me?" he asked, hoping the moment was right to ask.

"I think so," she said. "Give her a minute. Hard for her to climb over that stubborn streak a hers."

"I understand," he said, although he didn't. Since the moment he'd heard that his dad had cancer, he hadn't understood a goddamn thing.

Elaine woke up. It was late—the sun outside had the clarity of a day well under way. With the "new section" of the tree house separated from the original side, no one woke her with smells of breakfast or sounds of pots and pans. This was good and bad, she realized. A little prodding toward the living world could only help.

She sat up in her old childhood bed. A single bed. Rapunzel's bed. She hadn't slept in that room since the night before she married. The next room over had a double bed, and she and Carson always stayed in there together. Even when she visited the cabin without Carson, she stayed in the room with the double bed. Mick always slept in her old room. It was a room that belonged to a kid.

After the funeral, without thinking, really, she'd gravitated toward her old space, a room that had never been part of her life with Carson. Mick quietly moved out without asking why, taking his things one floor down to the bedroom that had belonged to Elaine's parents. It was the largest in both sections of the cabin. Elaine told Linnie years before that she should claim it, but her aunt preferred to stay in the old section near the den and kitchen. She kept the newer part of the house closed off when she was alone to save energy.

Elaine looked around her old room, noticing for the first time how archival it had remained in spite of Mick's use. Her parents, before they died, and Linnie, after she moved in, left the bedroom intact. High school ribbons, her books from grade school on up . . . everything seemed to be there. And now, she was back, sleeping in a single bed, feeling as if her adult life might have been a dream.

Dreams. She'd hoped to dream of Carson. A friend in Chapel Hill whose sister had died told Elaine that her sister visited her when she was sleeping.

"Sometimes I wake up and tell Bill, 'Dottie came around last night.' And Bill says, 'How's old Dottie doing?' I know it sounds crazy, but I have the most fun in those dreams."

After a week of restless nights, Elaine had yet to have a visit from Carson. She'd begun to feel irrationally angry with him for his absence.

The closest she'd come was the night before when, as she washed the Pyrex dish that Mattie had brought, she felt Carson . . . surround her. She couldn't think of another way to describe it. Of course, she didn't want to describe it—to anyone. Grief made you odd anyway. She didn't need to appear any crazier than she already felt. But something had happened. She felt *held* somehow. She'd loved the man for decades. She knew what it felt like when he was in the room. The occurrence brought a fleeting absence of pain.

As she slid her fingers along the smooth Pyrex glass, along the bottom of the dish, she felt a piece of masking tape, and she turned the clear, wet dish over to see G. Forsyth scrawled on the tape.

Hours later, in bed, she wondered if the occurrence had, in fact, been a dream. Had she really washed the dish? She was sure she had. Either way, Carson's presence had been palpable.

A god-awful sound came through the window. Morty had his drill out, repairing something outside. She got out of bed and went over to the closet, sliding the wood-paneled door open. In the week that she'd been sleeping in the room, she hadn't once opened the closet. She would throw her dirty clothes in a pile on the floor and they'd appear clean and folded on the chair the next day. Linnie. Doing what she could to make life bearable. So Elaine had no use for closets.

When she slid the door open, she saw that all her old possessions—some in plastic bins and some thrown in loose and scattered—filled the space. Her clothes had either gone with her at some point or had been given away, but everything else seemed to be there. Books, a few dolls, pom-poms, and the radio she'd taken down to the pier every day in the summer during high school.

On a high shelf off to the side, she saw the wooden corner of a framed corkboard. A box overflowing with notebooks sat in front of it, so she couldn't tell if it had been left untouched or if her mom had taken down the final selection of photos and put them away.

She pulled her old desk chair over to the closet, stood on it, and slid other things to the side. There were still pictures attached with thumbtacks to the board, offering up the final slice of youth that had been recorded there. She'd had the board at college with her, then brought it home when she graduated. Pictures were put up and then taken down as new rolls were taken and developed. The last posting was from the summer she'd gotten engaged to Carson—the summer she found out she was pregnant. She'd moved home after graduating from Chapel Hill and worked at the library. Those months seemed frozen in place, tucked away to commemorate the end of one life and the beginning of another.

She pulled it down, climbed off the chair, and propped the photo board on the desk. Sunlight, bright even when filtered through tree branches, dated the photos as old, archival. Most of the pictures featured her with Carson. Some were taken in Lowfield during his visits home to see her. Some were from her visits to DC.

Georgetown was a long day's drive from Lowfield, so the trips back and forth took tremendous effort for both of them. But they'd managed. She wondered why she hadn't moved there, just moved in with him. But in the 1980s, with his mother and even his grandparents alive to disapprove, it hadn't seemed like much of an option. Her parents wouldn't have objected. People who decide to build a tree house and live in it were not the sort of people to make a fuss over premarital cohabitation.

But living in Lowfield, there was still gossip—and not about her and Carson. Elaine and Wallace. A lot of the talk was fueled by Greta. Hell, most of it was fueled by Greta. But the flame was stoked by others in Greta's church, including Wallace's mother and his aunts.

Tacked on to the board, amid all her smiling poses with Carson, there was a picture of her in a bathing suit, sitting beside Wallace. She's smiling there, too. Why wouldn't she be? She loved Wallace and he loved her. It had been a source of tension, the time she spent with Wallace, but Carson had been so far away. Before the final blowup, Carson had tried to accept her friendship with her high school friend. Still, the talk always bothered him.

She looked closely at Wallace and wondered what he would be doing now. He'd lived in Lowfield until a few years before. She'd heard he moved away, but she didn't know where. A devoted teacher, he would still be saving the world, somehow—one kid at a time. It hadn't occurred to her when they were so close, but it did now, that Wallace had been very much like her dad.

She'd seen Wallace's two sisters at the graveside service. They didn't come up to her—had left just after the service, in fact, so she didn't have the chance to ask what he was up to these days. Just as well; with Greta sitting stonelike and within earshot through the service and the burial, the fewer reasons to bring up Wallace, the better.

"Elaine?" Linnie called her from outside the door.

"I'm up," she said. "Come on in."

Linnie opened the door. She had a cup of coffee in her hand, steam rising from the blue mug.

"God bless you," Elaine said, smiling.

"It's almost eleven," Linnie said. "You've got to be hungry."

"I am," she lied. "Just let me wash my face and I'll come over to the kitchen."

"That's the last of the pot," Linnie told her. "I'll make another one."

"Is Mick up?" Elaine pulled on her robe, even though the air was too warm for another layer.

"Up and gone," Linnie said, going back into the hall. "He took the dragon lady's dish from the kitchen and left over an hour ago."

Elaine felt an urgency to call him, to tell him to come back. The dish. That had been something tangible that led her to Carson. She understood how insane the notion was, even as it moved through her thoughts. Then a slow, uneasy question took hold.

"Why did he take the dish?" she asked.

"He didn't say." Linnie leaned on the door frame. "I can only think of one reason though."

"Dammit to hell," Elaine mumbled. "He didn't go out there. You think?"

Linnie shrugged, let out a sigh. "Come on," she said. "You'll feel better with something in your stomach."

Just thinking of Mick at that woman's house, Elaine felt the solid weight of dread in her stomach. Swallowing anything else, even Linnie's perfect eggs, might be next to impossible.

Mick heard Greta before he saw her. She was moving around in another part of the house. He guessed it was Greta. Or maybe there were more children around and more adults who went with them. Then he heard a voice call out Mattie's name, the quality of it both familiar and new to him. Had he heard her speak before?

Mattie went into the back room to talk with Greta, probably trying to coax his grandmother out to the main room.

He sat on the blue couch while children, the three he'd seen in the yard, plus at least two others that he counted, leaned their foreheads against the screen door, jockeying for position.

They made no attempt to come in and fled the moment Mattie emerged from the other room.

"She'll be right out," Mattie said, seeming not to notice the squealing kids and the general stampede back into the yard. "How's your mama holding up?"

"Not bad," he said, "considering."

Mattie nodded, but didn't press him for more detail. He looked away from Mattie, feeling the betrayal of even mentioning his mother in Greta's house. His eyes found a framed print on the wall, a likeness of Jesus: a pale-skinned Messiah with a passel of white children gathered at his knees. A floral-trimmed portico arched behind him, and donkeys looked on from the periphery of the scene.

He and Mattie fell into a silence that he could barely stand. Then after a few moments, to his great relief, she began to hum a tune—a hymn he knew but couldn't quite name. She continued the song as she busied herself in the chair by the window. She was mending the hem of a little girl's dress.

Jesus. People did this sort of thing. Sat around humming hymns to themselves while they mended clothes and sipped on glasses of iced tea. He'd never before spent time with his dad's side of the family. It was a whole different world, he realized, than the one he'd known with Grandma Ginnie and Pop, his mom's folks. They had been a prototype for hippies before there were hippies. Mending hems had never made it to the top of the to-do list. Better to have cutoffs, anyway. He used to chop wood with Pop sometimes, though. That was pretty old school. What Grandma Gin didn't use in her kiln, they burned in the outdoor fire pit after dark.

"Michael." The voice sounded stern—his name a reprimand—and it startled him.

There she was. Greta. Standing about four feet away from

him. At close range, she was taller than he expected. Damned imposing.

"Stand up to greet your grandmother, son," Mattie said.

He did. Her condition made her appear to be looking at him and through him at the same time, as if something of greater significance lay just beyond where he stood. He remembered being in a room with his parents, watching their silent conversation, their need for each other palpable. He'd always felt entirely loved, but sometimes, it seemed to him that Kayla had been the first—and one of the few —who'd regarded him without distraction, who afforded him that brand of respect and admiration.

He walked to Greta, and when he stopped about a foot away from where she stood, he saw her eyes find him. Brown eyes, bright, even in their scattered focus. She stuck her chin out, mouth slightly open, as if examining a creature at the zoo. But Jesus, she looked so much like his dad.

She seemed to catch herself staring at him. She closed her mouth and pulled back slightly. "I'm sure you've heard about my difficulties," she said, and it sounded almost like an apology. "Anything beyond a short distance tends to blur. Even close it's not perfect."

"Well," he said, "in that case I'm wicked handsome." The Rhode Island expression didn't translate well to Southern ears, he realized. Greta scowled and Mattie appeared stricken. "I just came to return your dish," he said quickly. "I don't mean to interrupt your morning."

"Interruptions are what we live for," she said.

Mick wondered if that was an invitation to stay longer, or a sarcastic jab at his arrival. Before he could decide, she said, "There's no particular need for us to stand, is there?"

She turned toward a sofa chair opposite the couch, selecting the seat as her intended target.

Mick reached to take her elbow, and at his touch, she wrenched her arm away as if his intention leaned toward assault rather than assistance. "I'm quite capable," she said. There was the Greta he'd heard about. A Greta he remembered. His vague recollection of the porch, the yard beside the house, became a firmer image in his mind.

"You've returned the dish," Greta said, her tone suggesting disapproval at Mattie's little outing to the lake. "Was there anything else you need before you go back to your mother?"

Exactly what had he expected from her in the first place? No one said she'd see him and suddenly get all warm and fuzzy. But he'd envisioned a demystification of sorts. Clearly, that wasn't going to happen.

"Greta," Mattie spoke up from her sewing spot by the window. "This boy is your kin." Her words were equally stern. One thing seemed clear, they'd had conversations about him before. "He's making an effort. You could do the same."

Greta turned to him. She'd reached the chair but remained standing. "Carson was my only kin. I have no blood relatives remaining." She spoke in response to Mattie, but she kept her damaged eyes on Mick, as she braced herself with her hand on the back of the chair and settled into it. "You should get home to your mother, Michael. Faithless as she is, I expect she's still capable of worry. If she knows you're here, it won't sit well, I'm sure."

Mick stood, paralyzed. Unable to believe he'd heard her correctly. Faithless? She sounded as if she'd come from a colony of Puritans. "What do you mean, I'm not your blood kin?" His voice had taken a high, Southern turn, as if either mocking her or reaching for some slight toehold in her world. He sounded strange, even to himself.

"Ask your mother about Wallace Jamison," Greta said. He stood in the middle of the room as if the target of interrogation.

His grandmother's unfocused gaze gave him the sense of being disregarded.

"Thick as thieves while Carson worked at that degree of his," Greta continued. "You ask your mother about that. If she's honest with you, she'll tell you the truth after all this time."

"What the hell are you talking about?" Mick's voice ran to an even higher register. "Who's Wallace Jamison?"

Greta settled back in her seat and turned slightly away from him. Clearly, she had no intention of enlightening him further.

"Greta," Mattie said. "Get close to the boy. Look at his features. What I told you is true."

"I've seen all I need to see," Greta said.

"What about Carson? Think about what he would want from you."

"Carson had a blindness worse than my present condition when it came to that woman. He wouldn't see what's clear to anyone with sense." Greta spoke as if Mick had already left.

"What's she talking about?" He turned to Mattie.

Mattie walked over to him. "Son," she said, her voice as gentle as Greta's had been rigid, "you've already done what you could here today. You've put out a hand to your grandmother. I thought a close look at you might do her good, but she's got her mind set. Go back to your mama now. You're blameless in all this mess." This last part seemed again directed at Greta.

Greta remained motionless on her upholstered throne, and Mattie guided Mick back out onto the porch. She let out a sigh, and the two of them stood together looking out over the yard. The children weren't in sight, and the canvas of green and brown became the setting once again for something remembered. Dark clouds, nettles of rain, and Greta yelling at him to stay out of her home.

Stop calling him Daddy! Stop it . . . She was near him, her fingers gripping his shoulder and arm in anger as Carson yelled from a small distance for her to leave him be. He'd slipped away from his daddy and gone to the porch. He wanted to get out of the rain.

Mick remembered the woman's strong grip hurting his skin. Carson reached him, pulled him away, and when her fingers gripped him harder, Carson pushed her. She fell, and the yelling stopped. Then Carson had lifted him, gathered him up and carried him toward the car. They stopped long enough to see Greta rising from the ground, muddy but unhurt. Mick remembered how his dad appeared stunned at his own actions, Greta staring back at them, hard and unyielding.

The context of it now had been something young Mick would have registered only as confusion. He wondered how much was true memory and how much he simply filled in with imagination. The woman's fingers digging hard into his flesh. That had been real.

"Don't you let her get to you." Mattie's voice, a whisper. "And she might come around, yet. Lord can do anything, big or little. Little steps will still get you from the barn to the henhouse."

"What?" Mick looked around, caught in a time warp of memory. Irrationally, his eyes searched for his father to help him, and he wondered if he'd lost his mind. *I'm in the middle of nowhere with some woman who is saying I'm not a Forsyth. Fuck that.* She sounded sane, but she'd apparently lost her mind to some delusion. Did anyone know how crazy she was? His mom knew. His mom had told him to forget about her.

"I was here with my dad once when I was little," he said.

Mattie nodded, inclined her head in a way that suggested pity. "You can only go forward, son," she said. "Let go of the past." She put her hand on his arm. "There's so much good in that woman, Michael. I swear that's true."

What could he say? That he'd keep trying? That was a lie. He was done with his grandmother. So he said nothing and moved to leave. Mattie followed, stopping at the bottom of the stairs, as he continued on through the yard. He felt disoriented and was glad when he reached the shade of his car.

As he turned on the engine, children again dotted the landscape around him, a chorus of eyes.

Not her blood relative?

On the seat beside him, three brown eggs sat, obviously a present of sorts from one of the kids. He reached over and touched one. It was still warm, and the unexpected sensation made him pull his hand away.

"Jesus." The small exclamation escaped his lips, but he held little faith that help would come to him from that particular source. The gentle, white savior and his cherubic Caucasian brood were, apparently, tending to other matters.

"Why would he go there?" Elaine paused between bites of toast and scrambled egg. She found that, in spite of everything, she had an appetite after all.

"I don't understand why *you* don't go out there," Linnie said. "She is Carson's mother and you're both hurting right now. It might be good for the two of you to sit in the same room."

"She wouldn't help me get through this," Elaine said. "She could only make things worse." The pronouncement sounded self-centered. It made her wince a little to play it back in her head. Maybe Carson's mother could help Mick. Maybe they could both help Greta. But Elaine didn't feel up to offering clemency—any more than Greta seemed inclined to ask for it.

"Well," Linnie said, putting another glass of orange juice in front of her, "Mick has to work things out his own way. He is her grandson. That's got to count for something."

"She's never considered him family." Elaine stopped there. She didn't want to admit—even to her aunt—that some of Greta's accusations hit close to home. Linnie didn't know the

whole story when it came to Wallace Jamison. Elaine hated the
pain she had caused Carson, but that was her business—and
Carson's. Greta had no right to interfere or to judge. Not then.
Certainly not now. "Carson kept up with her, saw her from time
to time. But she never made the slightest effort to be a part of
Mick's life."

"Mick's an adult." Linnie sat beside her with a fresh cup of
coffee. "He gets to decide if he wants to try with her. He looks
like you, but he's Carson through and through. That sly humor
of his. If he spends five minutes with her, she'll see that much."

"I don't think Greta will find anything about Mick funny."

The phone rang and Linnie got up to answer. Her voice
dropped low, and she slipped off to her bedroom with the cord-
less receiver.

Elaine could see the house next door through the kitchen
window. Morty walked out his back door and over to a storage
shed near the road. She went outside to get some air and say hi
to Morty. The climate had changed overnight. Spring to summer.
That was the way in the South. Seasons began and ended with
an abrupt declaration.

"Hey, Elaine," Morty came out of the shed and called up to
where she stood on the landing. He was carrying an armload of
what appeared to be old blankets and towels. "Heading over to the
animal shelter. Wanna come?"

She'd pulled on jeans and a T-shirt when she got up, but
hadn't dressed to go anywhere.

"I'm not really put together yet for the day," she said, running
a hand through her hair to confirm what a mess she was.

"Nice thing about dogs," he said, grinning. "Scratch 'em
behind the ears and they don't give a pig's ass what you're
wearin'."

She laughed. "What about the people who work with the dogs?"

"You kiddin'? They live with dogs—got more fur on 'em than Sasquatch. You think they care?"

"Okay," she said. "Let me tell Linnie where I'm going." Any diversion would be worthwhile.

"Linnie," she called, going into the house.

Linnie was in the kitchen. She turned, and for a moment looked almost apologetic, then the expression passed and she smiled. "What's up?"

"You okay?" Elaine asked.

"Fine," she said. Clearly something was up, but her aunt didn't elaborate.

"I'm going to ride over to the animal shelter with Morty. Looks like he has a bunch of old towels and bedding to give them. Wanna come?"

"No. I've got a class in forty-five minutes, so I have to get to town."

"Okay," Elaine said. She looked at the expression on Linnie's face. "You're sure everything's all right?"

She nodded. "I'll talk to you later, but things are fine. You go with Morty. It'll be good for you."

She was right. With the exception of taking a swim once in a while and a couple of visits out to Carson's grave, Elaine hadn't left the tree house since the funeral. "I'll plan on making dinner tonight. You've been doing too much."

"We can argue about that later," Linnie said. "Go. Let Morty entertain you."

As she headed down the stairs, Elaine felt a flush of adrenaline move through her. She was leaving her place to go face other people for the first time as a widow. At the funeral, it had been a role she played. The Widow. This time, it would simply be her identity.

Every damn thing—even going to the dog pound—would be

a first for her now. Everything she did for the foreseeable future would be delineated by the before and the after.

"Grab a handful of those for me, would you?" Morty pointed toward the shed where more blankets were stacked.

"Where'd you get all this stuff?"

"I play cards with some fellas over at Merle's Marina on Tuesday nights. Fellas and gals, I guess I gotta say. Merle's daughter, Gabbie, who runs the place now, she took me for everything in my wallet two weeks ago. Anyway, got all my poker buddies to go home and clean out their closets. Dogs need a soft place," he said. "'Specially dogs with no people." His tall frame seemed to stoop slightly with the pain of the suffering animals.

She went to grab a handful of blankets from the shed. "You're a softy, Morty," she said over her shoulder.

"Don't go tellin' it."

Elaine missed her dad, especially when she was at the lake. But Morty had become as good a substitute as she could imagine.

"You're safe with me, Morty," she said, picking up a load of old blankets.

In a day or two, he'd leave. First, he'd go with his mom to Chapel Hill. He'd make sure she was going to be okay, then get back to Rhode Island. That was the plan. Trying to get to know Greta at this point was bullshit. He'd been crazy to even ride out there. Why had he wanted to talk to her in the first place?

He'd forget about the crazy stuff the woman had been spouting. If that bizarre crap had any sort of truth to it, he'd have heard about it. His parents wouldn't have kept something like that from him. If his mom had screwed around . . . (*Shit! Why was he even thinking about this?*) His mom wouldn't, and the two of them wouldn't have been married and happy if she had. Greta had lost her marbles. End of story. Fuck Wallace Jamison, whoever the hell he was.

Still, he had to fess up to his mom about talking to Greta. He'd tell her the truth. He'd done it because he had the idea that Carson would have wanted him to try.

In his mind, he absently prepared another explanation. The one for Carson. This would be the explanation of why he didn't intend to try again with his grandmother. Then he realized there would be no opportunity to tell his dad anything. Ever. A shot of panic traveled through his nerves. Never. His dad would learn nothing new about him, would never see him improve. The thought gutted him.

Once, in Rhode Island, the garage apartment where he lived had lost power for almost a week. By the third or fourth day, his longing for light and warmth became overwhelming. It wasn't so much the idea of comfort as the idea of "normal" that he craved. Driving away from Greta's house, he felt that again. Going to see his grandmother had only made him feel worse. He didn't want to let his dad down, but he couldn't make peace with the woman any more than he could wish Carson alive again. His inability to succeed with Greta wasn't his failure—all that was on her. She played the mind games—with his mom, with him. Hell, she'd messed with his dad's head, too, and she'd actually loved Carson.

Seven decades on the planet ought to teach a person something, but it didn't always work that way. Just because Greta had lived seventy-plus years didn't mean she was automatically wise and misunderstood. Grandmothers could be assholes just like anybody else. Hell, he had to let it go.

To his right, he saw Benny's, the burger joint where he used to hang out. He could go for something greasy. He pulled into the parking lot and put the car in park. He thought he'd put thoughts of Carson behind him—at least for a time. But without warning, a fierce longing for his dad slammed him. A rogue wave. It had happened before, the rising panic. No tears. He wished to hell he'd just cry. Instead, his chest tightened and his heartbeats grew faster, as if trying to escape. He made himself breathe, tried to roll with it, but the muscles in his neck only clenched in response. He would either die or live through it. Slowly, he felt himself gaining control. *Breathe . . . breathe . . .*

Looking inside the burger place, he could see people sitting. Eating . . . talking . . . Others came through the door with their takeout. White bags stained with grease through the bottom and sides. *Breathe . . . breathe . . .* It passed, eventually. Though he had no idea how long he'd been sitting there.

The people coming and going took no special interest in him. No one knew he'd just lost it. He looked like a guy hanging out in his car. Okay. That seemed like a good sign.

As his panic gave way, the other feeling settled back in. The one that told him what a fuckup he was. Since graduation, he couldn't think of a single thing he'd done to make his dad proud.

He hated that thought, and that nasty little voice stayed pretty quiet when he was in Newport. Rigging boats kept him engaged in technical challenges. His demons were never quite gone, but when he was hoisted midway up a thirty-foot mast, he tended to keep his concentration on the matter at hand. After a day of that, drinking with guys who didn't think so much about every damn thing took care of the rest of his time.

In Rhode Island, Kayla wasn't on his mind every day either. That was the other reason he needed to leave Lowfield. Before he'd screwed things up with Kayla, the town was a playground filled with fishing, baseball, and a girl he loved. After, it had been a place he'd rather not see. After that, Lowfield only reminded him of what a dick he really was.

No matter where he went, one image wouldn't leave him— the look on Kayla's face when he told her that coming for homecoming wasn't such a good idea. Her eyes, green with just a hint of blue—so incongruous in the landscape of her warm, brown skin—those eyes had looked at him with profound disappointment. Mick, the great guy. Mick, the enlightened son of a professor who was blind to race and social standing. Mick, who fell in love with Kayla Grimes, daughter of a black lunchroom lady and a white mechanic. That Mick didn't exist. There was only the Mick who faced introducing Kayla to his Chapel Hill friends and then bailed.

"Have you asked somebody else?" She'd kept some distance between them, standing in her front yard.

"No," he said. It was the truth. "It's not that."

"What is it?" Her voice had gone flat. Her eyes dulled, looked ordinary.

He tried to think of how to answer her. A rooster walked close enough to brush his pant leg. Three cars sat rusting in the side yard, and only one of them had a working engine. *This.* He looked around the property. *This is why.* It wasn't race. It wasn't because she was poor. It was because his friends would eat her alive. Her world was a Faulkner novel.

Someone would make a reference to a winter ski trip their parents had planned to Sun Valley. They'd ask her if she'd ever been. "Do you ski?" they'd ask her. Not because they expected an answer, but to see her stare at the question. And when a panicked look of incomprehension came across her face, they'd turn their heads and laugh—not even caring if she saw.

The minute he really thought of her arriving in Chapel Hill, his mind saw it happen as if it were already a memory. What did that say about him? That he'd become friends with people like that? They were on teams with him. School clubs. They didn't even know they were elitist because they didn't know anyone who wasn't. Maybe he would have never known either if he hadn't spent his summers at the lake.

He couldn't let them do that to her. Kayla was a separate room in his life. A safe place. If he pulled her out of the world they had created, they'd both be destroyed.

"You're ashamed of me," she said.

She said it as a statement. He'd thought she might cry or get pissed as hell. He'd fashioned what he would do, what he would say. But the flat, dead stare of someone who suddenly had reason to despise him? For that, he had no response.

"I'm not ashamed of you." This was true. But he couldn't bring himself to say the rest of it. *I'm ashamed of me. I'm ashamed of my friends. I'm ashamed that I want both worlds.* To have both worlds, he couldn't let them collide.

Then he didn't have either. Kayla had refused to see him again. He couldn't stomach the sight of his friends, blaming them for a scene that never actually played out. By the time he graduated, he couldn't wait for fall to come so he could leave North Carolina for Vermont.

What kind of asshole treated somebody like that? Maybe he and Greta did have something in common. Maybe it skipped a generation, but still ran in the family. Not Greta's blood? What a joke. He was more like her than his dad had ever been.

Enough. He needed to do something mundane. Something absolutely regular. He picked up his cell phone and dialed his mom.

"Hey," he said when she picked up. "You need anything? I'm at Benny's getting ready to grab a bite."

"No, that's okay," she said. "I'm riding out with Morty to the animal shelter right now."

The animal shelter? That was pretty random. But hell, at least she was out of the house—and going somewhere besides the cemetery.

"I was thinking," he said, "that I should get out of this town pretty soon. I can go back to Chapel Hill with you for a few days and help get things settled there. Then go back to Rhode Island. What do you think? You said you were about ready to leave."

"I'm thinking the same thing. I called work this morning and told them I wanted to come back."

"You think you're ready for work?" he asked. He was planning on going back, too, but his work required boat hardware and marine paint, not creative energy and dealing with an endless parade of performers and artists.

"I don't know," she said. "Guess I'll find out." Her voice had lost the confidence he'd always known her to have. "Do you think I should wait?"

"No, I didn't mean that," he said. "Whatever you think." He felt as if there was more to say. He tried to imagine what his dad would have told her, but drew a blank. Carson's had always been the opinion she needed. It had been fine for him to be a kid. Everywhere—but especially with his folks, and for as long as he could remember, he'd longed to be given serious regard. Well, he'd gotten his damn wish, and he didn't know what to do with it.

"I'll see you when you get home," she told him.

"Okay."

He got out of the car and walked into Benny's Burgers. He wanted cheese and grease. He might even get a milk shake. With any luck, the meal would kill him before he had to think any more about what to do the next day—and the day after that.

Several people came in the door and got in line behind him. He glanced back. Directly behind him was a girl. A damn pretty girl, actually. Brown, curly hair. Long, gorgeous neck. He looked back again. A sliver of porcelain belly showed between her T-shirt and the waist of her jeans. Damn.

"Hi, Micky," she said.

Damn.

"Hey," he said, moving his eyes up to her face again, trying to place her.

"Can I help you?" The boy behind the counter sounded irritated. Mick's turn had apparently come up.

Mick gave his order. Chili cheese dog. Onion rings. Chocolate milk shake. A ten-year-old's order. Maybe it *would* kill him. If that was the case, he'd try to die looking at that girl behind him. He paid, took his ticket, then stepped aside to wait. The girl moved up to the counter to order.

"I'll have a plain burger on a bun," she said, "and a Diet Pepsi with lemon."

"Just meat and bread?"

"That's it," she said. Then she looked over at Mick again and smiled.

He found himself hoping that his order would take a while. He loitered around the condiments and straws, watched as she stepped over and got her drink from the girl filling the orders.

"I forgot to get a soda," he said, absently, contemplating the long line that had formed at the order window.

"If you sit with me, I'll share," the girl said. She came over and stood beside him. She smelled like strawberries. "You can give me some of that milk shake."

"You're not worried about my germs?" he asked, grinning.

"I'll take my chances," she said. "Besides, I had daydreams about your germs when I was eleven."

Clearly she knew him. But she was . . . what? Nineteen? Twenty? She did look a little familiar, but he couldn't place her. That smile again. Straight, white teeth. Deep pink lips.

"Forty-five and"—the girl behind the counter looked at the tickets in her hand—"forty-four." Both their orders at the same time. A sign, maybe?

"Let's sit over there," she said. "Tell you what. I'll share my drink *and* I'll read your palm."

Whoever she was, this was clearly a girl who could get him out of a funk. At least temporarily. He sat down across from her and she took hold of his hand. Good God, she was pretty.

"This line means that you're going to have a bunch of kids," she said. Her voice lost its definition around the edges, as if she had a Life Saver tucked at the back of her throat. "And this line . . ." She tapped his palm with a slender finger. "Well, that one means you're going to have *fun* having 'em." She drew out the word *fun* as if it had two long syllables between the *f* and the *u*. She raised her eyebrows and smiled, then sat back and offered him a sip of her drink.

The dog was in the backseat. They had taken one of Morty's blankets and spread it over the leather of his Acura after he'd convinced Elaine to take the dog.

"Sometimes, the critters, they know more than we know," he'd said to her as she stood looking at the pitiful mutt.

The animal had been abused and it showed. His hay-colored fur looked two sizes too large on his thin frame, and neglect hadn't even been the worst of his problems. The creature had endured the cruelty of teenagers who had hurt him for sport. He'd come to Elaine immediately, sat down between her feet, as if she was the shelter he'd been seeking all along.

"That dog done claimed you, darlin'. You don't take him, well . . ." Morty scrunched his eyes, made a face that said he couldn't bear to think of the bad things that could happen if she denied fate. "Go on," he said. "Tell him you're his person now."

"What am I supposed to do with a dog, Morty? I can't even take care of myself."

"Give and get." He nodded as if what he said made sense to her.

So she'd taken the dog. If she was lucky, Linnie would fall

for the animal and keep him at the lake. She'd already e-mailed everyone at work that she'd be back by the middle of the next week. A dog did not fit into her plans.

A whimper from the backseat gave her the eerie notion of protest in response to her thoughts.

"God help me," she mumbled to herself. "What have I done?"

"Done the right thing." Morty looked pleased, as if he'd brokered a successful deal. "The right thing," he said again.

She found a loose pretzel in her purse and handed it back to the dog.

"If this doesn't work out, I'm putting the dog on your doorstep and walking away," she said, half believing she would do it.

Morty smiled and turned down the road that led back to the lake.

She'd known Morty forever. He'd been back and forth from New Orleans a lot when she was a kid. Never staying long, but never staying away long either. She knew from local talk that he'd had a wife once, but Elaine had never met her. The story never seemed clear.

"Did you get tired of New Orleans?" she asked. "Is that why you moved up here full-time?"

"No," he said, keeping his eyes on the road ahead. "I love Louisiana. Especially that city. Every bit as much as I love it here, just in a different way."

"Why move here then?"

"I needed the rest. When you make your money in one place, leisure is always someplace else, darlin'. After I made all the money I needed—more than I need, truth be told—I couldn't stop thinking about ways I could turn it into more. It was like a game with no end in sight. Everything around me made it a habit. Just couldn't relax. That's when I loaded up the car and drove here for good. Live here, visit there—instead of the other way around. I'm better keeping it like that."

"Do you still have family there?"

"Some," he said. A silence followed, leaving the blanks unfilled for a moment. "Two brothers," he said, finally. "One sister. Started out with six of us, but two are gone now. My wife passed years ago. She was young." He shook his head. "I was young."

"Was she sick for a long time?"

Again, he shook his head. "Aneurism." He snapped his fingers. "Like that."

"God, Morty. How awful." She thought of how cheated she felt, losing Carson in the middle of their life together. Morty was a kindred soul. "It's weird. I always thought you were divorced for some reason."

"I let people think that sometimes," he said. "Avoids the pity." He glanced over at her. "People mean well, but it still crawls under your skin."

"Yes, it does," she said, grateful for his honesty.

"Anyway," he said, "my family is still thick in New Orleans." He perked up. "God's honest truth, I've got a hundred-year-old aunt still kicking there."

She smiled. "I'm glad you're here."

"Me, too," he said, nodding, still keeping his eyes ahead.

The dog's breathing, something between a grunt and a snore, kept odd time with the sound of wheels over a stretch of unkempt highway near the outskirts of town.

"I'm not going to do this if you don't pay attention," the girl said. She'd taken up Mick's palm again after finishing half her burger. This time she seemed more serious about discerning the fate that awaited him. "I need your attention," she repeated, raising one eyebrow.

He didn't doubt that for a minute. She clearly assumed he knew who she was—had offered no introduction before sharing her drink and her carnival skills. The mouth . . . he could almost place the mouth. She bit her bottom lip in concentration, and he had a flash of recognition.

The kid. She was the kid who came to all his baseball games. Her older brother had been on one of the other teams in town. She used to show up early and hang around Mick while he warmed up. She made posters for his team and stuck around after the games to help load the equipment into the coach's car. The kid. Joy. Joy Brown.

He remembered the last time he saw her. One of the games before everything went to hell with Kayla. Back then, he was living without worries, looking forward to more summers in Lowfield. Joy, ten or eleven at the time, came up to him after the game—a win.

"I'm going to marry you someday, Micky Forsyth," she said.

He'd bent down to kiss her on top of the head. An odd gesture for him. An older man's gesture. Something his dad might have done. But it thrilled the girl. She'd looked up at him, smiling wide. Straight, white teeth, even then.

"What's so funny?" She was staring at him.

"Those posters you used to make," he said. "I just remembered them. They must have taken you forever."

She shrugged. "I had nothing but time back then. Mama and Daddy didn't make me work at the fruit stand until I turned twelve." She let go of his palm, picked up her burger again. "You acted like I bugged you," she said, grinning. "But you looked for me. I could tell."

Had he? Maybe. He didn't remember half the things he'd felt back then.

"What are you doing these days?" he asked, thinking the answer would likely include some mention of work at the Cut and Curl on Route 3.

"Graduation was a week ago," she said. "I'm working at the stand this summer."

Her folks' produce stand was a fixture on the highway that led to the lake. He passed it going back and forth to town. The adjoining fields spread out in all directions behind the roadside operation.

He was about to ask her what was growing so early in the season when the reality of her words set in. Graduation. Holy crap, she was barely out of high school. He straightened up in his seat and leaned back, as if a few more inches between them would make everything he'd been thinking about her go away.

"College?" he asked, buying some time.

"Georgetown. This fall. I almost decided to go to Duke and stay closer to home, but Georgetown put a big push on with financial aid."

"Georgetown . . ." he said, echoing the word. He sounded like a moron.

"My application essay was about the psychology of selling roadside produce. Lucky for me, rural kids are all the rage right now."

"Wow," he said. "Georgetown. And Duke. That's impressive."

"Yeah," she said, "even my folks were shocked. Neither one of them liked school, but their kids—we're totally into it. They thought my older brother was a fluke—couldn't believe it when I got put in with the bluebirds, too."

Bluebirds. Redbirds. Yellowbirds. They'd had that in Mick's elementary school. As if kids wouldn't notice the intellectual hierarchy of the avian system.

"It's like some recessive gene reared its nerdy little head with my generation."

He stared at her, trying to recalibrate his thoughts.

"Is everything okay?" she asked.

"Yeah. My dad was in grad school at Georgetown." Mick felt himself sliding, shifting to neutral on the personality scale, blending in with the sun-washed posters of milk shakes and soft-serve scotch-taped to Benny's floor-length windows. All this, over a girl who barely had her cap and gown in the closet, for crissake. "What do you plan to study?" Holy shit. He'd bottomed out. *What do you plan to study? Jesus.*

She hesitated. "I haven't decided yet," she answered, finally. She tilted her head to the side, clearly wondering what the hell was wrong with him. "You sure you're okay?"

"Yeah, I'm fine." He wasn't sure what fine was anymore, but he was nowhere near it. "It's just been a weird time—with my dad and all. I kind of fade out sometimes."

"What's wrong with your dad?"

She didn't even know that's why he was in town. He couldn't say it. He just couldn't. But he had to. He had to get used to saying the words. "My dad died last week. We had the funeral here."

"Oh my God, Micky . . ." She didn't lean in. She didn't put her hand on his arm. She didn't do anything that girls did to make the drama all about themselves. She just sat there looking stunned. Finally, she said, "I didn't know."

"That's okay," he said. "It's good that you didn't know. It kind of took me out of it for a while."

She'd eaten all her food. And they'd established that she was a scholar and he was fatherless. What else was there to do?

"I don't know how long you'll be around," she said. "But I'm here this summer. Let me know if you want to get together, Micky. I've waited a long time to be old enough to tell you that."

She had no pretense at flirtation when she said this. He found that he didn't want to leave. Her eyes, her voice . . . everything about her made him feel better.

He tried to think of something light to say. Something just right. But before anything came to mind, she said, "But you'll have to call if you want to see me. I don't hang out at the baseball field anymore."

"Yeah," he said. "Neither do I."

He followed her into the parking lot, leaving most of the milk shake and a half-eaten chili cheese dog behind. He felt guilty, chasing after happiness. But his dad would understand. His dad would *want* him to find something good in the middle of such a hard time. But how old was she? She had to have turned eighteen.

"Are you around tomorrow?" he asked. "Maybe we could do something."

"I need to sort out when Mama and Daddy want me at the stand," she said. She pulled out her cell phone. "What's your number?"

He told her, and a second later felt his phone vibrate in his pocket.

"You have my number now," she said. "Call me."

Mick looked beyond her, saw how she stood in bright relief against the backdrop of the town as it stretched into a tintype of brown and gray. He needed a diversion. "Okay," he said. "I'll call you tomorrow and we can figure something out."

She nodded, gave him that smile again, then got into her car, an old Toyota that had seen its best days a while back. "And Micky?" She looked at him through the open window. "I'm really sorry about your dad."

"Thanks." Didn't change a damn thing, but it was nice of her to say it.

He watched her drive off and walked back toward his mom's car. Someone was standing beside the door on the passenger side and, as he got closer, he saw that it was Kooper Grimes, Kayla's brother.

"Hey," Mick said as he neared. He looked closely at the guy's face, searching for any likeness of the girl he'd loved. What would she look like now? She'd be beautiful. He registered a flush of nerves in his cheeks, his temples. He hoped it wasn't obvious. He felt desperate to get out of the sun.

"Hey, Mick." Kooper looked at the ground and then back up at him. "New girl?" He nodded toward the parking spot that Joy had just vacated.

Mick shook his head, trying to read into Kooper's intention with the question. "Just an old friend."

Kooper nodded. "You got a few minutes?"

"Sure." Mick waited for the follow-up.

"I'll ride with you." Kooper opened the door and got in.

"Ride where?"

Kooper nodded in the direction of town. "Got something to show you."

Okay. Mick went to the driver's side. The day couldn't get any more weird. "Where to?"

"Go through town first," Kooper said. "Just want to talk for a minute."

Mick pulled out, blending into the early afternoon traffic. He glanced at the gas gauge. A quarter of a tank's worth of conversation. Since he'd never heard Kayla's brother string more than four sentences together at a stretch, Mick figured he'd be safe with that. He made a left turn and headed toward town.

Five

Elaine sat cross-legged on the wooden dock, the puppy asleep in her lap. Across the lake, the green lawn of some year-round resident stood out in the middle of the mostly wooded shoreline. A mismatched piece of jigsaw puzzle. She could make out the Watson family's A-frame. Beside it, the cabin that looked to be made of giant Lincoln Logs. She knew the lake shore to shore, but even a place so familiar seemed strange without Carson.

She shifted her legs to ease a cramp, and the puppy, nameless still, stirred, but didn't wake. His chin rested on her ankle, blond tail spilling over her leg. The dog was a mutt. Best she could tell, cocker spaniel with a little hound dog thrown in. She stroked the bald spot behind the dog's ear, a scar, likely permanent, that remained red even though it had mostly healed. She looked at the droopy left eye, an injury noticeable even when the animal slept.

Shelly, who'd run the shelter for a decade or more now, said the dog had been mistreated. Bad stuff. The puppy was outside with Shelly when Morty and Elaine drove up.

When the dog made a beeline for Elaine, Shelly had been astonished. "I'll be damned," she said, coming over to them. "You're the first person he's gone to on his own."

Morty had petitioned hard for her to take the animal home, and she had argued against it, but even as she spoke, she felt the comfort of the dog pressing against her.

"I know things are hard right now," Shelly said. "It was a beautiful service. I can't imagine . . ." She stopped. Shelly had been divorced twice, lived by herself, and said she planned to keep it that way. Elaine thought it might be nice to have Shelly up to Chapel Hill for a visit sometime. They'd been friends in high school—had kept up a little over the years. Elaine didn't have many single friends.

"So what happened to this little guy?" Elaine shifted the dog's weight in her arms. She wanted to get away from the subject of Carson's funeral.

"Kids," Shelly said, "teenagers old enough to know better . . ." She shook her head. "They set fire to his head just to watch him thrash around and run. A neighbor saw it and called the law. He told the deputy that he'd seen people kick and swat at the animal, and that was bad enough, but lighting his fur on fire . . ."

She said the dog was just shy of five months old and skittish as a gerbil.

"Good God, what kind of people would do that to a puppy?"

Shelly made a face to register the shame of it all. Even in high school, she'd had a higher regard for animals than for most of the people they knew. "You'd be amazed at what people do. I see it all here at the shelter."

"Did they get arrested, at least?"

Shelly laughed, a thick, humorless sound. "Scolded a little.

That's all they got. I'm just glad the deputy who went over there brought this fella to us." She scratched the puppy behind the ears. "One thing's for sure. He takes to you. I thought it would be months before he trusted anybody. I've thought of taking him and working with him myself, but I'm not sure he'll ever forget that I was part of the worst day of his life."

The wood slats of the dock felt warm under her. Elaine listened to the slap of the waves as they reached the muddy bank. She felt the animal relax against her legs, and from up the hill, she heard a car door slam.

"Hey, little no-name," she said, "you get to meet Mick." At least she thought it must be Mick. Linnie had called and was still at the studio trying to herd a bunch of third graders through an improv movement session. Elaine had kept quiet about the dog. She had no idea how to explain the temporary insanity of adopting a pet.

She heard a man's voice call to her. "Hey, how're you doin'?"

The shade from the oak trees and the house built high in them kept his face hidden from view. A low growl came from the puppy, and she felt the vibration against her knee.

"Can I help you?" she asked.

"Hope so."

"Are you looking for my aunt, Linnie Phelps?"

"No, ma'am," he said. "Came to talk to you."

She squinted, made out that he wore a uniform of some sort. He worked his way down the flagstone walkway to the dock. He was medium height with a gut threatening to take over his middle, but his shoulders looked as solid as door beams. She felt the dock shimmy as he stepped onto the boards.

The dog crawled off her lap, and Elaine stood up as the man came toward her.

"Ronnie Allsap." He stuck his hand out. "With the Sheriff's Department."

"Elaine Forsyth." She hesitated as she put out her hand to meet his. "My last name was Tyson when I was growing up here." The dog's growl segued into a muttered bark as he took cover behind her leg.

"Yeah, we were in school at the same time," he said. "You were a year back from me. Your husband was in my grade. I'm awfully sorry. I know you had the funeral last week."

"Thank you." The call-and-response of sympathy and acknowledgment had become an awkward necessity.

The officer nodded, looking shy and suddenly uncomfortable, as if he'd forgotten his purpose for arriving on her dock in the middle of the afternoon. He did look familiar to her. *Ronnie Allsap.* She recalled the face—younger, of course, but with the same eyes—framed by the window of his blue Ford pickup. Her friend Laura had liked him briefly. But then Laura had liked most anybody with facial hair and a driver's license.

"You still drive a truck?" she asked.

He grinned, warming to her recognition.

"Naw," he told her. "They gimme that Chevrolet up there to drive when I'm working. I got a Corolla at home." He looked down, as if embarrassed at owning such an ordinary car.

She pictured him again, sitting high in his pickup, arm hanging out the window while Laura leaned against the door. Back then, he'd looked good in a truck. Unfortunately, the years had not been particularly kind to Officer Allsap.

"You came here to ask me about something?"

"Oh, right," he said. "I hate to bother you about this so soon after your loss, but I didn't know how long you might be around."

"I plan to leave in a couple of days. What's up?"

"The Forsyth woman," he said. "Your mother-in-law?"

"Greta," she said. "What about her?"

"We've been approached by this fella trying to buy her property." He shifted his weight from one foot to the other, looked down at the weathered boards at his feet. "He's interested in expanding some livestock operation—raising these animals for their fur. You can make a lot of money apparently, and she hasn't been real open to selling, I guess."

Elaine thought of Greta opening the gates to free the *evil* alpacas.

"Anyway, guy's been around at the courthouse, looking at multifamily zoning issues. Seems she's turned some buildings on her property into housing for a couple of families. The fellow tells us there are children all over the place."

It had been dark when she'd dropped Greta at her place after the Roseville drama, but from what she'd seen—the yard and the houses—everything looked well kept. Mattie lived with Greta and had mentioned some of her family living on the property. It hardly sounded like what the man described.

"I don't recall Greta's place having any close neighbors, so I'm not sure why anyone would complain. What's he worried about?"

"Well, technically, there are restrictions within town limits on use of property for multifamily dwellings. Since the old Forsyth property is so close to the town line, this guy has put in a request to get a surveyor out there to check whether she's really on county or town property. His property isn't in town, but hers might be. To be honest, he's just drummed up these zoning issues to try and rattle her. Get her to sell. But I've got to follow through."

"I don't know what this has to do with me," Elaine said. "Greta and I aren't really on good terms."

"I know," he said. "It's just that the land . . . Well, you'd be next in line—you or your boy—and it might be in your interest to see what she plans to do with her place, when . . . Well, you know." He stopped, looked up at her briefly before moving his gaze out toward the lake. "The county is pretty keen on expanding any industry that comes in this direction. He's wanting to make a bigger operation out of raising the animals and shearing them for wool. So I'm getting pressure to look into the stuff he's saying."

"Officer . . ."

"Ronnie," he said. "Just call me Ronnie."

"Ronnie." She tried to imagine any scenario where she would care about Greta's land or what she decided to do with it. "I doubt very much that Mick and I are featured in Greta's will. Even if we were . . . I live in Chapel Hill. Mick is out of state. We buried Carson here because that's what he wanted, but other than my aunt and this place . . ."—she gestured up the hill toward the tree house—"we really don't have any ties here anymore. Who is this guy anyway?"

"He's a fellow up from Atlanta. An actor. I've seen him on a couple of commercials, but I've never run into him here."

"And he plans to make a business out of the alpacas?"

"Makes most of his money with his voice in commercials," Ronnie said. "He does the voice in that commercial for that big antacid pill . . . I can't remember the name of it just now, but you'd know the one. Fellow's got a real distinctive sound when he talks. You'd probably recognize the voice before you would the face."

Elaine looked out toward the lake, hoped to see Morty outside. If she could flag him over, he'd come to her rescue. Morty could talk a blue streak with types like old Ronnie, but she wanted to run and hide.

"I'm not sure what I could do to help," she said, hoping to wrap up the discussion.

Ronnie shrugged. "I just thought you might have a stake in the whole business. I know you and your mother-in-law have had your problems, but . . ." He stopped, realizing he'd stepped into conversational quicksand. "It's just that the land could be worth something. If you could convince her to consider what the man has to say . . ."

"She would take any suggestion I made and do the opposite. And as far as any claim Mick and I have to the property, we haven't planned on being heirs to anything Greta has to leave." He looked so deflated that she added, "But I appreciate the concern."

"Well, you can think it over. Talk it over with your son."

"I don't mean to be difficult," she said. "It's just that Greta's property is the last thing on my mind at the moment. I'm sorry you came all this way out and I'm really not much help."

"S'okay," he said. "I come out this way for lunch a lot anyway. Go to Merle's to get a sandwich or something."

Merle's Marina. Morty had been talking about that place the other day. She hadn't been out that way in a while, but she suddenly craved a sandwich in the worst way. "I heard Merle's retired, that Gabbie's running it now."

"Yeah." Ronnie shook his head. "Merle's living down at the beach now. Retired after last summer. Said he don't want to look at another lake for as long as he lives. His daughter's doing a good job with it, though. She'd taken charge of most every-thing for a while before he left anyway. Gabbie's a good ol' girl. Don't play cards with her though."

"That's what I hear," Elaine said. "I haven't been there this year."

Before Carson's diagnosis, they had come down to visit Linnie for the weekend, had lunch at Merle's, and gassed up the boat. That night Carson, wide awake at two in the morn-ing, nudged her.

"Let's take the boat out," he said.

"Now?"

"Full tank of gas. Full moon. It'll be pretty."

They'd gone out to the middle of the lake and sat on the floor of the boat for the longest time, looking up. Carson wanted to make love, but the boat was too tippy and they both got the giggles. They rode back to the cabin and spread a towel out on the dock.

Ronnie shuffled his feet slightly. He looked toward the shoreline beyond Elaine's dock. The water was low, exposing a muddy bank that ran around beyond the point, all prime lakefront that Morty owned. Ducks, three of them, hung around Morty's boathouse, waiting for him to arrive with his daily offering of bread crumbs.

"You see those blue lights over the lake the other night?" Ronnie changed the subject with such force that it startled her. "Some of the reports came from around here."

"No," she said. "When was it again?"

"Tuesday before last," he said. "Early morning. First call came in before sunrise."

The morning Carson died. She felt the muscles in her throat tighten. She would *not* cry in front of Ronnie Allsap. She recalled looking at Carson's face while he looked out the window. He'd talked about lights, close in. Lights that looked like some pattern he recalled. She thought he was talking out of his head, but if what Ronnie said was right, Carson had actually been *looking* at something. She wished she'd turned to see it, too.

"People over here saw it first." Ronnie rambled, nervous maybe that she'd gone so quiet. "Later, we got calls from folks changing shifts at the mill."

Greta had asked her in the car if Carson had seen the lights yet. She felt overcome with the possibility that something had been there. Something there to help him. Ronnie was staring at her. The last thing she wanted was to share Carson's last moments with a man she barely remembered from high school.

"I've had a lot on my mind," she said. "I haven't had time to think about any UFOs." Emotion made her voice sound low and cracked. It added a harsh quality to her words. She hadn't intended to be unkind, but she really wanted the man to leave.

"Sure, I understand," he said. He looked down, as if scolded by a teacher. "So, like I said, let me know if you change your mind about getting involved with your mother-in-law and her property. Good to see you again."

For a moment, it looked as if he might say more, but then he turned and went up the hill. His back stretched solid inside the cotton shirt of his uniform, and drops of sweat dotted the space between his shoulder blades. She opened her mouth to say something, but before she could think of what might be right, he'd disappeared over the ridge. A moment later, she heard the rumble of an engine—the overjuiced squad car sound that scared the shit out of high school stoners. The noise grew fainter as Ronnie Allsap fled the scene.

Standing beside her halfway up the hill, the puppy looked up and regarded her with a droopy eye that for all the world seemed to be a reproach.

Mick's day had taken a major turn. He'd gone from being treated like some kind of disease by Greta to hanging out with arguably the prettiest girl in a three-county radius. Next, for unclear reasons, he was riding in a car with Kayla's brother.

For someone who said he wanted to talk, Kooper had very little to say. Mick kept making turns and circling behind town and then back through Main Street.

"Turn off and take it to the baseball field." Kooper spoke as if continuing a series of instructions rather than initiating a single directive.

Mick turned right and within a couple of blocks pulled into the crowded parking lot beside the ball field. It was the first time he'd seen the place in years. He would have still been dating Kayla the last time he'd been to the field. Looking at the park, he felt the same old excitement at the sight of the diamond. He'd forgotten how much he'd loved being out there.

Kids who looked to be in early elementary school populated the field while parents and other children filled the stands. Mick rolled down the windows and turned off the engine. He looked at the other man and waited, but Kooper kept his eyes on the game.

"I need to get back to my mom pretty soon," Mick said. "I appreciate you coming to the funeral. I know I'm not your favorite person."

"You hurt her," Kooper said, still looking at the field.

Had he tracked Mick down and made him drive all over town just to rehash what a shithead Mick had been when he was a teenager?

"I know," Mick said. "I live with it. I wish she was still living with it. I was an asshole. I'd go back if I could, but . . ." What did the guy want from him? Mick used to think that he might grow into forgiving himself, but somehow, he'd just grown to feel worse about it. Maybe if she'd lived . . .

"Kyle plays like shit," Kooper said without any segue in the conversation.

"What?"

Kooper nodded toward the field, and Mick recognized the smallest Grimes. They were playing T-ball, and Kayla's little brother was up at bat. He swung and missed the whole damn thing. He didn't hit the ball or even the tee. Nothing but air. He tried again. Same thing. Kooper was right. The kid sucked. But hell, he was little.

"Not everybody gets their coordination at his age," Mick said. "He'll be all right."

"Gets teased," Kooper said. "Not quite black. Not quite white. Fucks up in every direction out there."

Mick watched the boy's final swing. Finally making contact with something, he slammed the bat into the midsection of the tee, and the ball hopped off its perch and rolled a few feet. Some kid picked it up and tagged Kyle as he made an unusually awkward sprint toward first base. As he walked back to the bench, he muttered to himself—Mick could only imagine what—and shook his dark curls in disgust.

"I can play football," Kooper said, looking at Mick. "Wide receiver. Pretty good at basketball. But Kyle's settled on baseball." Kooper paused, made a face. "And he's *bad*."

Mick laughed. Then Kooper laughed. For a second or two, the tension left the car.

"I don't know a damn thing about baseball, except I can barely stand to watch it, much less play it. It's what turtles would play if they had sense enough for a game." Kooper looked Mick steady in the eye. "I thought you might could help him. This is your thing. Man, when you were out there, I used to watch you sometimes and wonder how you made that slow-assed sport look like it had something to it. I ain't got the patience to work with him. I'm tellin' you the truth on that. I would if I could."

Mick didn't know what to say. Kooper's request hadn't been on his radar. He looked at the field again. Kyle's out had put the other team at bat, and the boy stood in the outfield—as far out as they could position him. Any kid who could hit a ball off a tee far enough to reach Kyle deserved a run.

"I'm leaving soon," Mick said. "I'd like to help him, but I've got to get back to Rhode Island."

Kooper nodded. Looked down at his hands. He moved his thumb over the tips of his fingers in a nervous motion, then pulled a pack of Kools out of his shirt pocket. "You mind?"

"No problem," Mick said.

Kooper lit up, pulled in a long drag, and let it out. Then he turned back to Mick. "I hear you say you might do something with that girl," he said. "You going to be around long enough for that?"

"Kooper," Mick said, "I don't know what the fuck I'm doing. I buried my dad a week ago, and I'm feeling my way blind at the moment. Please don't pull this bullshit on me. Your little brother will figure it out. Not every kid is good at sports. He's what? Six?"

Kayla's brother nodded. He kept his eyes steady on Mick. "He's six," he said.

Mick motioned toward his cigarettes, and Kooper handed him one along with a lighter. Mick usually only smoked when he was really drunk. He took a drag and wished he *was* really drunk. Kooper didn't say it, but if Mick could hear the man's thoughts they would be saying, *You owe us a little something, Mick Forsyth. You treated Kayla like shit. You can teach her little brother how to throw a ball—how to hit the damn thing off the top of a stick.* And if Kooper actually said all that, he wouldn't be wrong. For years, through college and beyond, Mick had managed to keep Kayla mostly out of his thoughts. Back in Lowfield, he couldn't escape her. He couldn't escape himself.

"I'll be here for a couple of days," he said. "I can ride out to-morrow for a little while if you want."

Kooper nodded. His face softened. It was almost a smile. Mick found a scrap of paper and a pen in the middle console and wrote down his number. "Call me in the morning sometime and I'll know more what I'm up to."

"That's solid, man," Kooper said. "Thanks."

They sat and smoked, listened to the familiar sounds of kids playing, parents talking and calling out.

"You stay on the lake, right?" Kooper asked.

"Yeah," Mick said, watching a kid who had to be a foot taller than the rest slam a ball that sailed by second base.

"I remember Kayla sayin' it was a tree house. A real one."

Mick nodded. "Kind of weird, I guess. My grandparents built the place, and my mom grew up there."

"Speaking of weird, you ever see any of them lights they been talking about?" Kooper tossed his cigarette out the window.

"What lights?"

"UFO lights," Kooper said. "Blue things in the sky shaped kind of like a stop sign."

Mick shook his head. "Never seen anything like that," he said. "I've heard people talking. Probably something out of Fort Bragg, don't you think?"

"Naw, man," Kooper leaned forward, looked more animated than Mick had seen him. "Horace, my stepdaddy, he works that shift at the mill that changes before it turns light outside. He saw 'em the other morning. Said he just stared at 'em and got to wishin' he could just float on up there to 'em. Didn't know why he was thinking that. It was like the lights made him think it. He said it was like any problems you have might go away if you could just pass through that blue light.

"Horace don't talk about shit like that. Not ever. He's an engines-and-football kind of talk man. And he sees lights and starts to sound like some goddamn psychic infomercial. Said they were a blue he's never seen before."

"I don't know," Mick said, trying to imagine looking up and finding something like that in the sky. "The military is into all kinds of crap we don't know about."

"Horace been in the military," Kooper said, sitting back. "What he saw, it had nothing to do with Fort Bragg. Said he knows that much for sure."

Kooper seemed disappointed. He'd wanted something from Mick. Maybe something as simple as corroboration that his stepdad wasn't losing it.

There was suddenly nothing else to say. A car pulling into the parking lot crunched on the loose gravel, and the dusty dirt rose and hovered in the warm air.

"You want me to take you back to Benny's?" Mick asked.

"No." Kooper looked at the game. "Got a friend picking us up here."

Kyle had moved closer infield, seemed to be in a spasm of advance and retreat as a ball arced in his direction. Before he had a chance to miss it, another kid ran over and caught it.

"Besides, I gotta stay here and watch this train wreck," Kooper said. "He gonna need some damn ice cream or something to cheer him up when it's over. Same thing every Saturday."

Kooper got out of the car and walked toward the stands. He motioned good-bye with one hand, but didn't bother to look back at Mick.

As Mick pulled out of the lot, he heard a cheer go up from the crowd. He didn't look, but he seriously doubted little Kyle was the hero in whatever scenario had just played out. Helping the kid would matter to Kayla. Very few things were that concrete, but if she was alive, she'd have done the asking.

The day had started pretty dismally with his grandmother. But doing something right for Kayla's family combined with his Joy Brown encounter moved things into the win column overall, giving him some small reason to feel better than he had three hours before.

The only hurdle left was to tell his mother that he'd been out to Greta's. That, and to fill her in on the fact that Greta had, indeed, gone off the deep end. Still, something nagged at him. He couldn't quite let it go. Regardless of how insane it was, if his conversation with Greta was to be put to rest once and for all, he'd have to take his grandmother's advice and ask Elaine about this Wallace Jamison. Jamison had to be a real person, at least, and his mom could tell him why Greta thought the guy had anything to do with Mick. He'd waded deep into the family muck, and it would be better to push through than to turn back.

At least, he hoped to hell that was the case.

From the kitchen, Elaine heard Mick come in. She took a bowl of pretzels into the den to meet him.

"Good God," she said, "you smell like a day-old campfire. Have you been smoking?"

"Just one," he said, sprawling onto the couch, laying his head back as if exhausted. "Kayla's brother hijacked me at Benny's. He wanted to talk about something. By the end of the conversation, a smoke seemed like a good idea. Sorry. Your car probably stinks, too."

"Great," she said. But her mind wasn't on the car; she was wondering what the girl's brother wanted with Mick.

Linnie came around the corner, hair still in a towel from a shower. "What have you been up to all day?" she asked Mick.

"Well," he said, "for one thing, I ran into this girl at Benny's. Mom? Remember Joy Brown, that kid who used to follow me around?"

"Yeah, I do," Elaine said, mentally conjuring a pretty dark-haired child. "She made those elaborate posters and brought them to your games."

"That's her," he said, sitting up, shedding his lethargic pose. "Well, she was in line behind me and, I've gotta say, she's looking pretty good."

"She can't be more than sixteen, Michael." Elaine didn't want to discourage anything that might cheer him up, but Jesus, the girl had to be too young.

"She's eighteen, I think," he said, seeming none too certain. "She just graduated from high school. I know that's young, but it's not crazy young."

"Well, it's not criminal, but . . ." Elaine said, wondering what little Joy would look like at eighteen.

"That depends on what you're planning on doing with her," Linnie piped in. "She can't legally walk into a bar. You realize that, don't you?"

"Jesus, I've had one conversation with her," he protested.

"Sorry." Elaine smiled. He seemed more like himself somehow. That was a good thing. "We're not trying to jump on you."

He leaned forward, propped his elbows on his knees. "I need to ask you something," he said, changing tone.

"Shoot." Elaine sat down in the sofa chair, took a few pretzels from the bowl on the coffee table, and settled back.

Mick hesitated. Outside on the lake, a WaveRunner buzzed in frantic circles in front of the dock, stirring a wake that sloshed against the shore. Linnie made a face at the disruption.

"Do you know anybody named Wallace Jamison?" he asked. He went still waiting for her to answer.

Elaine felt a sliding sensation in her gut, and her face flushed hot. Linnie caught her eye and, with a look of sympathy, gestured that she'd be in the other room. Mick didn't seem to register her departure; his eyes stayed intent on Elaine and whatever response she could muster.

"You went out to Greta's," she said, finally, buying time. She had to force calm into her voice.

He nodded. Waited.

"Greta has been obsessed with Wallace for thirty years," she said. "He was a close friend from high school, and my best friend in town during the two years when your dad was away at Georgetown. He was never more than a friend, but Greta didn't believe it. She had been close friends with Wallace's mother, Tilda. They went to church together. The whole thing added fuel to an earlier falling-out between those two. It was kind of a mess."

She provided only the CliffsNotes to that period in her life. The fewer details, the better.

"Your dad trusted me," she said. "He had every reason to trust me. And Wallace . . ." She smiled—couldn't help but smile when she thought of him. "Wallace was a remarkable friend."

"I've had friendships with girls," Mick said. "They work okay. But usually one of us would make it something else if it could happen that way. Was he in love with you?"

She thought of how to answer and, in her hesitation, Mick took the nonresponse to mean something.

"You shut him down, right?" he asked. "You never cheated on Dad. Even before you got married—you couldn't. Right?"

"No," she answered. "I never cheated on your dad." It was all she could do to say the words. They were true, of course. In light of what Mick was asking, they were certainly true. But there were all kinds of betrayal.

"So Greta's full of shit." Mick's heel tapped on the wood-slat floors in a disjointed salsa kind of rhythm. Elaine felt nervous, just watching him. "She even implied that I'm not Dad's kid. Completely full of shit, right? That's what you're saying."

"Michael." She stood up and went to him, sat beside him, pulling him close. "Every vein in your body has Forsyth blood running through it. Look at me." She looked into his beautiful blue-green eyes. Carson's strong chin and her colorful eyes. What a combo. "You are Carson's son in every way. So, yes, as you so aptly put it, Greta is full of shit."

"Were you still friends with him after all that?"

For an absurd moment, Elaine thought he was referring to Carson, as if her son somehow knew the difficulty they had during that long summer before they got married. Then she realized he meant Wallace.

"Wallace did the right thing," she said. "He saw how things

looked with us hanging around together all the time. And even though none of it was true, he stepped away."

"Where is he now?" Mick asked.

"I don't know," she said. "He lived here for a long time. He taught history at the middle school for years and married one of the other teachers. I don't think it lasted though. I'd see him in town sometimes, just in passing. I know he moved away a couple of years ago, but . . ." She shrugged her shoulders. What was there to say? Wallace was intensely part of her life for a short while. She would have liked to keep their friendship, but some things you did for love. Letting go of Wallace was one of those things.

"Okay," Mick said, his fingers drumming silently on his knee. "Okay."

She felt relieved to have it over, and in some ways, glad he'd brought it up. Why shouldn't he know why his grandmother acted the way she did?

Linnie poked her head around the door that led into the kitchen.

"It's fine," Elaine said. "Come on in."

Mick stood up. "I think I might go for a swim." He headed for the porch that connected the tree house sections.

Elaine was about to suggest that they all take the boat to Merle's for dinner when Mick called out from the other room. "Whose dog is this?" He came back into the den. The animal trailed him, but cowered and then retreated when Mick turned to regard him.

"Believe it or not," Linnie said, "your mom lost her mind today at the shelter and adopted the damn thing."

"You brought home a dog?" Mick looked at her. "What's wrong with his eye?"

The poor creature made his way to Elaine and pressed tightly against her leg. Mick too closely resembled a teenage boy for the pup's comfort. It would take some work to get him to trust her son.

"He'd been abused by some kids," Elaine said. "I couldn't help myself. He kind of chose me."

"What's his name?" Mick asked.

"Doesn't have one yet." Elaine knelt down and scratched the animal under the chin. "I'm waiting until the right one comes to me."

"You plan to take him home with you?" Mick asked. The dog raised his scarred head to look at her as if waiting for her answer.

"I don't know what I'm going to do with him," she said. "I'm trying to talk Linnie into keeping him here until I get things settled at home."

"I can't," Linnie said abruptly. Too abruptly.

Elaine stood up and looked at her aunt. "What's up?"

"I've had an offer," Linnie said. "I hate to even bring it up. I feel like I'm abandoning you."

"What kind of offer?" Elaine tried to sound upbeat, as if another shift in her world would be nothing at all.

"The company," Linnie said. "They need me to go to Europe with them."

"What company?" For a moment, she pictured Linnie sitting in a conference room with a crowd of suits around her and it seemed comical.

"My old company," she said. "They're launching a tour."

"You're going to dance again?" Mick couldn't mask his astonishment.

"No, no." Linnie laughed. They all laughed, but it had an awkward note to it. "The rehearsal director has had to bow out. I did it for years," she said, "that and all the other administrative crap that has to be done when the company travels. They need somebody who can step in without being trained and I . . ." She looked around the room. "After a few years of peace and quiet here, I could use a little chaos."

"I understand, Lin," Elaine said. "I'm going back to Chapel Hill anyway. Mick's got to get back to Rhode Island. It sounds like this is the right thing for you."

It was. Linnie looked excited. Elaine had to fight the selfish urge to want Linnie in the tree house just so she could have the notion of her *home*—her childhood home—still open to her. Linnie had kept that going after Elaine's folks were gone, and she was grateful.

Elaine thought of her aunt's description of movement onstage. Pirouettes required a single spot, fixed and easily seen, that the eye could find each time around. That way, you knew where you were, she had explained. Elaine feared that with Linnie flying off to parts unknown, there would be no fixed point for her, nothing on which to hang her balance as she struggled to reinvent life without Carson.

Ridiculous. She was a grown woman and she needed to act like one.

"You'll have a blast," she said to Linnie.

"That's great, Auntie Lin," Mick said. His words had a forced, anemic quality, and Elaine wondered if Linnie had been his fixed point, too.

Outside, the full hive of WaveRunners closed in, churning and turning until the lake's surface looked scattered beyond repair.

Six

Mick sat on the screened porch with a mug of coffee. It was after nine in the morning and he was barely awake. In Newport, he would have two hours of work behind him at the yard by now. He'd been feeling the itch to go back, to get into his old routine again. But that had changed. He could feel Joy's fingers on the palm of his hand, fingernails tracing the life ahead of him.

He looked at her number on his phone. Too early? He should wait until ten, at least. Besides, Kooper hadn't called yet to sort out the thing with little Kyle.

He twirled the phone around in his fingers. The age difference was weird. She hadn't even started college yet. Hell, he only planned to ask her to a movie.

The wind quickened, giving rise to goose bumps on the lake's surface. He'd spent a lot of time on that water. With his dad in the boat, with baseball buddies in the summer, with Kayla. Especially with Kayla.

Joy looked and acted nothing like Kayla. Still, he couldn't help comparing the two. Maybe being in Lowfield invited it, but it seemed to him that Joy engaged a part of him that hadn't felt anything since he was seventeen.

It had to be the place. He looked at the pier. If Kayla appeared there, it would seem so natural. Being at the cabin made his time with her feel closer to him than his own breath.

W ater's warm." Kayla was sitting on the edge of the dock, her foot dangling in the lake. Not fully naked, just in her underwear, she lowered herself down the ladder into the water. Mick's grandparents had gone to bed, and he had taken her to the dock. Stripping to his boxers, he went in with her, and they'd floated together toward the middle of the lake.

All the while, she talked about pictures she'd drawn, a few that she'd painted. Some were at her house, some still in her head. The best ones were still in her head, but she'd turn them into real pictures someday.

"Art supplies are expensive," she said, "but the art teacher at school said my charcoal sketches are good. I'm thinking I'll stick to those for now. Then, when I can afford other kinds of stuff . . ." She gave a little kick, and the motion propelled her into a slash of moonlight that fell across the water.

"Robert Rauschenberg didn't have money for a canvas," he said, floating up next to her. The moon, near full, exposed them to anyone awake and looking. He felt the risk. "Rauschenberg, he just had to paint, so he took his bed and painted on it. Crazy paint on the bedspread and all over. It's in a museum in New York. You can actually see it if you go there. I went with my folks a couple of years ago."

She turned onto her back. Her bra, soaked through, lay like thin adhesive over her nipples. He felt himself getting hard under the surface. He kept some distance from her, kept talking about the famous artist who painted his own mattress, and aroused as Mick was, he could still picture the damn paint-splattered bed in his head.

"What did it look like?" she asked. She sounded breathless, and he wondered if it was because of him or the art.

"I read that some people thought it looked all cozy, like a bed they could crawl into," he told her. "Other people said it looked like somebody had been murdered there, and it freaked them out. I didn't see it as a bed at all. I let it get blurry, so that it looked like liquid bits of color."

She rolled over and swam away from him. He followed, wanting her to turn onto her back again. Wanting to see her breasts under the thin veil of her bra, wanting to hear her thoughts about paint-splattered sheets and artistic vision just because the words would be her voice.

A little later, still damp from their swim, they made love. He'd spread out a boat tarp over the pier and used cushions from the deck chairs as pillows. It wasn't their first time together, but he was nervous anyway, and she still seemed shy. Even so, he felt an urgency that she matched breath for breath. It would have taken a freight train to stop them.

That night—the water, the moon, her body, her voice—he kept it fragile as an ornament inside his thoughts.

He took another sip of lukewarm coffee. A boat passed close to the pier below, the deep wake dividing the larger lake from the shore. Was anything ever as intense as it seemed at seventeen?

He didn't mind diminished expectations, but he didn't want

to believe he'd never find another real relationship—ever. He didn't want to think about life without the kind of partner his parents had been to each other. With Joy, for the first time since his teenage summers in Lowfield, he felt the possibility. He pulled out his cell and dialed.

"Hey there," she answered her phone. "I wondered if you'd follow through with a call."

"I'm a man of my word. You feel like a movie tonight?"

"Mama said she needs me to help with some stuff tonight. How about we hang out at the lake this afternoon?" she suggested. "A friend of mine called and told me to come over to her lake house. She said it was fine to bring you."

"I don't know," he said. "I'm not really ready for a party."

"I know," she said. "I wouldn't ask you if it was a party. This is just me and my best friend—laying out and swimming."

Joy in a bathing suit. If he passed on that, they might as well tag and bag him. "Maybe for a little while," he said. "I've promised to throw the ball with a friend's kid brother. Why don't you give me the address, and I'll join up with you after that."

He'd track down Kooper's number and get the baseball lesson out of the way early.

After the call to Joy, he tore the address off and put it in his pocket. A thread of pleasure went through him, and he again felt guilty. What was the timeline after losing somebody? Was even the barest hint of something good acceptable so soon?

His dad had spent some of his last days sitting where Mick was at that moment. He'd smiled during that time. Even laughed some. Mick could smell the cinnamon and clove tea Carson drank from morning until night because it was something he could keep in his stomach. *Take happiness when it comes.* That's what Carson would tell him.

Already his father's voice and the other one, the voice of his own thoughts, were beginning to merge. That was okay, too.

There were worse voices to have in your head than that of Carson Forsyth.

An hour later, he was driving the same road he'd been on the day before. This time, he wasn't going to Greta's place, thank God. He would go past Whitesill Road and on to a playing field near a church. Kooper had suggested the spot. It was near the house where he and Kyle lived, the house that Kayla had lived in before she died. Mick was glad he wasn't asked to go to their home. Seeing Kayla's parents, standing in the yard, or worse yet, going inside—that might have been too much.

Church would be in full swing, so Kooper had said to park on the street and walk down to the field. A cemetery separated the field from the building, so they'd have plenty of room to practice with a bat and ball.

A couple miles past the road to Greta's, Mick saw the white steeple. The parking lot was full, but the service had begun, so no one except Kooper and Kyle remained outside. The brothers stood in front of the church as if charged with greeting late arrivals, only they were both dressed in jeans and big T-shirts. Kooper's was solid white. Kyle's sported a graphic that looked like house floor plans.

"Hey."

Kooper nodded, picked up a bat and ball, and turned to walk down to the field. Kyle didn't move. He had a glove on his hand and a look of pure misery on his face.

"Hey, buddy," Mick said to the boy. "I'm Mick. Want to throw the ball a little?"

Kyle didn't answer, but he turned and began to walk toward the field as if doing penance.

Mick caught up with Kooper. "He doesn't seem real excited about this," Mick said. "I don't want to make him stay out here if he doesn't want to."

"I set up one of those tee stands over here," Kooper said, ignoring the observation. He pointed to the far side of the field where a bar rose out of the grass. "I got something I need to do," he said. "Y'all go ahead and I'll be back in a few."

Mick watched Kooper as he retreated. What the hell was he supposed to say to the kid? Okay, he'd been a counselor one summer at camp.

"So, Kyle," he said. "Let's start with batting." He walked over to the tee stand and Kyle followed. He put the ball on top and picked up the bat. "You don't want to hold the bat with too tight a grip," he said. "That will make you tense up. You just want a solid hold, keeping your shoulders relaxed."

Kyle looked at him. His eyes were a startling shade of blue. Mick had to fight through the resemblance the boy had to Kayla. He wanted to be anywhere else. Kyle seemed even less keen on the coaching session than Mick. "When's Kooper coming back?" Mick asked.

Kyle shrugged his small shoulders, looked around as if Kooper might appear, but they were alone in the field. The refrain of an old hymn traveled through the walls and stained glass. It reached them in muffled tones.

"Do you want to take a swing?" Mick asked, inclining his head toward the ball.

Kyle shook his head. He looked both defeated and defiant in his quiet refusal.

"Come here," Mick said as gently as he could. Kyle approached him slowly.

"Kooper said you like baseball." Mick sat on the grass, motioned for Kyle to sit beside him. "Do you?"

Again, Kyle shook his head no.

"Why does Kooper think you like it so much?"

"He knows I don't like it," Kyle said. "He knows I don't like to play on any teams." He pulled blades of grass from the ground, one at a time, and never looked up at Mick. "I'm slow, and when the ball comes to me, it hurts my fingers."

"What *do* you like?" Mick asked.

For the first time, Kyle's face eased away from the deeply concerned expression that Mick had decided was more or less permanent. "Models," the boy said.

Mick tried to remember when he started thinking about the opposite sex. Maybe as young as Kyle. "I can't argue with that," he said. "I like girls a lot, too."

Kyle broke into a grin. His whole face changed when he smiled. "Not supermodels," he said. "Ewwww. I like to build stuff. Sometimes model airplanes, but mostly buildings. I did one that looks like the Empire State Building. I got that kit for my birthday."

Mick thought of Kayla, the way she'd talked about drawing. Her little brother had the same sound in his voice.

"So why do you play baseball if you don't really like it?"

Again, the frown. Mick had forgotten how mercurial emotions were when you were six.

"Horace says a boy ought to play some sport," Kyle told him. "I don't like any of them, but baseball's better than the others. Mostly, I get to stand there unless the coach yells at me to do something."

"Horace?" Mick asked. Kooper had mentioned the stepdad— one who'd seen weird blue lights after his shift at the mill.

"Horace is our new daddy," Kyle said. "Except he's not really new. Mama married him when I was three. My white daddy died before that. I don't remember him."

Another lost father. Mick felt the slide inside his gut that would lead to a thickness in his throat—and worse. He really didn't want to lose his shit in front of the kid.

"So I'm guessing you don't have dreams of being in the major leagues," he said, changing the subject.

"I want to be an engineer," Kyle said, and there was nothing childlike in the way he announced these intentions.

"Do you get good grades?"

Kyle nodded. "I get all A's and check-plus marks." He looked almost shy about admitting it.

Kayla told him once that she didn't talk to her folks about wanting to draw. They told her there were too many things that had to get done to waste her time like that. At least they let Kyle build stuff. That was an improvement. Then again, he had a different dad in the house.

"That's good," Mick said. "Engineers have to have really good grades."

So Kooper had coughed up a major lie about the boy liking baseball. Why would he do that? The ball still sat on the T-ball stand, looking entirely disrespected.

"While we're here," Mick said, "you want to try and hit that thing?"

Kyle shrugged. He didn't look as if he particularly objected any longer. They got up together and walked over. Mick carried the bat.

After trying for a half hour, Kyle managed to go from never making contact with the ball to about one hit in five tries. It didn't go very far, even when he made contact, but hitting it at all was such an improvement that Mick got a few high fives out of him.

That ought to make his turn at bat less painful—for everyone. Catching, it turned out, was pretty much a lost cause, and throwing was only slightly better. But Mick worked with him and, to his amazement, Kyle seemed to be enjoying himself most of the time.

A crowd began spilling out up at the church, and Mick realized Kooper had been gone for almost an hour. He couldn't leave the kid alone in a field, but he'd promised to catch up with Joy at the lake by early afternoon.

"Let's get the tee stand and head up toward the road," Mick said. "We can wait for Kooper up there."

"I can just get with Mama," Kyle said. "She'll be mad that I skipped Sunday school, but Kooper said he'd tell her it was his idea."

"Your mom's at the church?" Mick pulled up the ball stand and stopped. He didn't want to run into Kayla's mother.

"There she is." Kyle spotted her in the church yard. "Come on," he said to Mick. "You can tell Mama how I hit the ball."

"Wait, Kyle . . ." But the boy was off and running toward the crowd, and Mick could do nothing but follow.

Kyle was standing beside Mrs. Grimes by the time Mick reached the church. Then it hit him that she wasn't *Mrs. Grimes* anymore, and he wondered what he would call her. She wore a deep purple dress that went high at the neck and low at the knees. He used to see her in her lunch lady uniform. Like Kayla, she had a delicate structure, and all that shiny fabric overwhelmed her, made her look like a child playing dress-up.

"Hello," he said, avoiding the name altogether. "It's good to see you again. I was just helping Kyle with his batting."

"What are you doin' here?" The look on her face told him that Kooper had not cleared this baseball lesson with the folks. A man walked up to join her—obviously Horace, the new dad. The weathered surface of his deep brown skin reminded Mick of an older wooden boat, the hard-won texture that spoke of wind and rough seas.

"Horace Ames." The man introduced himself and extended a hand. As Mick offered his own hand to shake, Horace's welcoming expression began to fade. He saw his wife and picked up the hostile vibe she continued to throw in Mick's direction.

"Hello, Mrs. Ames," Mick said. "It's been a long time." She still didn't speak. "I'm Michael Forsyth," he said to Horace. "I didn't mean to upset anyone. Kooper just asked me to help Kyle . . ."

"You need to stay away from the boy," Kayla's mother said.

"Mama!" Kooper came running over from his car across the street. "I was . . ."

"I don't care what you were doing. I was just telling Michael that he needs to stay clear of your little brother."

He'd been ambushed by Kooper, and for the life of him, he couldn't figure out why. Poor Kyle had gone mute. He hugged the bat as if it might be a blanket or a stuffed bear, a necessary comfort. He seemed to have regressed in age by several years, no longer the articulate budding engineer he'd been just moments before.

Kooper stopped trying to explain. The standoff had rendered them all speechless, even poor Horace, who was apparently a quick study in family conflict. His severe expression mirrored his wife's. A Mount Rushmore of discontent. Clearly, Kyle's mother hadn't found forgiveness for Mick over the years, regardless of her time spent at the church behind her.

"I am sorry for your loss," Kayla's mom said finally. "Your daddy was a good man, by all accounts. But I have to ask you to keep your distance from Kyle. It's best that way."

"Mama . . ." Kooper had a surprisingly stern tone when he addressed her, but he stopped when she turned to him. Mick couldn't see her eyes, and he realized that was a good thing. Compared to this woman, Greta had been almost welcoming.

"I should go," Mick said. "Kyle . . . Hey, buddy, you did great. Remember. Loose shoulders. Eye on the ball. Listen, I really liked hanging out."

"Me, too," Kyle said in a voice so small Mick had to read his lips to figure out the words.

As Mick walked by, Kooper touched his arm. "Listen, man, I

thought I'd get back by the time they came out." He shook his head. "I'm sorry."

"If you were sneaking this whole thing," Mick asked, "why did you have us come here? Did you want me to run into your mom? Why would you put either of us through that?"

"It's complicated." He kept his voice low, cut his eyes over toward his folks. "Trust me. It's really fuckin' complicated." He took a deep breath and put both hands in his pockets. Apparently, that was all Kooper had to say.

Mick nodded and walked off toward his car without looking back. He wanted to get the hell away from all of them. How was it that he only came to Lowfield for his dad, but he kept getting demonized by people for trying to be a good guy? The crazy part was that in spite of getting yelled at by yet another God-fearing woman, he actually felt good about the time he'd spent with little Kyle.

The kid seemed great. He'd never be anything but the goat on any playing field, but he was a terrific little guy. Mick didn't know anything about kids that age, but it seemed to him that Kyle had a lot going for him.

Mick just barely heard the siren before the ambulance swerved around the curve ahead of him, and he startled, jerking to the right. His front tire slipped off a high shoulder, giving him that awful sensation of being yanked off the road in spite of himself. As he fought to correct, a tree seemed to jump dead in his path and he swerved farther right, deep into the woods. It took him a second to realize the car had stopped, and a second more to process that he had hit nothing more than scrawny undergrowth. At worst, he'd have a few scratches on the paint.

The siren grew faint, and he felt himself trembling. He had the small presence of mind to turn off the car. Beyond that, he was lost.

He thought of Kayla. Of the tree coming at him. Only the tree in front of her had kept coming. Before he knew it, his tremors had turned to heaving sobs, less crying than expelling something toxic inside of him. He let it happen.

Anyone watching would have thought he was crazy. A car positioned in the woods with a guy rubbing his face, letting out growls and sobs before finally giving in to simple tears. The world outside the car became a parallel universe as he surrendered to feeling everything he had grown accustomed to tamping down, keeping in check. He felt it driving through him, through nerves, skin, bone, and blood as if he'd become a conduit for something larger than himself. It made him feel clean.

He knew without a doubt that his time with the kid was tied into all of it somehow. He didn't know how he knew, just that he felt he'd done something right for the first time in a very long time.

When it all settled, when he looked at the time on his phone, he realized he'd only been sitting there for fifteen minutes. A little less, actually. Joy had called, but he hadn't heard the ring. He could have sworn hours had passed. It was as if he'd been pulled out of his body to a place where the time/space continuum ceased.

He turned the key and, another miracle . . . not only had the ambulance and the tree missed him, but the car engine turned as if nothing had happened. Before resuming his drive to the lake, he dialed Joy, left her a message saying he was on his way. Then he moved back onto the empty stretch of road, grateful to obey the stern directive of the GPS as she reminded him how to find his way.

The paramedics made everyone else clear out of the kitchen. Greta watched as best she could from the other room. She could make out the shape of one fellow hunched over Mattie, while another one went back and forth bringing in what they needed from the truck.

Greta had been sitting by the window in her room while Mattie cleaned up from lunch when she heard the other woman suck in her breath, hard and fast. It sounded like Mattie had stepped waist deep into ice cold water. Dishes, cups, glasses—Greta still didn't know what all—crashed to the kitchen floor.

For an instant after the sound, Greta's mind went to thinking about all the old china that was in that cabinet—registering how sad it would be if it all got broken. Mattie must have been putting something away, or else getting something out. In that moment of disassociated calm, Greta let herself picture all the pieces on the floor. She even registered an unexpected relief—as if the treasured belongings held her captive somehow and she'd been unexpectedly set free. This was all before she collected herself and called out to the other woman.

"Mattie!" She called out the name, but only heard a kind of animal groan. "Mattie, what happened?" Thoughts of dishes disappeared as a panic set in.

Outside, the young folks and their children were getting out of their cars coming back from church. She'd skipped the morning service, was going to have Mattie drive her to the smaller evening sermon.

"Ayla! Rae!" She called out the window as she put both hands on the little table by her chair and pulled herself up. "Somebody, get in here! Something's happened!" She didn't hear a response.

Every step felt like she was pushing her body through a wall of sand. She knew the house as well as she knew her own face in the mirror, but trying to get to her friend, she seemed to forget where she was. She could recall with clarity the ease that unclouded eyes had afforded her.

Shapes of furniture, the light that came through the kitchen door, all of it seemed foreign as she made her way to the kitchen.

Shattered china and glass crunched under her slippers, and the sharp edge of a broken something went clear through to her foot. She screamed out in pain, but kept pushing forward to the place where Mattie lay on the floor. She slid her feet along to avoid stepping down on more jagged edges, and she felt her own blood soaking the cloth of her slipper.

Where were they all, that passel of kids always underfoot? Mattie's granddaughters hadn't heard her. What could she do?

She reached Mattie and felt relief loosen the muscles in her arms and chest as Mattie spoke.

"Greta," Mattie said, her voice weak as a bird, "Lord, I done broke everything."

"Hush," Greta said. "Don't worry about dishes. Good Lord, that's nothing." The floor had become a sea of shards.

"Some . . . thing . . . wrong," Mattie said.

"Where does it hurt, Mattie? Did you cut yourself? Are you bleeding anywhere?" Bending low, she got close enough to see that there were only scrapes on Mattie's arms and face, but nothing deep.

"Hurting stopped now," she said. "No more."

"Hang on, Mattie. If it's the last thing I do on this earth, I'm going to get you some help."

The phone was across the kitchen and, with the same slide-step motion of her feet, she pushed through the breakage. It must have been a whole shelf in the china cabinet that had come out when Mattie went down.

Before Greta got to the phone, she heard one of the children stomping around on the porch calling out some game.

"Get your mama!" she yelled as loud as she could. "Mattie's hurt! Go get your folks."

"Okay!" A child's voice yelled back.

She kept her progress toward the phone, but before she

reached it, Ayla came running in with her husband, Robeson; Rae and all the others followed.

"Thank you," Greta intoned to God and Mattie's kin, her heart slowing to some semblance of normal, and she turned again and made her way back to Mattie.

Robeson called 911 while Ayla got a cold cloth to put on Mattie's forehead.

"She's dripping with sweat," Rae said, "wet as a dishcloth. Granny Mat? You still hear me, Granny Mat?"

"I hear you, child," came a voice too soft to be Mattie's, but it was.

Greta went back to Mattie, brushed china pieces to the side with her foot, and eased herself down beside her friend. She found the buttons of Mattie's dress near her neck and undid the top few so Mattie could breathe better. With every other part of her body trembling, Greta marveled that her fingers still worked.

"You children stay out of here," Ayla said. "You'll get cut on this mess."

The children left the room, but Greta could hear them nearby, waiting on the ambulance.

"You hang on, Mattie," Greta said. "I've lost too much. You won't be going anywhere, you hear? I'm stubborn and I'm selfish and I won't let you."

Greta had a hand on Mattie's shoulder, felt the slight motion of her chest rising and falling. Good. *Keep that breath coming and going,* she thought.

"Greta . . ." Mattie's voice came out as a whisper. "I worry about you. You are stubborn." She stopped, caught her breath again.

"You stop trying to talk," Greta said. "I'm going to be just fine. You worry about your old self. I'm not flat on the floor, am I?"

"Let your family help you," Mattie managed. "You hear me?"

"You're my family," she said. "Now stop trying to talk."

Then she'd heard the noises of the siren. As it came closer, the wail dominated the sounds of the country, subdued them with an urgency normally reserved for busier streets. She tried to sort out how long it had been since they arrived. Could have been twenty minutes, could have been two hours. If her soul depended on it, she couldn't have told anyone which it was.

She sat on the couch, listening for anything that meant Mattie was all right. While the EMTs—three of them—tended to Mattie, Ayla, the older of Mattie's two granddaughters, went to work cleaning the cut on Greta's foot.

"Don't worry with that," Greta said to the girl.

"Rae's in there with her. It's better if I keep busy," Ayla said, dabbing the cut with something that stung like hellfire.

After a moment, one of the paramedics came out with supplies and took over wrapping the wound.

Then they waited. Greta heard one of them radio in to the hospital. He said something about Mattie's heart. Something about a possible stroke. She'd never understood Catholics and the need for those beads they called a rosary, but she suddenly wished she had prayers at the ready. Her mind was spinning so fast, she couldn't think of actual words to pray. She wished she had something memorized, so that bead by bead she would pray Mattie back to being okay.

Elaine stood in the yard spraying water on Linnie's crepe myrtle bushes. Her aunt's attempt at sprucing up the landscape had achieved minimal success. The cheerless patch of bushes huddled to the side of the wooded slope to the lake. Keeping them alive seemed to be a point of pride for Linnie, so Elaine decided to do her part. Standing there, not just alone, but profoundly lonely.

Mick had taken off in the car and Linnie in her truck. Linnie was off tracking down some flea market—a weekend obsession— and Mick . . . well, she had no idea what he was up to. He'd babbled on about playing ball with some kid and then swimming at a friend's lake house, but Elaine didn't think he'd kept up with any of his Lowfield buddies. Maybe it had something to do with the Brown girl.

So Elaine and the dog, still shamefully unnamed, were left to their own devices. The puppy sat at attention beside her. She looked at the animal, tried to fashion a proper moniker for him. Looking at the eye brought the name Droopy to mind, but that just seemed cruel. After that, she drew a blank. Maybe just Dog would stick. Clean. Minimalist.

The lake was quiet. Eerily so, for a Sunday. She almost missed the noise of engines and people yelling back and forth. The quiet left too much space to fill in her mind. Whenever that happened, the absence of Carson became an unavoidable reality. Maybe people would pile into their boats after church.

She directed showering sprays of water over the leaves. The dog went off a few feet sniffing at something and Elaine watched as he dug at the ground. A slight breeze rattled branches. The air moved over her damp skin.

The dog came toward her with something in his mouth, and she turned the sprayer off and knelt beside him. He'd found a leather pouch, weathered and muddy from time spent in the yard. The drawstring at the mouth was secured by a clear blue bead with the string threaded through a hole in the middle. While the pouch felt stiff from the elements, the bead looked as clean as if it had been kept in a drawer.

Carson had lost the pouch months before. She remembered his search on the dock and in the house before they took off for the drive back to Chapel Hill.

"What's in it?" she'd asked him.

"I keep my lures in there," he said. "A few favorites. Maybe it'll turn up."

She took the pouch from the dog's mouth and pulled at the drawstring opening. Inside, a piece of chamois cloth had been rolled into a cylinder. She took it out to unroll it. With every rotation, a small lure revealed itself. Delicate little items with hooks hidden inside the wisps of feather and sparkles of metal.

On the lake, a weak, puttering engine went by. Holding the pouch made Elaine feel as if Carson might be close, as if nothing more than mist separated the two of them. She thought she heard the mumbling of voices. She turned to find nothing, not even a squirrel or a bird in the yard. The puppy had settled into a comfortable, flat-bellied sprawl on the ground. He stared up at her, unconcerned.

"Carson?" she said it out loud, and her voice broke through the odd moment and left her feeling foolish. But to her relief, the gutted emptiness had left her.

"Come on," she said to the animal. "Let's take you for your first ride in the boat. If we go to the marina now, we'll beat the afternoon crowd."

At her change in tone, Dog stood, ready for anything. She went to the side of the utility building and turned off the spigot and headed toward the dock with the puppy in tow. Morty came out of his house with a bag of cat food in his hand. He met her in the yard, and they walked down to the water's edge.

"Did you have your television on really loud a few minutes ago?" she asked.

"No darlin'," he said. "Don't turn that thing on until it's time for the news. If I have it on for anything else, all those shiny, good-looking people moving and talking get me too distracted to accomplish a damn thing."

She laughed. "So is this your attempt to get all the fish over your way?" She pointed to the cat food. Morty routinely sprinkled it in the water to increase the chances of catching something off his dock.

He shrugged, walked over toward his pier. "Food got old. Cat won't touch it, so I figure I'll let the poor fish have a go."

"A last meal for the condemned?"

"You folks aren't plannin' to catch 'em," he said. "I might as well have a shot. Linnie don't so much as swat flies, much less put a worm on a hook and try to kill a fish. Double homicide."

"You're right," Elaine said. She thought of Carson's lure pouch in her pocket. Maybe Mick would take up fishing again someday. Maybe he still did. She'd lost her usual awareness of Mick's life during Carson's illness.

"I'm gonna catch these fish for all of us," he said, grinning. "Linnie don't kill 'em, but by God, she eat 'em, huh?"

"We'll take whatever you give us and be grateful for it," Elaine said, stepping onto her own dock and retrieving the boat key from a metal box attached to a post. "We're down to crackers and canned corn up at the cabin," she said. "I'm going over to Merle's Marina to pick up a few things. You need anything?"

"No darlin'," he said, pausing with a handful of cat food. "Be careful when you do your shopping in that place."

"Why?"

"Grill is still good as ever, but Gabbie, she loses track of inventory, I think. The grocery section's got baked beans that date back to Old Ike's second term. Check the expiration before you get to the register. She's just like old Merle. Don't like to give refunds."

Elaine thought of Merle. He'd been a disheveled creature behind the counter—wearing a stained apron, flipping burgers and complaining about the "damned Arabs" and their "dang robbery" of people trying to make a living selling gas.

"Have fun," Morty called over to her as he sprinkled liberal handfuls of cat food near a fallen tree trunk in the water by his dock.

"Will do," she said. She lowered the lift and let the boat settle into the lake. The old aluminum outboard had belonged to her daddy, and between Carson and Linnie, it had been kept up beautifully. Elaine steadied it against the dock, motioning for the dog to get inside.

"On second thought," Morty called out, "you can bring me a pack a Salems, darlin'."

"They'll kill you," she said.

"Oh, sweetness, I'd be gone if that was true," he said, heading over to sprinkle on the other side of his dock. "Besides, I've cut back to only a few a week. I'll pay you back."

"Pay me in fish," she said, starting the engine and slowly backing the boat out into the water. The dog hopped onto the seat beside her, paws on the side of the boat and nose tilted up.

Lake Riley, built between two dams, ran for eight miles—a clear, deepwater pool where bass the size of sheep held court in the lower depths. Elaine felt the vibrations of the outboard's rumbling churn. She looked behind her. Her boat parted the slick surface, leaving a lovely, symmetrical V of unchallenged wake. The tight response of the steering made it feel like an extension of her limbs as she willed the boat toward the place of her choosing. Her choosing. For better or worse now, she got to choose everything. She passed the bend that took her dock out of sight.

A mile down, as she saw the entrance to the cove that would lead her to Merle's, she eased toward the mouth of the inlet and slowed her speed. The dog, registering a change in momentum, stood on the seat, front paws on the side of the boat. Then, for unclear reasons, he scrambled up and over, launching himself into the water.

"Jesus! You crazy mutt!" Elaine put the motor in neutral.

The dog must have realized that he had no idea where he was going. He began to paddle furiously, making little or no headway.

"I thought all dogs were *good* swimmers," she said. She cut the motor entirely and went over to try and reach him.

He began to move in circles as it became clear that there was no shore in the immediate vicinity. At this point, he paddled back toward the boat. "Hold on," she said. "I'll get you back in." She leaned over the edge, nearly toppling the boat, distributing her weight sideways across the beam in an effort to keep everything stable. "Don't fight me or we'll both be in the water."

She leaned out as far as she could go and got a hand on one of his paws. Slowly, she began to haul the animal up over the side. He felt like a sack of rocks, his weight doubling as the water soaked his thick fur. She pulled at him and he yelped, then snapped in her direction.

"Dammit! Don't you bite me or I'll leave you in the lake."

Finally, she got him over the side. Noises of distress came from deep in his throat, and she sat on the floor and coaxed him into her lap as the boat rocked from side to side. In spite of his weight, she saw just how skinny he was under all that fur. She also saw the mix of fear and gratitude in his eyes.

"You poor thing," she said. "We're quite a pair." She held him close, feeling the lake water soaking through to her skin. After a few minutes, when the puppy seemed to have recovered, she reluctantly eased him off her lap and, once again, got behind the wheel. Nearly as drenched as the dog and smeared with mud from the floor of the boat, she found a grungy towel that did little to help.

"Do we go to the marina looking like hobos, or do we go home?" Her stomach growled again. "I've got nothing to prove to people around here."

She looked at the dog. "Hobo." She said it aloud, and the dog's ears perked up. "Hobo," she said again. "You like that name?" He walked over and settled his head against her leg. In the distance, she heard a rumble of thunder. Her wet shirt pulled at her skin, making her shiver.

"Perfect," she said as clouds took away the last of the sun.

Mick climbed the ladder to the top of the boathouse. On the pier below, Joy lay sunning herself on a towel. A black-and-green bikini revealed her flat belly, pink from the early season exposure. She couldn't have been more than five four or five five, but the suit made her small body look long and lean. He sat on the edge, looking down at the water. He'd climbed up to dive off the board, but he was having second thoughts. The hot sun felt nice.

"Don't bother showing off," Joy called up to him without opening her eyes. "I'm not looking at you."

Joy's friend Teresa lounged on top of an inner tube, floating just off the pier with a cigarette in one hand and a wine cooler in the other.

Mick knew the house. He'd been there on occasion with Teresa's older sister, Laurie, during his summers in Lowfield. Looking down at the floating girl, he could have been looking at Laurie eight years before.

Now he heard from Teresa that Laurie ran the hardware store with her husband, Aiden. Mick remembered Aiden, too, a shy, awkward boy, always on the outskirts of the in crowd. Laurie, in her glory days, wouldn't have looked twice at Aiden Spence. She'd planned to move to Atlanta to be a model and "make even more money than my daddy can give me."

Aiden must have been thrilled when, as Laurie's options dwindled, he rose higher and higher on her list. They had a baby girl a few months back, Teresa said.

"Jump already," Teresa yelled up at him. "And don't splash me. You'll put my cigarette out."

"Don't rush me," he said. "I like it up here."

It had been Laurie, all those years ago, who teased him about slumming it with Kayla. She'd had no idea how serious his relationship was and when he'd snapped at her, told her to worry about her own love life, she'd seemed genuinely surprised at his anger.

"Don't get mad. She can't help it if she's trailer park, Mick," Laurie, still clueless, tried to explain. "Your daddy's a college professor. Hell, even I'm a little low rent for your uptown shit over there in Chapel Hill. Kayla Grimes? Are you kidding me? Those things just don't work out."

He hadn't given a damn what Laurie Pascal thought. But later, he wondered if he hadn't heard her voice as a preview of the things his friends in Chapel Hill would say. Had he let that get to him before homecoming?

Maybe Kayla wouldn't have fit in, would have been humiliated. Maybe that was something he'd known all along. Or maybe he'd been too damn insecure to put their two worlds in the same room and let people deal with it.

"If you want something to drink," Teresa said, "there's a bottle of Jack in the plastic bin where we store the seat cushions up there."

"Great idea." What had gotten him thinking about Kayla again? It seemed he couldn't go anywhere in the county without his thoughts coming around to her.

He went over and lifted the hinged lid. Sure enough, a bottle of Jack Daniel's stood upright in the corner, a stack of paper cups beside it. He poured, downed it, then poured again.

"Pascals know how to get it done," he mumbled.

He finished the second and then, against all good sense, climbed onto the board.

"Remember," Teresa said, "don't splash my cigarette."

"I'd be doing you a favor," he said, tossing the cup beside the diving board. "I thought you were working as a nurse or something at the hospital. Don't they make you quit that shit before they hire you?"

"I'm volunteering, asshole," she said, "to get credits for community college this fall. And I only go in on weekday mornings. I can do whatever I want on the weekends. It's not even like they're paying me. Besides, I'll quit when I have my first baby. That's what Laurie did, and she said it was easy as peeing in a pool."

"Remind me to give you plenty of space in the water."

She took a drag and closed her eyes. Even with her hands full, she managed to shoot him the bird with her drink hand.

He thought of doing a backflip. But he hadn't tried one in several years, and that choice had the potential for substantial humiliation and pain. He opted for a clean dive, no frills. The cool, deep water momentarily cleared the alcohol from his brain. He swam toward the pier, and when he came up near Teresa, she lightly grabbed his shoulder and he stopped.

"What's up?" he asked.

She motioned for him to paddle out a little farther.

He glanced over toward Joy. She lay motionless on her back. He followed Teresa until they were out of earshot of the pier.

"She likes you, you know." Teresa sounded like someone's stern and irritated mother.

"I'm glad," he said. "I like her, too." He wondered what the hell he'd done wrong.

"I mean," she said, "that she *really* likes you. She'll probably sleep with you if you let it go that far. There are a lot of reasons why that's probably not a good idea."

"What are you? Her mother?" he said. "Besides, I just saw her again for the first time in seven years yesterday."

"Yeah, and seven years ago you were playing mind games with another local girl. I know all about you from Laurie—all about you and that black girl who died. Joy's my best friend. She has been forever."

Mick stopped moving, forgot he was swimming for a second. His head slid under and he came up blinking, wondering what people had said about him back then. No wonder he couldn't get Kayla off his mind.

"That was a long time ago," he told her. He had no intention of discussing Kayla with another Pascal.

"You messed that girl up pretty good. You probably don't even know the half of it."

"You're out of line." He started to swim away, but she grabbed a section of his hair. "Stop it," he hissed, glancing over again at Joy.

"People still talk about it," she said.

"*People*," he said, "would be your sister Laurie. She's got a lot to say about everybody. Always has."

She sucked in the dregs of her spent cigarette and dropped it into the water. The slight breeze took it along the surface like a toy boat. "You're fucking clueless," she whispered.

"What's that supposed to mean?" Mick paddled slightly away from her, as if the distance would bring clarity to the bizarre exchange.

She paddled lightly and followed him. "Joy's not like me," she said. "I'm not a slut or anything, but I do know how to have a good time and then let it go. She talks pretty gutsy, but she hasn't been serious with anybody before."

Teresa gave him a hard stare.

"Like I said, I saw her yesterday for the first time since she was a kid." Jesus, he wanted the conversation to end in the worst way. "She's got nothing to do with Kayla—and neither do you."

Teresa unnerved him. She continued to look at him. Maybe only seconds went by, but the silence seemed to go on and on, turning their conversation into a standoff.

"All I'm saying is that taking it too far might not be the best thing for her," she said, still whispering. "That's all I'm going to say."

"Noted." He'd heard enough. He'd never let Laurie Pascal get away with her crap, and he certainly wasn't going to take it from her sister. He swam away, and as he looked up at the dock, he saw Joy watching him, her face full of questions.

"Hey," he said.

"Hey," she said back. "What was that all about?"

He shrugged. "She's just being a Pascal."

Whatever that meant to Joy, she seemed inclined to leave it alone. He pulled himself up to sit on the edge of the pier. The sun went behind a cloud, bringing chills to his wet skin. Seconds later, it began to rain, stinging pellets accompanied by rumbles of thunder in the distance.

Teresa paddled her way in, and Joy was up and moving toward the shelter of the boathouse. Mick followed, and once Teresa was inside, she went to a cabinet and pulled out dry towels for all of them.

"Joy," Teresa said. "Look behind the oil can on the shelf. That's where Daddy keeps his bourbon."

"Wow," Mick said, securing his towel around his waist, "this is a full-service boathouse."

"My brothers stash it up top," Teresa said, seemingly unbothered by their exchange in the water, "and Daddy's stuff is down here."

Sure enough, Joy pulled down a fifth, half full. Maker's Mark. Mr. Pascal kept it top shelf, even in the boathouse. They sat down, legs dangling beside the boat lift, and passed the bottle back and forth. After a few swigs, Mick realized that he and Teresa were the only ones drinking. Joy had stopped after a sip or two, but the bottle looked woefully low.

"Will you get in trouble?" he asked. "Your dad's going to notice how empty this is."

"He'll blame Scott," Teresa said. "And Scott won't snitch. For a brother, he's pretty good about backing me up. Besides, both the boys get off easy with Daddy."

Mick listened. He missed his dad. Strange, how grief seemed to have actual weight. If he stepped on a scale, he'd swear it would register. Teresa talking about her dad and her brothers seemed pointed and cruel. It wasn't meant that way, of course. She had no idea.

"We should head home," Joy said. "Mick, are you okay to drive?"

"Yeah, I don't have far to go," he said. "Just down the lake." He thought of what Teresa had said out in the water, tried to balance those words against his urge to mindlessly escape by taking things with Joy as far as they would go. He liked her. He liked her a lot. But he was leaving town. He would not be an asshole with this girl. She didn't deserve that.

He and Joy gathered their things from the boathouse changing room and picked up their wet towels from outside. The squall had passed, but the clouds remained.

He looked at her as she slid behind the wheel of her car. The lines of her wet bikini top showed through her white T-shirt. Tight jean shorts and tanned thighs completed the pinup image. She might be more innocent than Teresa—Courtney Love might be more innocent than Teresa—but Joy knew what she was doing to him. She had to.

"Whatever Teresa pulled on you," she said, "don't worry about it. I love my friend, but I don't plan to ask her for dating advice. It's nice to see you again, Micky—to get to know you. It's all good. Okay?"

It felt strange. Between his morning with little Kyle Grimes and his afternoon with Joy, he'd been more connected with Lowfield in one day than he'd been with Newport in two years. There, coworkers had turned into drinking buddies. Women streamed through his existence, but never paused long enough to be memorable. Trina, his only true friend in town, tended bar at his favorite dive. She looked a little like John Wayne in drag and routinely fell for rowdy, unattainable sailors who saw her as one of the guys. Her nickname for Mick was "Professor"—and it was said without any hint of admiration. Something set him apart from the people he knew up north—allowed him to keep his distance. But his father's death had left him flayed. Both Kyle and Joy had found the opening.

"You're quiet," she said, interrupting his thoughts.

"Sorry," he said. "Sorting through some stuff."

"Anything I can do?" She glanced up at him as he stood beside her car.

He looked at her, wanted to tell her yes, wanted to kiss her, wanted to let her soothe his serrated nerves.

"No," he said. "I don't think so."

She moved close to him. Again, the smell of berries permeated her hair, her skin, breaking through the suntan lotion and sweat of the afternoon. He wondered if the scent had settled on her skin after all the hours at the family stand. She tilted her head up and seemed to be waiting, then before he thought about it too much, he bent through the open window and kissed her. She felt like water, like something elemental and fluid. She pulled away too soon.

"Maybe we'll do something this week?" She didn't really look at him when she spoke.

"Yeah," he said. "I'll call you."

She offered a small wave before pulling away.

He stood there and watched her go. The dull feeling of being drunk had eased into a more pleasant feeling of being a little loose. The headache hadn't crept in yet, and he decided to try and enjoy the sweet spot. He took out his cell to check in at the cabin.

Linnie answered.

"Hey," he said, "what are you guys up to?"

"Your mom's not here. I just walked in from the flea market and she and the dog were both gone. I saw Morty. He said she'd taken the boat to Merle's Marina to pick up a few groceries."

"Okay," he said. "I'm heading home now. You need for me to pick up anything?"

"I think I'm good," she said.

"Okay."

Driving back to the cabin, his mind wandered through a collage of images from the day. Little Kyle finally getting his bat to connect with the ball—opening up and talking, smiling even, about building his models. Joy. All that dark hair and white skin.

A sheriff's cruiser passed him and made a U-turn, bringing his thoughts to more practical concerns. The blue light came on behind him and he wondered just how fast he'd been going—and how much bourbon was still in his system. He didn't feel at all drunk. Maybe he was okay. Jesus, he was getting too old for this shit.

He pulled over, rolled down his window, and offered his most sober smile to the approaching officer.

Thunder rolled in the distance. Greta sat on the blue couch in her living room. She knew she wasn't alone, but Lord, she felt it. Robeson, Ayla's husband, had stayed behind with her and the kids while Ayla, Rae, and Dane went to the hospital to be with Mattie. Greta's eyes couldn't recognize a face from ten feet away and yet she had the vivid image in her head of Mattie being carried out the front door. Mattie, dark skin against that white stretcher. Men lifting her with no more effort than it took to pick up a child. It made her friend seem slight—and that wasn't Mattie. Mattie had more substance, sense, and will than any ten people put together.

With Carson, Greta had been sad. She'd known it was coming after he told her he was sick. But with Mattie now, she was scared. She hated feeling scared. Helpless, scared emotions were worthless. They came to no good in this world.

Greta wasn't sure just when she and Mattie changed—when the two of them went from employer and hired help to two peas in a pod. It happened before Mattie moved in. Maybe even before Taylor died, Greta wasn't sure. Tilda Jamison noticed it before Greta. Tilda began as Greta's closest friend, then turned hateful and small-minded. Maybe Tilda had always been that way and, over time, Greta had grown up enough to notice it.

"Why do you and that colored woman always have your heads stuck together like a couple of hens?" Tilda had said one day when she and Greta were shopping in Greensboro. Taylor had been gone for several years, and Mattie had begun to spend more and more time at the house.

"Her name's Mattie, Tilda. And she's a good, Christian woman."

"And she's a colored."

Greta had looked at Tilda's puffy face. Her light hair teased the same way for twenty years and counting. "You sound like a bigot, Tilda Jamison."

"I am not." To the woman's credit, she'd looked more offended than angry. "I just don't know why my best friend would rather sit and shell peas with a colored woman than come over and watch television with me."

Greta had tried to think of why that was true. She *would* rather sit with Mattie, and she found it harder and harder to stomach Tilda's increasing tirades, not only about black people, but also about *low-rents* and *the Catholics*. Tilda had been fun in high school, but she'd become just plain mean. That very day, Greta decided she needed to distance herself from Tilda Jamison.

In the thirty or more years since, she and Mattie had understood each other. Helped each other.

Let your family help you. That's what Mattie had said. Why had her words carried such urgency?

Let your family help you. Greta heard it again in her head, not with Mattie's voice, but with Carson's. Clear as a bell. *Mattie is my family. Her kin are closer to me than those I'm told are my own. You're gone, Carson. You left me. Leave me be, now.* Her mind answered her son, angry to be bothered at such a time.

She pulled herself up, unable to sit any longer, and made her way to the window. A world of gray pressed down around her. Thunder grew louder, but no rain came with it. In the hazy gloom, she could almost see the ambulance sitting in front of her house. She could play it over and over, the men putting Mattie into the back.

They'd turned off the siren, but the lights pulsed red the whole time, throwing color into the overcast light of the day.

As Greta looked out the window, the dots of color still floated in her field of vision, only they were no longer red. They pulsed blue, bright to dim and back to bright again. It was a blue she remembered and she hoped against hope that it was her imagination and not real. Her unreliable eyes grew wet with tears.

Don't take anybody else from me. Don't leave me here again while somebody I love has to leave.

They didn't always come to take. Sometimes they came to comfort. Sometimes to celebrate. Sometimes to warn. That's what she'd always heard. Greta stood there and prayed. She prayed for Mattie. She prayed for herself. And she realized that the two prayers were interchangeable. She left it to God to sort that one out.

From the water, Merle's Marina formed a collection of docks, connected in haphazard fashion along one side of the cove near a small bridge. The random configuration—sections tacked onto existing sections—looked a little like a game of dominoes. The owners clearly added on as needed.

The squall had come and gone—was over by the time Elaine pulled the boat alongside Merle's temporary tie-up near the gas tanks. In that time she'd gone from damp to soaking wet. Hobo licked the rainwater from her leg as she leaned over to secure the boat to the pier.

Shiny patches of oil floated on the water near the fuel pumps. Familiar smells of engines, gas, mud, and fish surrounded the place. The scents had predated the years when her dad brought her to Merle's as a kid.

The aromas fascinated Hobo, too. He ran to the edge of the bank and then back to the path that led up the hill. She hadn't bought a leash yet and wondered if Hobo would stay put outside while she got something to eat. After his stunt out in the lake, she didn't trust leaving him in the boat. Maybe Gabbie would have a leash for sale. "You're going to have to behave," she said.

"Hey, there," a voice from behind startled her.

She turned to find Ronnie Allsap walking over from the parking lot toward Merle's. She still felt bad about her behavior at the cabin. She'd been kind of awful. But if he saw it that way, he didn't let on.

"I got you craving some food from this place, huh?" He grinned.

"I guess you did." She was actually glad to see him again.

"I pulled in up here just in time to see you out there hauling that wet ball of fur back into the boat. Thought you were going to flip for a second."

"You waited out here all that time just to give me grief?" Hobo sniffed in Ronnie's direction, but kept his distance.

"No. I left my phone in the car. Just came back out to get it," he said. "Razzing you was just a bonus."

She smiled in spite of herself. "Glad I livened up your afternoon. I'm sure it was entertaining."

"It was that," he said, opening the door to Merle's.

"Hobo, stay," she instructed the puppy. Did he even know what *stay* meant?

"Good God, what happened to you?" Gabbie boomed from behind the lunch counter. Merle's aging daughter hadn't cut her hair in over a decade, best Elaine could tell. It hung in a loose ponytail—mixed brown and gray—down to the small of her back. She'd evolved from homely to comfortable-looking over the years.

"You look like you fell in," the woman said, shaking her head.

At least Ronnie hadn't shared her misfortune with the rest of the crowd. Elaine could suddenly feel the mud, sweat, and dog hair that clung to her rain-soaked body and clothes.

"Dog fell out of the boat," she said to an audience of diners.

"What dog?" Gabbie looked over the counter, down at the floor.

"I left him outside."

Ronnie nodded toward an obese black lab wearing a skull-and-crossbones bandanna settled by the counter in front of the grill.

"As long as he doesn't pick a fight with Jolly Roger there," Gabbie said, "I don't care if you let him join the party."

Somebody had beaten her to it and opened the door for the

pathetic-looking Hobo. Ears back, fur clumped, and head down, he made his way over to Elaine. Jolly Roger raised his eyes in mild interest, then settled down again.

Gabbie looked at Hobo and shook her head in pity. "Only a mama could love that one." Then she promptly lost interest in the dog. "I'm awfully sorry about Carson. He was a good man." She looked as if she meant it. Anyone who remembered Carson loved him, even people who still had their suspicions about Elaine. Elaine was sure that Greta's opinions about what happened back then must have become the version of record.

"He was a very good man," Elaine said, hoping for the sympathy conversation to end.

"Grill or groceries?" Gabbie asked.

"Both," Elaine answered, settling at the counter.

"Good. We'll get you fixed up in a few." Gabbie turned to Ronnie. "Yours will be up in a second."

Ronnie sat down beside Elaine.

"Let me ring you up over here," Gabbie yelled to someone wanting to pay for an armload of groceries. "I'm running both sides till my sorry-assed son gets here."

"Omelet? Burger?" Gabbie's general inquiry was directed at Elaine while she rang up the man's purchases. Then, before Elaine even answered, she'd washed her hands and was slapping mayonnaise on a bun. She added a grilled patty and served it to an aging black man sitting at the very end of the counter.

"Cheese omelet," Elaine said, hoping that counted as giving her order.

Gabbie nodded her way, threw another burger on the grill, and cracked three eggs into a Teflon pan. Elaine felt dizzy watching her. She was a large woman, but she moved like a gymnast.

"They upped my cost on gas again," she announced to no one in particular, sprinkling cheese on top of the egg. "People think

I'm getting rich off those pumps, but I don't get a nickel more, no matter how much it goes up."

She didn't mention the Arabs, but for the most part, it could have been her father talking.

"I'm going to go wash up," Elaine told Ronnie. "Would you keep an eye on Hobo for me? He's a bit skittish, but he's getting better around people." She looked down at the dog. He'd planted himself under her stool.

"You bet."

As she headed toward the bathroom, Gabbie called out, "Let me know if we're out of soap in there. It's that squirt kind, and them kids use a handful every time they go in."

Inside the restroom, the gray walls gave her skin a dull pallor. A slash of mud down her cheek told the rest of the tale. *What am I going to do?* The question flashed through her mind but took on such a broad reach that she didn't even know where to begin with an answer.

She pumped soap from the dispenser and washed her hands, then wet a paper towel and wiped her face. She ran damp hands through her tangle of hair, beads of water resting on her dark, untamed curls. It made her feel better. Not a lot better, but she would take anything in that general direction.

When she went out, Gabbie was putting the omelet at her place and Elaine sat down to eat. Hobo accepted small pieces of toast and bacon from Elaine without begging for more. His expectations were so minimal that it made her want to cry.

"So has that Atlanta fellow been to see you yet?" Gabbie asked.

Elaine glanced over at Ronnie. Had he been talking about it with Gabbie?

He shook his head. "I didn't say anything," he said, "but the guy's been making a lot of noise around town."

"I haven't seen him yet," she said.

"It's a matter of time." Gabbie rang up the older black man's ticket. "Man's on a mission. I heard Greta tried to set his livestock loose." She laughed. Shook her head. "He'd have hauled her haughty backside off to jail if he didn't want to buy the land from her. I told him you'd just lost a husband and didn't need him bothering you. That's probably why he hasn't been over there yet."

"He seems nice enough." A younger woman in blue jeans and a batik shirt spoke up from one of the booths. "He has a great voice. I'll say that much."

"Antacid commercial," the old man at the end of the counter mumbled. "Seen that thing a hundred times if I've seen it once. Know that voice anywhere."

"That's what I told her the other day." Ronnie nodded in Elaine's direction.

Elaine looked around. She recognized most of the faces but had no names in her memory to go with them.

"People are all dazzled 'cause the guy's been on TV," Gabbie said, shaking her head. She scraped crusted grease from the grill with a spatula. "Doesn't make him special in my book."

"What is he?" the old man asked. "Mexican?"

"Venezuelan." Another man in shirtsleeves and a tie spoke up from the corner.

"Not sure what he wants to do with all that land out there anyway," Gabbie said.

"Raise llamas," the man at the counter offered.

"Alpacas," Ronnie corrected him. "They're called alpacas."

"Their wool, or fur, whatever you call it—it's worth a fortune," the younger woman said. "I've got a sweater at home I had to take out a second mortgage to buy. Damn, it's soft, though," she said, turning back to her grilled cheese.

"He wants to expand," Ronnie explained, "but he's got that corner lot. He's hemmed in on two sides by state roads and Greta's land on the other two. Got nowhere to go with it unless he buys her out."

"Plus, I heard she's got that natural spring on her property," the man at the counter piped in again. "It runs between them two houses that the old black lady's kin live in out there. Spring would mean fresh water for the . . . what are they?"

"Alpacas," Ronnie said again.

Good God, everybody knew about this man and his interest in Greta's property. Elaine tried to remember the place out there. She hadn't seen it in daylight in years. What the Atlanta man didn't know was that Greta would give it to him free before she'd leave it to Elaine or Mick.

"I wonder why she hasn't just sold it to him?" Elaine said, wondering out loud more than asking the question.

"My cousin works with one of the young black fellows who lives out there," the man at the counter said. "Guy who married Mattie's oldest granddaughter. They help Greta keep the property up. Probably couldn't manage out there without 'em. Mattie wants the kids to buy it from Greta, make a home place out there, but they aren't that keen on it anymore. Don't want to hurt Mattie though. Logical thing would be for you and the boy to have it eventually." He looked at Elaine.

"She might have left it to Carson," Elaine said, "but she sure as hell won't leave it to me or Mick."

People avoided her eyes. All of them seemed willing to chime in about everything else, but no one wanted to touch that one.

"Well"—Gabbie stopped for the first time, leaned over, and rested her elbows on the counter—"all I know is, that man wants it done yesterday. He may have a smooth voice, but from what I've seen, he don't have a penny's worth of patience."

"Everybody's got a price," the older man chimed in as he put money on the counter for Gabbie and made his way to the door. "High. Low. Everybody's got one."

Elaine wanted to go home. She'd heard enough about Greta and the "Voice of Antacid." Ronnie had finished his burger and ordered a cup of coffee. She left Hobo cowering under her stool at the counter and went to gather up a few groceries. She remembered Morty's request and asked Gabbie for a pack of Salems from behind the counter. She didn't know if he smoked menthol or regular, so she went with regular. The news would make it from the lake to town in no time: Carson's widow had taken up smoking to calm her nerves. She eyed the pack of cigarettes in her hand. Might not be a bad idea.

"How much do I owe you for everything?" she asked Gabbie.

The small total for the meal and groceries combined made her wonder how Merle's daughter managed to make a living. Then again, it took less to live in this place than Chapel Hill.

As she turned to leave, Gabbie said, "See if you and Hobo there can stay out of the lake on the way home."

"We'll do our best." Elaine smiled. She felt like a regular. "Bye, Ronnie," she added.

"I'm on my way out, too," he said.

"And, hon?" Gabbie added.

Elaine stopped and turned around.

"If I can do anything . . ." The offer trailed off. Gabbie wore gentility like someone else's clothes.

"Thanks," Elaine said.

Ronnie opened the door for her and walked out at the same time. He waved good-bye and headed to his car—his civilian vehicle with no pizzazz, but good mileage. A tinny, urgent "Devil Went Down to Georgia" ringtone reminded her of the transistor radio sound track of junior high. She smiled when she realized that it came from Ronnie's phone. Perfect.

Until that afternoon, she'd never considered the notion of staying around for a while, but at some point, it had crept into her thoughts. All she had left in Chapel Hill was a job that no longer seemed important. She'd enjoyed working when it had been part of her life with Carson. She couldn't imagine that it would be enough on its own.

In the decades that she'd been away, Carson and Mick had been her center. But Mick needed to fashion his own adult life, and she needed to refashion hers. The absence of Carson left her emotionally homeless in their adopted town. Was Lowfield home again? She didn't know.

Maybe that was why Carson had wanted to come back at the end—as much for her as for himself.

"Elaine." Ronnie came up behind her as she was nearing the dock.

"What's up?"

"I just got a call from one of the other deputies," he said. "He said a call went out on the radio looking for you."

"For me?" Her thoughts went to Mick and a small panic rose up inside her.

"The deputy pulled your son over thinking you might be in the car," Ronnie said. "I guess something's happened out at Greta Forsyth's place, and they're trying to find you."

"How'd they know to call you?"

"Your son said he thought you'd come to Merle's place here," he said, "and, well, it's no secret that I stop in here all the time." He seemed a bit embarrassed that this was common knowledge. "Anyway, I guess if you call the station, they'll fill you in."

"Has something happened to Greta?" She felt conflicted at the possibility. Greta had been an irritant for Elaine's entire adult life, but it was almost as if she had concern by proxy. Elaine loved Carson. Carson loved Greta.

"I think it's the black lady who lives out there," he said. "But I don't know the details."

"Thanks, Ronnie."

"You need me to drive you to town?"

"No," she said, looking down at her clothes. "I need to get the dog home and clean up before I go anywhere. I'll call and sort things out on the way."

He nodded. "All right," he said. "Let me know if there's anything I can do." She believed he meant that. She wouldn't have recognized him on the street two weeks before, but he'd now taken on a mild accountability for her well-being.

She got Hobo into the boat and then fished her phone out of her bag. She'd missed a few calls. One from Linnie, two from Mick.

She turned the engine and got herself away from the dock. Then she dialed. It seemed that regardless of what they both wanted, she and Greta couldn't be finished with each other.

Mick pulled into the driveway at the lake, grateful to arrive without a DUI. The boat wasn't in the lift, so his mom hadn't gotten home yet.

As he walked into the tree house, Linnie made a face. "Good God, Mick. It's four in the afternoon. What have you been drinking?" She sat at the table, stitching a border onto a toddler-sized dance costume.

"Mr. Jack Daniel's would be the culprit there. The rest of the story involved two girls in bikinis, a rainstorm, and the Pascals' dad's stash of Maker's Mark in the boathouse," he said.

"Ah, the Pascal place. I dipped into that hooch myself back in the day," she said. "I don't know. Wild bunch back when I knew them."

"The tradition continues," he said.

"Damn!" She nicked her finger with the needle and jerked her hand back in pain. "I'll miss the kids, but I won't miss these damn recital costumes. I don't know how I get stuck doing half this stuff. These children all have parents, for God's sake."

"Mom come back?" he asked, sitting in a chair beside her.

"Not yet." She tied off a thread and bit it. "I tried to call her, but she's not picking up."

"Yeah, me too," he said. "Have you listened to the machine?"

"Nope," she said. "I hate those things. I liked it when people couldn't find you every waking second."

"There are messages, I'm sure. A deputy was looking for her and found me instead with Mom's license plate number," he said.

"You're lucky he didn't make you walk a straight line," she said. "What did they want with Elaine?"

"Something's happened out at Greta's. To Mattie, I think. I don't know much more than that."

Linnie put down her sewing. "Oh God, I hope she's okay. She seems like an awfully good soul."

Mick liked Mattie, too, but he knew there was another reason to be concerned. Greta relied on Mattie. Without her, Mick's grandmother had only Mattie's progeny and the remains of her own fractured family.

"Greta could manage, right?" He didn't even like the woman, but the thought of her in some retirement community felt wrong—like caging a bird of prey.

"I don't know," she said. "If she lived in town, maybe, but out there in the country . . ." Linnie's face registered significant doubt.

Technically, he was Greta's only blood relative—regardless of what she believed.

"Do you know the whole story about my mom and Greta?" he asked.

"I thought your mom explained that to you."

"Not really," he said. "There has to be more to it."

"This is not my conversation to have with you, hon," she said. Linnie wasn't going to cough up more than he knew already. "But I will say this. Your folks had an amazing marriage."

"I know," he said. "I had a front-row seat."

After he'd showered and gotten some food into his system, he took off again. Linnie gave him the keys to the truck. She didn't ask where he was going, only if he was sober enough to drive.

"Stone cold sober," he said. It was true. He'd never felt more alert.

Before he left, he'd made a phone call. There were two Jamisons in the phone book. Different addresses. He'd picked one number and dialed.

"Hi," he'd said when a woman answered. "This is Mick Forsyth. I'm trying to find out how to get in touch with a Wallace Jamison. Is he related to you?"

He heard breathing on the other end of the line. Another voice mumbled, and then the woman on the phone mumbled back, "Keep Mama out there."

"Wallace is my brother," she said, returning to her conversation with him. "He doesn't live in town any longer."

"I'm Elaine Forsyth's son," he said. "My mom and your brother used to be close friends and I . . ."

"I know your mother," the woman said. "And . . . I'm sorry for your loss." Her voice softened as she found her manners. "Why do you want to talk to Wallace?"

"I'm trying to sort out some old family stuff," he said. "I thought he might be able to help."

"Your mother could help you," she said. She was stalling, but she didn't sound unkind. He thought he'd probably like her if he ever met her.

"My mother's going through a hard time right now," he said. "I don't want to put her through more. But . . . Wallace was obviously important to her."

Wallace's sister had been reluctant, but in the end, she gave him a phone number. Before hanging up, she added, "It would be best if you didn't call here anymore. My husband and I live with my mother, and I'd just as soon she didn't know I'd put you in touch with Wallace."

"No problem," he said. "And thank you."

The area code turned out to be a number in Rockingham. The land of NASCAR. He wondered if Wallace was a good ol' boy. The bad boy with rough edges compared to Carson's role as the smooth, professorial suitor.

"Hello?" The man's voice on the other end of the line had been deep.

"My name is Michael Forsyth," Mick said. "I'm looking for Wallace Jamison."

"I'm Wallace Jamison," he said, the words emerging as a lyrical rumble of sounds. "You're Elaine's son."

Wallace had agreed to see him. He'd agreed with very little explanation on Mick's part. Then again, the drama of whatever happened had played out in this man's life, too. Down the road, the man might even be a friend to his mom again. That thought got weird, so he let it go.

He felt a little guilty, driving to Rockingham. But he'd feel worse pressing his mom for more. If he was going to help his mother sort out the problem of helping Greta, Mick wanted to know what the fuck he was dealing with. How much baggage was stuffed into his great-grandmother's emotional closet?

As flat stretches of fields gave way to the outskirts of Rockingham, Mick felt the unease of a questionable plan put in motion. What if he found out more than he wanted to know about his mom and the guy?

He pressed on. Knowing couldn't be any worse than wondering.

Elaine steered the boat into the lift. The electric pulley raised her level with the pier. She didn't get out. Getting out meant she had to begin dealing with the mess down at Greta's. She wanted to be a casual observer to the ordeal. Someone who felt bad for Mattie because she was a nice person. Someone who dropped food by to help out until she got better. She didn't want to be the person responsible for Greta in the absence of her longtime companion. But who else was there?

Greta had been awful to her—harsh and insulting. Then she had rejected her own grandchild. But of all the negative exchanges Elaine had endured with her mother-in-law all those years ago, there were only two she would have to struggle— really struggle—to forgive.

The first one was the hatefulness she'd shown to Mick when he was so little. That visit to her house had been a disaster, nothing less.

The other one also had to do with Mick, but earlier, before he was born. Greta had called Carson at Georgetown before Elaine could reach him. She'd told him what Tilda Jamison walked in on, and Carson dropped everything to drive to the lake. By the time he reached Elaine, he'd been in the car for hours—angry, confused and, most of all, hurt.

She said you slept with him."
    Elaine was drying her hair and she hadn't heard his car pull into the driveway below. Her mom had let him in and he had come straight to her room. She turned off the hair dryer but

couldn't think of what to say to him. Then he spoke. *She said you slept with him.*

It was the middle of the week. He had classes to teach and graduate work due. But Greta reached him and told him that Tilda Jamison had found Wallace and Elaine together. Tilda went to wake her son for work and discovered Elaine there in bed with him.

Elaine wished Carson had called, wished she could have explained before he spent hours driving in that state of mind. His words were full of confusion, but, even so, it wasn't phrased as a question. *She said you slept with him.*

"I tried to call you," she said. She had tried and gotten no answer. She thought he must be in class. And then she'd tried later. Again, no answer.

"What's going on?" he asked. "Why would you do something like that?"

Elaine had been in Wallace's room all night. That part was true. Wallace held her all night—first while she cried and then, when she'd exhausted herself, while she slept. He'd planned to wake her and take her home, but at some point, fatigue got the best of him, too.

Wallace had tried to calm her, to reassure her. "Carson will be happy about this baby," he told her.

"He's not even done with grad school," she said. "He can't afford to be distracted with this right now."

"Well, he's got *this* right now," Wallace said, "and my bet is, he'll figure out how to make it work. He's a great guy, Elaine. He loves you."

"I don't want to screw everything up for him," she said. "He's worked his ass off at Georgetown."

"Elaine," Wallace said as he sat up and looked her in the eyes, "he already wants to marry you. He'll want to be a family.

I know the timing sucks, but it will work out. And if for any reason he lost his mind and didn't want to work this out with you . . ." He stopped. Elaine was still reeling from imagining a scenario without Carson when Wallace pulled her close. "If that happened, I'd marry you myself. You won't go through this by yourself. No matter what."

Wallace had been serious. He'd been that kind of friend. He'd been the friend who drove her two towns over to a doctor no one in Lowfield knew. The friend who sat in the waiting room and the friend who took her out afterward to get her prenatal vitamins. Then he'd taken her back to his house and let her cry and talk and cry and talk until they both fell asleep.

The next morning when Wallace's mother walked in, the sight confirmed everything she'd been telling Greta Forsyth. That crazy Tyson girl who said she was Carson's girlfriend was after her Wallace. And it looked as if she'd succeeded.

Elaine should have called Carson then, but she wanted to figure out how to tell him about the baby before she spoke with him. By the time she picked up the phone, he'd spoken to his mother and was halfway to Lowfield.

"I fell asleep, Carson," she said when he walked through her door. "That's all. You know I wouldn't be with anyone but you."

"That's all?" He paced back and forth. "You spent the night with Wallace Jamison and—that's all!"

"Listen. I have to talk to you. Sit down."

She told Carson everything. The missed periods. The trip to the doctor with Wallace.

"He was just looking out for me," she said.

Carson sat on the side of her bed, hunched over with his elbows on his knees. The entire time she talked, his head had been down, resting in his hands. He was upset—she thought about the baby—but when he looked up, she saw anger. Anger?

"You think you're pregnant with *my* baby," he said, "and you tell *him* first? You let *him* drive you to the doctor? You cry on *his* shoulder and stay in *his* room? What the hell, Elaine? I want to have a life with you. I've always wanted that. But this . . ." He shook his head.

"Carson?" She didn't know where to begin. Defending her friendship with Wallace hadn't been part of the speech she rehearsed over and over. "Is this some kind of caveman bullshit?" She felt herself getting angry back at him. "Wallace is my friend, and a damn good one. Either you believe what I'm telling you or you don't trust me."

"I believe you, Elaine," he said, "but you, running to him. It still makes me feel like shit. I believe you didn't do anything with him, but to let him have that place in your life. To hear about a baby before you even tell me there might be one. To let him take you to the doctor . . . For months and months, every time I come home, he's around. He goes and gets a burger with us and the two of you have this language . . . these jokes . . . I've tried not to let it get to me. I know you need friends. But this is too much. The doctor? Jesus."

"I never saw it that way, Carson," she said. "When you came home, I never knew you felt that way. You could have said something before."

"And be the jealous asshole who tells you he can't be with you all the time, but you can't have friends either?" He stood up and paced toward the door. For a second she'd feared he might just leave, but then he turned around. "He's waiting, Elaine. He's waiting to be there if things don't work out for us."

The laughter escaped before she could stop herself.

"You think this is funny?"

She shook her head, no. No, it wasn't funny at all. Wallace had said he would marry her, and he would have. That was Wallace being Wallace. But what Elaine had with Carson? That was something Wallace had never wanted.

* * *

In Wallace Jamison's neighborhood, each house was nearly identical in size and style to the other fifteen or twenty homes that lined the street—a mixture of mostly brick and siding split-levels with a few ranch models thrown in for good measure. The houses looked perfect for modest family types who prayed on Sunday morning, then went to Shoney's for lunch. Elaine had said he'd been a middle-school teacher in Lowfield. Is that what he did in Rockingham? He'd been married, she said. Did he have kids? A new wife?

Mick found the right house number and pulled over to park across the street. Wallace's house had a driveway, but there were two cars parked side by side, and he couldn't pull in without blocking one of them.

Adrenaline took over as he got out of the car, and by the time he rang the doorbell, he could feel his own heartbeat thumping inside his ears. He stood outside the storm door and, as the inner wooden door began to open, an unexplained sense of calm came over him. It reminded him of tipping over the highest climb on a roller coaster.

Through the clear glass, Mick saw a man about his own height, but younger than he'd expected. Late thirties or early forties. The man opened the storm door to let him in, and he took a few steps into the foyer. Several pairs of shoes lined the wall in the entry. Mick wore Top-Siders with no socks. He stepped out of them, feeling a little ridiculous in his bare feet.

"You must be Michael." The man's voice was as smooth and polished as his appearance.

"Wallace Jamison?" Mick didn't want to address him by his first name, but found *Mr. Jamison* too awkward.

"No." The man's tanned features opened into a broad smile. "I'm Jason. Wallace is in the kitchen." He leaned over closer to

Mick. "He's a bit on the nervous side." This last part was confided in a whisper.

They walked together into a beautiful den with polished hardwood floors, modern furniture, and a rug that, to Mick's untrained eye, looked pretty damned expensive. Maybe they'd finally started paying teachers what they were actually worth.

"Have a seat," Jason said. "I'll be back in a minute with Wallace." Jason gave his shoulder a friendly pat and went off toward what Mick guessed was the kitchen.

Mick settled on the chestnut leather couch—deep set and comfortable. Across the room, tall, fresh cut flowers fanned out from a crystal vase on a table near the window. The vase had been situated on top of a round mirror, so that the flowers were reflected from below. Everything in the place looked intentional, but not stuffy. So much for the assumptions about a NASCAR aficionado.

"Hi, Michael." The deep voice from the telephone. Wallace. He came into the room without Jason, and Mick stood up to shake his hand.

"Call me Mick," he said. "Michael was only for when I got in trouble—which was fairly often, come to think of it."

"Well, you're not in any trouble now." The older man smiled. "And I'm always Wallace—regardless of the circumstances."

Like Jason, Wallace was tall, but with a sturdier build. He might have come off as imposing, if it weren't for his basic demeanor, which seemed kind and a little shy.

"I've just made a pitcher of tea," he said. "Would you like some? If you're hungry, I've got some wonderful cheese Jason picked up at the farmer's market last weekend." His offers seemed part hospitality and part nervous ramble.

"I'm fine," Mick said. "Thank you." He sat back down, and Wallace settled to his left in a wing-backed chair. "I probably shouldn't have bothered you, but I'm trying to sort out some things about my grandmother."

"Ah, Cruella." The words came out of Wallace's mouth almost as a reflexive response to the mention of Greta. "I'm sorry," he said. "Sometimes I have trouble editing my thoughts before I say them."

"I'm familiar with that particular affliction myself," Mick said. He felt an immediate affinity for Wallace. When Elaine said the man had been one of her best friends, Mick had thought it was odd, but meeting Wallace, he could see it.

"I know you were a good friend of Mom's," Mick said, "and I know Greta read a lot more into it than that. But I don't see how the whole thing could make Greta hold a grudge for twenty-five years."

"Have you talked to your mother?" Wallace asked.

Mick nodded. "She gave me some of the story, but I knew there must be more."

Jason popped his head around a doorway and waved. "I've got to run off now," he said. "It was great to meet you, Michael."

"Mick," Wallace corrected him. "Michael means he's being scolded."

"Oh, my Lord," Jason said, grinning. "Then, Mick it is. Anyway, I'm out of here. I'll be back in a while," he said to Wallace, then gave a small nod that seemed like an offer of encouragement to soothe the older man's nerves.

A silence followed Jason's departure. It was as if, even from another room, the other man's presence had been a source of courage for Wallace. Mick wondered how to begin.

"The house is beautiful." Lead with a compliment. "How long have you lived here?"

"I moved in about three years ago," he said. "It was a mess when I bought it. Would have stayed that way, I suppose. But Jason took pity on me and made it a real home." He stopped and, for a second, looked like some kind of cornered creature. He'd opened his world up to Mick, and it was clear he was suddenly having second thoughts.

"We'd been seeing each other for a while—when I was still in Lowfield. He moved in after I'd been in the house for a few months." Wallace kept steady eye contact with Mick. "He started out with heirlooms that his grandmother left him. I had a few things I brought from home, but my ex-wife got most of the good stuff." He smiled. "Guilt made the divorce settlement a pretty lopsided deal, I'm afraid. But Jason's things are beautiful. That table with the flowers and the chest in the entryway when you came in. He has a really good eye. From there, we went to estate sales . . . and of course to High Point . . ." He trailed off. It was as if he simply ran out of words.

"So how long have you and Jason been together?" Mick asked. His tone was a little too jaunty.

"I moved to Rockingham because he lived here," he said. "And because I had to stop pretending every day of my life that I was somebody else."

"How long have you known who you are?" Mick asked. He'd had a wife before Jason. Had he fancied himself Elaine's boyfriend, too?

Wallace waited to answer. Maybe there wasn't one answer. "By the time I was twelve," Wallace said. "Before, if you count the feeling that I was different from the other boys around me. But at twelve, I'd started to put a name on it. At that point, I became terrified that everyone else would put a number of different names on it. On me."

"What did you do then?" Mick asked.

"I became a good athlete. Laughed at jokes I didn't find funny. Never told anyone." He stopped there, looked at Mick as if trying to decide what more to say. "Except, eventually, your mother. She knew before I told her. No judgment. No baggage. Knowing that

I could be myself with even one person . . . She gave my secret a home until I could come around—begin to own it myself. I think it saved me, her friendship. I'll always be grateful."

"So you never . . ." Mick stopped. Jesus. How do you ask a guy if he slept with your mom?

"No." Wallace smiled. "We never. She was my closest friend."

"And you got married?" Mick shifted on the couch. Outside a dog began to bark and a car horn sounded in two short bursts—as if alerting someone that their ride was there. It was a normal street, but Mick had never before had a conversation like the one he was having with Wallace Jamison.

"It's hard to explain," Wallace said. "Even to myself sometimes. I was teaching with Carol. I genuinely liked her. I thought I could settle into a life that seemed normal. And it thrilled my mother. It was almost worth it, just to see Mama that happy."

"When Mom told me about your friendship," Mick said, "I thought you must have been in love with her. Willing to hang around in case she and Dad split. I thought maybe she even slipped up and cheated with you—even though she told me she didn't. It never occurred to me . . ."

"I felt bad about your parents' problems with Greta," he said. "I wish I'd had the courage to tell everyone back then. But I was struggling to fit into the only world I knew, and it never seemed to happen. Like I said, I even tried that pathetic attempt at getting married—just to see if I could live that way. It would have been so much easier if I'd . . ." He dropped his head, took in a deep breath. Mick figured he'd tipped over the peak of his own roller-coaster ride. Good or bad, it was all in motion.

"And you were right about one thing," Wallace continued. "I did love your mother. I've still never had a better friend. I should have been stronger for her. She and your dad protected me. And it cost them. Especially your father. He was a really good man."

"I know," Mick said, feeling the words catching in his throat.

His own emotion embarrassed him. Wallace turned away. Mick looked down at his bare feet, then over to his Top-Siders, sitting worn and dirty by the front door. Shoes from his life on boats. Could he ever return to that?

"So," Wallace said, changing his tone. "In answer to your question about the house. All the lovely little touches in the house are Jason's doing." He inclined his head toward Mick and smiled. "Contrary to popular assumptions, I have no flair for decorating."

Mick laughed.

"Does your family know?" Mick asked. He thought of the woman who answered the phone at the Lowfield Jamison home. The awkward conversation and whispered asides.

"My sisters know," he said. "My father died last year, and there's no reason to tell my mother. She wouldn't accept it. It would be too hard to try and make her understand at this point."

"She was Greta's friend." Mick was putting things together. Elaine told him that Greta and Wallace's mother used to be close, but had been at odds for years.

"They were best friends," he said. "But then something happened, even before my friendship with Elaine. Mom felt slighted by Greta somehow. And then my mother thought that I had as much right to Elaine as Carson Forsyth—that he should bow out gracefully. I don't think my mother put it that nicely, but you get the picture." He stopped—shrugged and smiled for emphasis. "And the real kicker was that neither Greta nor my mother could stand Elaine, but it was a point of pride for them that she choose one son over the other. All of it got lumped together. Caused quite the drama at Calvary Baptist."

Mick could only imagine.

"I guess it makes sense that Greta and your mom would think what they did," Mick said. "I mean, if you and Mom spent a lot of time together. Anything else you can tell me that would help me understand?"

Wallace smiled. "I'll stop there. Your lovely mother had the kindness and grace to honor my private matters," he said. "I would do no less for her. I would do just about anything for her, as a matter of fact."

"I bet my mom would like to see you," Mick said, standing. "She could use a friend."

"I'd like that," he said. "I'd love to see her. I don't want to overstep, but maybe I'll call when I'm in town visiting my mother. You have my number, and I'd be delighted if she called me. Are you staying at the lake?"

"Yeah," Mick told him. "That's where my dad wanted to be at the end, and we've been there since the funeral. I'm supposed to head back to Rhode Island soon, but I can't quite think about getting back to my regular life. Nothing seems normal."

"What do you do in Rhode Island?"

"I work in a boatyard. Mostly on sailboats. Rigging, doing repairs, sometimes transporting them for people. It's free sailing at least." He smiled.

"We have a boat at my family's place on the lake," Wallace said. "An old Catalina 27. My brother-in-law is the only one who uses it anymore. You're welcome to take it out sometime."

"Thanks," Mick said, wondering how his mom would feel about him borrowing the Jamison sailboat. He'd give her Wallace's number. It was up to her whether she got in touch or not. "I should get back."

Wallace walked him to the front door.

"Again, I am very sorry about your dad. It's a loss for everyone when the truly good ones leave us so young."

Mick nodded, but didn't know what to say, really. As if sensing a change of subject was in order, Wallace added, "Hey, did you happen to see those UFOs they've been talking about? The blue lights? I heard they were over the lake near your place."

"I missed them," Mick said. "Just as well," he added. "Given my experiences with uniformed individuals, blue lights are usually not a good thing."

Wallace laughed, and he stood at the door until Mick got into his car. By the time Mick pulled away from the curb, Wallace had gone inside.

Well, I wouldn't have predicted that one. Mick made his way toward the highway. Of all the explanations running around his brain, finding Wallace in love with a guy named Jason had not been on his radar. He smiled to himself, thinking that—occasionally—you had to give the world a little credit for originality.

Wallace had been the one to tell Carson he was gay. She'd promised to keep his confidence and she did. But when she told him how Carson reacted in her room, when he saw beyond the anger all the way to the hurt that the other man felt, he'd broken down and told Carson the truth.

"Elaine is the only person in the whole damn town—the whole damn county, I guess—who knows."

"That helps me to understand," Carson said, "but it still doesn't take away the fact that she let you be that person, *the* person she came to when she was scared and upset. Christ! You took her to the doctor." He turned to Elaine. "I'm supposed to be that person for you. We're supposed to be that for each other. We can't be a family any other way."

He'd been right. Elaine had made a mistake, even though she didn't see it that way as it was happening. They all paid for that mistake. Carson with his damaged trust, with the hurt he felt. Elaine and Wallace paid with their friendship. She told Wallace that, as much as it pained her, after everything, she knew that Carson would feel it with every mention of Wallace. Wallace agreed and, overnight, they became people who smiled and spoke on the street or in the grocery store.

Carson had forgiven her, of course. But she'd wounded him. The injury caused residual aches here and there, but it also made them both aware that trust is, by nature, fragile. It requires care. She hadn't considered telling her problems to Wallace to be any kind of betrayal. But it had been. Then there'd been the humiliation. The entire town had an opinion about Elaine and Wallace. Elaine and Carson.

In the setting of all that, Carson had kept Wallace's secret. Wallace told them he'd understand if they had to tell Greta, but Carson refused. "My mother would tell your mother," he said, "no question about it. And your life here, your job, your family, everything would be on the line. I won't do that, Wallace. My mother will have to believe me about Elaine, and she'll have to do it without turning your life upside down."

Even when his relationship with Greta was circling the drain and Elaine and the baby to come were not welcomed in his mother's home, he refused to sell Wallace out. Through all the years, he never had.

Elaine stepped out of the boat and lifted Hobo onto the dock. With a bag of groceries in one hand and a pack of cigarettes in the other, she cut across the property to Morty's place, up the hill from his pier.

When she'd left in the boat just hours before, her world had been a different place. After Ronnie's news that something had happened at Greta's, she'd called home and talked to Linnie.

"I reached Mattie's grandson," her aunt said. "Or maybe the husband of the granddaughter, I don't know exactly who he was. Anyway, he'd stayed behind with the kids and Greta while everyone else went to the hospital with Mattie. They think it was a stroke, but she may have also broken something when she fell."

"How's Greta taking it?" Elaine asked.

"She's sitting in a chair, he said, not talking much. He no-

tices her mumbling sometimes, thinks she's probably praying."
Linnie took a breath and let it out. "Elaine?" she said.

"Yeah?" At her aunt's change in tone, Elaine cut the motor,
let the boat drift.

"Ayla and Rae," she said, "they've got their hands full with
Mattie and their own children. He told me they're going to want
to move closer to town. We need to think about Greta. What
she's going to do." Linnie said *we,* but she was only trying to be
supportive. It fell to Elaine and Mick to sort things out with
Carson's mother. Greta was a smart woman, could decide for
herself what she wanted, but with her limited sight, few options
made sense. Elaine could not imagine Greta in a retirement
home. What the hell were they going to do? Elaine felt her own
head shaking no—an involuntary response to everything that
was certainly headed toward them.

"Elaine?" She heard her aunt again. She'd forgotten that
Linnie waited on the other end of the line.

"Is Mick still there?" Elaine asked.

"He asked to borrow my car," Linnie said. "Just took off
again."

"Don't suppose you know where he went, do you?"

"Didn't say. Maybe to see the girl again?" Linnie ventured a
guess. "The parenting business isn't for the weak, is it?"

"No, ma'am," she said. "And doing it alone is downright ter-
rifying."

After ending the call, Elaine sat for a few moments. In the
distance, a woman made a razor-sharp cut with her slalom ski
behind a boat. Overhead, a crane passed, heading into a quiet
cove. All around her the world continued with direction and
purpose—while she floated. She and her pitiful dog.

The next call she'd made was to the sheriff's office to let them
know she'd gotten the messages and would be in touch with
Greta. She could barely believe she was saying the words. She'd

spent a quarter century avoiding Carson's mother. Little did she know she'd always been a heartbeat away—and poor Mattie's heartbeat at that—from having Greta back in her life.

She wanted to sit in the middle of the lake forever.

Delivering the cigarettes to Morty was one small reprieve before she had to act. Morty owned prime property at the end of the small peninsula. His house looked like something out of Grimm's fairy tales. And not the Disneyfied version, either, but the old scary ones. His two-story house had begun as a single A-frame. Over the years, he'd built on, but kept the same design as the original, building a smaller A-frame section connected at ground level by a short hallway. The result looked like a lopsided M. Given his name, Elaine wondered if that had been his intent—an architectural homage, of sorts.

"I got your Salems," she said when he answered the door, "but only under protest."

"You're a fine woman, Elaine Forsyth," he said. "Want to come in? I got hot water and some tea that's supposed to cure angina and make you handsome."

"You don't have angina, and you're already handsome," she said.

"Works then, eh?"

She laughed. "I should get home," she said. "I've got some family stuff to deal with. Looks like Mattie's had an episode and is in the hospital."

"Oh, no." He looked genuinely concerned. "I like that Mattie. She's a good soul. I hope everything's okay."

"Me, too." She thought of Mattie, casserole in hand, arriving after the funeral. "This leaves Greta in a bad way," Elaine said. "I need to step in, I guess, but I don't know where to begin. Listen, Morty, did you ever have to move your folks into retirement homes?"

"Both of 'em." He shook his head. "Oh, it's a hard one. My

pop, he'd gone a little . . ." He tapped a finger on the side of his head. "My ma, she was sharp as needles. Called me names I don't want to repeat." He stopped, looked past Elaine as if his mother stood there over her shoulder. "Hard business."

"I don't know how Greta will get along without Mattie," she said. "Maybe she's already thought it through."

"Did Mick go out there? I saw him leaving in the truck a while back," Morty said.

"I don't know. He keeps taking off. Hell, maybe he'd rather not be around me right now."

"Why wouldn't he want to be around his wonderful mother?" Morty leaned against the door frame.

"I'm another person as damaged by Carson's absence as he is," she said. "I don't know if that divides the pain or doubles it for him."

"How about for you?"

"Worrying about him is a distraction," she told him. "For a parent, it's different. I was half of a parental whole with Carson. In terms of what Mick has come to expect, I'm only half the package and he needs twice the effort at the moment. I'm losing ground everywhere I turn. I don't know if he's trying to work through things or trying to escape. He won't sit still long enough for me to figure it out."

"Does it matter?" Morty asked.

"You're right," she said. She'd always liked Morty. But in the month she'd been at the cabin—first with Carson, then as a widow—Morty's role in the family had taken on weight. He'd actually become like family. "Thanks, Morty."

"For what, darlin'?"

"For making sense when I can't." She looked around for Hobo, realizing that the dog had already become part of her general landscape.

"You're doing fine, Elaine. Under the circumstances, better

than average, I'd say." He cleared his throat, looked out toward the lake. "My bet is, your mother-in-law will find out some things about herself with all this."

"What do you mean?"

"I've seen her here," he said, "back and forth to visit Carson. Talked to her a little. She's relied on Mattie, that's true, but Greta's a strong woman. You're a strong woman. Just don't work when you two are so hard against each other. Figure out how not to do that, and things might be okay."

"A lot of it is out of my hands, Morty." She felt the slightest irritation at what sounded like a reproach. When had he become such a big Greta fan anyway? Maybe she was too sensitive. She had to figure out what was best for Mick—and what Carson would want from her. More and more, her mother-in-law could not be separated from those two equations.

"I should go in. Start making some calls. I'll see you later, Morty." She handed over the cigarettes she was still holding. "Don't smoke the whole pack at once. I'm not making another run for you."

"Yeah, yeah . . ." He waved away her scolding. "I'll bring some fish over later," he said. "Fry it up for you if you don't feel like cooking it yourself."

"Plan to eat at our place either way," she said.

She caught a glimpse of Hobo over by Linnie's shrubs. He moved on to the flowerbeds under the house. Above him, her home seemed to rest on air and promises.

Before she reached the second landing, she saw Linnie's truck coming down the road. Mick, arriving home. She waited for him and when he came close, she saw through the window of the car that he was smiling. The sight of it cheered her.

Seven

Mattie was damaged but alive. She'd had a stroke when she fell, and a second, smaller one on the way to the hospital that had affected her ability to put words together. Greta's prayers had become as involuntary as the breath going in and out of her. Mattie lived, and that was all that mattered. Except that it wasn't true. Other things mattered. Like *how* Mattie lived. Like *where* Mattie lived. Since the sound of that crash in the kitchen, Greta's thoughts had become raw, painful fears. With Carson, there had been the resigned sadness of losing her only son, but with Mattie, a layer of panic coated her emotions.

Greta sat at the small table by the window in her bedroom. She could hear Ayla in the kitchen, finishing up lunch with the kids—her two and her sister's three children. Since Mattie's episode Ayla and Rae had been taking turns at the hospital with Mattie while the other stayed home with Greta and the kids.

Both of them had lived in the main house themselves when they were small, then moved to the smaller houses on the property after they got married. But without Mattie's presence, the comings and goings of the girls left Greta nervous and unsettled.

Greta and Mattie had been sharing the same space for twenty-five years. In that time, the patterns of their lives had grown to fit each other. The absence of her companion, her friend, made Greta a stranger in her home. Worse yet, she didn't know what Mattie was feeling. No one could tell her the degree of fear, suffering, or comfort Mattie experienced day to day. Because, while Mattie was conscious, she wasn't able to speak—only to nod and shake her head, offer small gestures with her hands when she needed to point.

Greta felt trapped inside unfamiliar circumstances. Mattie was trapped inside her own head.

"Greta?" Ayla had come into the room. "I've got some chicken and dumplings here. You need to try and eat. A half a piece of toast is all you've swallowed all day and it's nearly two o'clock."

"Thank you." Greta took the bowl and Ayla left the room, came back a minute later with a glass of iced tea.

She hated being waited on. With Mattie, there was a give-and-take. Greta would find a bowl of green beans on the table, and she'd sit and begin snapping them. When she was done, the hot water would be boiling and Mattie would put them in the pot. Tasks moved seamlessly start to finish. Mattie did more, but Greta made herself useful and the days didn't feel long. Suddenly, they had become endless.

Ayla stood in the doorway, as if deciding whether to stay or go.

"What's on your mind, child?" Greta had known the girl and her sister since they were babies. The idea that they were both married with children of their own still startled her sometimes.

"Granny Mat isn't going to be able to stay in the hospital

much longer." Ayla came closer to her and rested a hand on the small desk where Greta sat, the steaming bowl of dumplings in front of her, untouched.

"But she's sick," Greta said, putting down her fork and turning toward the young woman. "They can't make her leave if she's not able to get along."

"They say she's stable." Ayla came over and sat on the bed near Greta. "She needs help, but not the kind they can give her in the hospital. The doctor said the next step is rehab—a place where they can work with her and get her walking and talking again."

"Is this a place where she'll stay?" Greta asked. "Is it like a hospital?"

"No," Ayla said. The girl was measuring her words, and Greta grew eager to know what she *wasn't* saying. "She'll just have to go every day for a few hours."

"Ayla, I have known you since you made pies out of mud in my good baking tins. If you have something hard to say, I'd rather you come on out with it. I could never abide tiptoeing through a conversation, and you know it."

"I'm sorry," the girl said. "Granny Mat's got a long road, they say. Rae and I have gone over and over how we're going to make this all work. The facility—this rehab place—is right in town. We're thinking we need to rent a house close by where it'll be easy to go back and forth with Granny and still get the kids to the pool and to their camps. If her treatment goes into fall, the schools are close by and . . ."

"You don't have to explain, Ayla." Greta felt the need to stem the bleeding on poor Ayla's conscience. "I know this is hard on everybody."

"Greta, this place has been my home for so long. It breaks my heart—Rae's, too—to think of leaving. But if we were in town, Robeson and Dane could even pop in during the day if we needed them." She stopped there. All those words came out and then she just quit.

Greta stared at the girl in front of her. Ayla was looking down. The poor girl couldn't even make herself look at Greta. Greta realized that she'd been expecting to hear everything Ayla had told her. She'd been dreading it. It came as a relief to have it over with. Even before Mattie's fall, the girls and their husbands had been hinting at a move. Mattie never wanted to hear it, dismissed it as just talk. But Greta had seen it coming. The situation had accelerated the need for a decision. Obviously, one had been made.

"How did you end up getting stuck delivering the news to me?" Greta made herself smile. She worked hard to keep her voice free of the panic welling up inside her ribs.

"Rae said if I told you, she'd tell the kids when it comes time to put the dog down. Poor thing's failing by the day."

Greta had the sour thought that she'd somehow been put on par with the family pet. The thought hit her, and she felt so angry at her own self-pity that she literally expelled a noise, somewhere between a cough and a grunt. The suddenness of it caused Ayla to jump.

"Well, let's think of what we can do then," Greta said, although she had no ideas, only a crawling dread that nothing good would follow their discussion.

"You've got blood kin, Greta." Ayla's small voice barely got the words out in the open. "I know we're your family, too, and I know there's tension with Elaine and her boy." She said everything quickly, as if it took both nerve and velocity to get it out. "I'd have you with us in town if I thought it would work. You know I would. Rae, too. But I know you don't want to leave this place, and with Granny Mat and the kids taking so much of our time . . ." Her voice broke. Greta heard the girl's quiet sobs and knew that she couldn't press Mattie's people to consider the farm to be their responsibility. When did she get so full of need? In two days' time, it seemed.

"You go check on the children, child," Greta said. "I'll sort out something. You don't have to worry about anything but getting Mattie on her feet again."

"We can make a place for you with us, Greta," Ayla insisted. "I'll talk to Robeson. We can find a bigger house than the one he saw and . . ."

"Ayla." Greta made the name into a command. "I've got kin, you said it yourself. Now go check on your children." She reached into a small drawer in her table and pulled out a handkerchief, one of a half dozen or more that Mattie kept clean and ready in there because Greta didn't like the feel of paper tissue. "Get those eyes good and dry," she said, handing over the dainty cloth. "You don't want those kids wondering what's wrong."

"Yes, ma'am," Ayla said. She took the handkerchief and stood. "You don't show many people what a soft side you've got," she said. She laid a hand on Greta's shoulder. Her fingers felt light as dust.

"No use spreading that rumor around. Won't do me a bit of good in the real world. Could be that you're mistaken, anyway." Greta made herself smile as she spoke.

"No, ma'am," Ayla said as she pulled her hand away and walked toward the door. "There's no mistake."

After she was gone, Greta's mind began to make a list. She was good at keeping lists in her head, had done it all her life. This one was a list of possibilities. Hiring somebody to come into her home. Moving to a place like Spring Gardens. Asking Elaine Forsyth to take her in.

She would not go to Spring Gardens. She might as well be in jail, and she'd certainly rather be in the ground. Some people enjoyed those places, she knew, but she wouldn't be one of them. Maybe if she sold off part of the property to that man with the ridiculous creatures, she could afford to get somebody to stay with her. But that would mean paying somebody a fortune to be underfoot, driving her crazy. She needed time to consider. She had no time.

She looked across the room, and through the shadows and gauze of her pitiful eyes, she made out the shape of the phone on the nightstand by the bed—an old rotary she'd never wanted to replace. She despised that woman. The woman despised her. And still, Carson's wife had driven to the police station to get her.

She didn't know what listing that tree cabin would be under. Probably that Linnie woman, but she couldn't remember her last name. She could have Ayla look it up. Then there was the other number she knew by heart. The one she'd been calling. Carson's cell phone. Those numbers ran through her mind and she felt as if, in the act of dialing them, she'd be calling the great beyond.

If she used that number, would anyone answer? If someone did, what in the world would she say?

"Listen, man . . . I just wanted to say I'm sorry again for all that last weekend." A message from Kooper. Mick had seen the number come up on his cell and let it go to voice mail. "I know it seemed like I tried to . . ." The message ended abruptly. A lost connection.

Mick wasn't in the mood to talk to the guy. He wasn't in the mood to talk to anybody. It had been three days since his afternoon with Joy at the lake. Three days since he visited Wallace. Three days since Greta had somehow become the responsibility of him and his mother.

He sat at a desk in his room in the tree house. Outside, the wind was up and eager bands of whitecaps peaked and rolled. He reached over and raised the window, listened to the nervous tattering of leaves just outside.

His mother had been pissed when she found out about his trip to Rockingham.

"Why the hell would you go there without telling me?" She'd been outside when he drove in from the visit.

"You weren't *telling me* something," he said. She looked hurt and he felt like a shit. "I'm sorry. I didn't want to push you, but I really needed to understand what happened. I know why you cared so much about him. Wallace is great. I know you wanted to protect him, but he's living with a guy now. His sisters know. You can lighten up a little."

"You went behind my back, Mick," she said. Both Elaine and the dog looked like they'd been through the wash cycle. "You could have talked to me."

"I'm talking to you now," he said. "I know you didn't sleep with the guy. I know Greta's full of it."

"I told you that before. You just wouldn't take my word for it."

"I'm not an idiot, Mom," he said. "I could tell there was more to it. There still is." He looked at her and she looked away. "It's okay. I promise I'll let it go now. At least I understand why you seemed so protective of him. You could have told me. I've had gay friends all my life; so have you. I'm not Greta."

"I know," she said. She seemed to be struggling to understand her own feelings. "With Wallace, it never seemed right to talk about his life without his permission. I know I could have told you, but I guess old habits die hard."

He felt bad. She'd obviously had a crappy day. "I'm sorry," he offered again.

"We've got to sort out what's going on with Greta," she said, changing the subject.

"Okay."

She put a hand on his arm. "I'm just exhausted. I'm not mad."

It had been three days since that conversation, and they were no closer to resolving the Greta issue. He pressed a key to hear the next voice mail.

"Lost you, there," Kooper said in a follow-up message. "Anyway, I wasn't trying to set you up," he explained. "I just . . . Kyle, man. The kid's got stuff going on. Stuff I don't understand, and I just thought you might know how to talk to him." Pause. Mick wondered if the message had ended. But then he heard an intake of breath. "He's like Kayla, man. You got what was going on with her more than any of us. That art shit she liked and everything. He's like that . . . Anyway, I just wanted to apologize. That's all."

Then the message was over for real. After that, there was one from his boss in Rhode Island. He stopped before that one played. If he'd gotten his ass fired for staying away so long, he'd just as soon not know it yet.

He should have already been back in Chapel Hill with his mom, sorting out her life, planning to return to his own up north. He'd felt better after his visit with Wallace. Even before that, with Kyle and Joy. He'd felt as if he'd made progress. Then the thing with Greta had taken on a life of its own. In the days that followed, his mom had talked to both of Mattie's granddaughters. They'd found a place in town and planned to move within a week or so. That would leave Greta alone on her property, and they all knew that wouldn't work for long.

Mick looked out the window again. Middle of the week, and he could see a half-dozen boats sitting in the water, pitching and rocking with each gust. In the topsy-turvy fishing boats, people without worries were taking the morning to cast a line. Beyond them a sailboat made use of the freshening breeze. Lucky bastards, all of them.

He hadn't seen Joy since he'd left her at the Pascal place. He'd stayed close to the cabin for his mother—at least that's what he told himself, but even he didn't know exactly why he was avoiding a girl he wanted to see. And so far, he and Elaine had only sat around and stared at each other—powerless to come up with any solution for his grandmother.

Who died and put me in charge? The irony of the thought brought him up short. He laughed—a nervous gurgle of sound. It was a joke his dad would have made.

"Something funny?" Linnie was at his door.

"Nothing worth repeating. What's up?"

She came in and sat down on the end of the bed. "I'm going to cancel on the company," she said. "I can't leave you and your mom right now."

"Great. Mom needs to be pissed off at you in addition to everything else. I can't wait."

"I don't care, I . . ."

"Yes, you do. You care too much," he said, interrupting her. "You have a life, Linnie. I'm going to stay here and figure this out with her. Greta's got to come around to the idea of a . . . what's the current euphemism? An adult community. But that isn't any more or less likely to happen with you hanging around."

"Mick," she said, "listen, I can't just leave."

"Okay, and then she'll start worrying about you, too." He looked at his great-aunt. He envied her. She *had* to go. It would be worse for his mom if she didn't. That was the truth. "You don't have a choice any more than we do, Lin. It'll make her sick if you give up this opportunity."

"If I go," she said, "I'll have to leave by the end of the week."

"We'll have a big send-off for you. You, me, and Mom. Maybe Greta, the sightless wonder, will join us. We already have the most pathetic-looking dog on the planet. It'll be a blast."

"Invite your underage girlfriend to round out the cast, and I might take you up on it."

"She's eighteen," he said, smiling. "And don't tell me you haven't dated younger men. I've heard shit. Want to share your stories, Auntie Lin?"

"Yeah, keep dreaming," she said. "It would take booze and a full moon to get that out of me." She got up to leave. "I don't feel good about this," she said, back to fretting over her planned departure.

"Feeling good isn't on the menu for any of us at the moment," he said. "But you're headed in the right direction if you go. Seriously." He looked past Linnie into the hall. Something was missing. Elaine. She'd have barged in on the discussion if she'd been around. "Where's Mom?"

"She rode to the shelter with the dog," Linnie told him. "Shelly told her to come by. The vet was visiting this morning, and Hobo's got some kind of rash on his belly."

"That dog gets less appealing by the day."

"She's always loved strays," Linnie said. "Was always bent on saving them."

Mick *felt* like one of her strays. But he had to behave like a partner with her on this Greta thing. It was time to grow up. When he was younger, he'd wanted his parents to turn to him. Ask his opinion. Just once, he'd wanted to feel valued in that arena. That regard had been handed to him and he had no idea what to do. Maybe he'd begin with his own life.

"Do you need the truck right now?" He followed Linnie into the main section of the tree house.

"Nope. All yours." Linnie wore leggings and a cotton tunic that hit her midthigh. She walked over and lifted her foot so that it rested lightly on a barre she'd set up along the side wall of the den.

He watched her bend as if taking a bow, arm extended. Most of the girls Mick knew were decades younger than his aunt and couldn't move like that if you paid them.

"You need anything while I'm out?" he asked.

"Don't think so." Leg still on the barre, she lifted her torso and bent backward, the graceful branch of her spine forming an arc. Behind her, the sliding glass doors framed a collage of limbs, leaves, and lake.

Sometimes at night with the lights on, Mick felt conspicuous in the tree house. But during the day, his mother's home became chameleon-like, their lives invisible in plain sight. He'd taken Kayla up once, when his grandparents were out in the boat. She said that if she lived there, she'd look out and draw one section of bark every day until she had dozens of them. And when she was done, she'd make the grouped sketches into a single installation.

"The texture of each piece of bark tells a different story," she told him.

Kayla had taught him to stop and look at things like that, scenes broken into pieces until each section looked like something different than the whole. He wished she could see through his eyes at that moment, and then, maybe because he wanted it to be true, he felt weirdly as if she *could*. As if his eyes offered it all to her. The line of Linnie's arm. The leaf that rested on the porch rail.

The wind had gone still on the lake, and the white sail he'd seen before went from full to slack in an instant.

Linnie had stopped. She stared at him. "You thinking about your dad?" she asked.

He shook his head. "Somebody else."

She walked over and pulled him into the lightest of hugs. He put his head against her hair and gave in to the comfort of someone who'd known him forever.

"In college," he said, still leaning into her embrace, "I took a course that looked at the ties between physics and spiritual traditions."

Linnie pulled back, her gaze intent. "What did you get from that?"

"Nothing that I've thought about until recently. The professor talked a lot about consciousness existing outside of time and space—of that being the real *us*. Everything we experience here is known to our larger consciousness, he believed, but inside our bodies here, we're cut off from knowing the full scope of that existence."

"Did he say why?" Linnie didn't act as if he'd gone nuts. It made him feel safe, and bold.

"He had theories. Mainly, he believed that the whole point of *here* is to give our larger selves unique perspectives, experiences. Knowing everything would take away our specific context."

"What do you think?" she asked.

"I thought it was interesting bullshit at the time," he said. "Now, because it matters to me, I've had it on my mind. Dad has to be somewhere, right? Kayla? Everything they thought and felt? It has to still *be*—don't you think?"

"I wish I knew, hon," Linnie said. "I can tell you that with all the traveling I've done in my company days, I've gotten to see a lot of spiritual traditions in different countries. The Eastern countries, the mystics, all had theories similar to your professor's ideas. Not from the point of view of physics, of course. But essentially the same thing. If I had to believe something, I guess that would be it. It seems to make sense." Linnie paused. "Did you love that girl, Kayla?" she asked.

"Yeah." Mick had never admitted it to anyone but Kayla herself.

"Wish I had the answers," she said. "I wish I knew where they all are. But at least I can tell you the questions aren't crazy."

"I'm really going to miss you, Lin," he said.

"Back at you." She picked up the keys to her truck off the table and handed them to him. "Now, go. If I don't finish this barre work, I'm going to be a creaking mess. Get out of here."

"Call me if Mom needs me," he said.

"Will do."

Outside the air had actual weight. It pressed full against his skin. Heat was supposed to rise, but as he descended the stairs, the ground seemed to radiate warmth.

He got into the truck and turned on the air. He'd left with a vague sense of purpose, but once the steering wheel was in his hand, he had no idea where he wanted to go.

Aside from all the issues with Greta, something else nagged at his brain. He'd been avoiding Joy. And as much as he wanted to blame it on his grandmother, he knew that wasn't it. Teresa Pascal. The stuff she'd said. Even more, all the things she hadn't said. That was still playing in the back of his thoughts. Joy's friend all but told him he was bad news. Pascals had considerable faults, but their opinions were honest and often not wrong.

He knew where he was going. If Teresa Pascal didn't want him to get in deeper with Joy, she had to cough up more than she'd given him at the lake. Not hints, but solid reasons. She'd be at the hospital working. She'd said she volunteered weekday mornings. He put the truck in gear.

The blacktop of the hospital parking lot gave off an oily, toxic smell. In the years when he'd come to Lowfield every summer, the hospital had still been privately owned and staffed by local docs. But the local doctors had long since fled to retirement with no reinforcements in sight. So for several years, the facility had been a satellite operation for a medical center in Greensboro.

Carson, who had been in a couple of times during his final weeks, said it was a shame that small-town doctors no longer had a solid stake in the community.

"Used to be you knew the guy prodding under your clothes,"

he'd said over dinner after his appointment. "Not anymore."

"At least they kept the hospital open," Elaine said. "I thought it would have closed."

"There's my glass-half-full girl." Carson had grinned at Elaine. Mick remembered feeling invisible in that moment. It was easy to feel invisible around the two of them.

The temperature dropped better than twenty degrees as Mick walked through the hospital's revolving doors.

"Can I help you?" The girl behind the desk seemed too cheerful for the illness that lay beyond her post. She could have been serving ice cream somewhere.

"I'm looking for Teresa Pascal," he said. "She's volunteering today, I think."

"Yeah," she said. "Terri's up on four. You want to go up, or you want me to page her?"

"I'll just go up," he said. "Thanks."

She nodded and sent him off with a wave.

While half the world was screening for weapons, it felt nice to walk into a place without an interrogation. He wondered how long that would last. Probably until some nutjob took a shot at somebody in the emergency room. He had to stop veering to dark places in his head.

When he came off the elevator, he nearly ran into a woman who looked vaguely familiar. She had brown skin and kind eyes, and she smiled as she regarded him with familiarity. His first thought was that she might be one of Kayla's relatives.

"Are you here to see Granny Mat?" she asked.

"Uh, yeah. I was in town and thought I'd stop by," he lied. "How is she?" The woman had to be one of Mattie's daughters—no, granddaughters. He wasn't sure how she recognized him.

"She's still not talking," she said, "but she can move things on her right side pretty well, and she gave me a smile this morning. Looked almost like herself for the first time since it happened.

Come on in and say hi. I'm Rae, by the way," she added. "I saw you play baseball a few times—back in the day. Granny Mat said you came out to the house a few days ago."

"Yeah, I did," he said. "In retrospect, it might have not been my brightest idea." He followed, feeling entirely like the impostor he was.

"Greta gets set in her ways," Rae told him, as if his grandmother's rejection amounted to a distaste for peas.

"Granny," the younger woman said gently as they entered Mattie's room, "you got a visitor here. Mick Forsyth is here to see you."

Mattie opened her eyes. Her lips stretched slightly, and she looked as if something unpleasant had occurred to her.

"See," the young woman said. "She's smiling at you, too."

Mick wasn't at all sure that was the older woman's intention— she'd been pretty stingy with smiles even before the stroke—but he smiled back and nodded as if he agreed.

"My mom sends her best," he said. In for a penny, in for a pound. "We're glad you're getting better."

Mattie's right hand began to move in a kind of fluttering motion, her right knee, too. She was clearly agitated at something.

"What is it, Granny Mat?" Rae asked. She leaned in close, as if proximity to the injured woman would offer some answer.

With great effort, Mattie lifted her hand. She pointed to her eyes, closed them, and pointed to her closed eyelids. Unseeing eyes. She could only be thinking of one person. Then she opened them again and shifted her index finger toward Mick. The pleading expression told him the rest of the story.

"She's worried about Greta," he said, then realized he shouldn't be talking about her as if she couldn't hear. "You're worried about my grandmother."

Mattie relaxed, offered the smallest of nods.

"We'll take care of things, Mattie," he said. "You can't worry about her right now. We'll work something out."

Even in her compromised state, Mattie looked imposing, and altogether unconvinced.

"I should go," he said. "But don't worry about Greta. Really. Everything will be fine."

One lie begets another—and another.

Rae walked out with him into the hall. "I don't know if you heard," she said, "but we're getting a place in town. We haven't said anything to Granny Mat yet. She's going to be upset, but it's the only thing we can do to make this work."

"No one blames you for doing what you have to do," he said. Did Greta blame them? Did she feel abandoned? Without Mattie and her family—and his own dad just buried—the woman truly had no one. He felt an unexpected wash of sympathy for his grandmother. "It's up to us to sort something out for her," he said. "We'll figure it out."

Rae looked grateful.

"We're still close by," she said, "you know, if you need anything or . . ."

"We're making this up as we go along," he said, tired of not saying it. "You got blindsided by this. But shit happens all the time." She winced, and he made a note to check his language. "I'm just saying that nobody blames you for taking care of your family."

"Greta's a hard one. Stubborn as the day is long." She shook her head, but the words were delivered with affection. "She was wrong to push you out of her life. Granny Mat told her as much all the time. But she's got a lot to her that you don't see unless you look for it."

"Well," he said, trying and failing to sound light, "the trick is to get close enough to see it without losing an arm."

Rae smiled. "She's strong. That's a good thing. I should get back to Granny Mat."

He nodded, watched her as she slipped in and closed the door behind her.

What would Carson tell him to do? His dad would do the right thing, whatever the hell that was. Mick walked away from Mattie's room with no answers.

Teresa stood behind the fourth-floor nurses' desk. She wore khakis, tennis shoes, and a pale pink polo shirt, looking like the valet at a surf-and-turf place.

"Wow," he said as he approached the desk. "You have an L.L.Bean photo shoot after work?"

"They make the volunteers wear this shit," she said, keeping her voice low. "I'm going to burn these pants when the summer's over. They ride up into my ass every time I sit down."

"An image I'll cherish."

"Asshole," she said, putting a manila folder into a drawer. "What are you doing here?"

"You got time for a break?"

She raised one eyebrow.

What the hell? He'd never done anything to any of the Pascals. "I just want to talk for ten minutes. Can you sit down with me for a sec?"

"Sure," she said. She looked over her shoulder. Two nurses rested their elbows on the desk, talking about a movie they'd seen over the weekend. Other than that, an anemic-looking orderly was the only other person in sight. Nothing appeared to be urgent.

Teresa steered him toward an empty room where the bed, linens crisp as a Saltine, waited for some poor soul. Everything smelled like cheap mouthwash. Teresa sat in an imitation leather recliner by the bed. She popped up the foot section and leaned back. Mick pulled a straight-backed metal chair over next to her.

"Don't ask me what Joy's said about you," she told him. "We're not in middle school. Call her, for crissake. She said she hasn't even gotten a text from you since the lake. I told you to be careful with her, but I didn't mean for you to be a total dick."

"We had a family crisis," he said.

"You mean one worse than your dad dying?" She leaned forward close enough so that he could see the creased smudges in her blue eye shadow. But then she pulled back, as if catching herself. "I'm sorry. That was a crappy thing to say."

"Don't worry about it." He leaned over, resting his elbows on his knees. "You're right. I should have called her."

"Okay," she said. "Are we done?"

"No."

Teresa's eyes narrowed.

What *did* he really want to say? He'd driven to the hospital to get some answers, but he suddenly couldn't think of the questions. Her remarks at the lake had been cryptic, at best. Something about people still talking. Gossip about him and Kayla.

"You said some stuff at the lake. You said it wasn't fair to drag Joy into something when people still talked about me. About me and Kayla. Kayla's been gone for years. What would anybody have to say about us now?"

"Mick," she said. She let out a breath. Stalling. Debating. Jesus, what the hell could she be worried about? "Why don't you just go back to Maine or wherever it is you've been and forget it. You'll be better off and Joy will, too."

"Dammit, Teresa. You're a Pascal, for God's sake. Just spit it out. That's what you guys do."

"You guys? Fuck you." She sat up.

"I'm sorry. I just meant that you, Laurie, your brothers—all of you say what you mean." He dove into recovery mode. "It's not a bad thing. Don't act all pissed off. Just tell me what you were talking about."

She settled back again, looked at the clock on the wall and then at the door.

"Please," he said.

She looked at the window, seemed to be considering his request. After a moment, she sat up and put her feet on the floor, leaned in closer to him. "You hung out with Kayla's little brother before you came to the lake."

He nodded.

"Why?" It was a quiz more than a question.

"Kooper—the older one—he asked me to help his little brother learn how to hit a ball."

"Why?"

"What do you mean—why?" He was getting irritated.

"Why you? Why did Kooper ask you to help the kid?"

"Because I know how to play baseball." He didn't mention that Kooper had guilted him into it. That was none of her damn business.

"Mick," she said, looking more agitated than he'd ever imagined a Pascal could be, "when that kid, Kayla's little brother, showed up, people had a lot of questions. I was in sixth grade and I remember hearing about it. Laurie knew, too."

"Knew what? What do you mean, he *showed up*? When he was born?"

"He wasn't born here," she said. "Kayla left school at Christmas and she didn't graduate in the spring. She and her mom went away. When they came back, she had a *little brother*." Teresa looked at him. "Mick? People said it was Kayla's kid."

Mick felt a flutter of panic. Hot chills around his neck and nausea rising in his gut.

"What the hell are you trying to do? Are you saying I've got a kid? That Kayla had *my* kid?"

"I'm not trying to do anything, Mick." She sounded almost timid. "I'm just telling you what I heard . . ."

"Fuck what you heard!"

Teresa looked toward the door, then got up to close it. "Listen," she said. "You're right. I was eleven years old, and I was listening to my sister and her stupid friends. It was gossip."

"Then why are you repeating it?" He felt as if he was climbing but continued to lose ground. He couldn't make headway.

"Mick, I haven't repeated it to anyone but you. Just now." She returned to the old Teresa—the one who could bust any guy's balls with one look. "If you notice, I haven't even repeated it to my best friend. I mean, she hasn't been under a rock, so maybe she's heard some of it, too, but I get the feeling she doesn't know. And she likes you a lot. I'm not going to dump on that. But Mick, Joy and I have been like sisters for as long as I can remember. That's all this is about for me."

The panic had left him, and he felt strangely empty. One last try. One last question, then he'd give up. "Was Kayla seeing anybody?" he asked. "You know, after me?"

Teresa shook her head.

"Nobody else?"

"Laurie said she barely talked to anybody at school after you guys broke up."

"Well, Kayla wouldn't have talked to Laurie. They weren't friends." He grabbed at thin air and he knew it. "Laurie wouldn't know who she talked to."

"Laurie knew everything about everybody. You know that. Laurie said Kayla hung around, kept to herself, sitting and drawing on some sketchpad. Then she disappeared. When she got back—boom . . . a baby brother."

The antiseptic smell in the room overwhelmed him. He stood and tried to fill his lungs. When he couldn't take in a full breath, when the pressure felt like iron in his gut, he went into the bath-room, half coughed, half retched over the toilet.

"Mick . . ." Teresa came in after him.

"Go away," he said. "I really want you to go."

She stood a moment more, put a hand on his arm, but he pulled away. The touch felt dangerous. Everything around him suddenly put his world at peril.

She left. He went to the sink and splashed water on his face. There was no towel, so he dried it on his own T-shirt. He thought of Kooper's insistence that he hang out with Kyle. In an entirely new context, he saw the frantic look on the face of Kayla's mother when she saw him with the boy.

"What the fuck am I going to do?" His voice sounded pa-thetic in the sterile, empty room.

He made his way to the elevator. Teresa called his name, but he pretended not to hear.

Shelly took the towel she'd given Elaine and handed over an an-tiseptic wipe and a large bandage. Hobo had slunk to the corner of the room and was doing his best not to be seen.

"I'm sorry," Shelly said. "I should have realized the vet would freak him out. The poor thing's only association with the guy is pain. He doesn't know the difference between the pain he's having when someone's trying to hurt him and the other kind—when someone's just trying to help."

"It's okay," Elaine said. The alcohol wipe hurt like a son of a bitch. "It's not that deep. He panicked and snapped, but he didn't bite down. I'm fine." She put the bandage on the place where Hobo's tooth had sliced into the heel of her hand, just below her thumb.

"Here's the ointment for the rash on his belly," Shelly said, handing her a tube. "Doc says it's on the house." She went into the other room to check on the vet's progress with the rest of his charges.

Elaine walked over to the dog. He wouldn't look at her. Ears down, tail down, hunched shoulders. If every creature in the world felt remorse so thoroughly, there would be no wars.

"Come here, little buddy." She scratched his neck. "Come on." The animal relented and crawled into her lap. "It's okay."

"You made up." Shelly came back in and sat on a stool.

"Yeah," Elaine said. "Friends again."

A long howl from the adjoining room sliced through their conversation. She felt Hobo's back tense.

"So you didn't finish telling me about Greta," Shelly said. "What are you going to do with her?"

"She's a person, Shell. Not a used couch."

"Sorry." Shelly exhibited none of Hobo's aptitude for guilt. "I'm just saying that after the way she treated you and Mick, you don't owe that woman a damn thing." She spun around on the rotating stool. The childlike activity suited her. "She's got a house she can sell and get herself fixed up in Spring Gardens or someplace like that. End of story."

"I know how Carson would feel about that. I need to think about it. I've got to make her talk to me, but I've been avoiding that particular trip to hell."

"Honey," Shelly said, getting off the stool and coming to sit beside Elaine on the floor, "Carson's not here. You've got to make decisions that are right for you, not Carson."

"I can't separate those two things." Elaine looked at her old friend. Shelly was divorced. She always said she cared more for her animals than her exes. She had no point of reference. "Carson and I . . . if you tried to find the dividing line between the two of us, you couldn't come up with a clean break. If he's not here to help her, it's my job to take that on for him."

"Does Greta even want you involved?"

"I don't know," Elaine said. "She called Carson's cell phone yesterday. I saw her name come up on the screen, but she hung up before I even said hello. Even dialing the numbers had to be a big step for her."

Shelly nodded, but Elaine knew she still didn't understand. Time to change the subject.

"Hey," Elaine forced a change in her tone, "the good news is I'll be around a little longer. I've called them at work and told them I'm taking a longer leave. If I'm here, that means we can go to dinner and really catch up."

"Anytime." Shelly dug her fingers into Hobo's fur. "My calendar never gets too full."

Twenty minutes later, Elaine pulled out of the shelter's driveway. Instead of turning to go back to the lake, she went the other way. Ayla had called her the day before and said that she and Rae had gotten everything set up with the rental in town. They planned to move and get Mattie settled within a few days. Everyone spoke as if things were up to her—everyone except Mick, who seemed to think it was his job to solve the Greta problem. But Greta wasn't a child. She was a grown woman who could take some responsibility for what happened to her. Elaine needed to be an adult and talk to her mother-in-law. She'd just drive to Greta's and get it over with.

She turned out of town and onto the two-lane highway that led to Carson's old homeplace. Instead of getting worked up about how the interaction would go, Elaine pushed her thoughts in another direction. Wallace.

Mick had been out of line going to see him, but it cheered her to think of her old friend talking to her son. She thought about calling Wallace. She could use a friend. Even after so many years, Wallace would understand her. Did she still owe it to Carson to keep her distance from him? It seemed ridiculous, but it was something she couldn't help but consider.

In all the years since she and Carson left Lowfield, Carson had been enough. She'd had casual friends, work friends, neighborhood buddies. Situational attachments. She'd missed Wallace. She realized part of her had always missed Wallace. There was no reason not to call him sometime. Carson wouldn't blame her. Her actions, not Wallace's, had been painful to Carson. Wallace was simply collateral damage in her betrayal of Carson's trust.

In the backseat, Hobo put his paws up to the window as if he recognized their destination. He let out a bark or two, then sat at attention—waiting.

"What's up with you?" she asked absently.

As they turned into the bumpy drive that would lead to Greta's, she passed a fenced-in field. On the other side stood a half-dozen alpacas. She slowed to stare at them. They looked like oversized stuffed animals—puppet-faced, with puffy heads and woolly fur all over, even down their legs. She knew Greta found them menacing, but Elaine thought they fell somewhere between cuddly and mildly unsettling, like when toys came to life in a kids' television show.

She pulled over and turned off the engine, then let Hobo out of the backseat. The dog ran to the edge of the fence and sniffed at one of the animals that stood about two feet away. Elaine thought that it disregarded the dog entirely until she looked more carefully and saw that while its head remained motionless, its eyes followed Hobo with a fair amount of interest.

"Not as dumb as you look, huh?"

"Excuse me?" A man approached from the side of the pasture.

"Sorry," she said, "I was talking to myself."

"They're somethin', aren't they?" He grinned at a brown-and-white creature grazing beside him.

"They are something," she told him. The man didn't seem polished enough, or Latin enough for that matter, to be the actor she kept hearing about. "I'm Elaine Forsyth, Mrs. Forsyth's daughter-in-law. Do you own the property here?"

"No, ma'am," he said. "Joe Timmer." He walked toward her, stuck his hand over the high fence to shake hers. "Mr. Morales hired me to help him look after the place. My wife and I live down the road a ways. He's off in Atlanta this week."

"Well," she said. "Nice to meet you. Are you from around here originally?"

"No, ma'am." He put his hands in his pockets. He looked like a young boy at a dance, suddenly shy about making conversation. "Moved here from South Carolina to take this job. I worked for a guy who bred horses down there. These here," he said, finding his conversational momentum, "they're easier than horses. Then again, they don't get the same treatment. Throw a saddle on one of these guys and I guess I'd find out just how easy they are, right?"

"So you like working with these . . ."—she started to say *things,* but decided that might be insulting—"animals?"

"Best job I ever had," he said. "They act like big dogs. Except when they get to squalling. Sounds like a damn pterodactyl attacking a donkey. Make your hair stand up."

She hoped to never hear it.

"Listen," he said. "I hear tell that black lady got sick. Is that right?"

She nodded. "Mattie had a stroke a few days ago."

"I am sorry about that. She seems like a real nice person." He looked off toward Greta's house, bit absently at his bottom lip. "I know it's a bad time over there. Things need to settle down some. But I'm sure you've heard that Mr. Morales wants to expand. I don't know what Mrs. Forsyth's situation is exactly, but he's suggested a real fair price. Might be a good time to think about it. She won't get a better offer."

"This is her home, Mr. Timmer," she said. "It's a hard decision for her to make."

"I understand. And I'm not all about money or anything. If I was, I'd be doing something else with my life. But in my experience, having the money situation eased a little makes living with a decision a lot easier."

"I'll pass that along."

He offered a nod, acknowledging the exchange. Hobo had slipped under the fence, walking among the alpacas as if he belonged. It struck her that it was the first time she'd seen the dog so confident, easy inside his own damaged little body. "Sorry," she said. One alpaca bent its head to softly nudge the dog. The gentle gesture warmed Elaine to the creature. It had a kindness about it. "Come on, Hobo."

The dog started toward her, but stopped and looked back. He seemed conflicted, but in the end did as he was told. "You like it with the critters?" she asked when they were in the car.

A grunting sigh came back in reply.

Greta heard a car turning in. Ayla was back over at her place with the kids, and Greta felt exposed, alone in the big house. Something was going on down at the road. After a moment, the car came closer and pulled in the drive just in front of the porch.

She walked away from the window, sat on the couch, and waited. Footsteps landed on the porch steps, along with the scratchy sound of a dog's paws on the wood. It wasn't the dogs that lived on her property. They stayed outside, never came on the front porch.

"Greta?" a woman's voice came through the door, along with the sound of knocking. Elaine.

"Come on in." She might have known the woman would just show up without calling first. It didn't matter. The conversation was coming sooner or later. Might as well be sooner. "Close the door behind you so it'll stay cool in here." She could hear the low panting sound of the animal that was with Elaine. "You have a dog with you?"

"Hobo," Elaine said. "Do you mind if he's in the house?"

"Suit yourself." Greta had thought about getting a house dog at one point a decade or so ago. She thought it might be nice to have a small pet, something other than the big dogs Mattie's people kept. But as her sight declined, she didn't want one more thing to worry about. She remained on the couch and jumped slightly when the dog's moist nose touched her ankle. Without thinking, she reached down and scratched the animal's head. Her fingers touched a slick, furless place behind one ear. She bent low and saw a bald spot behind his ear. "What happened to him?"

"Kids set him on fire," Elaine said. Carson's widow settled into a chair opposite the couch. "It's healed, but he's got scars on his head, and his fur won't grow there."

"Kids at your place?" Greta thought of the boy Michael— bringing friends over so that they could harm the dog for sport. Almost made her sick to imagine it.

"God, no!" Elaine sounded genuinely insulted. "I just adopted him. What is it that you really think of us, Greta?"

"I don't know," Greta said, feeling too tired to hold up her end of the long-standing battle. "You said kids, and it follows that it might be your boy."

"My child is Carson's child," she said, "whether you believe it or not. And we didn't raise him to hurt animals."

"My mistake." Greta kept her voice even, void of any inflection that might let the other woman know how frightened she had become inside her own life.

"You've made a lot of mistakes, Greta. A lot of wrong assumptions and . . ." Elaine trailed off. Greta could see her rigid form on the chair. She could hear the deep breathing of a woman trying to calm herself. "Do you mind if I put some water in a bowl for the dog?" Elaine was standing again, waiting for an answer.

"Use one of the plastic bowls in the cabinet to the far right," Greta told her. She looked around for the mutt and realized he'd settled himself at her feet.

Elaine walked by and Greta saw that her hand was taped up with gauze. "What happened to you?"

"Hobo didn't like the vet and took it out on my hand."

Greta reached down and touched the dog's ears. Elaine left the room, and Greta let her shoulders relax. The dog raised his head to watch Elaine leave, but he stayed by Greta's side as if keeping a post—a sad excuse as a sentry, for sure, but the intention seemed touching.

Greta heard the refrigerator door open. The woman's snooping brought her simmering irritation back to a slow boil. This feeling was followed immediately by a wash of embarrassment. The small selection of food in the kitchen reflected a missed trip of grocery shopping. Mattie usually drove Greta out each Monday and they selected meals for the week. Anything to be found in the fridge was likely beginning to look old and maybe even smell.

Since Mattie's stroke, Ayla and Rae had brought food over every day, but with a sudden yawning hunger, Greta realized they hadn't brought anything for lunch. She'd found a few dry crackers and eaten them with jam in the early morning, but that wasn't going to hold her much longer. She didn't blame Mattie's girls, of course. They had their hands full—a sick grandmother and five kids between them.

Elaine put a water bowl down for the dog. "Have you had anything to eat today?" she asked, too casually, over her shoulder.

"My appetite hasn't been much," Greta lied.

Elaine sat down on the other end of the couch from Greta.

"We need to stop arguing with each other. At least a temporary cease-fire. I know you don't like what this has come to. You hate that Mick and I are the only people left to help you."

"The church folks said they'd set up a schedule of bringing meals . . ."

"You need more than meals, Greta. Maybe if you were closer in town that would work, but out here you're too isolated. Keeping the house up, doctor's appointments, sorting laundry . . . I know you're strong, and God knows there's nothing wrong with that stubborn brain of yours, but even if your eyes were perfect, this would be tough."

"So what is it that you think I should do?" Greta realized it was less a question than a challenge.

"That's what I'm here to sort out with you," Elaine said, her tone even and not taking the bait. "I don't know. Honestly, I don't."

They fell quiet. The refrigerator cycled and hummed. Crows made a ruckus outside and then stopped. Greta wished she'd had the television on or maybe the radio—anything to break the sound of the two of them breathing. She put her elbow on the armrest of the couch and her stomach growled, bringing a humiliating flush of heat to her face. She adjusted herself to a more comfortable position. As she did this, her foot pushed lightly against the dog, who'd gotten up to drink and then settled again. She put her hand down and touched his back. Thick fur gave way to the skeletal outlines of spine and ribs held thinly in place by the dog's skin.

"You feed this animal?" Again, she'd offered more of an insult than a question. She didn't know how to talk to the woman without doing that.

"I've only had him a little while," Elaine said, not taking the bait. "He wasn't accepting much food at the animal shelter, but he's doing better at the house. Believe it or not, he's put on weight since I got him."

Greta nodded. She had to remind herself that the woman had made the effort to drive out and felt no more affection for Greta than the other way around. Again, the flutter of panic beat its wings inside her chest. She'd become a creature as vulnerable as the animal at her feet, but acknowledging this to Carson's widow . . . she wouldn't do that.

"If you want to stay here," Elaine said, "there are people you could hire to help out. Somebody who could do what Mattie did around here and . . ."

"Mattie is not some kind of nursemaid." Greta heard the edge in her own voice. She wanted to be rational, but she couldn't pretend to accept Carson's widow running her life. "This is Mattie's home. No one coming in would belong here." She thought of a stranger in her house, rummaging through cabinets and drawers as she sat helpless. Having to constantly remind herself she'd invited the intrusion. That would be worse than Spring Gardens. But the thought of going to a place like that brought her right back around to the anxious drumming of fear.

"Greta"—Elaine's voice sounded strained—"I'm trying to find a solution. If you have any ideas, please give them to me."

"Just leave me be," Greta said, wondering how she would manage if Elaine took that suggestion to heart.

"I can't do that," Elaine said. The woman stood up and went to the window. Greta could make out her back as she looked out at the porch and across the yard. "I haven't been here in a long time," she said. "And I've never really looked at the place.

Carson must have had a great time when he was a kid. You've got that stream running right behind the house. Animals. Fields and woods to explore."

Greta closed her eyes. She could see Carson as a boy. Hours spent tossing up a baseball and hitting it into the field with a bat. He'd retrieve the ball—sometimes with difficulty in the tall corn they had planted back then—and do it again. Ever since, she'd enjoyed listening to baseball on television. The crack of a ball hitting the wood.

"He was happy," Greta said. "At least until his daddy died. Even after, it was hard, but he mostly had good times, I think."

"You tell me what we're going to do, Greta," Elaine said. "Just tell me."

"I don't know." Greta let herself breathe. It took conscious effort, it seemed. "I never planned on Mattie's absence. And it never occurred to me that her kids wouldn't want to stay here and raise their children. I don't blame them, mind you. I understand why they want to go. But, for the life of me, I can't think of what to do. Other than worrying about Mattie, it's all that's on my mind."

Those were, she realized, the first unguarded words she'd presented to Elaine Forsyth in a quarter century.

Somewhere, in the course of twenty minutes, maybe less, Elaine had begun to see Greta as a person instead of a problem. Given this, there was one small thing she could tackle—the *person* Greta seemed to be in need of a decent meal.

"Let's ride out to town," Elaine said.

"Why?"

"We'll grab lunch," she said. "People do it all the time. Why not us?"

Greta offered a nod, which Elaine took to mean she acquiesced.

"We could go to the diner," Elaine offered, trying to think of the options in town.

"That place is always full of old men who don't have jobs to keep them busy anymore," Greta said. "Wives won't let them hang around the house, so they live at the diner. People say hens gossip, but I'll tell you—roosters crow. And they both spout the same nonsense, only the roosters are louder." She seemed to consider for a moment. "Carson used to stop off at Benny's on the way to the house sometimes. He'd bring a bag of hamburgers so we didn't have to make lunch. They tasted pretty good, as I recall."

"I like Benny's," Elaine said.

"Let me change into better slacks." She went off to the back room and it seemed to be settled.

When she came out, Greta's short hair looked combed and styled, her lipstick in place. She'd put on low-heeled pumps and gotten her bag. None of that seemed to matter, though, because she wore slacks that were pale green and a blouse of another, deeper green. Her eye condition must involve some problems with color recognition because the greens clashed. It gave Elaine a glimpse into her mother-in-law's reality. Mattie had signed off on Greta's clothes each day. Without that help, the older woman simply did her best to get along.

Elaine felt a tug of sympathy. The feeling, without precedent in their history, left her with no template for how to proceed. She considered simply telling her, but didn't want to embarrass the woman and set their progress back to square one. Maybe something over the blouse.

"You might want a sweater," she said. "They turn the air up in those places."

"I have one in my room," Greta said.

"I can get it for you," Elaine offered. The older woman turned to look in her direction.

"My legs are fine."

Everything seemed hard. Too hard. They had only one common denominator, Greta and Elaine, but the thing they shared had left them both empty and bruised by grief. Maybe that was enough to go on. Elaine waited for her mother-in-law by the door.

She took a moment to look around. Furniture, worn but well made. A framed replica of a famous Seurat painting on one wall and a flea market print of Jesus in a garden with some oddly contemporary children on another. A smooth wood floor covered by one large, hand-knotted rug—the oversized pale roses on the rug mirrored the damask on the couch upholstery. The rug had faded so that the original color of the wool strands emerged in places. All of it was new to Elaine's eyes but as familiar to Greta as her own skin. Leaving meant more than walking out the door to the woman. It meant giving up what her mind could still see.

"All right." Greta was standing in the room. Elaine didn't know how long she'd been there. The beige sweater masked the clashing of the greens.

"All right," Elaine said.

Greta led the way out onto the porch, sure-footed until she reached the yard. As her steps grew careful, Hobo quietly flanked her. Elaine followed and watched how the dog seemed to lead the old woman—without getting underfoot—through safe passage to the car. When they arrived at the sedan, Greta reached down and—as Elaine had seen her do several times—touched the dog's head, before opening the car door and settling herself inside.

Elaine got to the car and let Hobo into the backseat. "Good dog," she said, as she found the keys in her pocket and got into the driver's seat.

Mick drove away from the hospital with no destination in mind. The only place he didn't want to go was home. He didn't want to run into his mom or Linnie. They'd know something was up.

He could let it go. Just let it drop. Life would be no different than it had been when he woke up. But that wasn't true. He didn't recognize his life anymore. Every day he was lifted and delivered to a different location. A video-game life. After meeting one challenge, he kept finding another, more difficult level ahead.

Main Street looked quiet. Lunch hour. He pulled the truck over and parked between the slanted lines of a curbside spot. Coffee. He'd get a cup of coffee. If someone had been peddling bourbon or a joint, he would have opted for one of those, but at noon on a weekday, alcohol and weed were out of the question, so coffee it was.

He put his hand on the door of the downtown diner, then stopped before going in. Retired guys huddled over laminate tables that had been wiped down daily since the '50s. The place was full of older men—eating lunch, talking earnestly. If Mick went in, at least one of them would get started on knowing Carson when he was Mick's age. Mick stepped away and crossed the street. He could go to Benny's. It was only one block down, but, standing in the sidewalk heat, he'd lost his desire for coffee—or anything else.

In the days since he'd said good-bye to Carson, he'd spent his time driving from one end of the county to another trying to find answers. With more than a little irony, it occurred to him that issues of paternity held court at the center of all his questions.

He was standing in front of the hardware store. The door had a paper clock that read BACK AT . . . across the top. The hand pointed to 1:00 P.M. He looked at his watch: 12:15. He turned to leave, but saw someone moving at the back of the store. Laurie Pascal—she was Spence, now, he guessed—stood in the doorway of what must have been the back office. She had half a sandwich in one hand and a paperback in the other. He knocked on the glass door and a look of irritation crossed her face until she recognized him and the expression morphed into a grin.

She motioned for him to wait, then disappeared and emerged a second later with a key in the hand where her sandwich had been. As she came toward him, her broad, familiar smile calmed him. Her blond hair fell straight, just past her shoulders—the way she'd always worn it. If he didn't look too carefully, she could still be sixteen. What would he do if he could go back to those years, start with a white canvas and new paint?

"Hell's bells, Micky Forsyth," she said. "I was wondering when I would see you. Come in real quick before I have to let some customer in here. I get about an hour of peace on Wednesdays when I'm running the place by myself—Aiden takes off and fishes one day every week. I hate being on my own here and, by God, I take every second of my lunch break. How are you?"

He started to say *I'm fine,* then realized she'd most likely hear within the hour from Teresa that he was anything but okay. Instead of an answer, he just shrugged his shoulders.

"Yeah, I know, hon," she said, touching his arm. "I'm sorry I didn't come to the funeral. The death thing kind of freaks me out. I know I should get over it and do better. It's got to be hard losing somebody like that. And you and your daddy were pretty tight."

"Yeah." He nodded.

She locked the door behind him, motioned him to the back of the store. "Sylvia's asleep back here, so we have to be kind of quiet. This office is a mess," she said, gesturing to the desk, a paper-strewn landscape. "I'm no better here than I am at home. At home, I use that baby as an excuse, but here . . ." She lifted her hands, palms up. Offered him another grin.

"I saw Teresa this morning," he said. "At the hospital."

"Yeah? She keeping that attitude of hers in check over there?"

"Apparently." He kept his voice just above a whisper. What was he doing with Laurie Pascal in an empty hardware store? He would make a little bit of conversation then leave. It seemed he didn't belong anywhere. "Hey, you look the same," he said. "And Teresa told me about your baby. Hell, I can't believe that."

"We've turned the storage closet into a nursery here." She inclined her head toward a door at the side of the room. "She's five months old now. You want to see her?"

He had the vague sense that it was probably wrong to stick a baby in a closet, but he let it go.

"Sylvia's just about the prettiest little thing in the whole damn world," Laurie whispered. She opened the closet door—to Mick's relief, it was a really large closet—and he saw a small lump of flesh inside the crib. He followed Laurie over to the child.

The baby's eyes were closed, but her mouth rooted at the sheet as if searching for a nipple. The girl's nearly bald head had the wispy beginnings of Laurie's blond hair.

Laurie stood looking at her daughter, and the expression on her face was one he would never have associated with the teenage girl he'd known seven years before. For the first time in his recollection, Laurie seemed tender, unaware of herself, of what her own presence was saying to everyone. After a moment, she put a finger to her lips, then motioned that they should leave. They walked back into the office, and she closed the door gently behind her.

The Laurie he'd known would have laughed at her current incarnation. He didn't know if he liked the change or not. Laurie ought to be Laurie. Something in his world ought to make sense.

"What's going on with you, Mick?" She cleared a stack of manila folders from a chair so he could sit down, and then she sat behind the desk.

"It's a weird time," he said, not wanting to settle into a drawn-out session of catching up. "Listen, has Teresa talked to you about me?"

"She said you're trying your best to get into Joy Brown's size-two jeans. From what I hear, you're the first if you succeed. I don't know if that sort of thing makes it more or less appealing to you."

He had no idea how to respond, but something of the old Laurie had returned, at least. "I like Joy a lot," he said, which was saying nothing, really.

"Okay." She raised her eyebrows.

"Did Teresa tell you she doesn't want me with Joy?" He put a hand on his knee to stop the urge to move. "She's heard a lot of rumors—most of them from you, I guess."

Laurie let out a huff of air. "Oh hell, she told you she thinks that black kid is yours, didn't she?" she asked, irritated at her younger sibling. "Goddamnit, Teresa. How can she even remember all the stuff I yak about?" she muttered under her breath. "I told her to leave you the hell alone. Let you and Joy have fun if you want and not drag up all that old shit."

"If he's mine," Mick said, "it's not exactly something that can be over and done with. He's a person, not a banged-up car or something. How many people think I'm Kyle's dad?"

Laurie let her head drop. "I don't know," she said. "I haven't taken a poll. Kids at school talked about it at the time, but that was years ago. Most people have moved on, and no one left would care anymore. It's old gossip."

In a town the size of Lowfield, there was no such thing as old gossip. Stories looped back on top of themselves until they became lore.

"Let it go, Micky. That kid's settled. He's fine."

"His brother called me out to teach him how to play baseball. I didn't know why at the time, but Kayla's mom saw me with him and freaked out."

Laurie got up and came over to him. She squatted beside him so that her face looked up to his. "Half the girls I know have babies whose daddies are long gone. Other people step in and the kids do okay. You didn't even know about this. Kayla didn't want you to know. Hell, he *has* two people raising him. That's one more than he'd have with you. What do you think you're going to do? Be a daddy all of a sudden?"

"I don't know what to do." He thought of Kyle. He thought of Greta at the other end of his responsibility spectrum. Wasn't he supposed to be forty or something before he felt sandwiched in by two damn generations of family?

"You're making it all too complicated, Micky. You always did. You think there's some code of behavior that makes everything come out equal in the end. If that was true, sweetheart, there wouldn't be all those big-bellied babies starving in Africa while my little Sylvia sleeps fat and happy in her crib. Hell, if it was really true, I'd be a model in Atlanta right now instead of running a True Value on Main Street. You can't expect life to make perfectly round circles all the time. Sometimes you just have to live with lopsided things and thank God it's not worse than it is."

She looked sad. Talking about his problems was making her regard her own life—the things she wanted and didn't have. He looked at the even line where she parted her hair on top of her head, the pink flesh that was her scalp. She smelled like vanilla. Maybe it was her shampoo, her lotion. From his vantage in the chair he could also see a little way down her shirt, post-baby breasts sloping into the lace edges of her bra.

"So have you slept with Joy Brown?" Her words sounded small.

"No." He couldn't imagine why he was answering that question. Laurie had a way of making the truth seem like something owed to her.

"Well, maybe you should," she said. "You're about as nervous as a squirrel." He realized he'd been tapping his heel—a rapid staccato against the tile—and he forced himself to be still. She leaned over a little more, and her bra gaped enough to see the brown edge on one of her nipples. He wondered if she'd done it on purpose.

He tried to pull his focus away from her chest. "I don't think my problems have anything to do with—"

"Listen, Micky," she interrupted him, still keeping her voice low. His growing erection pressed tight against his jeans. "We were good friends back in the day. We never did it, but I thought some about it at the time. It's just that you were all sloppy for your girlfriend, and I figured we were made for conversation and that was it. But maybe I was wrong." She looked up at him, her expression straightforward. Nothing coy. No apology. "Maybe it wasn't the right time back then. Maybe the right time is now."

"Jesus, Laurie," he whispered. He made his voice register surprise, but the truth was, he didn't feel nearly as shocked as he should. Maybe he'd crossed the street knowing that this very situation was possible. Maybe he wanted to do something stupid and wrong. Maybe he couldn't change.

She stood up, walked to the edge of the desk, and gestured for him to come over. As he did, she unbuttoned her shirt.

"Stop, Laurie."

She didn't move, didn't button her shirt, but didn't go any further with her striptease.

"You look like you could use a little fun, Mick," she said. "You've had a rough few weeks."

"This would make it better for five minutes," he said. "And then it would make it worse. I've got to figure out how to handle shit without screwing up all the time."

Her mouth curved into a smile, but her eyes didn't follow. With that baby just behind the door, he figured she was as sick of being responsible as he was of fucking up. She buttoned her shirt.

"Thanks for talking to me, Laurie. You've always given me your opinions straight up. I appreciate that. We could be real friends, you know."

She sat on the edge of the desk, her fingers still touching the top button on her blouse. "I thought we were."

So much for getting things right. She looked sad, and it was his fault. "I should go, Laurie," he said.

She handed him the key to the front door. "Leave it in the door. I've got to open back up anyway."

He left and she stayed in the back office. When he turned to wave, she was sitting at the desk with her sandwich and her paperback again, not bothering to regard him at all.

Greta ate a hamburger the way Grace Kelly might have approached the sandwich at a state dinner. She used her hands, but the delicate care employed elevated the Benny's staple to a higher level of dining. Elaine knew Greta had been hungry, but even so, Carson's mother took her time, kept her posture, sipped her soda from the edge of the cup and not through a straw. Elaine had finished her meal and even thought of going back for a swirl cone—still, Greta had more than half a burger left.

"Why are you watching me?" Greta asked.

Elaine wondered what she actually saw of her surroundings and what she guessed at based on experience and gut feelings.

"You're very neat—even with fast food."

Greta almost smiled, but seemed to catch herself. "It's because of my mama," she said as if there were blame attached to it rather than praise. "She never liked living in the country. Never wanted to be considered country. She said, 'We may live on a farm, but we don't have to eat like pigs.' I guess I took that much of it to heart." She appeared to be talking to herself more than Elaine. "But all I ever wanted was a farmhouse. A lot of space around me."

Elaine wondered if they were back to talking about the house. Greta's situation. Even a day before, she would have guessed everything Greta did to be calculated. She wasn't sure of that anymore. She wasn't sure of anything.

"I understand that these are hard decisions to make," Elaine said.

Greta had stopped eating. The remnants of a hamburger and fries sat in front of her. "I have two choices," she said. "One's no better than the other. I suppose I could flip a coin and be done with it."

At a table beside them, kids, teenagers—three boys and two girls—were laughing at something. Nervous giggles followed by shushing noises. Elaine heard one of them say something about "Grandma Leprechaun." The laughter began again, and they seemed unable to contain themselves. Elaine realized that Greta had slipped her sweater off and put it on the back of the chair.

Elaine looked in their direction. She didn't know whether she wanted to scold them or plead with them to stop. She'd been stupid in high school. Everything was funny, and adults had no feelings, weren't vulnerable.

Greta put her hands in her lap. For a moment, Elaine thought she hadn't heard, but then the older woman's face lost color. Her mouth became set in a tight line that Elaine knew was a defense against showing any emotion at all. She inclined her head in Elaine's direction. "Do I have on a brown blouse and light green pants?" she asked, her voice low.

"Your blouse is green, too," Elaine told her.

"You wanted to see me look ridiculous?" The question was loaded, but her tone suggested a more casual exchange.

"No, Greta," Elaine said. "I just didn't want to get into it. I didn't know how you'd react to my suggestions."

Greta nodded. Seemed to accept the explanation.

"I'm finished when you are," Elaine said. "We can leave any time."

Greta didn't respond. For a moment, she sat, her color still off, looking like a waxed version of herself. Elaine watched her take in a long breath and turn in the general direction of the teenagers.

"When you've lived for more than seven decades," she said, her voice shaky, but projecting well beyond the intended target, "if you've kept your wits and your eyesight, you might do better than I've done today with my . . . ensemble. But then again, you might not. It's okay to enjoy your youth, but try not to do it at the expense of other people." She turned back to Elaine, as if they had a conversation to resume.

The kids' fish-mouthed stares gave way to nervous small talk among themselves.

"They don't realize . . ." Elaine spoke in low tones.

"It doesn't matter," Greta said. "I have bigger concerns."

"I know. That's why I drove out today." Elaine shot a stern glance over at the kids who had resumed a low chatter, their heads bent low together like cattle feeding at a trough. "There has to be . . ."

"We both know the direction this is going." Greta stopped her from finishing. From saying something they both knew was a lie. "I told you before, I have two choices," she said. "I can either invite a stranger into my home or give up my home."

"In the long term, you're probably right," Elaine said. An idea had been in the back of her thoughts. Something unthinkable, but at the same time, inevitable. "But there's another choice in the short term. It would buy us some time."

"And what currency would be required to *buy* this precious time?" Greta asked. "Other than the property I own, my resources are limited."

"This solution may cost you a little pride."

"That vault has already been raided, I'm afraid." Greta inclined her head toward the teenagers.

Elaine didn't know how to respond.

"That was a joke," Greta said. "An effort at one, anyway."

"Okay." Elaine forged ahead. "Well, you're not going to like this idea very much." She didn't much care for it either, but it was the right thing. It's what Carson would have asked of her. "Come to the tree house and stay for a while," Elaine said. "Linnie's leaving at the end of the week to tour with the dance company she was with all those years. The main section of the house will be empty. Mick and I are in the other part of the house."

"How long are you planning to stay in town?" Greta asked. "I thought you'd be going back to Chapel Hill right away."

"Summer is slow at the arts council," Elaine said, hoping to stay vague. She didn't want Greta to know that she'd already changed her plans based on what had happened. "Besides, I'm not ready to go back yet. I told them I'd be taking more time than I originally thought. It's too soon for me to try and find a new normal for myself. I'm going to stay at the lake. You could move in as early as this weekend."

"Why would we do that to ourselves?" Greta's question seemed genuine. "One civil lunch doesn't mean the last twenty-five years never happened."

The teenagers got up to leave in unison—an exit that appeared choreographed. They walked past Elaine and Greta, avoiding eye contact.

"We don't have a lot of options," Elaine said. Her shoulders and arms felt weak. Stepping around the shards of conversation with her mother-in-law had exhausted her.

"I'll pay someone to come in." The statement came from Greta in Tourette-like urgency. It signaled the level of panic underneath Greta's neutral expression. "I'll just do it."

Elaine wanted to agree. To say, *problem solved*. Regardless of what Elaine offered in the short term, circumstances would lead to the same decisions for Greta in the end. Did doing something that would break Carson's heart count if Carson wasn't there to see it? She wanted to scream at him to stop. To leave her alone. Then she wanted to take it back. Tell him to never stop nagging at her.

"Ride out with me," Elaine said. "A quick trip out to the cabin. You can get a feel for it and decide if it could work. If not, we'll put an ad in the paper for someone, and we'll figure out how to pay for it."

"Will the boy be there today?"

"Goddamnit, Greta." No matter how hard Elaine tried, the old Greta would not go away lightly. She hated to let Greta get to her. She made herself breathe and speak with a calm she didn't feel. "His name is Mick. Michael. Carson and I gave him that name. I told you this arrangement would cost you a little pride. I'm working hard here. I really am. But could you please take a step in my direction?"

At first Greta didn't seem to even hear her. Elaine watched, waited. The older woman let out the breath she'd been holding. The ridges around her mouth and eyes relaxed, making her look almost pleasant.

"I don't have anything much planned for the afternoon," she said. "Unless you count picking out a change of clothes." She glanced down at her outfit. Elaine recognized a little of Carson in the sly smile that came across her face. "You could have told me, you know."

"I can only imagine how well that would have gone," Elaine said.

Greta sat still for a moment, then neatly wrapped up her un-eaten food in the hamburger wrapper. She put it on the plastic tray with the other trash.

"On the way out," she said, "I think I would like one of those soft ice cream cones they have here."

"Outstanding," Elaine said. "I could eat some ice cream, too."

"I'll get it," Greta said.

Elaine watched as Greta stood up. Following what must have been shadowed images and memory, she made her way to the counter.

"Two cones please," Greta said.

"What kind would you like?" the girl behind the counter asked.

"Swirl for me." She half turned in Elaine's direction, raised her eyebrows.

"The same," Elaine said.

"Two swirl cones," Greta said to the girl.

Elaine felt as if she'd climbed a large hill, with steeper terrain to follow. But she had come to a pause, with finally a moment to rest.

Outside the hardware store, a pillow of humidity pressed against Mick's lungs. He felt light-headed. Questions about Greta and Kyle had been pushed aside—Laurie's post-pregnancy breasts proved an amazing distraction—but as he made his way toward the spot where he'd parked the truck, his concerns caught up with him.

Maybe Laurie was right. Maybe everyone would be better if he forgot about Kyle. And Greta? She ought to go where people go when they can't see three feet in front of them. If she'd ever done one damn thing for him, it might be different, but she didn't even like him.

He wasn't cut out to be anybody's savior. That had been Kayla's mistake—expecting too much of him. He'd tell Joy it had been great, but no thanks. He'd help his mom get her life sorted out. Everybody else could just go to hell.

"Mick?" His mother stood in front of him on the sidewalk. She held a half-eaten ice cream cone. Beside her, his grandmother held an identical cone and was bending to take a bite before one entire side of the cone collapsed out of her hand.

"Mom?"

Seeing the blue extraterrestrials descend, settling to the hot asphalt of Main Street, would not have startled him more.

"What are you two doing?" he asked. And what the hell was his grandmother wearing? She looked like she'd been assigned to be the green bean in a 4-H pageant.

"We're getting ready to ride out to the tree house," Elaine said, as if *that* made sense. "I've offered to have Greta stay with us for a while if she wants."

Inside his mind, he was shaking his head. No. But all he could do, facing the two women on the main drag in Lowfield, was nod. Across the street through the large glass storefront of the hardware store, he saw Laurie holding little Sylvia over her shoulder, giving the sales pitch for a riding lawn mower to some gray-haired man who openly stared at her chest.

"Why not?" Mick said, a little too loud. People around him on the street turned to stare. "Why the hell not?" He semi-addressed the onlookers in a voice worthy of Ringling. He felt an insane grin spread across his face. "Would you like to ride with me, Grandmother?"

"Have you been drinking?" Elaine asked.

"No," he said, aware, suddenly, that his bizarre behavior was making the situation even harder for his mother. "That's something I haven't done today." He shifted his attention to the older woman. "We should get to know each other, Greta," he said. "I'm serious. Come on. I'll give you a ride."

She ditched the remnants of the cone in a nearby trash can and wiped her hand with a tissue. "I'll go with your mother," she said in a voice far too dignified for her St. Paddy's Day getup. Clearly—and with good reason—Elaine had quickly become the lesser of two evils.

"I'll meet you at the lake then," he said, taking keys out of his pocket and turning to leave.

As he walked away, he saw Laurie standing near the window inside the store, still holding the baby. She watched him for a moment and gave him a glare that would wilt flowers on the spot, then turned away. Even when he did the right thing, he was a fucking disappointment.

Greta took careful steps over the gravel in the driveway, but she gained confidence heading up the stairs. Elaine stayed near but gave her space to navigate on her own. If Greta came to stay, Elaine would not be a nursemaid.

"Hi, Greta." Linnie came out of the house and greeted them at the top of the landing—Hobo at Greta's heels. "Welcome."

"Thank you," Greta said, only slightly winded from the climb.

"Come on in. I've got a batch of cheese straws in the oven, and I've just made a pitcher of tea."

Elaine, reaching the top of the stairs with Mick trailing just behind her, watched her mother-in-law. Greta didn't seem to know what to do with Linnie's hospitality.

"I haven't had homemade cheese straws in a decade or more," Greta said. "I stopped baking, and Mattie doesn't care for them."

Having exhausted their greetings, they all went inside, into the den. Elaine wondered what she had hoped to accomplish in dragging Greta to the tree house.

"A nice breeze has come up," Linnie offered. "Want to settle out on the screened porch?"

"Sure," Elaine answered, grateful that Linnie was taking charge of the situation. Elaine had called her aunt on the way home. With Greta in earshot, Elaine hadn't been able to speak freely, but Linnie seemed to have a handle on everything.

"Before we go out, why don't you get a feel for where everything is, Greta. I know you and Elaine talked about having you visit for a while. My room is close to everything, and I'm leaving at the end of the week. It would be a good spot for you."

They stepped into Linnie's bedroom. "This is where Carson was," Greta said. "I sat with him in there."

It was a simple statement, but it stopped everything. Mick steadied himself with an arm on the bedpost, the sturdy, carved wood becoming his crutch. Elaine felt something shift inside of her. Unable to be in the bedroom any longer, she went back out to the den and sat on the couch.

Of course Greta had been in that room. Elaine had never stayed around, but Greta had come to see Carson on multiple occasions. And now they talked of moving her in there.

The others returned to the den, and Mick walked to the picture windows and stared out. Still no one spoke. Elaine registered a small horror when she felt wet streams on her face.

"Actually, the porch can wait. No one here needs to pretend this isn't hard." Linnie helped Greta into the Queen Anne chair and then sat beside Elaine, laying a protective hand on her arm.

"Did he pass in that room?" Greta asked. She didn't seem troubled by the possibility of staying in a bed where Carson might have died.

"No," Elaine told her. "We were in here. Sitting by the window. He was in the chair that you're in now. I pulled up another chair beside him."

"He had his wits about him?" Greta regarded the window, as if imagining him there.

"Mostly," Elaine said. "Right until the end. He wasn't in as much pain as they expected. He talked a fair amount. Sometimes to me. Sometimes he seemed to be directing his thoughts toward things I couldn't see."

"Tell me," Greta said, then added, "if you don't mind. I'd like to know about how he was at the last."

Mick came to the couch to sit on the other side of Elaine. Flanked by those two, Elaine looked at Carson's mother. She had high cheekbones and pale skin. For her age, there weren't many lines. She must have been stunning as a very young woman. And something else Elaine saw for the first time—the architecture of Greta's face had been replicated in Carson's features. Mick had made note of it at the funeral. No wonder he'd wanted to go see his grandmother.

"We talked for a long time about anything that came to mind," Elaine said. "Vacations we'd particularly enjoyed. Students who stuck out in his memory. We talked a lot about when Mick was little. Laughed about the funny things we both remembered. He told me things about his own childhood. He said when he was about eight or ten, you and Taylor took him on a weekend trip to the beach. The first time he'd seen the ocean. He said there were other trips like that, but the first one came back to him the most clearly."

Greta nodded. "Every morning at the beach, we went to a pancake house for breakfast. Carson ate his weight in pancakes. Other than those trips, I cooked breakfast every morning of Carson's growing up. I felt so free, sitting there eating—watching him and Taylor eat, and knowing I had no breakfast dishes to clean up after. You could smell the salt water from the restaurant.

"We ate dinner out, too, but we did that at home sometimes. Dinner never bothered me much anyway. But making breakfast then cleaning it up . . ." She shook her head as if to shake off the burden of so many mornings.

"He talked about the pancakes," Elaine said. "About how much you enjoyed them. I don't think he knew that what you really liked was not cooking." Elaine smiled.

"You said he said other things . . . things that you didn't understand."

"He talked about the lights," Elaine said. "The blue ones that other people saw. I thought he was a little delirious, but then there were the reports so . . ."

"Weather blues," Greta said. "I've seen them myself. People have their opinions, but I think they were there for Carson."

Did Greta really believe that aliens came and took her son away?

"We have to take some form when we pass," Greta said, as if hearing Elaine's thoughts. She looked again toward the daylight coming through the picture windows. "Whatever those lights are, they're there to help. You can call me crazy, but like I said, I've seen them a few times. Not just at somebody's death, but certainly that's most common." Her words had a defensive timbre, and she sounded more like the old Greta than she had moments before.

What had Carson said about the lights? *It's all there. Everything. It's all there.* And when she'd reminded him that she was sitting with him in their real world . . . in the cabin—he'd smiled and told her she was both here and there. *That's the amazing part. You're everywhere.*

"He saw me," Elaine said. "Wherever he was going, he said I was there, too."

"Consciousness," Mick said. His voice sounded rusted, a strain for him to use. "At Middlebury," he said, "one professor told us about theories of consciousness where we all exist outside of time. The experiences we have here . . . we have all those memories there. Ours and everyone else's. Everything. More than we can possibly retain in our limited brains."

"That sounds like your mother's folks," Greta said. She seemed to sense that offending her hosts would be less than productive. "People have a lot of ideas about what comes after. None of us will know until we're there, I suppose."

"I saw something once," Mick continued. "Just before sunset on a boat out in Narragansett Bay. The sun made the sky and the water turn into these incredible colors. Then there were points of blue in the sky that looked like mirrored reflections of the water, but three dimensional. A shape I remembered from geometry. I thought it was some illusion of the low sun."

"What shape?" Elaine asked.

"Dodecahedron," Mick said, as if the word might be common in his everyday life.

It made Elaine smile. "Once a math major, always a math major," she said.

Greta turned as if she could see him. "Did anything happen around that time?" she asked.

"What do you mean?" Mick asked.

"Did anything important happen?"

He thought for a moment. "Dad called sometime later that week," he said. "His initial test results had come in. The bad ones. I remember because that night out on the water was the last one before we started pulling boats out for the season. Dad called the first week we were hauling out. I'd forgotten about that sky."

The words seemed to have ended. They sat and no one spoke until the harmony of their breathing made Elaine feel that they were a single creature.

"I'll get the cheese straws," Linnie said. She stood up. "Mick, why don't you help Greta get settled on the porch? Your mom and I will bring out the food and drinks."

Elaine waited for Greta to recoil somehow from Mick's outstretched hand. The older woman did hesitate, but only for a moment. She took his hand and stood. For an instant, the back-lit image of the two of them allowed her a vision that stopped her breathing. The light rendered a pair of matching profiles; either of them might have been interchangeable with Carson's.

Then, for the slightest part of a moment, Elaine felt as if she'd seen three instead of two. *There you are.* The thought came and went. But the afterimage remained. In that flash, existence had collapsed into the purest distillation of a particular feeling—something like happiness, but without a name.

Greta and Mick moved toward the porch. Linnie made kitchen noises, gathering the food. And from her high vantage, Elaine searched the sun and shadows on the lake below.

For what, she didn't know.

Mick helped Greta to a chair. She felt the breeze through the screen. The lake smelled of clean dirt and laudable decay—the kind that spoke of growth rather than destruction. The creek on her property had hints of that same smell, but the shallow-moving water offered a different brand of service to the surrounding land. Nevertheless, the creek had more commonality than difference with the lake in front of her.

When considering bodies of water, only the ocean was a different creature altogether. The few times she'd seen it, she'd loved it for setting her nerves on edge. Anything could happen when you kept company with that much water, entire worlds of it. Unless you had a particular set of skills, you simply stayed out of its way. Apparently the boy knew how to handle himself on the ocean. Sailing in those boats. That was something to respect.

The boy had yet to sit down. He stood, his entire posture aimed in her direction, and though his features remained fuzzy, she could tell he was regarding her. He was also having trouble keeping still.

"You're staring at me," she said.

"Sorry," he said, sounding anything but contrite. She heard his agitation, nervous movement building. "You know," he said, as if responding to some challenge on her part, "my whole life, you've been a character. A myth, almost. Dad saw you, but you were never real to me. Then, you pretty much threw me out of your house the other day. Now you're sitting here, and I have no idea what to say. What am I supposed to say?"

"I don't expect you to say anything," she told him. "I don't know what your folks told you. But I've had my reasons for keeping a distance from you and your mother. These current circumstances . . . they're not of my choosing."

Again, she heard his breathing, listened as he paced to the far side of the porch and back. The dog came out onto the porch. She heard the *tac-i-tac* of his nails on the wood floor, then felt him settle at her feet, his back giving slight pressure to her leg. "I can make do with very little conversation," she told the boy.

"Well," he said, sitting beside her, "you're out of luck because I intend to keep things lively."

She tried not to smile, but she couldn't help it. He did seem like Carson up and down sometimes. Understandable. The man had raised him, after all. "All right," she said. "I can do lively, too." She heard movement from inside. The other two would be out soon. "Let's start with you. So what is it that you do?" she asked. "I know you live up north somewhere. Do something with boats."

"Rhode Island," he said. "I work in a boatyard—do a little of everything there."

"What kind of boats?" Greta thought of hot sun and strong wind. Cool waves colliding with sand. Did he see the ocean all the time? Was it for him like looking at the backyard used to be for her?

"Mostly sailboats," he said. He sounded wary. Maybe he

didn't trust her interest. She didn't blame him. She didn't trust
him, either.

"You take them on the ocean?" she asked. She'd never talked
to anyone who regularly spent time on the sea.

"Sometimes. I do a lot of inland coastal sailing. Narragansett
Bay."

"I don't understand," she said. "Is that the ocean?"

"Part of it. Salt water. Tides. Big water, only protected by the
land surrounding it."

Questions flooded her thoughts. She couldn't get her visions
of the broad, blue expanse to go away. "You ever see anything
out there? Animals?"

"Mostly dolphins," he said, like that was the most regular of
his sightings. Dolphins to her were just shy of fairies and elves in
the fascination department. She'd seen two dolphins swimming
together one time and had never lost the vision.

"Occasionally whales when they're migrating," he went on.
"Sharks and seals. But dolphins come to us, run with the boat
sometimes."

"What do you mean *run*?" If his dolphins had feet, she
planned to ask *him* about the mermaids he'd encountered.

He laughed as if he might have heard her thoughts. "It's an
expression," he explained. "They swim alongside sailboats, a lot
of times at the bow—the front of the boat. Keeping up."

"Why?"

"I don't know. For fun, I guess. I couldn't say for sure. I mean,
that dog follows you around." He leaned over, elbows on knees.
"Dolphins are smarter than dogs. And social like them. It makes
sense they'd want to play with us."

He leaned in, was close enough for her to make out his face.
She saw what Mattie had said was true. He had the mother's
features, but when he turned to look out at the lake, the line of
his face—forehead to chin—could have been Carson. She hadn't

shed tears when they laid Carson to rest, but the sight of her son in the boy's face brought a stinging wetness that caught on her lashes. By some blessed benevolence, the tears stayed shy of her cheeks.

She turned away from him—allowed the tide to recede.

"The iced tea's fresh," Linnie said, coming onto the porch with a tray. She put the drinks on the table. Elaine followed her with two bowls. Greta figured one of them held the cheese straws.

"What's that smell?" Greta asked. Taking in the amalgam of spices, Greta could have been in her own kitchen, forty years before.

"Molasses cookies," Elaine said. "Linnie made them for Carson one night here a few weeks ago and put part of the batch in the freezer. He mentioned to her when he was eating them that they were your favorites."

"You're very thoughtful." Greta turned to face the shape she knew belonged to Elaine's aunt. "Very kind, actually." Greta wouldn't cry again. She knew how to keep outward emotion at bay, but she couldn't stop the rolling waves of sadness inside her, and Linnie's efforts made it worse.

Everything Carson's other people did for her only underscored the loss she felt. She'd fashioned a world from her beliefs. But all along, the boy had been Carson's. Carson tried to tell her, but sitting there, she knew it for the first time. She'd denied herself her very own grandchild. Denied Carson the act of sharing him.

When Carson passed, she'd leaned on her anger. After all this time, if she even existed without that hot core of animosity she'd carried through the years, she didn't know how.

"Sweet tea?" Linnie was asking.

"Yes, thank you," she heard herself say.

She was grateful when the commotion of someone else's arrival provided a distraction.

"Morty," she heard Elaine say. "Come on in."

The boy stepped past her; his leg brushed her arm. It left her with the most profound sort of regret.

Elaine went into the kitchen to refill the bowl of cheese straws and to see if anything in the refrigerator could be turned into a meal. To everyone's surprise, Greta had given no indication that she felt compelled to go home. It stood to reason that food would be a concern before too long.

Elaine had called Ayla to let her know that Greta would be staying at the tree house for dinner. The younger woman sounded relieved not to have feeding Greta on her list of things to do for the evening.

Greta had grown quiet. Not the surly sort of quiet that would have seemed normal, but a pensive variety. Elaine couldn't make sense of it. The woman had seemed characteristically prickly and animated not long before, but something had turned for her.

"What are you doing?" Mick came into the kitchen.

"Looking to see if we have anything to eat," she said. "I brought Greta here thinking I'd take her home before dinner. But I'm not sure she's eating regularly out there. Mattie's girls are doing the best they can, but they have to be distracted."

"Does that pizza place in town deliver out this far?" he asked. "I could go for that."

"Why don't you go out and ask Linnie. I've never ordered it here, but if they don't deliver rural, they don't have much of a customer base."

"I don't want to go back out there." He was picking at a corner of peeling wallpaper. He looked five years old.

"Why?"

"She's freaking me out a little," he said. "Greta," he clarified, as if there was any question.

"How?"

"Asking me questions about my life." He sat on the edge of a stool near the counter. "Looking at me in a weird way when I'm close to her."

"She can barely see beyond a foot or two, Mick. If she's going to see anything, she has to stare."

"I know," he said, standing up again. "It's just that I liked it better when she seemed to be pissing on everything I said."

"Yeah," Elaine said. "She is acting odd."

"What's the powwow about?" Morty had come into the room.

"We're trying to sort out what's going on with my mother-in-law," she said. "I know how to spar with her, but I'm not sure I know how to talk to her. Mick's having the same trouble."

"Try pretending you just met her," he said. "She's an engaging woman. Speaks her mind, but has the kind of dignity you don't see much anymore."

Elaine glanced at Mick. He raised his eyebrows, gave a slight shrug. Changing the subject seemed like a good idea. "Do you know if pizza delivers out this far?" Elaine asked him.

"Oh, yeah," he said, "they bring it to you. They'll do anything to take your money, darlin'. But it's a day old by the time the delivery boy turns in your driveway. You don't want to do that. I'll run over to my place. See what I got. I'll be back in a sec."

He turned and left, didn't give anyone a chance to respond. Morty never waited to act—not a second between the decision and the execution of his plans. It was a solid wonder to Elaine.

"That man is a gift," she said, looking out the window as he went down the series of landings that led to the ground outside.

"What's up with Greta being 'engaging'?" Mick asked, a grin on his face.

"Beats me." Elaine looked out toward the darkness of the den. Beyond, a yellow glow from the porch came through the door at the far end of the room. "Greta is apparently different things to different people. For us, she might be a character-building exercise. For Morty . . . ? Who knows?"

Elaine settled back against the counter and looked at her son. He was so close to being a man, but he hadn't outgrown the need for parenting. Would she be enough for him? "Your dad would like it that she's here with us." She inclined her head toward the other room and the light beyond.

Mick nodded. Agreement? Resignation? She wasn't sure.

The evening turned cooler. Not what Mick considered cool in New England—a fleece after sunset in the dead of summer—but a temperature that meant you could exist outside without feeling punished.

Greta declared it *comfortable,* and so they did something Mick remembered Pop and Grandma Ginnie doing all the time when he was a kid—they moved the kitchen table out to the porch to eat in the open air.

Morty had returned with an overabundance of perch, already breaded and ready to panfry in sizzling oil. He pulled out every pan in the kitchen suitable for frying and set up all four burners.

"In New Orleans, we were always feeding a crowd. Didn't know how to cook for a few. This is going to be good. I promise you that."

The meal seemed to be men's work all of a sudden, so Mick hung out in the kitchen and tried to be useful but, for the most part, Morty put on a one-man show and Mick kept him company.

While the fish sputtered and browned, Morty rooted around and found rice, along with cans of black-eyed peas and a few pieces of leftover bacon in the fridge. "Look-a-here," he declared. "Even got us some hoppin' John." Obviously delighted with the discovery, he set his sights on the spice cabinet. Mick admired his enthusiasm for something as pedestrian as making dinner.

Just after dark, they sat down to the meal. Tea was replaced with glasses of wine, and, to Mick's surprise, Greta accepted her glass from Morty with a pleasant nod. He'd always figured she didn't drink. But then, what did he know about the woman?

Morty positioned himself beside Greta and offered a brief grace. The latter seemed to be a nod toward her expectations. Maybe it helped that Mick was starving, but with his first bite of fish, an unexpected feeling of well-being arrived, slipping in out of nowhere. The sensation proved to be the leading edge of a calm he hadn't felt since his dad's diagnosis.

"How in the world did you pull together hoppin' John out of the pantry?" Linnie asked Morty, her fork suspended midbite.

"No magic to it, darlin'," he said. "Problem with cooking is that people want to do something new when the old is still the best. Didn't do a thing my mama didn't teach me."

Afternoon had made its final turn toward evening. Mick felt securely held by the yellow light inside the screens of the porch. The light must have seemed odd to anyone looking on from a distance—an unlikely orb of domestic life suspended amid silhouettes of leaves and branches. All of it pressed against the last remnants of a salmon-colored sky.

Mick could squint and see the gatherings of his childhood. Grandma Ginnie and Pop, his mom and dad and Linnie . . . the scene remained the same even though the cast of characters had evolved. Greta and Morty instead of his mom's folks and his grown self instead of Carson as a younger man. In a startling insight, he realized that if the gatherings continued, it would be up to him to fill in the roster. A wife. A kid. Kids. Had he already made a contribution to this effort? The notion didn't terrify him the way it should have. Probably the wine working on him.

"Come on, Hobo." Elaine stood up. "Let's get you some food. It's not fair to let all these smells drive you crazy."

"Here." Linnie handed her a napkin that held a few fish scraps. "I checked this for bones. Put it in with his food."

Elaine took the napkin, and the dog followed her into the house.

Morty sat beside Greta, and Mick noticed that in the most subtle of ways, he assisted her with the meal—passing food and settling it back after she was served, slipping her wineglass into easy reach, picking up her napkin after it fell to the floor. Stranger things had happened, he supposed.

Elaine came back to the porch. "Dessert will be a disappointment after the feast Morty cooked up, I'm afraid. We've got ice cream in the freezer and some store-bought pound cake."

Mick stood and began to clear plates. He heard a car door slam below and, moments later, footsteps on the stairs heading up to the landing.

"Hello!" A voice called from the landing. Everyone peered around the side of the house.

"We're on the porch!" Linnie called out to the new arrival.

As the man on the landing leaned around the edge to greet everyone on the porch, the front door light revealed his features. Mick recognized Wallace Jamison.

"Wallace?" Elaine had frozen, a stack of dirty plates in her hand.

"Hi," Wallace greeted the gathering. "I don't mean to barge in. Since it's on my way, I thought I'd ride out after I visited with my mom and sisters this evening. Hope I'm not disrupting anything."

"Just a sec, I'll let you in," Elaine said, looking momentarily disoriented by her old friend's appearance. "Actually, it's open," she added. "Come on in." Mick saw that his mother's tanned face had taken on a gray cast. She looked as if she might throw up. She left the porch to intercept Wallace before he found himself in the presence of Greta.

Mick looked at his grandmother. Her expression held the entire story of how the next few moments would go down. Any progress that they had made as a family had been wiped clean. Not a thin residue of goodwill was left on the woman's face.

By the time Wallace and Elaine got to the porch, Mick knew that he'd been briefed on the situation. "Hi, everyone," Wallace said.

A thick sound emanated from Greta's throat. Mick wondered why Elaine and Wallace didn't just tell Greta the truth. What if he blurted it out? How could that hurt anything?

"It's great to see you again. I shouldn't have dropped by without talking to you," Wallace addressed Elaine but clearly spoke for Greta's benefit. He sounded more than a little desperate. "My goodness, I haven't seen you in years. I thought I'd come tell you myself how sorry I was to hear about Carson." His words sounded staged, as if read from a script. Mick felt sorry for him. Mick felt sorry for all of them, even his grandmother. "Hi Mick," he added. "Great to see you, too."

Greta looked not so much angry as caged. She brought a hand to her cheek, then lowered it to the table again, picked up her napkin and rubbed the white tissue between her thumb and forefinger. All color had left her face.

"Are you all right?" Morty asked.

"I'm not feeling quite well," she answered. "I think I should be getting home."

Mick couldn't read her tone. If she was angry, she kept it in check. She appeared confused, as if she didn't know the proper response to Wallace's arrival.

"I need to pick up some milk for tomorrow," Morty said as he stood also. "I'll drive you in, darlin'."

"I can't ask you to do that, Morty," Elaine said. "I'll run Greta home." Mick saw the bluff in his mother's eyes. She was hoping to God Morty didn't take her up on the offer.

"Won't hear of it," Morty said. "You folks clean up that mess I made in the kitchen, and I'll be delighted to play chauffeur for the lady."

No one protested. Cleaning dishes was a bargain under the circumstances. But as Greta and Morty stood to leave, Mick felt the loss of something. The calm he'd felt just moments before had disappeared. Anxious, unnamed fears claimed him again.

"Thank you for having me out," Greta said. She addressed Linnie specifically, as if she couldn't bring herself to direct her gratitude elsewhere. She turned and walked toward the door to the house, Morty at her elbow to guide her, Hobo at her heels.

Morty stopped and looked down at the animal and then back up at Elaine.

"He can ride with you," Elaine said.

As Greta passed by Wallace, Mick saw him make note of her green-on-green ensemble and quickly look away.

Morty slipped Greta's sweater over her shoulders. He turned and offered a nod of assurance to Elaine—trying to convey that everything would be all right. And for a moment, no one moved. Mick looked around and took in the patch-quilt gathering.

Greta and Morty stood paused at the screen door. Elaine had retreated to the corner of the porch, standing shoulder to shoulder with Wallace. Linnie, the only one still sitting at the table, held her wineglass and looked up at Elaine. Even the dog remained motionless, as if pointing toward game in a field. The tableau lasted long enough for Mick to regard the scene before it dissolved into motion again.

"I don't know you well, darlin'," Morty said to her, "but you seem to be awfully quiet."

Greta had no words for what had happened in the tree house. Elaine, the boy—and that Wallace fellow—maybe they all thought she was just Greta being Greta again. But the truth was, the Jamison man's appearance had left her so conflicted she couldn't untangle her own thoughts. She'd been wrong about Carson's son—of that she was certain. She saw it. It was almost as if the scales had briefly cleared from her vision and she saw her son again as a teenager.

Straight on, the resemblance wasn't strong, but from the side it became unmistakable. She thought of the decades she'd denied herself a grandchild. Wallace Jamison's arrival had at least given her actions a thread of legitimacy. Mick might be Carson's son, but if Elaine Forsyth had never betrayed her boy, then why would the man show up like that, unannounced, with so little time passed since Carson's departure?

She could hold on to that small validation. It was the only thing that kept her free of the unbearable regret. Morty waited for a response. Still, she didn't know how to put a voice to it. He was a patient man.

During the meal, she'd alternated between a complete sense of loss and an equally certain joy at everything that surrounded her. Even Elaine—having made the effort to get her and bring her to the tree house, offering to take her in—had made strides in Greta's estimation. Then Wallace Jamison was there, and Greta felt like a fool. Leaving had settled her down, but it had done nothing to lessen her confusion. Behind it all, in the back of her thoughts, an alternate life, an unlived reel of memory, mocked her.

"Greta?" Morty gently prompted, her name said quietly, so as not to startle her.

"That man," she said, "that Jamison man. He's the one who started this business that has gone on for so long."

"Even before the Wallace fellow arrived, something was on your mind." Morty turned off the car radio—easy jazz—and the sudden quiet amplified his words.

Only two people in her life had taken notice enough to read her the way Morty just had. Mattie and Carson—they could follow her thoughts and read her emotions with only a handful of words to go on. Taylor hadn't even been able to do that. She'd loved her husband, but for him, the less said about any kind of emotion, the better.

"With Michael," she said, "I made a mistake. From a certain angle, he's got Carson's exact features."

"From the side, "Morty said. "You're right about that, I think."

"Close up with the sun behind him, even I couldn't miss it. After his daddy died, Carson used to get lost in his own head. He'd stare out a window and I'd watch him. It was that face I saw today. It was like Carson had come back, just for a second or two. I couldn't decide if it was the best or worst thing that could happen. I still don't know."

"Then Jamison showed up."

She nodded. "It was a relief to get angry again. But that didn't make what I'd seen—what I'd realized—go away. I hoped it might, but it didn't."

Morty let the miles go by. He didn't turn the radio back on. He didn't tell her she deserved what she got. He just let her be.

"What do you think I should do?" she asked.

"I'm not inside your lovely skin, darlin'," he said.

"What would you do?"

He gave it a moment, as if considering. "I think I'd try to live with what is. It's true that Mick's a grown boy, but both of you have time to be something to each other."

"It might be too painful," she said. "I just don't know."

"Might be."

"And Elaine," she said. "I feel like I'm back where I started with her."

"I can't speak to that one," Morty said. "I don't have any bad history to climb over. But I can tell you that Elaine's a person I'm glad to know. Proud like you—and that's not a bad thing—and a worthy soul. Don't get me wrong. I'm not laying any judgment on your feelings about her or hers for you. I can only offer one opinion."

"I trust what you say, Morty," she told him, "but I don't think my habits have any room to yield after such a long time."

He didn't ask why that was. If he had, her reasons would have sounded thin, and she knew it. But making a change so profound was another thing entirely.

Eight

The tree house seemed cavernous. Elaine sat in the predawn dark. The day before, Linnie had packed up everything in her room and stored it in the ground-level shed that housed the water tank, washer/dryer, and AC unit. Greta had declined the offer to move in, but Linnie said she'd clear out anyway—in case something changed.

An hour before, Mick had loaded two large suitcases in the truck and had taken off to drive Linnie to Charlotte for a 7:00 A.M. flight. Elaine had opted not to go, but sitting in the dark, too awake to sleep and too tired to move, she was thinking her decision was a mistake. Even the dog was mopey.

It didn't make sense that the place seemed so empty. Linnie's room was the only thing that had changed. She pulled the sofa chair over to the window, exactly where Carson had been on the night he died. She looked out over the lake, up at the sky, and made a nonspecific plea for something. She didn't know what.

A whisper from Carson, a sign in the movement of the trees outside . . . even those damn blue lights. She wanted assurance that he was still *somewhere,* still accountable for feelings they promised wouldn't end. Were the times they shared still with him somewhere, or was she the sole keeper of their life together?

She was a senior in high school and he was home for the weekend from Duke. They sat in the car outside Sally's, a barbecue joint on the near side of Roseville, waiting for a table to open. The place stayed crowded in spite of the fact that it sat in the middle of nowhere.

"Muscadines are ripe," Carson said. An anemic-looking hedge of vines clawed at the undergrowth at the edge of the woods.

"Muscadines aren't good for much unless you know how to make jelly," she told him. "And I don't know how to make jelly." She looked at the straggling crop that lined the dirt driveway. "The skin's too thick, and the seeds are sour."

"Are you kidding me?" With only a month of college under his belt, he already seemed older to her. More man than boy. "You're missing out, girl."

At that moment, Hal, the owner of Sally's, came onto the front stoop. "Dennis!" he called out to the crowd milling around.

"Yup!" A man yelled back.

"Y'all are up!" Hal told him.

"Hey, Hal!" Carson called through his open window before the man turned to go back inside. "How long until we're called?"

Hal leaned inside the door. "Janie," he said. "How far down is the Forsyth boy?" He looked back at Elaine and Carson. "Twenty minutes," he said. "Maybe twenty-five."

"Thanks." Carson opened his car door. "Come on," he said to Elaine. "Let's walk."

"Walk where?"

"Come on," he said again with no explanation. Then he was

out of the car and pulling her from her seat. He reached in and grabbed an empty brown bag lying on the backseat of the car.

He led her down the dusty road until it tapered into a path, and, on either side, she saw that there were more muscadine vines—healthy ones, thick with grapes.

Carson pronounced it "musky-dines," recalling something pungent and overripe. Elaine felt overripe when she was with him—every part of her—and so she followed him, hoping their stroll would lead to a little privacy off the path.

"Where are we going?" She laughed.

"Here." He stopped.

The damp ground smelled of brown leaves and old rain, fodder for thirsty grapes. Carson pulled off a handful and put a single grape to her lips.

"Hold it with your teeth," he said. "Bite gently. Just enough to split the skin."

She offered slight pressure with her teeth and the tough skin gave way on one side. The sour fruit slipped into her mouth, and she made a face.

"Let it go down whole," he said.

She did. It went slippery and tart down the back of her throat.

"Now take your fingers and squeeze the rest out of the hull." He smiled. Eyes intent on her face.

The juice left inside the skin tasted like syrup, only lighter, more delicious.

He filled the brown bag with grapes, and they began walking back. All the way from the vines to the restaurant, muscadine skins littered the ground, trailing them at their particular leisure. It was a desultory path until they heard Carson's name called loudly in the distance. Hal only allowed a minute, maybe two, so they walked quickly to claim their spot.

* * *

Elaine wished she had pictures of every second, a stop-frame account of her full life with Carson.

She watched the apricot light edge the horizon; the full sun would appear soon. Every part of her ached. She'd heard this. That grief could manifest as true, physical pain. What was Greta feeling? Losing Carson. Mattie taken away. Elaine didn't want to care. She had Mick to worry about and her own struggles, for God's sake. She didn't want to think about her mother-in-law. Especially since she'd already made an effort with Greta and the woman rejected her. But Greta had no one. Elaine couldn't get that out of her thoughts.

Elaine considered precious recollections of Carson. Greta had memories, too. Parallel memories. Greta had insights into what Carson had been like as a boy. If no new experiences could be had with her husband, Elaine wanted the old ones. She wanted every scrap of him that she'd never asked for when he was alive.

She and Greta could have helped each other. But Greta wouldn't talk to her. It was as if they'd hadn't had a day of almost getting along. Damn bizarre to have come so far as to actually *want* to interact with Greta. Elaine wondered what the hell the woman was doing. She'd called, but Greta wouldn't answer. Mattie's kids had moved out over the weekend. Morty had seen her and said she was getting along, but he wouldn't elaborate.

The cell phone rang.

"Hey, Mom." Mick sounded tired from the early morning drive.

"Linnie get off okay?"

"Yeah," he said. "She called me twenty minutes after I left her and told me to turn around. Said she'd made a mistake and shouldn't leave."

"What'd you do?"

"I told her to get on the damn plane," he said, "that you

wouldn't let either one of us in the house if I came back with her."

"Good. She worries too much."

"I don't know," he said. "We're pretty messed up."

"What's going on with you, Mick?" she asked for the millionth time in three days. She'd watched his normal, nervous movement progress into overdrive since the day they brought Greta to the tree house. Something had happened. Something beyond missing his dad. "You've got to talk to me at some point," she said. "Whatever it is, it's obviously not going away."

"I'm sorry, Mom." He stopped at that, and the dead air hung between them.

She wouldn't press, not over the phone. She let the uncomfortable silence hold the moment.

"This one's on me, Mom," he said, finally. "I've got to figure it out. If you could help, I'd let you."

"Sometimes talking helps," she said.

"Sometimes." He sounded like his dad. The unyielding nonargument.

"I'm here," she said. "You know that."

"I know," he said with some impatience to get off the subject. But then, after a second, he said, "I really do know that."

Hot tears blurred the new dawn in front of her.

"I'm going to drive around for a bit if you don't mind," he said.

"Okay," she said. She wanted him to come home in the worst way. She wanted to hear someone else breathing and moving in the space she occupied. She'd never minded being alone before. But alone had never really been alone—not the way it was without Carson. "Be careful."

"Will do."

Every joint, every muscle required absolute stillness to keep the hurt at bay. Hobo padded up to her. The compassion in his puppy eyes looked old. Then he walked to the door that led outside and looked back at her.

"You need to go out?" She felt relief, the sudden task momentarily curing her ailments. "Keep me busy, Hobo. Maybe I'll get through this."

Outside, the lake smells mixed with something else, something sweet. Whether memory or magic was at play, she smelled the muscadines. Out of season and nowhere to be seen. Maybe Mick's professor was right. Maybe thought and consciousness did exist out there somewhere, relying on puppet bodies to offer tactile elements to our eternal selves. A scratch-and-sniff experience that traveled to the beyond.

If that was true, Carson had packed up their decades of memory and taken it with him when he left. He'd taken the parts of his life spent with Greta, too. Maybe all of it existed still outside of time and space.

The sun had arrived over the trees across the lake. Hobo had finished his business and had begun the fun of digging—frantic muddy paws excavating the shore of a lake she'd known before her own memories began.

Mick turned off the car. It was early still, but first light had finally arrived. He sat by the road staring at Kayla's house. The place looked beaten—curling chips of paint scattered on weathered wood siding, porch steps giving way to the incline of the yard. Kyle lived in that house. Mick didn't want to judge. The family did the best it could, he was sure. But Kooper wanted more for Kyle. College. Travel. All the things Mick had taken for granted. Mick had the impulse to drive away. But he couldn't.

Someone was awake, he realized. Smoke rose from a stone fire pit in the yard. Mick had seen open fires only when he was camping—and a couple of times when his granddad burned leaves in the fall. But it was only the beginning of summer—not the time for leaves. And somehow, he doubted that Kayla's folks planned to roast marshmallows in the yard.

After about fifteen minutes, Kayla's mother came onto the porch. When he'd seen her in her Sunday best, she hadn't shown the wear of the decade it had been since he first met her. But in a shapeless housedress, her hair under a net, she looked a thousand years old. He watched her walk down the crooked steps into the yard, pick up a random chicken that walked by and tuck it under her arm. It was over before he realized what she'd done. Her hand on the bird's throat, she'd twisted hard and fast, as if securing the lid on a jar. The movement was so deft and quick, his mind's eye had to backtrack for him to understand that the bird was dead.

"Jesus."

Before the hen's body had even stopped moving, she carried it to the fire by the side of the house. She pulled the feathers off in ragged handfuls and held the naked chicken high over the flame to singe the small feathers that remained. He watched her go back into the house, swinging the chicken like a purse by her side.

The violence of what he'd seen left him shaken. It was part of Kyle's everyday life. Part of his survival. Kooper was right. Kayla could have helped the little boy navigate from that world to an easier one. If Mick had tried, he could have helped Kayla.

"You okay, son?" Horace Ames, the man Kyle knew as his stepdad, had come up beside the car from behind.

"I wanted to see Kooper," Mick said. "But I didn't want to wake anyone."

"We're all up early. He's probably in the garage trying to get that car of his to run. Come on. Let's see if we can find him. Leave your car here." Then he added, "You'll want to stay clear of my wife."

Mick thought of the demise of the chicken and decided the man offered sound advice. He wondered how much Horace Ames knew about him, about his relationship with Kayla—his possible relationship to Kyle.

The garage opening was closed, but Mick saw through a side window that lights were on. Like the house, the building was in need of a coat of paint, but overall, it looked less ramshackle than the family's home. The older man took him around the building to a side door.

"I know what Kooper's doing, son," Mr. Ames said. "I'm not saying he's wrong." He stopped before opening the door to the shed. "But my wife loves that little boy. Not just her; I love the child like he's my own. You need to keep that in mind."

Mick didn't know what to say. Did that confirm it? Was Mick Kyle's real dad? "Sir," Mick said, "I'm not here to mess up anybody's world. I'm just trying to figure out what's going on."

Mr. Ames nodded, then reached out and turned the knob to the door to let Mick inside. Early rays of sun fell between loose boards onto sacks of chicken feed and a collection of farm tools. A bright, bare bulb poured light onto an old-model Impala in the center of the room. Mick had to squint to pick out Kooper's features as he leaned under the hood. He heard a faint undercurrent of sound. The churning, voice percussion of a rap song—its urgent punctuated cadence leaking out of headphones on Kooper's ears.

Mr. Ames went over to Kooper, tapped his shoulder, and pointed to Mick.

"Hey, man." Kooper took the headphones off. "Sorry, I didn't see you." Kooper looked at Horace Ames. He didn't say it, but the question was asked. *Did Mama see him?*

"Your mama's inside the house."

It occurred to Mick that the remaining members of the Grimes family were all lucky to have Horace Ames around. He didn't remember Kayla's real dad as a particularly reasonable man—and certainly not a warm one. Mr. Ames seemed to be both.

"Where's Kyle?" Kooper asked his stepdad.

"He's finishing a bowl of cereal. I'm driving him to that camp at the community center before I go to work." The man shook his head and smiled. "Science camp," he said, as if it was funny. "Remember. Don't upset your mother."

Kooper nodded. Then Mick found himself alone with Kayla's brother, and he had no idea what he intended to say. Even if he asked straight out, would Kooper tell him the truth? Maybe Kayla's brother had intended from the beginning to tell him, or, at the very least, to let Mick figure it out, but Mick needed to know—to really believe— that whatever Kooper told him came without an agenda.

"When I was showing Kyle how to bat," Mick said, making up a scenario—a crazy scenario, but he went with it anyway, "he leaned his head against me. After I left you, I found a few of his hairs on my shirt. Hairs have DNA." He was flying blind, lying his ass off. "Kyle isn't Kayla's brother, is he? He isn't your brother. He's your nephew. You obviously wanted me to figure this out. What was your plan, Kooper?"

"You check him against your DNA?"

"What do you think?" Mick said. His heel tapped wildly on the dirt floor of the shed. His heart felt as if it might fly out of his chest. He couldn't stop it. He couldn't stop anything that was happening. "You wanted me to begin wondering about it. You had to. You put it in motion. I'm not fucking stupid."

"I'm sorry, man," Kooper said. "I wasn't trying to trick you or nothing. It's just . . . That kid's got nobody who knows how to help him get out of . . . this." He gestured around him. "I wasn't thinking everything through. Honest to God. I just thought if I could get you curious. Interested. You might help him. He *ought* to be yours. Even after the way you treated her, she wanted him to be yours. If she could have changed that one thing, she would have."

Holy shit. Kyle *wasn't* his. His arms, his legs . . . everything felt liquid. If he'd dissolved and trickled through the rivets in the dirt floor, it wouldn't have surprised him.

"Who was she with, Kooper? Who was it?"

"Don't matter." He leaned, braced himself on the open hood of the car. "Old news."

"Try telling that to Kyle."

"I'm not telling Kyle shit." Kooper's head shot up. For the first time since Mick had first met him, he looked capable of doing harm.

"Then tell me," Mick said. "I'm not going to run to the kid. It's not my place. I know that. And damn it, Kooper, I don't want to ruin anybody else's life." So much time had passed and still, the thought of Kayla—gone—nearly broke him. He took a long breath. "I know I don't deserve it, but if you want me to help Kyle out, I need to know what happened after I split with Kayla."

Kooper's mouth formed a thin, hard line. He looked Mick in the eyes as if to assess how much he could trust the guy who mistreated his sister.

"Fucking piece of shit art teacher," Kooper said. His body relaxed suddenly, as if he'd expelled something toxic. "For a while, she was doing nothing but staring into empty space. Then she started drawing again. Drawing at home, staying after school in the art room. That piece of shit had been after her since she sat herself in that class the first day. She ignored that part, let him teach her his stuff. After you . . ."—his shoulders fell—"she stopped ignoring that other part. Started saying to herself, *What the hell? Why not?*"

"What did the guy do when she got pregnant?" Mick felt

numb asking. If he let himself picture it, believe it, he didn't know who he would hurt—maybe himself—but he'd have to destroy something. That wouldn't help Kayla. It wouldn't help Kyle.

"Said the right shit at first," Kooper said. "Said he'd help her—but she couldn't tell anybody. His job. His wife. It was about him, him, him." He slammed his open hand against the side of the car. Jangling metal rang hollow in Mick's ears. "Then one day, the motherfucker's gone. Just up and gone. Principal hired a substitute for the rest of the year. Somebody said that man mentioned a school in Tennessee that offered him a job. Nobody knew for sure."

"Your mama doesn't know about any of this." Mick thought of Kayla's mother outside the church, frantic that Mick was standing beside Kyle.

"Mama and Horace both think that boy's yours. Kayla never said a thing. Not to protect the guy, but because she was ashamed, I think. She made me promise not to tell it. So, yeah, Mama is scared to death you're gonna figure it out. Try to take Kyle."

"But you," Mick said, "you wanted me to think he was mine."

"Man, I just want him to have something. Get a shot at something for himself. I didn't have a scheme, if that's what you mean. I'm not some kind of Dr. Evil, planning everybody's life. I see Kyle and he looks lost. Thought you might help him find a way to not be lost. That's all . . . that's it."

"You think it's my fault?" Mick asked. "You think it went down like this because of the way I treated her?"

Kooper nodded. "Most of it. Yeah."

Mick couldn't think of any reasonable argument that might refute that notion. Not a single one.

* * *

The woman sat watching a morning news program. Greta tried to remember what her story was. Kate—that was her name—attended Greta's church, though Greta didn't know her well. Kate had only been involved in the congregation for about eight years. In her sixties and never married, the woman told Greta that she volunteered to share the blessings life had given her with others. Greta wished she would share her blessings in front of somebody else's television.

When the call had gone out that a "longtime parishioner" was in need of some assistance, the sign-up sheet filled before the Wednesday evening service ended. Greta hadn't known about a sign-up sheet, would have never made herself anyone's charity case. But Ayla had gone to the pastor with a well-meaning inquiry about people in the church who might be looking for work, and the result had been not an employee for Greta, but a potluck-style schedule of volunteers who were to arrive on her porch (a different one every day best Greta could tell), watch her television, and generally disrupt what small amount of peace she'd managed since Mattie's accident.

Greta took a sip of the coffee-flavored water the woman had brewed. Kate said she had to have her morning cup, but since the acid bothered her stomach, she kept it weak. Greta needed five minutes to herself—that's all there was to it. She'd been touched by the response from people at Calvary Baptist, but if this visiting business kept up, Greta reasoned she'd lose what was left of her mind.

"Don't get up, Mrs. Forsyth." Kate stood the minute Greta moved her chair to stand. "I'll be happy to get you anything you need. That's what I'm here for." The cheerful note of her voice, her sheer eagerness to please, made Greta feel ungrateful and guilty.

"So what do we want?" the woman asked.

Sweet Jesus, we want you to leave. "I was just going to the necessary room." Greta stood up. "I don't imagine you need to follow
me there."

"I can give you a hand. I don't mind," Kate said.

"No." The force of her gut response elicited a chirp of surprise from the startled Kate. "No," she said more calmly. "I can
manage fine, but thank you." She made her way out of the room
and hoped the woman wouldn't follow.

She didn't even have to use the bathroom. She only wanted
an excuse to get away by herself. She couldn't hear herself think
with that woman sitting there. And there was so much to think
about.

Mattie. She hadn't seen her friend in two days when Morty
had driven her home from that tree house. It had been his idea
to go by the hospital. She was so agitated. He asked her if it
would soothe her nerves to sit by her friend for a few minutes.
It had. The others had all gone for the night, and Morty was
kind enough to slip off for a cup of coffee while she sat and held
Mattie's hand.

Ayla and Rae planned to move Mattie out of the hospital in
the next day or so—into that house they'd rented in town. That
had to be a good sign, didn't it?

Greta felt better when she was with Mattie, but began to
worry about her friend again the minute she left her. Greta
wanted to hear Mattie say something. Anything. She wanted
to know that she was still in there. That she wasn't scared or
in pain. Helpless. Mattie, the strongest, most sensible person
Greta knew, had been rendered helpless. That's how Greta felt,
too. Helpless.

She could go stay at the lake. Elaine had called more than
once. Greta knew that her daughter-in-law thought she'd simply
reverted back into their feud. And she had to some degree. But
her real problem was the overwhelming sadness she felt, the

anger with herself for not listening to Carson and, at least, embracing the boy.

That evening at the lake, she'd allowed herself to indulge in a moment of thinking only the future mattered. When Wallace had arrived, it brought that fantasy to a painful end. She wasn't sure why, exactly. It would have happened without him eventually. Decades were lost. She couldn't make up for them. Carson was lost. Being with her grandson could only bring all those missing years into bright relief. With hot shame, she remembered Mick's visit as a small boy. How could she have been so cruel to her own son? Her grandson? She'd allowed pride and resentment—and loneliness, too, she guessed—to turn her into something hard that day.

In the absence of all that lost time, prideful stubbornness seemed to be the only thing she had left. She'd been content to stay closed off from Carson's family. Over time, she'd settled into that life, and she hadn't been unhappy. Feeling her losses made her unhappy, and not feeling anything—well, it was better.

But even if she shut off her feelings about Michael, other losses remained. If only Mattie could come back.

She thought of what she'd be doing if Mattie were with her. They'd be checking the plants in the small garden out back. Ayla and Rae had been so distracted, Greta was sure it had gone to weeds. The girls did feed the chickens, she knew, but when they moved to town, the next day or the day after, she'd have to work out something. She couldn't imagine sending members of the church brigade out to the coop.

If Mattie was there, she would have made a decent pot of coffee and the two of them would be in the kitchen, talking or not talking. It didn't matter.

She closed the door to her bedroom and sat down on the bed. Even though it was early yet, Kate had closed all the windows and turned on the air conditioner. Greta felt cold and sealed off from the world. Maybe that wasn't a bad thing. The one problem with vowing to remain self-contained was Morty. She hadn't been flustered over a man since before she married Taylor.

Morty. She ran his name through her thoughts just to hear it and found herself smiling without cause. *Stop making a fool of yourself, Greta Forsyth.* The state she was in. He was being charitable. That was all. Driving her home, and a few days later coming out to make dinner for her.

When he'd arrived unexpectedly, that nosy Thea Meyer, the first to sign up at the church, had just left, and Greta was madder than fleas that these people were going to be traipsing in and out of her house. But before the dust from Thea's car had settled, she'd heard another car coming down the drive.

"Didn't call," he said, "because I knew you'd tell me not to bother."

"How'd you know that?" she asked him.

He stopped unloading a bag of groceries he'd brought into her kitchen. "I know your type. Been a sucker for a beautiful, stubborn woman my whole life." He was already busy with water for the spaghetti. "Forgot to buy oregano, darlin'. You find me some?"

She went to the cabinet. It took her ten minutes to pick up each jar and get the label close enough to read. He didn't get impatient. Didn't hover like a parent overseeing a child. He simply went on making the sauce and thanked her when she handed him the jar.

Don't be a fool, Greta.

"Are you all right, Miss Greta?" Kate called from the other room.

Miss Greta. She wasn't ninety, for heaven's sake. She was less than a decade older than *Miss Kate* out there—and, with the exception of the woman's 20/20 vision, Greta was in better shape, too. Greta let herself make an ugly face at the closed door. She had to let it out before she returned to the den and made nice again. And she would make an effort. In spite of her irritation, Greta knew that the woman did not deserve all her mean thoughts. Kate had offered her time and her kindness, and it wasn't the poor woman's fault if Greta was simply contrary.

"I'm fine," Greta called back. "Just a minute." She *did* need to go to the bathroom, after all.

Thank goodness for that, she thought, a few more minutes to herself.

When Greta returned to the living room, the television morning show had gone off and a game show blared from the TV. Not one of the game shows that she liked, but some new thing that had some self-satisfied contestant answering multiple-choice questions for money. The show moved at the pace of a caterpillar on a branch.

"Lyndon Johnson!" Kate yelled at the television. "I can't believe that man doesn't know that."

Greta heard the car. Her pulse went into double time. Teenagers got all jittery over things like that. Greta was no teenager.

Kate was up, staring out the window. "You got a visitor, Mrs. Forsyth. A visitor in a *very* nice car."

Greta was glad she'd taken care to put on a little lipstick that morning. If she leaned in near the mirror, she could manage to get face powder in the right place, too. After the *green* incident, she'd taken special care to choose her clothes more deliberately. She was reasonably certain she looked presentable.

"Mornin', ladies," Morty said after Kate let him in. "I'm Morton Connell," he said to Kate.

"Kate Madsen," she said. "I go to church with Mrs. Forsyth."

"Very nice to meet you," he said.

Greta saw the dark imprint of his shape moving through her den toward the kitchen. She heard the rustle of bags as he put things on the counter.

"I stopped early at the produce stand and bought too much," he called out from the other room. "Thought I'd come and share the bounty."

"Well," she said, hearing him come into the room. "I appreciate that."

"Would it be rude if I asked you to let me steal Mrs. Forsyth away from you?" Morty asked Kate. "I've gone and bought an overabundance of cucumbers from the produce stand out on Highway 109," he said, "and I thought she might lend some of her expertise with putting up some sweet pickles."

"No," Kate said, "I certainly don't mind. But I'd be happy to help out. I use my grandmama's recipe for bread and butter pickles and . . ."

"I appreciate the offer," Greta spoke up. "But I'm afraid I'm going to impose on Mr. Connell here for a few small chores in exchange for my kitchen secrets. I'm sure you have things you need to get done. I hear you're just about the busiest woman in the congregation."

"I do find myself running from dawn to dark," Kate said.

"Why don't you take off," Morty chimed in. "I'll take good care of our lady here."

To Greta's amazement, Kate began to gather her things.

After she left, they both moved into the kitchen. It seemed a natural place to be. It was where she'd always sat and talked with Mattie in the mornings.

Morty poured himself a cup of Kate's weak coffee and joined her at the table. The light scent of aftershave mixed with the laundry smell of his clothes. For a man living alone, he knew how to put himself together. She liked that.

"If your church friend's pickles are as bad as her coffee, we did ourselves a favor in getting her out of your kitchen." He got up and poured the contents of his own cup and hers into the sink, then set about making a fresh pot. "She'd be the ruin of some good cucumbers—that's for sure."

"Thea Meyer had a sour disposition," Greta said, "but she did make a good cup of coffee."

Morty seemed at ease in her kitchen, finding what he needed after opening a cabinet or two.

"I should be more charitable toward their efforts," Greta said. "I'm alone and they're trying to help. It's a generous thing."

"Appreciating the effort and enjoying the company are two different things," he said, sitting back down. "In fact," he said, as if something had just occurred to him, "if I'm getting underfoot, you got to give me the word on that."

"No, no." She sounded too eager, took a moment to breathe. "I'm comfortable around you."

"The both of us," Morty said, "we're too mature in life to dance around things the way we used to. I'm not showing up out here because of some sign-up sheet. I'm here because I enjoy your company. You seem to enjoy mine. That changes, you just tell me. Okay?"

"You'll be the first to know."

The coffeemaker gurgled, signaling the last of the water dripping through. He got up to pour and brought two cups back to the table. She'd taken a sip or two of the blessedly strong brew before it occurred to her that he'd put just the right amount of milk in hers—exactly as she liked it—without having to ask.

"Have you given more thought to your family situation?"

She wouldn't talk about that. Not to him. Not yet. He was Elaine's friend, and she didn't want to hear him make a case for some grand reconciliation.

"I've been concerned with more immediate issues," she said. "I've been a little worried about the garden out back."

"Well," he said, letting go of his inquiry, "you're talking to the right man. I do like a problem that can be solved. I was thinking we might ride in and visit your friend in the hospital again."

"I would like to check in on Mattie before they move her," she said.

"Since you got your going-to-town clothes on now, why don't we do that first," he said. "Then we can come back and tackle the garden."

She wondered why he was willing to do so much for her—with her. Pride wouldn't let her ask. "What about your pickles?"

"Maybe tomorrow," he said, taking their coffee cups to the sink. "If you've got the time."

Then he was up, helping her up, both of them moving toward the next thing.

Nine

The call to Wallace would be part of a compromise. Elaine negotiated with Carson, the dialogue occurring inside the half sleep she'd come to consider part of her night's rest. Maybe Carson was talking to her or maybe she knew his soul well enough to provide both sides without gaming her own position. Either way, she came to an agreement. A decision. Linnie had been gone less than a week, and already Elaine was going stir crazy. She would get in touch with Wallace because she needed a real friend, and all other options came in a distant second. In return, she would drive out to see Greta and make an effort that the woman couldn't ignore as easily as a phone call.

She knew from talking to Morty that Greta had been making do with help from him and some of the ladies from her church, but the situation needed a more permanent solution, and she felt resolved to find one.

Carson's blessing settled on her in the form of real sleep that lasted for maybe an hour. She woke with a warm body pressed against her and turned to find Hobo curled at her hip.

Three hours later, Wallace's small SUV turned into the driveway below the cabin. He wasn't alone. They'd agreed that Jason would drive him over on the way to a meeting in Charlotte, and Elaine would take him back to Rockingham after their visit so she could see his house.

"Elaine, this is Jason."

"Great to meet you," she said, extending her hand.

"Oh, come on," Jason said, pulling her into a hug. "We're all past the formal stuff."

They stood on the landing. Jason's easy smile held no demons. He'd had an easier time of things than Wallace. Either that or he was quite the actor. His smooth skin had the glow of care and vanity, but he had incredibly kind eyes.

"Come on in," she said. "I made some muffins. A box mix, I'm afraid; I'm not much of a cook. But they're warm."

"You take after your mother." Wallace smiled. "Every time I ate here, I think we had Chef Boyardee. Your dad ate it like it was prime rib."

"Unless Linnie was around," she added. "Then we'd get roast chicken with risotto . . . all the good stuff. She's off on tour with the company again. Can you believe it?"

"She was always the most glamorous thing," Wallace said. "If I could jump into her life for five minutes, I would. What a ride."

"Speaking of rides," Jason said, taking advantage of the segue, "I've got a meeting in two hours and there's no way to predict traffic, so I should be off. But I did want to meet you and see the famous tree house. This is every kid's dream, to grow up Swiss Family Robinson style."

"My folks certainly had a vision," she said. "For me, it was all I knew, so it was normal."

"Lucky you." Jason spread out an arm, indicating that the entire vista belonged to her. "My normal was a split-level three blocks from a Stop-N-Go."

"You were always ten minutes from a slushy," Wallace added.

"There was that," Jason agreed.

It was part of a shtick they'd developed, the way couples do. Elaine felt both happy for and envious of Wallace. She was the sad remainder of an act that had played for thirty years.

After Jason left, she and Wallace settled with coffee and muffins at the dining table just off the den. The morning light hitting the lake reflected back up at them, adding a bright wash to the wood-paneled walls.

"Is Mick here?"

She shook her head. "He's gone more than he's here. He has always had a hard time staying still, but it's been worse since Carson's been gone."

The rattle and snap of sails on the lake distracted them. As if to illustrate her conversation about her son, a sailboat came in close to shore and tacked back out. It bent to the wind, respectful of the power, but used the element to its own ends as well.

"You must feel amputated," Wallace said, going to the heart of things as he always had.

"With all the phantom sensations."

"Do you want to talk or do you want to be distracted?" Stray pieces of his fine brown hair lingered near his eyes and he seemed not to notice.

She reached up and brushed it back without thinking. She used to trim his hair for him back in the day, an act that struck her suddenly as a very intimate thing to have done. No wonder Carson had felt excluded.

"What do you think I should do?" she asked. "How do I turn into something different after all this time?"

He seemed to consider the question, to be weighing some decision. "Greta was sitting at your table when I got here the other night. That's an extraordinary accomplishment for both of you, and I set it all back."

"It was pretty tenuous from the start. Don't blame yourself."

"I think you might move on better if you make some kind of peace with her," he said, "and toward that end, I'm ready to do what I should have done years ago. My life is mostly out now. I might as well take this one last step."

"What about your mother? Do you plan to tell her, too?"

"I'd rather not. If she goes to her grave thinking I'm unlucky with women, it would be better for all of us. But that's a chance I can take. I used to have my entire life on the line. My work, my neighborhood, and my family were all here. That's not the case any longer. I'm not that vulnerable anymore."

"Are you sure you want to do this?"

He took a bite of the muffin and washed it down with her strong coffee. "I didn't see you and Carson for so long, Elaine. It was easy not to think about what keeping my confidence cost the two of you. What it cost Mick. I'm sorry. Let me make it as right as possible now."

It was true. Their lives could have been different. Better? For Carson. Maybe for Mick. Should she be angry with Wallace about that? If she was honest with herself, she had to admit she'd been happier with the Greta stalemate, letting Carson have his visits with his mother. Greta hadn't cared for Elaine before the Wallace trouble. It would have never been easy.

Carson had made the decision to keep Wallace's secrets, but Elaine could have petitioned her friend at any point over the years and she chose not to. Any anger she chose to direct at Wallace could be turned back on herself. Did posthumous resolution count for anything? She hoped so.

"As long as you understand that it's still taking a real chance,"

Elaine said. "I can't predict what Greta will say or not say to your mom, your old church."

"I'll ask her to be discreet. But if she feels she can't, then I'll suggest she give me time to talk to my mother. I think she'll at least be that reasonable."

"Maybe." Elaine didn't know which Greta they'd be encountering—the one who screamed at a four-year-old child or the one who bought her a swirl cone.

Wallace seemed determined to find out.

Joy ordered a grilled cheese. She sat across the booth from him at Merle's. Time in the sun had tanned her skin and lightened her hair, the dark curls showing flashes of auburn from certain angles. The low V of her T-shirt was enough to set him off, so he looked beyond her and made himself concentrate on the cash register and the large black dog that lounged on the floor beneath it. Shifting in his seat, he felt the torn vinyl scrape along the denim of his jeans.

"BLT?" Jake, Gabbie's son, brought their order to the booth.

"Mine," Mick said.

Jake put the sandwich in front of Mick and gave Joy her plate, melted cheese oozing onto the chips she'd ordered on the side.

Gabbie's son was manning the grill while Gabbie dealt with a problem down at the gas docks. She'd been yelling at some workman beside a pump when they arrived in the boat. Gabbie was nice enough, but Mick missed her dad, the guy the place was named after.

Mick had brought Kayla to Merle's a few times. They didn't go out to local places often because she didn't like the stares they got from older people with issues about a white boy dating a mixed-race girl. But the first time they'd gone to Merle's, a woman said something to her husband about what the world was coming to, and Merle suggested she eat her breakfast down on the dock if she didn't like the clientele inside his place. He was a gruff cuss, but Mick had always appreciated the way he'd made them feel at ease.

"What's on your mind?" Joy sipped her diet Sprite and fiddled with the salt.

"I was just thinking about the old guy who used to run the place."

He felt guilty reminiscing about Kayla while Joy was right in front of him, but he couldn't seem to stop. Kayla had been on his mind a lot since he'd arrived in Lowfield, but after his visit to see Kooper, he thought of her constantly. A weird cocktail of emotions kept playing with his mind—relief that he wasn't a father, but guilt and profound sadness at what Kayla had gone through. Then there was a strange hint of disappointment that Kyle wasn't his kid.

One thing had been clear to him after his conversation with Kooper—he wanted to call Joy. He'd been telling himself that he wouldn't see her, but he'd changed his mind. He wasn't going back to Rhode Island to resume his place-holding life. If Kyle had been his, he *would* have stepped up. That thought alone blew him away, gave him a valid reason to trust himself a little. And with that small bit of hope, he felt the stirrings of old ambitions. Maybe it was time to think about grad school again.

"I was thinking," Joy said, "that you should come see me for a football game this fall."

"Better not make any offers," he said. "You might regret it after you get there and guys start to fall all over you."

"I don't know . . . I was thinking about making you a real offer." She held her sandwich halfway between the plate and her mouth. For a second she remained bold, smiling and looking into his eyes, but then she broke character. Still smiling, she looked down and actually turned a little red.

He tried to come up with anything other than sex she might be talking about, but looking at her, the meaning was pretty clear.

"Where'd that come from?" He grinned, leaned toward her.

She shrugged. "I don't know," she said. "I was just thinking that it might be a good idea for me to . . ." She fired a new shade of red and didn't seem to be able to take her eyes off her plate.

"Joy . . ." He shifted again in his seat. His jeans were getting genuinely uncomfortable. "Look, we've only hung out a few times. Don't get me wrong; I'd be lying if I said it wasn't on my mind, but you don't need to do anything to get me to stay interested."

"I'm not." She looked up. Her color had settled, and she seemed to own herself again. "Listen, I was only thinking that I'm going to get to college and before long . . . I'm one of like four people I know who haven't already—and two of them are real freaks. I just haven't dated anybody who seemed special enough. And I didn't want to get talked about—like that. But when I get to college, I'm going to be the one feeling like a freak. I like you, Micky. I've liked you for a really long time."

He didn't know what the hell to say. She'd reasoned it out so that he almost felt like it would be an asshole move to tell her no. Shit, the last thing he wanted to do was turn her down. But there'd been so much crap churned up from the past in a week's time—all of the Greta, Kayla, and Kyle business mixed in with getting through his dad's death. He'd almost let his libido call the shots with Laurie, and that would have been a huge mistake. He didn't want to screw up with Joy. In fact, he wanted a real shot at getting it right with Joy.

"We've got time this summer." He put his hand out and took hers. "Let's see where this goes. You make me believe I can actually be a decent person. That I can be happy. I haven't felt those things in a while. I'm all in with the idea of being with you—in that way. I just want to make it right. I haven't always done important things the right way."

She looked relieved. He felt it, too, glad that something was on the agenda about the two of them—something more than flirting and playing around—but that it didn't have to be settled in five minutes.

"We can start with a serious make-out session?" She locked eyes with him, raised an eyebrow. "How about Landers' Island? You know where that is?"

He shifted again, managed a nod. Jake walked by and Mick caught his attention. "I can take the check anytime," he said.

The guy looked at their half-eaten food, shrugged, then pulled the ticket out of his apron and laid it on the table.

Elaine slowed so that Wallace could get a good look at the alpacas. The caretaker, Joe Timmer, had a posthole digger and worked down the drive a ways.

"I like these things." Elaine put the car in idle, looked at the grazing livestock. "They seem unexpectedly sweet."

"I kind of want to take one home," Wallace said. "I like them, too, but I can see where people might be conflicted."

"Greta says they have evil eyes." Elaine wished she'd brought Hobo along. He liked the alpacas. For that matter, he liked Greta. Go figure. "I think they fall somewhere between threatening and muppetish."

"Like clowns," he said. "Survey any ten people on clowns. Five say hilarious, and five say call an exorcist. Will that guy yell at us if we get out to take a closer look?"

"No." Elaine turned off the motor. "He's a nice guy—and this road is on Greta's land. I can't promise that Greta won't yell at us."

Timmer came over to greet them. "Hey again," he said. "I keep tellin' Mr. Morales we ought to put signs up on the highway and charge admission."

"Mr. Timmer, this is my friend, Mr. Jamison. Mr. Timmer looks after the alpacas."

Joe Timmer leaned over the fence and propped his elbow on the top of a post and extended his other hand. "Nice to meet you."

"Mr. Morales is an actor," she told Wallace. "He spends his time between here and Atlanta."

"Oh, I know. Mama's filled me in." Wallace turned toward Joe Timmer. "Your boss is quite the local celebrity. Mama also tells me that Greta is refusing to sell her land, even though Mr. Morales has been 'nice as can be' and offered her more than it's worth."

"It is a fair offer." Timmer looked a little lost, as if he'd missed a section of the conversation and didn't know if that was the proper response. And of course, he had. He'd missed a quarter century of dialogue between Greta and Tilda Jamison.

"We should go," Elaine said. "Greta's probably figured out that we're coming by now. I see Morty's car there."

Elaine had noticed the absence of Morty around his house. She'd guessed that Greta was the reason. Seeing his car confirmed it. She didn't know how she felt about Morty and Greta—together. She'd relied on Morty since arriving at the cabin with Carson. Greta seemed to be stealing away a vital friend and advocate. Elaine thought of what Greta had been like when she and Carson first got together. Greta had been a too-young widow herself at that time. Elaine knew she had dominated Carson's time. His thoughts. Maybe turnabout really *was* fair play.

"Good to see you again," Timmer said to Elaine. "You know, I saw that those families moved out of the green houses. I know Mr. Morales was raising a zoning stink, but you know, he wasn't going to push that one. He's just trying to get her to negotiate."

"They didn't move out for that reason," Elaine told him. "Both families are trying to take care of Mattie after the stroke. They thought that would be easier in town."

Timmer seemed relieved. "Well, you know I'm happy to help Mrs. Forsyth out if she needs anything. It's no secret that she and Mr. Morales have their problems—hell, I had to chase those dang things through the woods to round 'em up."

Wallace gave her a questioning look. She'd have fun filling him in on Greta's antics and the subsequent trip to the Roseville police station.

"I don't really blame her for being mad," Mr. Timmer continued, "and I don't have a thing against her. I'm happy to be a good neighbor."

"Thank you," Elaine told him.

It was becoming increasingly likely that it might, indeed, take a village with Greta.

Morty walked by with a basket in his arms. Greta threw a handful of weeds in as he paused in front of her. Up close, she could still make out the difference between a plant and a weed, but she could also do a lot by feel.

"Think we 'bout got it, darlin'." The garden had suffered considerable neglect since Mattie's fall. Morty took the basket over to a pile they'd collected on a cement landing near the storage shed. The weeds would dry in the sun and then they could burn them, along with other yard waste. Greta found great satisfaction in yard work. She always had. That was something she'd shared with Mattie.

Earlier, she'd gone to visit her friend. Morty had arrived at first light and he'd driven her into town. "She's saying more words." Ayla had gotten her up to speed on Mattie's progress in the two days since Greta had been by. "She's able to sit up for longer now. We're going to get her back, Mrs. Forsyth. I just know we will." The girl's words had sounded forced and, despite the pronouncement, profoundly unsure.

As Greta sat beside her friend, Mattie had moved her hand

and touched Greta's wrist with her fingers. Greta leaned in close. "Didn't . . ."—Mattie paused, gathering her thoughts and her strength, it seemed—" . . . want . . . to . . . leave."

Greta didn't know if Mattie referred to the illness that took her away immediately or the subsequent exodus by her family from Greta's land. Either way, Greta wanted to reassure her. "Don't you worry about that," Greta said. "We're both going to be all right. You don't fret about a thing. You hear me?"

"Blue . . ." Mattie stopped. Greta saw half her face soften into a familiar smile. The other side disobeyed and kept neutral. "Blue . . . lights . . . for . . . me?"

Greta smiled, but felt an uneasy pull inside her. "Not yet, Mattie." *Dear Lord, please. Not yet.*

W as that a car?" Morty called back to her from a flowerbed close to the house.

"I don't know." Greta's ears were keen. She listened, thought she heard the thump of a door closing, then another. "You might be right." She sat at a small table at the edge of her patio with a glass of Morty's favorite concoction, iced tea and lemonade. He said the drink was named after the golfer Arnold Palmer. "Let me know if it's another volunteer from the church. They should have put that business on hold after I called them, but you never know."

It had been a week or so since Ayla and Rae had moved into town with their families. One night, when a bad storm blew through, Morty insisted on staying the night. He slept in Mattie's room and told Greta it was more for his peace of mind than for hers. She'd spent the other nights by herself, her cell phone next to the house phone and both within easy reach. She didn't like it much, being so removed from another living person, but every morning, Morty would show up bright and early.

She knew they couldn't keep up the situation forever. Even

so, she'd avoided taking Elaine's calls. Each time a call came in, she felt as if a trapdoor opened underneath her, a sense of loss so overwhelming that the only way to close the door was to close her thoughts off from her grandson—and his mother. If the woman thought it was the old business making Greta keep her distance, so be it. It was, in part. That Jamison boy *had* walked right up the steps to that tree house, just like he belonged. That part was easier to think about.

"I'll go in and check to see who it is," Morty said. "Need more of your drink?"

"No, thank you," she said. "I'm fine." She could see smudges of dirt from the garden on her khaki yard pants. She'd asked Morty to root through a stack in her closet and find where Mattie had put them away. Then he'd helped her organize her everyday clothes in the drawer so that she could easily pick what to wear every day. She didn't know why she hadn't done that before. Mattie had just always laid something out and Greta got lazy over time, she guessed.

She heard the back door again and saw Morty's shape returning to her. He sat in a chair beside her. "We have ourselves some visitors," he said.

"Why didn't you bring them out back?"

She waited and heard him take a breath before he spoke. "It's Elaine," he told her. "Elaine and Wallace Jamison."

The trapdoor again, only it felt more like water underneath her than empty space. It seemed like she might be drowning. The scarce air pressed tight around her lungs.

"If you could ask them to leave, I'd be grateful." Used to be, she didn't mind saying her piece to anyone, anytime. But she wasn't up to the task and she knew it. She also didn't want to make a spectacle of herself in front of Morty. She hadn't worried about that kind of thing for a while either.

"I'll do what you want, darlin', but this situation is going to hang in the air until you get it settled. Elaine said she and Wallace got something important to talk about."

"She seem upset?" Greta asked. "You think something's happened to Michael?" Unexpected fear took hold.

"Far as I know, Mick is fine," Morty said. "She doesn't seem that kind of upset. Just wants to talk, seems like." He paused.

She knew he had always liked Elaine and had gotten more fond of her in the weeks that had passed. Morty was no fool. She didn't know what to think anymore.

"You say the word and I'll tell 'em to go," he said. "But I know it's been under your skin since the other day at the lake."

"I'll talk to them," she said.

Morty put his hand on hers and offered a small squeeze. Even with everything else happening, she felt a jolt in her pulse when he did that. Wonders never ceased.

Morty stood up, and she watched his tall frame blur into a shadow as he went to tell Elaine and Wallace Jamison that, against all odds, Greta Forsyth was willing to hear them out.

I don't understand," Greta told Wallace. She'd known the boy since he was a baby, couldn't imagine that what he was telling her was true. How could it be that he felt about other men the way Taylor had felt about her? The way Carson felt about Elaine. She knew about that sort of thing, but she had never known anyone personally. Or she thought she hadn't. No. The two of them must have cooked up a story. Although, for the life of her, she couldn't understand why he'd go along with this one.

She had moved closer to the house, and Morty sat by her on the glider. Elaine and Wallace flanked them in the patio chairs. She couldn't make out their expressions, but she could hear their voices perfectly. She simply couldn't believe *what* she was hearing.

"Is that the length you will go to?" She addressed Elaine. "You'd put this man up to this level of theater in order to squirm out of what has obviously never ended between you two."

"Mrs. Forsyth." Wallace pulled her attention back in his direction. "This is not a charade. I spent many years trying to convince myself it wasn't true and many more hiding it from almost everyone else. Elaine and Carson both kept the confidence for me. I promise you, Elaine hasn't orchestrated any of what I'm telling you. I offered to come here today. I should have offered long ago."

"You were married?" It came out as a question. She wasn't sure of anything anymore.

"If men who married women automatically became straight, a lot of Hollywood types would be very happy about now," Wallace said.

Greta could tell he was trying to make a joke, but she'd never felt less like laughing.

"My marriage couldn't survive who I really was," he went on, "and I regret that I put a good woman through the ordeal of it—trying to fit where I didn't belong."

She thought of Wallace's mother. Tilda didn't know. Couldn't possibly know. She would have been a big part of his silence over the years. "Your mother?" Greta managed.

He shook his head. "My sisters are the only ones in town, other than Elaine, Mick, and now you two. You know my mother. She's not open to things outside of her opinions. Never has been. I can ask you not to impose that on her at this point in her life, but obviously, I can't stop you if you decide to tell her."

"Carson knew this," she said. It had just occurred to her what that meant. "Carson knew and didn't tell me." She didn't know what to do with the anger that brought. What could she do with those feelings when he wasn't alive to explain himself? "Why didn't he tell me?" She turned to Elaine.

"We talked about it." Elaine had more softness in her voice than Greta would have expected. "I offered to tell Wallace that we couldn't keep it from you. Carson said that would be selfish, to change every aspect of Wallace's life—his job, his friends, his family—by forcing him to be open about it before he was ready. Carson thought he could convince you to trust him, to believe him. What he didn't factor in was the degree to which you distrusted me."

"He thought I would run to Tilda?" She was surely drowning. It was all too much.

"You two haven't been on good terms for a long time," Elaine said. "You saw her every week at church. Can you honestly say you wouldn't have slipped up, gotten angry with something she said and just blurted it out? I'm not saying that as an insult. I don't know if I could have stopped myself."

Greta wanted the woman to stop talking. She wanted everyone to leave her alone.

"Carson was upset with me." Elaine kept going. "I relied on Wallace too much in ways that I should have relied on Carson. But Carson didn't want Wallace to be used as a weapon any more than I did. Carson thought you would come around. I don't think he ever gave up on that."

"And you're saying I failed him."

"No, Greta, I'm not. You're still breathing, and you still have a grandson."

Greta thought of Mick's profile backlit by the light over the lake. And she thought of the regret that followed her realization that the boy carried Carson's blood—her blood. Always had. She hadn't imagined it could get worse. What had Elaine hoped to accomplish? Bringing this to her now?

"I need for you both to leave me now," Greta said. Her voice sounded hollow, even to herself. She wanted everyone to go away. Even Morty. If the breath she took in left her as well, it would be nothing but a blessing.

"Please, just go." She turned to Morty beside her. "You, too. Please."

Ten

A few days after his lunch with Joy, Mick dropped Kyle off at the Ames' house. Horace Ames came outside to greet him at the bottom of the porch steps.

"Is Kooper around?" Mick asked.

Horace shook his head. "They hired him up at the drugstore. Stocking shelves and inventory. He'll move up to cashier if he does a good job with that."

"That's good," Mick said. He looked past Horace to where Kyle had just run into the house. "That kid loves to fish. I let him drive the boat a little. I hope that's okay. I was right beside him the whole time."

"That's fine," Horace said. He nodded, offered a smile as if it was better than fine. "Good for the boy to know how to handle a boat."

"Is Mrs. Ames okay with me spending time with him?"

"She's nervous," he said. "But she appreciated the letter you wrote. Feels better having something signed saying you claim no rights to the little fellow. I told her we'd do better to work with you on this. You want to make a legal case, you can, but if we work something out . . ." Kyle's stepdad was nervous, too.

Mick wondered if Kooper ever planned to tell them that Mick had no rights to Kyle at all. If they found out, it would come from Kayla's brother. Mick made a promise to Kayla, wherever she was, that he would keep her secret. He made her a promise that he would try to help her boy.

"Good to see you, Mr. Ames," he said, putting the end punctuation on an uncomfortable exchange. "I told Kyle he could come over this weekend if he wants. I'll pick him up after his game and take him out again if that's okay."

"Be good for him to have something to look forward to after a ball game." Horace Ames made a face. "You understand that I told him he could quit." It seemed important to him for Mick to understand this. "It was his decision. He said he wants to finish out the season and leave it be next year. I think he don't want to get called a quitter on top of everything else."

Mick nodded. He didn't know what else to say. At least with Kooper grown up and a good stepdad in the picture, the kid had a posse of people trying to make his life better. That was more than Kayla ever counted on. He found himself wishing again that Horace had been around when she was young.

"I'll give you a call before the weekend," he said, "and make sure it's still okay."

Back in his car, he turned away from town, toward the back road that would take him to the produce stand. Life was falling into place. He had the summer with Joy, the summer to think about what he wanted to do. A Lowfield-Georgetown relationship. Hell, his parents had done it. And for the first time, the idea of grad school got him jazzed. He knew sailboats inside and out. Maybe his time working on them wasn't wasted after all. Maybe he could design them. Why not? He might even end up getting a degree at Georgetown. Like father, like son.

* * *

Joy stood alone behind an arrangement of okra and green beans. She wore the same midriff top with the ruffles that she'd worn the first time he saw her at Benny's. At the end of the table, small containers of strawberries rose on a display like spectators in a miniature stadium.

Joy glanced up as he pulled over. Something was wrong. She didn't meet his eyes at first, and when she did connect with him, it wasn't the face of someone happy to see him. Two days before—alone on Landers' Island—they'd both been pretty damn happy, and he'd talked to her on the phone the day before, making plans to ride out. What the hell could have happened?

"Hey." He greeted her as if he hadn't noticed her expression. Maybe it had nothing to do with him.

"Hey." She returned his greeting without enthusiasm.

Dead heat consumed the air. He looked at the splintered wood of the produce stand and imagined a spontaneous spark igniting the structure within seconds. A glorious explosion of flames with the smell of roasted berries thick in the air. He'd pull Joy out, console her, be the hero.

"We need to talk," she said. She was without guile.

"Okay," he said. "What did I do?" He went behind the stand. She sat down on one stool and motioned for him to do the same on another.

"The kid," she said. "The one that's supposed to be that girl's little brother . . ."

"Kyle."

"When were you going to tell me he's your kid?"

Up close, he could tell she'd been crying.

"Who's been talking to you about this?" He felt a small panic rising. This wasn't on his radar. "Teresa." Teresa had been so proud of keeping her fucking mouth shut.

Joy shook her head. "Laurie."

Mick thought of his last image of Laurie, through the front window of the hardware store, eyes shooting daggers through the glass. He'd refused to screw Laurie in the office. Now she was screwing him in her own way.

"I didn't know that he was Kayla's until recently," he said, trying to decide what to say—how much to say. "I had no idea."

"Apparently, other people have had that idea since the kid was born. Even Teresa knew and never said anything. I'm furious about that. I'm such an idiot."

"You're not an idiot," he said. "And I'm not . . ." Jesus. What was he supposed to say to her? "Joy, this isn't something that has anything to do with us."

"The hell it doesn't." There was a ragged scrape in her voice. She was angry. Sad. Helpless. He was on a first-name basis with all of those himself.

Before he could decide on a response, a car drove up and pulled over. Joy put on a cheerful face to greet the arrival. A heavyset man who looked to be in his sixties got out of a new-model Ford. He helped an older woman get out of the passenger side.

"Sugar," the man said, addressing Joy, "have you got any honeydew? Miss Effie here is just wild about honeydew, and I done promised her we'd find some before we get to Richmond." His voice sounded paternal, but his eyes scanned Joy without apology.

Mick stood up and moved to stand beside her. *Should she be out here alone?* He was even beginning to think like an adult. It wasn't fair that his adolescent years wouldn't let go of him.

"None of the melons are in yet," Joy told him. "It'll be a week or two. I'm sorry." She smiled at the old woman, and Miss Effie returned a vacant gaze.

"Well, that's too bad," he said, looking over the strawberries. "Maybe berries, Miss Effie?" he asked without looking up.

The old lady had wandered behind the stand and showed no sign of stopping there. She headed toward the open field with a determined gait.

"Sir," Mick said, "the lady just took off that way. I'm not sure where she's going."

"Dagnabit, Miss Effie." He took off after her.

"Joy," he said, taking the moment to dive back in. "Tell me what bothers you the most. I don't know what I'm supposed to apologize for here."

"I don't want an apology," she said. "We weren't far enough along for you to owe me anything, I guess. But what we were was new and it was good—and now it's broken."

"Jesus, Joy." He couldn't believe the conversation. "Nothing has to be broken." He paused. "If I'd told you . . . ?"

She shook her head. "It would have saved us the effort, I guess."

"Why?"

"I live in this place, Micky. I'm not a shallow person, but this is too much—even for me. I can't walk around and wonder if everybody's feeling sorry for me because I'm in love with that boy who had that kid with that girl when they were teenagers."

"Had that black kid with that black girl." The anger was creeping up on him. What decade was she living in, anyway?

"Don't put words in my mouth," she said. "It's not that. I'm not like that." She didn't seem to know where to go with her protest. "But this is a really small place, Mick. If you have a kid—anybody's kid—running around here . . . I don't think I'm strong enough for that."

"Is it the idea of me having a kid, or everyone thinking I have a kid?" he asked.

"Unless the whole thing could just go away," she said, "they're the same. Don't you see that?"

The man was returning from the field with Miss Effie in tow.

"Did you find me some honeydew, Walter?" she asked as they reached the stand.

"No, ma'am," he said. "We got to make do with strawberries."

She nodded, not appearing to be overly disappointed.

"You get on in the car and let me pay," he said, "but leave the door open or you'll suffocate." This time, Miss Effie did as she was told. As he paid for two containers of strawberries, he leaned over the table and confided in Mick and Joy, "Cain't never tell what she's going to do. That's what you git when you marry a woman for her money, I guess."

With that, he took his sack from Joy and walked away.

For a moment, it seemed as if they'd stepped out of their discussion, out of their own storyline, but then Joy brought it all back.

"Are you trying to tell me that little boy isn't yours?" she asked. "Laurie said no one ever saw her with anybody else. I mean, if he's not, you could just tell everybody the truth." It was the first note of hope he'd heard in her voice. He wanted to make it last, to tell her he could make everything right.

"No," he said, instead. "That's not what I'm saying."

He thought of Kyle. Someday the kid would hear rumors, too. Maybe not for a long time. Maybe not until he was Mick's age even. But at some point, he would hear about it. Was it better to hear that the boy his mother had loved is his real dad? The boy who turned into the man who spent time with him and took him fishing and cared about him? Or that the real dad was a married son of a bitch who weaseled out on his mom when she was pregnant?

"This is too hard, Micky. It's too much."

Promises to Kayla. Was she even anywhere to hear them? Did they count?

"I'm sorry, Joy."

"Yeah," she said. "Me, too."

* * *

"I thought I'd be able to cobble things together with Greta." Elaine sat in an Adirondack chair on Morty's pier with Morty in a matching chair beside her. Hobo had stretched out in a lone slice of sun that landed on the pier through the trees. It was late afternoon, and she'd gratefully accepted the beer Morty offered. "I thought knowing about Wallace would give her the assurance she needed about Mick."

"Turns out, the truth brings a lot of blame she puts on herself," Morty said. He took a last drag on his cigarette and put it out. "A lot of regret. If she backs away, it doesn't hurt so much. I guess I didn't consider that part of it."

"Why is it never simple with that woman?" Elaine asked. She smiled and glanced over in Morty's direction. "Does she know you smoke?"

"What she can't figure out with her eyes, she makes up for with that nose. I smoke three, maybe four Salems a week. She can tell every time. Tells me if I get the urge at her place to keep it outside."

Elaine looked at her pier. The boat sat slightly crooked in the lift. Mick had been teaching little Kyle how to maneuver it in, the two of them in the captain's seat together. Mick hadn't wanted to correct Kyle's effort, so he left the boat in a cockeyed position on the struts.

"Will she open up to *you,* still?" Elaine pulled her thoughts back to Greta.

"I was back out there yesterday and shooed off another one of those church ladies who've started up again. She didn't send me away, but she didn't seem herself. I tried to get her to talk about what she knows now. About what that could mean. But she said it was no use. Her ways are too set. If that's the end of the road for the two of you . . ." He looked over at Elaine. "You did your best. For Carson, Mick . . . for yourself . . . Even if she can't accept the offer, you've done right by the ones you love."

Elaine looked away from him. She let the swell in her throat, behind her eyes, subside before she turned back to him. "Thank you," she said.

"How about Wallace? He regret sharing things the way he did?"

"I don't think so." Elaine took a sip. A microbrew out of Asheville. The cool, bitter flow suited the moment. "He'd already decided to deal with whatever happens. He's a grown-up." She smiled. "I could take a few lessons from him at this point."

"We all hear that." Morty tipped his bottle toward her, clinked against hers.

"It seems right staying here," she said. "I don't know what I hope to accomplish, but at least I feel something here. I wish I had a passion to go back to work, but it's not there. Not now, at least. The work here might be more important."

"The work here still include Greta?" he asked, offhandedly. Did he want her to keep pressing with her mother-in-law, or let it go? She couldn't tell.

"Maybe," she told him. "And Mick. He's wanting to stay around for a while. We can afford to do it. We're lucky that way."

"I'm glad," he said. "Selfish reasons for sure, 'cause I sure like having you around." He looked out at the lake, drank deeply from his bottle, and put it on the pier. "Going to the Wednesday evening service with her tonight. My first time at her church." He stopped, let the implications of that settle.

"We all knew she'd end up in the same room with Tilda Jamison sooner or later," Elaine said. "You live in interesting times, my friend."

He nodded and picked up his beer.

Greta stood in the corner on the porch and leaned in close to the side of the house. If she looked up from that vantage, she could make out the dirt dauber nest against the wall. She stepped back, took the wooden end of the broom, and poked in the direction of the dark shadow she'd identified. It cascaded down in a crumbling mess, and she quickly swept it off the side of the porch. She hadn't held a broom in five years, maybe more. She'd let Mattie take over things she was still able to tackle herself. Time to take some of that back.

She'd had such high hopes of Mattie coming back, but the rehab was apparently not going as well as they hoped. Progress. But very slow progress. Greta couldn't dwell on that.

"Howdy, ma'am." The man's voice startled her, and she hit her elbow on a post.

"What in heaven's name are you sneaking up on me for?" She didn't know the voice, but he sounded tame enough.

"Sorry, Miz Forsyth," he said. "Joe Timmer, here. We've met. I work for Mr. Morales next door."

"I've told him I'm not selling," she said. "And he can call off those surveyors he's threatening, too. I don't have anyone on the property any longer."

"No, ma'am," he said. "I'm not here to bring that up again— although Mr. Morales gets back in town in a few days and will start up again, I'm sure."

"So what can I do for you then, Mr. Timmer?" Greta felt more like herself, at odds with an intruding neighbor. She didn't need the confusion brought on by her feelings for Morty Connell. She didn't need a grandson or a daughter-in-law. "I would appreciate brevity on your part. I have things to do."

"Bread?" He seemed flummoxed at what he perceived as an odd request.

"I mean, please be quick with whatever you need," she told him.

She heard him take in a breath. What was he stalling over? In the distance, his animals made those strange noises, as if calling out to him. Maybe she should be concerned about him, the keeper of those evil-eyed creatures.

"My wife," he said, finally. "She's a God-fearing woman, and she's at loose ends here, could use some work. I was thinking that there might be things around here she could do. I know you had folks who helped and they're gone now. Mattie. I think the world of Mattie."

Greta didn't know what to say. The man seemed decent enough, but the last thing she needed was another *God-fearing* woman underfoot. "I don't have a lot of income," she told him. "Not enough to hire help. And don't talk about the sale of my property. I'm not sacrificing my home in exchange for the means to hire a nursemaid. I don't need one."

"I was thinking," he said, "that we might have the arrangement your other folks had."

"What would that be?"

"The houses out back," he said. "I'm renting down the street right now. If I lived on the property—my wife and I, that is—she could be of help when you need it. I could, too. Live where I work, and you wouldn't be out here by yourself."

Greta intended to reject his idea and send him on his way. The words had formed and were nearly spoken. But something in it struck her as right. She couldn't imagine what. The man looked after a bunch of animals she didn't want around in the first place. She didn't want to like the idea of the man and his wife living—literally—in her backyard. But she had so few options to consider, and even she had to admit Timmer's was the best solution she'd heard.

"I don't know," she told him. "I'd need to meet your wife."

"Yes, ma'am. I think you'll get on with her just fine. If now's good, I'll go get her."

Greta tried to think of how it could be a mistake to follow through on the man's offer. She couldn't think of an argument against it. It wasn't his fault the awful alpacas had been brought there in the first place. Turning down the arrangement he suggested wouldn't change the situation in general.

"Now would be fine," she said.

"Appreciate it." Joe Timmer didn't make a big deal of it. She liked that. He gave her a small wave and went off to get his wife.

M orty was at the door, and she felt as nervous as a prom date. She hadn't gone with a man to church in decades. After Taylor died, an older widower would invite her to dinner once in a while. She'd proven too prickly for the men and found them unworthy of the effort it would take to change. Morty was different. She didn't want him getting under her skin, but he did.

She opened the door, and he stood close enough for her to see that he wore a suit. A tall man in a suit. Lord, help her.

"Ready to go?" he asked.

"I need my purse," she said. "And my sweater. Come in for a minute."

He waited in the den while she went to her room. Without meaning to, he brought with him a little of the sadness she wanted to push away. She'd have to separate Morty from thoughts about Carson's family. If she couldn't . . . well, she didn't want to think about that. She'd tell him later about Alice Timmer. Against all odds, she did *get on* with the woman as the man had predicted. Mrs. Timmer was a stern, farm-hardened woman of indeterminate age. But she kept her countenance and said she liked to cook. Greta needed little more than that.

"Tell you what. I'll go out and keep the car cool," Morty called to her.

She smiled. The man couldn't stay idle. He had to be busy with something. "I'll meet you there in a minute," she called back.

* * *

Attendance never reached more than twenty or twenty-five for the Wednesday evening service. Sunday nights were even less. That was why Greta liked those services better than the ones on Sunday morning. Fewer people to try and recognize. The smaller crowds she could figure out by their voices and their various shapes.

In the summer, the service started before dark set in. The church building had a stone wall that came waist high, with the rest built out of wide wooden boards. Over the years, Greta had seen the church painted white and, for a few years, a tan the color of khaki slacks. But before her eyes got so bad, Greta had helped them settle on a pale gray, and she thought that color suited the church and its surroundings best.

When she got out of Morty's car and walked across the gravel lot toward the church, she couldn't see who was staring in her direction, but she could feel eyes on her. From a short distance, she could hear Tilda Jamison talking. When the woman's yowling pitch suddenly ceased, Greta knew that she was looking, too.

Mattie had her own church, but she had always dropped Greta off and picked her up. Since Mattie's fall, others in the church had offered her rides. But this was the first time in a very long time that she'd been accompanied by someone. She'd forgotten how it felt.

"Greta," Pastor Freeland greeted her. "How are you this lovely evening?"

"Fine and grateful," Greta said.

"I don't believe I've met your friend?"

The preacher put out his hand, and Morty took it. "Morty Connell." Morty had his left hand on her waist, and he gave her a little squeeze as he introduced himself. Greta tried not to smile.

"What's the news on Mattie?" the pastor asked when Morty offered no further explanation of himself.

"About the same," Greta said. "I sat with her day before yesterday and watched the news. Her girls told me she's making progress with her movement. Talking about the same—a word here and there."

"Please tell her we're all praying for her."

"I certainly will."

The small gathering of parishioners had grown silent in their eavesdropping efforts. Tree frogs commenced the hollow, percussive rattle that would grow louder with the dying light. After a moment or two, a few people turned and went into the sanctuary, and others followed.

As Morty and Greta made their way to the door, Greta looked up to find herself inches from the familiar face of Tilda—the strange proximity to the woman stopping her progress. Tilda was often at services Greta attended, but they never spoke.

"I'm Tilda Jamison," she said to Morty, ignoring Greta. "My neighbor, Fred Alden, plays cards with you at Merle's sometimes."

"Fred's a good fellow," Morty said. "Very nice to meet you."

"You live beside that tree house, am I right?"

"Yes, I do," he said, cool as rainwater. "I was fortunate to meet this young lady when she came to visit Carson before he passed."

Tilda stepped slightly back from the two of them. "I was surprised to hear that you were in town with Carson's widow and her boy," she addressed Greta. "I wasn't aware that you had become friendly with those two."

The three of them were the only ones left outside. An owl had joined in with the frogs. "I wasn't aware that it was your business to know one way or the other. My daughter-in-law and grandson are suffering Carson's passing, the same way I'm suffering. We have that in common."

"Your grandson?"

She'd caught Tilda off guard with that one, and it cheered

her to no end. Morty offered another squeeze, and she worked to keep from actually giggling.

"My grandson," she said. It surprised her how easy it was to say the words. "I have nothing more to share with you about that particular subject, Tilda." *Not that I couldn't share a great deal more.* She pushed the thought down along with the temptation to utter it. Sounds of the opening hymn came through the closed door to the sanctuary. Stride piano and struggling voices. "The service is beginning," she added. "We should go in."

Morty kept firm pressure on her waist, guiding her away from Tilda Jamison and toward the sounds of "Standing on the Promises."

Pastor Freeland had kept it short. The air conditioner was working, but barely, and he had the good sense to know he couldn't hold the congregants' attention with the heat pressing in. On the stoop out front, Greta introduced Morty all around. With the women, he managed to be charming, without being flirtatious. With the men, he was friendly and quick to laugh at their jokes. Greta felt good, standing beside him.

"Greta's friend lives beside the lake house where Carson's widow grew up." Tilda Jamison's voice carried from behind Greta.

Greta turned in time to hear, "I believe she said Elaine and her grandson are staying there now. Is that right, Greta?"

"I don't believe I mentioned where they were staying," Greta said. "You must have heard it somewhere else."

Tilda walked over to her. Morty stood behind her, deep in some discussion with the preacher's wife about the best seasoning for catfish.

"Well," Tilda said, "if you want to claim that boy as a relative, more power to you because I can tell you what else I heard." She lowered her voice in preparation for whatever revelation was to come. "That Pascal girl up at the hardware store is telling anybody who'll listen that Mick Forsyth is the daddy to some little black boy in town. I would certainly hate to have that going around about my family. But then, you feel different about those people than most."

Greta didn't know what to do with the notion of Mick fathering a child—she'd get to that one later—but she certainly knew how to hold her own against the awful creature Tilda Jamison had become.

"I think *most* people regard *those* people as human beings, the same as anybody else. We're not living in the 1950s anymore, Tilda. You might want to catch up. And I don't put much stock in gossip—especially Pascal gossip. But if that happened to be true, I'd welcome the addition to my family." She heard Morty talking, which meant he wasn't listening to her conversation with Tilda. "I always thought it was a shame that Wallace's short marriage didn't result in any children. Especially a boy, you know, to carry on the family name." Even in the low lighting outside the church, she could make out the angry set of Tilda's mouth. She wanted to go on. She wanted—with no more than a sentence or two—to blow Tilda Jamison's small-minded world into a million even tinier pieces.

Her heart was racing and the words had already formed in her head, but she also registered the deep shame of lowering herself. Sinking to the swamp marsh level of the woman standing next to her. Wallace seemed like a decent man, and with the mother he had, he'd certainly beaten the odds.

"You asked me once why I preferred spending time with Mattie when I could have been with you," she said. "I guess it's for the same reason people try to attract songbirds to their yard instead of crows. I mean, who wants all that noise?"

Before the woman had time to even open her mouth, Greta turned and followed the sound of Morty's voice until she was standing beside him. She thought of the sermon, the preacher telling them how to act in a godly manner; how to become a better Christian than she felt like being at that moment. Best to leave, before any more of her buttons were pushed.

"I'm a little tired," she whispered to Morty.

He neatly ended his catfish discussion with Mrs. Freeland and said his good-byes.

She'd heard Morty laugh, but she hadn't seen him overcome before. She wondered if she should tell him to pull the car over until he collected himself.

She'd told him what she said to Tilda—none of it that funny in her estimation—and it set him off.

"Men can beat each other down to muscle and blood, but I swear women are the ones who carry the knives. Oh, my." He shook his head, then had another small fit before he settled.

"I didn't tell her," she said. "That's the important thing. That man has had nothing but a trial growing up with that woman."

Morty had calmed a little. "You're right." He reached over and gave her hand a pat. "I'm proud of you, darlin'. Couldn't have been easy."

They drove on toward her house. She had some chicken salad that Alice Timmer had brought by and left in the refrigerator. She could make a little supper for them out of that.

"So," he said, "you went out on a limb defending Carson's family. That mean you plan to reconsider spending time with them?" He asked it out of the blue. Morty didn't tiptoe around a subject, and that was usually a good thing. But he also wasn't given to interfering. She felt put on the spot with his inquiry.

"I've been honest with you, Morty. I've been through a hard stretch, and I've got to take the easiest route right now. I've been wrong about a lot of things, I won't deny it. But there was also information kept from me. Even Carson was complicit in that. If being with Michael can only remind me of the mistakes I made with my son—and the things he kept from me—it might be best to leave it all alone. I told you. I'm set in my patterns. Keeping my distance from Elaine and her son is second nature now. I don't see that changing."

"Being with me isn't exactly second nature," he said.

"Being with you isn't a painful reminder of anything. I didn't know you existed twenty-five years ago."

He drove in silence. Not angry silence, but it left Greta with quarreling thoughts inside her own head.

"I know what you're saying," she told him. "But the things I know now—thinking on it makes me angry. Angry with myself." She weighed whether or not she should—could—go on. "They make me angry with Carson. I can't stand that." She stopped. She had to swallow hard to keep her feelings where they belonged. "So then I get angry with Elaine and that's easier. I'm accustomed to it. Michael . . . he's just painful, and I don't know how to make that go away. I'm not . . . flexible. I guess that's the right word. I'm not flexible by nature, especially at this point in my life. The way it's been is still the easiest route now."

He didn't push beyond that. The man knew when to let something drop. But his continued silence left her coming back to what Tilda had said. Did Mick have a son? She remembered hearing years ago that he was seeing a girl in town—a girl whose mama was black and daddy was white. Talk went on for a little while and then stopped. She hadn't thought much about it. It was ridiculous for people to fret over black and white the way they did. But what if a child had come from that? Was she missing something else, another whole generation, by keeping to herself?

"I might be away a few days next month," Morty said, interrupting her thoughts.

"A vacation?"

"Not exactly. I'm going to visit my aunt in New Orleans for her birthday. She turns one hundred and one. Can you imagine?"

"That is something." Greta tried to imagine looking back on a century of life.

"People are living longer and longer," he said. "Just think, the two of us may have thirty years in front of us still."

And there was his point. She'd had a suspicion he was up to something. She lost twenty-five years with her grandson, but she could be denying herself that much again. Morty Connell was a sly one. But he was a Johnny-come-lately. Didn't understand a thing about what her life had really been like.

"Won't be gone for more than three days," he said. "Maybe four. Long enough to put on a pound or two most likely."

"You can stand it," she said.

Then again, she understood less about herself than she ever thought possible. The person who screamed at that little child all those years ago, grabbed his arm like a crazy woman—who had she been back then? Tilda Jamison had nothing on that woman. A bigger question loomed. Who was she now? What changes could she reconcile inside herself?

"What do you give a woman who's lived over a hundred years?" Greta asked.

"She wants me to sneak her some cigarettes," he said. "Place she lives won't let her have them."

"Sounds like she's a pistol."

"My kind of woman."

Greta smiled in spite of herself. She felt the turn and then the bump of her driveway underneath the tires telling her she was home.

Eleven

Designing sailboats. When he was in college, Mick had thought about going into engineering because he was good at that sort of thing, but he'd never seemed thrilled about it. Putting his ability to use with boats seemed to excite him in ways Elaine barely recognized. Mick had passion in his voice for the first time in years. He was on the phone, talking to an old professor. Mick thanked him for agreeing to write a recommendation. It calmed Elaine to see a path in front of her son.

She put out food for Hobo and glanced out the kitchen window toward Morty's place. No sign of him. She caught him for a cup of coffee or a beer when she could, but more often than not, his house looked lonely over there on the point. With no effort or even any intention, Greta had taken one of her lifelines. There was a certain symmetry to it, she supposed. Elaine thought of the day she spent with Greta, getting lunch at Benny's. Ending up on the porch with a crowd and a good meal. She'd liked that. She wanted it again—the gathering of family. But with Greta retreating to her old ways and Linnie off in Europe, a repeat of that day didn't seem likely.

Elaine took her coffee into the den and looked down toward the pier. Mick was heading down to join the boy where he stood fishing off one side of the dock. Kyle had certainly livened things up. Kyle. The official line was that he was Kayla's little brother, but she'd caught wind of rumors that would explain Mick's interest in the child. She didn't know what to make of it—if it could possibly be true.

The child had a family, and no one seemed inclined to mess with that. She'd wrestled a dozen times or more with the notion of bringing it up with Mick. She had to, eventually. But for the time being, she went along with the story that Mick wanted to be a sort of Big Brother to little Kyle. It seemed to make both of them happy. With all they'd both been through, she couldn't bear to rock that boat right away.

By all accounts, Kyle's mother wasn't thrilled with Mick's involvement—maybe with good reason. But apparently both the older Grimes boy and the stepdad thought time with Mick would be good for the boy.

She wanted to tell Carson about everything. Mick's plans. Little Kyle's newfound passion for fishing. Her efforts with Greta—that had come to nothing, but she'd tried. Greta and Morty. He'd get a kick out of that one.

She thought of Mick's notions of physics and philosophy. How consciousness and memory continued. For so long, her memories and Carson's memories had been interchangeable— even their thoughts sometimes. What was she supposed to do with the parts of herself she couldn't separate from him? Maybe nothing. Maybe he was still there somewhere, and she simply carried on for the both of them.

"Mom!" Mick called up from the pier.

She went out on the landing and waved.

"You should come down," he said. "See what Kyle's caught."

"Be right there!"

Hobo scratched at the door, and she let him out. Together, they went down the path to the lake.

"I had a huge one a second ago," Kyle called over his shoulder to her as she reached the pier. He bit at his bottom lip and refused to take his eyes off his line. "It almost broke my line, but then it got away."

"He did," Mick said, giving his own line a tug. "I saw it under the surface just before it broke free."

Elaine saw the large bucket on the pier that Mick had filled with lake water. In it, the smaller catches of the day flailed and wriggled. Hobo sniffed and jumped with each splash. The sun touched the surface of the bucket water, bringing up sparks of light.

"You'll probably need a larger hook to catch that big guy," Mick told the boy.

"You got some of his kin, though," she said.

Mick smiled, reeled in his line, and cast again.

"His kin?" Kyle looked at her as if he didn't understand at first, then he caught her meaning and broke into a grin. "Yes, ma'am. I did."

Morty came into the kitchen from the back door. Greta stood by the sink, lost in some thought or another. She looked out the side window. He wondered if she was staring from memory, imagining what she knew to be there. When he took time to really look at her, it always struck him what a lovely woman she was.

"The pole beans have come in," he said. "They'll need picking within a day or so."

She turned toward him and nodded. Didn't seem herself at all.

"Everything okay?"

She nodded again. "Just a feeling. I'm a little off, that's all."

She'd say more if she wanted to; he decided not to push. "To-matoes are on the way. Do you have any twine? I need to tie up one of the vines better."

"I think Mattie keeps it in the desk drawer there."

He went to the desk that sat in the open area between the kitchen and den. Inside the largest drawer, he found tape and glue, lots of pens and a stapler. Off to the side, he saw an envelope addressed to Greta. In the corner where the return would be, it simply said "Morales." The envelope had been opened.

"Your neighbor sending you love notes?" he joked.

"I think you know there's no love lost between me and Mr. Morales." She kept her vigil at the window.

"So what did he have to say?" He walked over and handed her the envelope.

She pulled it close to take a look, then handed it back. "I'll let you do the honors. This is the first I've seen of it." She could read a little still, but he knew it was a struggle for her to find the right focus.

Morty read the note out loud. An offer. A very large offer.

"Is that a number you've heard before?" he asked.

"Oh, my. No. I had no idea."

"So you really haven't seen this before?" He put the letter back in the envelope. "Who opened it then?"

Greta smiled. "I think there's only one answer to that. Silly woman. Thinking I'd get swayed by a bunch of numbers."

"Has he talked to you?" Morty didn't want to push, but money like that would bring her security.

"He's been after me. Came by once and called another time. Wants me to consider ten percent over his original offer. I didn't know what offer he was talking about, but I've been turning him down, so I didn't think it mattered much."

"You want to turn this down?" Morty was still coming to grips with the amount. He'd had no inkling the man wanted her property that badly.

"I'm not as old as your dear aunt," she said, "but like that lady, my needs are simple. A place to sleep and the health I have at the moment—minus the cigarettes, of course."

Seems that family ought to be included in that list. He kept that much of his thoughts to himself.

"Mattie had no business hiding it from you." He couldn't keep the irritation from his voice, but Greta only seemed amused by Mattie's deception.

Her mouth again spread into a small smile. "She must have tucked it in the drawer and forgotten about it."

"Forgotten."

"That's my story and I'm sticking to it," she said. The smile faded into a look of sadness.

Mattie was failing. He'd seen it, too. She looked that morning as if she'd had a setback. He wondered if she'd had another small stroke. He thought again of the money that envelope represented for Greta. But he understood how important it was for Greta to keep her home.

"You could consider an arrangement with that fellow," he said, working the notion out as he spoke. "Not necessarily an all-or-nothing proposition. The man's caretaker already stays out back here. Maybe a lease agreement for part of the land would work." The idea grew larger as the words came out of his mouth.

"We've talked enough about this," she said, a small thread of desperation running through her voice. "I don't want to think about that man or his animals anymore. I don't want to think about my grandson or his mother. Can't we let it all go, please?"

She'd opened her life to him. That was one change. He'd thought she might be capable of others. But maybe he'd been wrong.

She went back to her window staring. After a little more searching, he found a ball of twine in the cabinet over the dishwasher and went outside to tie up the tomato vine.

Mattie didn't see the blue, but she felt it. Always thought of blue as sad—people singin' the blues. But the blue she felt was joyful. She wanted to give in to it, but felt tethered by the hurt others might feel. Rae, Ayla . . . those children that swarmed around like butterflies. And Greta. She'd do anything to spare hurt for those people. But something inside the blue told her that the tethered feeling was her own doing. One place or another, that was an old notion.

She had words in her head. Her thoughts were full of sentences and memories. What she could get her mouth to say was another matter. It seemed it had gotten worse. Something else had happened to set her back. The little girls she used to care for were now fretting over her day and night. For the first time, it occurred to her that it might be time to stop fighting all the tiredness she felt.

She settled into a pleasant place in her mind. She sat with Greta, both of them young again, shelling butter beans.

Mattie smelled the clean dirt from the ground outside and the flowers that fed on it. The air in the kitchen was soft around her.

Hank was home, free of gigs for a few days, so she'd have to get to the house and make supper before too long. It was easier when he was gone. She felt guilty even knowing that to be true. Carson, a little thing, sat on the floor looking through a book of animal pictures. Giraffes, lions, and chimpanzees.

"I want to do a job like the man in this book," he announced.

"He work at a zoo?" Mattie glanced over at the book.

"No, ma'am," Carson said, very serious in his reply. "He looks out for them in the jungle. He rides in a Jeep and makes sure they're okay."

Greta, hands working quickly, threw beans into a large yellow bowl. She couldn't help but tease the boy. "You're not going to run off to some far place and leave me here, are you?"

Carson looked troubled, and a shock of that light hair fell into his eyes, but he didn't seem to notice. All of a sudden, he brightened. "We've got a lot of room. The animals could live here. That's what a farm's supposed to have."

Greta smiled at her son and his heartfelt response. A solution that kept the world as he knew it intact. It was always that way with him, it seemed.

Mattie came to herself again, looked around the room. Ayla sat beside her. Rae was off taking care of everybody else. Greta had been there for part of the morning, then had gone back to the farm with that nice Morty fellow. Morty was close to Carson's widow and the boy. Maybe he was the bridge. Maybe he could pick up where Mattie had left off.

She guessed it was time, after all. And with that, Mattie began to let go.

Morty came in from the garden again, took a rag from the pocket of his jeans, and wiped his forehead and his neck. He was done with work outside for the day. Late-afternoon heat had come on strong. He had work to do at his house, too. That would have to wait. His life existed in two places but it would all be reconciled eventually, he supposed.

"Greta?" he called. No answer.

He walked to the refrigerator to pour some orange juice for himself. The shelf looked empty, and he tried to recall what had been there. A bag of small apples. He'd brought them to make stewed apples for supper. He looked around the kitchen, but didn't see them.

He poured his glass of juice and took it into the den.

"Greta?" he called again, and still, he got no answer. A flutter of concern traveled through his stomach, through the nerves in his shoulders and neck. The door to her room was closed, but she left it that way most of the time.

He knocked.

No response.

The front door wasn't shut all the way. He looked out the window, over the driveway and beyond, and he saw her out there.

She stood at the fence, a gathering of alpacas crowding to be near her. In the crook of one arm, she held a sack. Apples. He watched her reach in and offer a piece of fruit over the fence. Flat hand open as anyone who'd been around horses knew to do. She did it again and again, trying to serve a different animal each time.

"Well, I'll be damned," he said, smiling to himself.

Morty sat his juice on the table by the window and walked outside. He made his way toward her, but she didn't hear him coming. As he drew near, he saw that she was smiling—and crying. Big wet tears rolling on her face, a startling sight on such a self-possessed woman. There was something powerful about the way she looked.

His presence would spoil it for sure, would embarrass her and do more harm than good. She was making her own way, and he'd do well to leave her to it. So he turned without speaking and headed back up to the house. Instead of going inside, he settled on the glider and watched. Over and over, her hand went in the bag, retrieving apple after apple—the burden noticeably lighter in her arm with each and every offering.

Elaine sat on the porch, Hobo at her feet. She heard Mick leaving in the truck with Kyle. He planned to get the boy some ice cream at Benny's and then take him home. It was late. The two of them had fished until the mosquitoes got too bad, then they'd brought the fish up to the utility shed and cleaned them, put them on ice for Kyle to take back with him.

Looking out, Elaine thought of something Carson had told her one time, a story about a day he came to the lake before they started going out. It was her freshman year in high school, his sophomore. On a whim, he'd brought his tackle and gear to the point near the tree house. He'd seen Morty outside and asked if he could fish off the bank there and Morty, being Morty, had agreed.

"I kept watching the cabin, hoping you'd come out," he'd said, smiling. "When the sun started to go down and the house lights came on, I saw you—at least I think it was you—behind a curtain in a high window. You were like something out of a storybook up there in the trees."

Hobo's head turned. His ears perked. Looking down over the lake, Elaine saw what captured his interest. She watched a flock of geese taking off, wings and webbed feet causing a ruckus on the water. After a moment, the small waves from their exodus lapped at the shore by the pier.

She wondered if Carson was out there somewhere, still watching her as she sat high in the branches, framed by the dim porch light against the fading day. She'd brought Carson from Chapel Hill to the lake thinking she was bringing him home. Turns out, he'd been bringing her.

From overhead, she heard them, circling back. A squadron of pleading geese, bellies lit gold by the last of the sun. They passed close enough for her to feel the urgency of their journey, and she understood their need.

But for a time, at least, the impulse to flee had left her.

About the author

2 Meet Jean Reynolds Page

About the book

3 Author's Note

6 Reading Group Guide

7 Writing in Southern:
Chasing a Good Yarn

Extras

10 A Few Favorite Recipes of
Grace Reynolds Massengill

Read on

12 Have You Read?
More by Jean Reynolds Page

Insights,
Interviews
& More . . .

Meet
Jean Reynolds Page

Andy Ziskind

JEAN REYNOLDS PAGE is the author of
*Leaving Before It's Over, The Last Summer
of Her Other Life, The Space Between Before
and After, A Blessed Event,* and *Accidental
Happiness.* She grew up in North Carolina
and graduated with a degree in journalism
from the University of North Carolina at
Chapel Hill. She worked as an arts publicist
for over a decade in New York and North
Carolina, then went on to review dance
performances for numerous publications
before turning full-time to fiction in 2001.
In addition to North Carolina and New
York, she has lived in Boston, Dallas, and
Seattle. She lives with her family near
Madison, Wisconsin. ∾

Author's Note

WHILE THE NARRATIVE THAT UNFOLDS
in *Safe Within* is entirely fictional, several
elements in the book are drawn loosely from
my upbringing in North Carolina and from
other real-life inspirations or experiences.
I thought it might be interesting to share a
few of those.

The Tree House

When I was eleven, my parents built a cabin
on Lake Tillery in the Piedmont section of
North Carolina. The lake is about a fifteen-
minute drive from my hometown of Troy.
That cabin was not a tree house and my folks
were anything but bohemian, but the cabin
was an important part of my middle school
and high school years and continued to be
an important place for my family after
I married and had my own children.

Over the years, I had made several
attempts to use the lake as a setting and
never came up with the right story. Then,
when driving from Washington state to
our new home in Wisconsin, we passed a
campground. I can't recall where in the
journey we were at the time, but I remember
in vivid detail the sight of a huge tree house
that overlooked the campground below. It
captured my imagination to the point that
I decided I wanted to use a tree house in my
next book.

It took some time (my wonderful and
very patient editor will tell you that it took
too much time!) for the idea to gel into a
fully realized narrative, but I eventually
put the two together and came up with
the setting for *Safe Within*. ▶

Author's Note *(continued)*

Elaine and Carson

My dad died from esophageal cancer when he was fifty-four. My
mother, who was fifty-two at the time, became a young widow.
With the exception of this circumstance, the story of Elaine and
Carson in no way resembles the lives of my parents, but watching
my mom reinvent herself after Daddy died gave me a great deal of
faith in human resilience and offered the inspiration for qualities
found in Elaine's character. Mom said to me once, several months
after the funeral, "I keep expecting to fall apart and I haven't. I suppose
I'm not going to." It seemed to surprise her as much as anyone that she
kept going with optimism and relative good cheer.

In telling Elaine's story, I wanted to capture my mother's spirit of
survival when, overnight, her world changed. The narrative doesn't
continue long enough for us to know exactly what Elaine does with
the rest of her life, but I feel that she is left in a position to allow family,
community, and her own inner resolve to take her to good places.

As for my mom, in time, she launched her own catering business and
got married again to another wonderful man—a man who became a
terrific grandfather to my kids. But Mom also kept my dad very present
in our lives. Because she never allowed sadness to consume her, it never
seemed sad to talk about Daddy and to recollect our lives when he was
around.

The Weather Blues

Several years ago, I was talking to my aunt when she mentioned
"weather balls." She explained that when she was a kid on my
grandparents' farm, they used to occasionally see bundles of light
that looked low in the sky, almost as if they were rolling just above
the fields near their home. It was most likely a phenomenon known
as ball lightning, described by Merriam-Webster's dictionary as "a
rare form of lightning consisting of luminous balls that may move
along solid objects or float in the air." The notion of something like
that suddenly appearing in the night became the inspiration for the
weather blues. (*Weather Blues* was also my working title when writing
the book. We almost went with it as the published title, but thought it
might mislead people into thinking it was a book about seasonal
depression.)

The Alpacas

It is a very loose association, but when I was a kid, we used to drive to an
attraction called the Buffalo Ranch. The story I heard (whether true or a

tall tale, I don't know) was that the owner had won several buffalo when gambling somewhere out of state. The animals were delivered to his farm and he initially let them graze with the cows and other livestock. So many people began to drive by to take a look—buffalo were very exotic in that part of the country, especially in the 1960s—that he decided to build a tourist spot around them and charge admission. I found the buffalo fascinating and thought it would be interesting to incorporate some type of unusual animal into the book. ∾

Reading Group Guide

1. Greta's dislike of Elaine precedes their first meeting. Greta disapproves of the unconventional way in which Elaine's parents have chosen to live their lives and raise their daughter. In what respects does Greta resemble Elaine's parents?
2. If Greta had known the truth about Wallace and Elaine decades earlier, what do you think would have happened? Would Elaine have had a closer relationship with her mother-in-law?
3. Did Carson and Elaine do the right thing when they kept Wallace's secret from Greta?
4. In a similar vein, does Mick make the right decision when he chooses to keep the truth about Kyle from Joy? How about from Elaine?
5. In their conversations, Kooper suggests that Mick bears some responsibility for things that happened after his relationship with Kayla ended. Do you think this is fair? Why or why not?
6. Elaine initially reaches out to Greta out of a sense of obligation to Carson. Do you believe it is important to "finish" the work of loved ones who have passed on and cannot see through to the end things that are important to them?
7. Was Mattie's friendship with Greta primarily situational or were they uniquely suited to each other? Was the relationship equally balanced in terms of benefit and control? Why or why not?
8. The alpaca farm next door proves an unwelcome distraction to Greta's home life. Why do you think she has such a strong reaction to the animals? ❧

Writing in Southern: Chasing a Good Yarn

I DON'T GET HOME OFTEN ENOUGH. That may contribute to the deep pleasure I feel when I return to the South each day at my computer. I have the opportunity—the privilege, really—of putting my memories and my longing for home to creative use. It still feels strange to me that more of my years have been lived outside the South than in it. Since graduating from Chapel Hill I've lived in the Northeast, another (too short) stint in North Carolina, the Southwest, the Northwest, and now the Midwest. In touring the country in five- to ten-year increments, I hear interesting stories everywhere. I love the variety of experiences I've had outside the South, but I haven't yet internalized them as voices in my head.

I have a good friend from Italy who told me that her son was troubled to find that, after living in London for a number of years, he began to dream in English. Did that make him less Italian? With my various migrations, my Southern accent has unintentionally moved toward a more generic sound and I don't know if I dream in Southern speak, but I do know that I seem to write only that way—at least in terms of a sustained narrative.

I can conjure the owner of a New York deli for a scene or two, but when it comes to knowing the blood and bones of a character, I have yet to venture outside the core demographic of *Southern Living* magazine. I've experimented on occasion, but I can't seem to make those characters fully come alive. So I go back to what works. For the most part, I don't employ extreme variations of my native dialect in my narratives, but I'm drawn toward the ▶

phrasing, cadence, and word choice that still sounds lyrical to me after all these years.

It is daunting to consider taking on narratives from a region that brought us Faulkner, Wolfe, and Welty—and more recently Reynolds Price, Lee Smith, and Jill McCorkle—to name only a very few. The South has a rich history of producing wonderful writers. I have a feeling this has something to do with the importance—in that neck of the woods—of a good spoken yarn. Not simply the story itself, but the way it is told. If you have a first-rate story in your pocket, you have a currency that buys you regard and, to some degree, respect.

I was reminded of this a couple of years ago when, on a visit with my ailing aunt, a neighbor stopped in to say hello and inquire about her health. When asked about his day, the neighbor launched into a story of his visit that morning to the local department store to buy a dress belt on his way to a funeral. I don't remember the particulars of the tale, but the upshot was that, in haste, he'd accidentally bought a belt several sizes too big, and because of the pressing event, he was forced to temporarily make it work. The story lasted a good ten minutes and not only held our interest but also left us thoroughly entertained. The only sentence I remember in detail was the one added as an afterthought at the very end.

"I'm goin' to go home now, cut off the extra, and make a dang dog collar out of it."

It's a gift, I tell you, this ability to take ordinary life and, in the telling, craft a story. It's one I have envied ever since I can remember remembering anything. To my dismay, I wasn't born this sort of raconteur. Because of the need to do readings and the like, I've gotten better at talking to groups and, on a good day, can manage to hold my own. But it doesn't come naturally and never ceases to be nerve-wracking.

Early on, I recall occasions when I attempted to find this quality in myself—usually with substandard, if not downright embarrassing, results. When I was in elementary school, I remember hearing about an engagement broken at the eleventh hour by a bride-to-be from our church who realized her mistake just days before the wedding. My clueless youth, coupled with my desire to be the center of attention, led me to relay this story for the entertainment of others. Unfortunately, I chose to do this during an open casket viewing at the local funeral home—with (unknown to me) the family of the no-longer-bride-to-be sitting directly behind me. Hard lessons all around.

With that misstep, I learned a lot about my own limitations in storytelling and—at the time, at least—in judgment. I learned the value of time and place when choosing to tell any story. And most important, I learned that spreading gossip at the expense of others is not the same as displaying a talent for telling a story. After this, I retreated at bit— until I realized that the written word afforded me more options. By middle school, I found that when I put anecdotes, stories, vignettes, and scenes on paper, I could engage people in a way that I could not when attempting to speak the same material. I could finally spin a yarn—albeit a written one that required crafting and redrafting to reach the desired result.

Childhood is a powerful time in life. I became a writer because from my earliest days, I wanted to be that person in school, in church, at 4-H, or at Girl Scouts who held court. The person who could turn a trip to the five-and-dime into an occasion for laughter with a neighbor. I wasn't that person, but my desire to emulate those who had the gift drove me to find another outlet for the lively voices that populated my days back then, and later my thoughts. My characters are rarely based on a single individual (and when they are, I promise, it is with consent). Still, they are drawn, with deepest respect (and with fair creative license), from the collected moments of my life.

So far I've written about Texans, South Carolinians, and, yes, Tar Heels. Maybe, in time, the voices that live in my imagination will venture into other regions where I've spent time. I'll never say never. But I do find that the older I get, the more I yearn for the red clay of home. So for now, my characters will eat black-eyed peas and collards for the New Year. They will tell you that miles of white sand is the only thing that can rightfully be called a beach. They'll say they really like that stuff served up in Kansas City, but it's not BBQ. In the telling, I hope I do justice to the remarkable region that raised me. ∾

A Few Favorite Recipes of Grace Reynolds Massengill

AFTER MY FATHER'S DEATH, my mother went on to start a catering business. She found great joy in both catering events, most often weddings, and filling the frequent orders she received for her remarkable hors d'oeuvres and cakes. Here are a few of the recipes that people requested most often from my mother's kitchen.

Chocolate Delight Cake

Icing
> 8 ounces cream cheese
> 2 sticks butter, softened
> 2 boxes of 10x powdered sugar
> 1 bar German chocolate
> ¼ cup hot water
> 1 teaspoon vanilla

Cream together cream cheese and butter and mix in sugar. In a saucepan, dissolve German chocolate in hot water over low heat. Remove from heat and add to cream cheese mixture along with vanilla. Reserve 3 cups of the icing in the refrigerator in a covered container.

Cake
To remaining icing add:
> 1 cup shortening (softened)
> 3 eggs
> 2¼ cups all-purpose flour
> 1 teaspoon baking soda
> 1 teaspoon salt
> 1 cup buttermilk

Preheat oven to 325° F. Mix all ingredients. Grease and flour three layer cake pans and pour mixture evenly into each pan. Bake for 25 minutes or until done (when knife comes out clean). Cool cake layers. Take reserved icing from refrigerator and allow to soften. Ice when cake is cool.

Olive Surprises

  60 pitted green olives
    (about 1½ regular bottles)
  1 (4-ounce) stick butter
  12 ounces sharp cheddar cheese (grated)
  1½ cups all-purpose flour
  1½ teaspoons paprika
  ½ teaspoon salt

Preheat oven to 400° F. Drain olives on a paper towel. Mix together butter, cheese, flour, paprika, and salt until dough forms. Dough must be firm enough to form a ball around each olive. Roll 1 teaspoon of dough around each olive. Bake on a lightly greased cookie sheet for 15 minutes.

Seafoam Salad

Mom used the recipe of her good friend Maxine Robinson

  1 medium (14.5 oz.) can sliced pears
    in juice
  1 3-ounce package lime gelatin
  6 ounces cream cheese
  2 tablespoons milk
  1 cup whipped cream
    (or whipped topping)

Drain and reserve 1 cup juice from pears (add water if juice from can does not equal a cup). Mash pears with a fork. Heat pear juice over low heat until it begins to boil. Remove from heat and mix in gelatin. In a separate bowl, mix together the cream cheese and milk, then add to the hot gelatin mixture. Cool and let thicken a bit, then mix in mashed pears and whipped cream. Pour into a serving bowl and refrigerate until firm, about three hours. Spoon sections onto small plates. Serve with whipped cream, if desired. ᗡ

Have You Read?
More by
Jean Reynolds Page

THE SPACE BETWEEN BEFORE AND AFTER

Forty-two and divorced, Holli Templeton
has just begun to realize the pleasures of
owning her life for the first time. But the
experience is short-lived. Her son, Conner,
has unexpectedly fled college in Rhode
Island and moved to Texas with his troubled
girlfriend, Kilian. This alone is difficult to
handle, but as Holli begins to understand
the depth of the girl's problems, concern
turns to crisis.

Conner's situation is worsening, and
as if that's not enough, Holli notices signs
of serious decline in the beloved Texas
grandmother who raised her. She has no
choice but to leave the comfort zone of life
in New York and return to her hometown
in Texas to care for the people she loves.

In the tight space between these two
generations, Holli initially feels lost. The
journey back stirs up so many unresolved
hurts from her childhood. But something
else happens in this uneasy homecoming.
Comfort arrives in the ethereal presence
of the mother long lost to her, and Holli is
surprised to find that as she struggles to help
her son and grandmother, the wounds of her
own past begin to heal.

The space between before and after—
easily the most challenging place she
has ever known—begins to reveal an
unanticipated hope for what the future
might hold.

THE LAST SUMMER OF HER OTHER LIFE

Jules is thirty-nine and is pregnant by a man she's decided to leave behind in California. Always the protected daughter, she must now relinquish that role and prepare to be a mother herself. But her efforts are upstaged by shocking allegations from a local teen in her North Carolina hometown. The boy has accused her of what the police are calling "inappropriate sexual contact." Three men rally in her defense: Lincoln, her brother, who flies in from New York to help her; Sam, her high school boyfriend, who after so many years still offers unconditional support; and Walt, the uncle of the teen, who charms Jules with his intelligence and unanticipated kindness.

Her search for the truth about the troubled teenager becomes, for Jules, a first step toward discovering the woman she wishes to be. But with so many wrong choices behind her, how can she trust herself with the future of her unborn child?

LEAVING BEFORE IT'S OVER

When Roy Vines married his wife, Rosalind, he traded his family and his inheritance for love—a painful choice that has rewarded them with years of joy nestled in rural North Carolina with their beautiful daughters, sixteen-year-old Lola and little Janie Ray.

But their happiness is threatened when Rosalind suddenly falls ill. Desperate to get her the help she needs, Roy does the one thing he swore he'd never do—turn to his heartless and bitter identical twin brother, Mont, for help.

The price is steep—and includes opening their home to a teenage boy who believes Roy is the father who abandoned him. As bad blood threatens to destroy her family,

Rosalind must make a difficult choice.
Should she walk away—like Roy once
did—for love, or try to mend wounds that
may never be healed? And will the pain of
choosing be more than her heart can bear?

Don't miss the next
book by your favorite
author. Sign up now for
AuthorTracker by visiting
www.AuthorTracker.com.